The Salty Rose

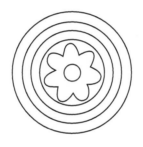

The Salty Rose

Alchemists, Witches & A Tapper In New Amsterdam

By Beth M. Caruso

For Chazz, Sky, & River

For the Justice Seekers and the Peace Keepers

CHAPTER ONE:

Marie's Story
New Amsterdam, New Netherland
Winter, 1664

The Director General slammed the gavel down with the harsh thud of an ending.

"Marie du Trieux, you are hereby banished from New Netherland forever!" he said.

As I held on to the railing of a departing schooner, I remembered the jarring finality of those stark words against me. Looking back one last time at my town, a little place in the wilderness that had grown up with me—I longed to stay in the home where I gave birth to all my children, the location of my loves and of my losses.

This is the best place to begin recounting the story of how I played a part in the transition from Dutch New Amsterdam to English New York, my dear granddaughter.

I suppose the English will have their own tales to tell about the events that transpired but I want you to know my personal and secret version of the history of my beloved city before I am gone.

Having left New Amsterdam for the first time on that cold winter day in 1664, I felt unsettled, not quite believing that the time for my departure had finally come. Where had the time gone? How quickly had it passed? It had been nearly forty years since I first set foot on the shores of Manhattan with my mother, father, and little brother.

The view from our vessel, *The Morning Star*, was unrecognizable from the one my family saw many decades earlier. We had arrived to nothing but marsh, forest, and a few Indian canoes that approached our ship in greeting and curiosity. It's easy to recall my excitement as a young girl of flowing dark hair seeing the Natives for the first time when we reached these shores many years ago.

But at the point of my expulsion I wasn't an adventurous, naïve child anymore. A mature and defiant woman who had faced her share of hardship and disappointment had taken her place. The Council of New Netherland and Director General Stuyvesant had told me they were finished with my repeated offenses and had given the order for banishment. I'd been in trouble with the authorities far too often they said. They'd insisted that my tavern be closed.

"So this is how it must end," I uttered in disbelief to my son Pierre, your uncle, as we huddled together on deck. We were passing the Stadthuys, a large brick building with stepped parapets in traditional Dutch style that served as the city hall. I struggled to pull my woolens and furs closer to guard against the cold wind.

A few minutes earlier, my sisters and brothers had met me at the slip as Pierre and I boarded our boat en route to Fort Orange. We had always been strong together, my proud Walloon family and I. My heart filled with gratitude,
knowing that my sisters would care for my littlest ones. What saddened me the most was to see my younger children waving goodbye, running along the shoreline for as long as they could keep their mother's boat in view. The separation wouldn't be forever, but I did not want it at all.

Little Maria, my youngest, was the one I worried about the most. She held me tight, hoping to never let go. She was only six but she had her older sisters, Anna and Alida, to help her get though the experience as well as her brother, Jacob, just a year older. Johannes, my other boy, was already apprenticed to a brewer. I vowed that I would do whatever I could to bring my family back together, whatever that might be.

After we said our tearful goodbyes, the skipper and his mate uncoiled the rope from the wood pylons on the slip and put up sail to take advantage of the high tide.

We passed the main canal where in warmer weather smaller watercraft plied their way past both cobbled and dirt streets lined with dwellings and trade shops. Most were of wood, but many new ones were built with brick and stepped gables. A couple of tall ships were anchored on the edge of the East River from ports of call all over the Indies, Europe, and Africa.

I had been a big part of that world with my beloved tavern near Maiden Lane, *The Salty Rose*, known by all the inhabitants and many travelers to New Amsterdam.

The skyline of our little Dutch town boasted some windmills for cutting wood and for processing grain. The wind blew them steadily as they creaked goodbye. I recognized townspeople whom I had known forever, waving to me from the waterfront against the background of the wooden Dutch church.

At the water's edge, tens of languages wafted in the air as citizen and traveler alike made trade deals between the docks and the warehouses. I heard some well-wishers as well.

"God protect you, Marie!" shouted Sara Kierstede within hearing distance from the shore.

"May you be well, Marie, my friend!" Judith Varlet cried out to me.

I had known both of them for many years. Our lives had connected in important ways. I waved back half-heartedly as another bout of crying commenced.

"Mama, please take the handkerchief and dry your eyes. Maybe we will come back one day," Pierre said as he tried to reassure me.

I could not stop the tears despite knowing that my departure from New Amsterdam was part of something much bigger than my family or myself. Sara Kierstede tried to warn me just how dire my situation was, but I didn't listen. Judith Varlet, feeling indebted to me, attempted to save me from the final decision her brother-in-law made against me, but it was to no avail. Even though I was exiled from New Amsterdam, I had been lucky that the Council members rescinded their original terms of banishment, deciding to be more lenient with me and allowing me to stay in the outer reaches of New Netherland.

"Mama, no need to make a fuss. Uncle Isaac will take care of everything once the Indian wars settle down again at Esopus. He will get you your tavern license again." Pierre said a little impatiently. He clearly looked dismayed to see me more emotional than usual, despite having witnessed some of my hardships. In his eyes, I had always been a strong woman, and he'd seen others view me as Marie the outgoing, resilient, and jolly tavern keeper with a sharp tongue, perfectly capable of taking care of herself.

Pierre was sixteen and anxious to set off on his own in the upper reaches of New Netherland. For him, leaving was his logical next step in life. He was excited to meet up with his older brothers, Aernoudt and Cornelis, in Beverwyck. They would take him to Fort Orange and teach him to barter with the Indians and to speak to them in their tongues.

I was sure that he wished he could have left on his own without the spectacle or the drama of his mother's banishment.

"Time will open new possibilities. It must," I said, resolving to be strong again. "Do not worry about your mother. We will find our future up north."

"I will miss the little ones, but we must be settled before they can join us. And who knows, maybe fate will be kind and allow for a return to New Amsterdam one day. For now, your brothers and sisters are in good care with your aunts and uncles. Aernoudt and Cornelis can help us get situated," I explained.

My sons made me very proud. Aernoudt was already a sought-out Indian translator. Cornelis was following his brother's lead and also trapped and traded, occasionally translating too. Pierre wanted to follow in their footsteps.

A deep chill was ever-present as we stood on the deck. Winter was stubborn and not quite ready to thaw. But I wanted to finish seeing our home, our lively, rowdy town of New Amsterdam, as we drifted past it.

"I know you loved it here, Pierre. It's the only real home we've ever known," I said, forcing a smile.

"You can come back any time, my son, if it suits you and life is not what you expect it to be in Beverwyck. Do not feel you have to protect me. Your mama will be fine. It is only me that Stuyvesant wants to be rid of," I said. "You have your whole life ahead of you."

"I know, Mama," he agreed.

Pierre was always my little champion. I know I doted on him a little more than the others since he was still a tender young age when his father, my first husband, Cornelis, died.

There were so many stories, my dear granddaughter.

The sight of a child tending his family's fowl on their lot bordering the shore prodded my memory.

"Do you remember the time that Jonas Hansen, our neighbor, hired you to watch his geese?" I asked Pierre as we continued to float past the town. I had to chuckle as I thought of that episode.

He nodded as I continued.

"It was your first job, and you were so proud, so determined to do your best for the cantankerous old man."

"I remember," he said. "I accidentally left the gate open. I feared that fierce old man. I went running home, begging for help," he laughed. "You formed the geese brigade with my older brothers, becoming full of feathers in the chase. You didn't stop helping me until the last one was caught, counted, and back in their pen."

"I couldn't bear for you to be yelled at when you wanted so badly to do a good job. The miserable old man needed to fix his gate anyway. It was ready to fall apart," I reasoned.

So many memories! Because of them all, there was nowhere else other than New Amsterdam that I wanted to be. I recognize now what a unique place it was—a Dutch frontier trying to emulate its fatherland but too mixed up in a human stew of many races and nationalities and too deep in its own aspirations to ever succeed in copying the identity of the fatherland. New Amsterdam was awash in commerce and desire, violence and conquest, defiance and free spirits.

As I continued to reminisce about my past, the fort came closer into view with its four corner bastions, each fortified with cannons on alert. Its walls of sod, dirt, and stone had deteriorated after many years. Privy to the numerous rumors of the English coveting our lands, Stuyvesant had thought it wise to start repairing it. So, on that freezing day soldiers with a few African slaves owned by the company had started to move fallen rocks and organize for the extensive repair. They barely looked up as we approached on our way to the North River.

The West India Company and Dutch flags waved in the ferocious wind. From the water, we could see Heerstraat, the main highway, snake upward and deeper into Manhattan. It had been the beginning of the old Wickquasgeck trail traveled by countless Indians before the Europeans came.

As we sailed a little farther out, the whole of New Amsterdam came into view—a mixture of clapboard buildings with rows of newer brick homes and businesses, each unique with its signature stepped-parapet facades, fruit orchards, and vegetable gardens. Even tulips would line the gardens of wealthier burgomasters and rich traders in springtime.

So alive was that place with the best breweries in the colonies and visitors from the entire world ready to make deals, drink, and dance. One couldn't be anything but entertained by life there. Yes, it had been scary too at times with the rising tensions between neighboring Natives. Of course, I would miss it, and despite the direness of my situation, the view of the town put everything into perspective.

Our schooner maneuvered around the tip of Manhattan, immediately passing the windmills and finally the far western end of the wall, the barricade that Stuyvesant so desperately hoped would keep English and warring Natives out of our little city. I had the distinct feeling that this was not my last appearance in New Amsterdam. A tiny inkling stirred that there was more to come.

"The Director General and Council of New Netherland have no idea what they have done or what I will do as a consequence of their betrayal," I whispered.

I left New Amsterdam that day, but I would be back. The walled barricade eventually receded from our sight as we sailed up the beautiful North River and through snow-covered and wooded highlands on either side of the temporarily expanding and widening river. Stuyvesant's fortification was not going to keep me out of my home forever. I doubted it would keep the English out either.

CHAPTER TWO:

Marie's Story
New Amsterdam, New Netherland
1638

I was only seven when I first boarded our giant ship to live in the vast landholdings of the West India Company across the sea. I was small but always loud and surprisingly boisterous. Papa said the Indians across the enormous ocean would realize we were coming and be ready to greet us days before our arrival. Papa accepted my nature. God bless his soul.

It was bittersweet for Papa to leave Holland and Leiden, knowing the grave of Mama was left behind. Truth be told, I hardly remembered her. I struggled and still strain to envision her proud and chiseled face, her work-worn hands, her long dark hair as it hung over me when she snuggled me in close to her for the night, singing an old French lullaby. I was just three when she died. Papa soon married her cousin Susanne.

It was a pity I didn't know my mother better, but that is the biggest burden in this life—to lose someone you love from time to time. In a way, it was a blessing that she died when I was so young. By seven, I was fully used to life without Mama, and Susanne was a good caretaker and companion. She also became my mother. She loved my father. And she also loved my brother and me.

After weeks on turbulent seas, what we arrived to was marsh and forest. No buildings. No streets. All we saw was a desolate yet beautiful wilderness. So I grew up in New Amsterdam and never adhered to the more cultured expectations of my European origins. I ran wild. We, the first Walloons, who came to this new world to work for the Dutch West India Company, suffered hardships that are difficult for most people to imagine. We had nothing and lived in dugout shelters for the first couple of years. I was schooled in the wilderness and learned how to survive even better than most of the adults. I was strong and adaptable, learning the languages and customs of the local Indians and of the other Europeans that eventually came to settle with us.

My family started out on Beaver Street, building one of the first homes in New Amsterdam, and my brothers and sisters were some of the first children born in the colony. Papa worked as a messenger for the Dutch West India Company under Director Kieft. Eventually, he moved us out to the edges of the town on lands granted to him in Smit's Vly, a beautiful valley. The family property overlooked the East River at a near distance from Maiden Lane. There Papa, with the help of his brood, spent most of his time tilling the rich soils of the family farm. I enjoyed living there with him and the rest of my family.

My papa, Philippe du Trieux, was always amused by my independence and shrugged his shoulders when people came to complain about my headstrong behavior and my lack of hesitation in speaking my mind. He was used to it and laughed it off. I was alarming to the newer settlers who had just left Amsterdam and expected that I should carry myself in a more subdued way.

As I matured and grew into the body of a woman, the men noticed. They liked to tease me because they knew how salty I was. But most who were familiar with me didn't dare cross a line because if they did, I could outsmart them and put them in their place. Other men such as transient sailors were not as wise. Some women in town only walked near the dock in groups or with their menfolk to avoid their unruliness. Not me. I wanted my freedom and I could handle them.

"Little lady, come here and let me see that beautiful rump of yours," a particularly repugnant one commanded as he leered at me and his friends laughed. Some of the time, it was worse than that. They were disgusting. My responses to defend myself usually had something to do with their inadequacies in pleasing woman.

A few times Papa was in earshot, but before he had the chance to intervene, I would deliver a spectacularly stinging insult and send them off in humiliation amongst the howling laughter of a growing crowd.

Sometimes Papa would even feel sorry for the idiots and would say, "Now, Marie, please tell me there are some thoughts that you know not to say out loud. Have a little pity, daughter. The desperate wretches are ravenous from being at sea."

"Papa, I say what must be said. Why should I be hushed by imbeciles?" I retorted. He would raise his hands and chuckle.

Other times, I blatantly spoke not for defense but out of a compulsion to point out the truth, like the time Hans Scheider was complaining about his fat wife. I told him that she should leave him for dallying with every woman that came to port. It was certainly better to be fat than to be an unfaithful and backstabbing ass.

"Ah, Marie, you will be who you are. Who am I to force the wild out of a child so free-spirited?" Papa asked, laughing to himself.

Now, don't misunderstand me. I was also a warm person and have become more so with time. I would help anybody to my own detriment. If I loved someone, I loved fiercely, and if I detested them, I did it with zeal.

One day Papa had had enough of my resistance to suitors and called for me. I'd rebuffed several who'd taken an interest in me.

"Papa, Susanne told me that you wish to speak with me," I said. Papa was in the shed next to the barn sharpening some tools before the harvest. I had a fresh tankard of beer in hand to give him some respite from his work.

"Marie, come here," he said as I handed him the tankard. He nodded in thanks and gestured for me to sit on a bench.

"Daughter, you are beautiful and skilled in many things. But no man can come near you. You push them away. You call them names. I laugh sometimes, but you cannot do this forever. Marie, I worry that I will not always be here to help you, your mother, and the other children. You must find a good man to help provide and give security. When will you not spurn each and every man you meet?" he asked.

"Maybe never, Papa. Most men are swine. I will be fine. I need no one," I insisted.

My papa, in his sweetness, tried to make me reconsider.

"Marie, you must give someone a chance. I cannot hold on to you forever. You are too comfortable here. Many girls your age have married already," Papa said.

"I am twenty-one, Papa. Not too old. What do you wish that I should do then, Papa, if they are of no interest to me?" I asked.

"Marie, I want you to go outside the farm and busy yourself with some kind of job in the town. I hear the Van Couwenhovens need help at their tavern on Pearl Street. You know the Wolfertsen van Couwenhoven brothers. A handsome lot they are, Marie. They need a barmaid. You will learn more about brewing beer and have a better possibility to meet men."

I made a face and shrugged my shoulders, unmoved by his pleas.

"Damn it, Marie. I've always been easy on you because I knew trying to change you would be fruitless, but I'm insisting now. Go do it and have a little fun too," he said winking at me.

Papa was always loving and affectionate but never very overly protective of me. He was always confident that I could handle myself. I realize now that if people expect you to be strong all the time, you are never allowed to be weak in their eyes. I loved Papa, but maybe he should have watched over me more instead of letting me be like a wild wolf cub.

Tired of the conversation and his persistence, I gave in to Papa's requests. Only for my papa did I do such a thing.

I was a hard worker and didn't want my family to think that I wasn't doing my part. The extra income from the tavern would help the family out.

I followed his advice and sought work at the Van Couwenhovens. In some ways, I'm glad Papa convinced me to work there in my youth. For it was there that I learned the ways of brewing and tavern keeping, a trade that became central to the rest of my life. It was not all that I took away from their tavern.

"Marie. Enough of this! Go roll out another barrel to tap. We are already out. These ravenous sailors will drink us dry with their unending thirst. And, think about minding your manners with the wealthy man at the window table," Mr. Couwenhoven scolded me as he glared in the man's direction.

The tavern was humming with activity, encased in a cloud of smoke and overflowing with not only beer but also boisterous laughter that night.

I'd rebuffed a lecherous traveler again. My mistake was that he was a repeat customer and one who had a little wealth to spread around.

"What shall I do? Let the letch grab me? You ask too much of me," I retorted. "Certainly, you understand I must protect myself against some of these animals," I emphasized.

Mr. Van Couwenhoven was a hideous man, only thinking of his coin.

"Listen to me quite well, you little Walloon," he retorted as his chubby face reddened with anger. "I'm giving you a chance to have a living, but you will end mine if you are not a little more lenient with my good customers! I don't care if you unleash that sharp tongue of yours with the foolish rogue sailors who are too drunk to remember what you say, but you will not chase away my better clientele. You understand me? Be polite!" he yelled.

I looked at Van Couwenhoven's son, Pieter, nodding as he raised his eyebrows at me, motioning to the back.

"Yes. For you, I can be ever so lenient," I said under my breath, staring into Pieter's bright blue eyes.

My heart raced a little at the chance to meet Pieter in the back. It was hard for me to take my eyes off his handsome cherub-like face, a face that hid the personality of a little rascal.

Mr. Van Couwenhoven ordered me to the storeroom one more time, not wanting to lose business.

"Marie, I said to go get another barrel of beer from the back. Do as I say!" Mr. Van Couwenhoven ordered me.

As mad as he was, he still liked me. It was worse when his wife was around too. The husband was greedy but only resented me if I got in the way of profits. His wife was another story. I knew she'd despise me once she got wind of my budding romance with her son.

"I'll help her, father. The barrel is too heavy for her. We need some wine too," Pieter offered.

Too engrossed in filling his pockets, the old man seemed too oblivious to care and waved him off to help.

We walked past the brewing room permeated with the odors of malt and hops. His mother had finished boiling the wort, a mashed barley and water concoction, and placed it in a vat that morning. She added the flavor of a nice, rich hops and cooked it down further. Now it was cooling. The spent grains were still not set out for the animals and added to other already strong aromas.

I loved that smell, but I loved Pieter's scent even more and I eagerly followed him.

"Have you thought about me lately?" said Pieter Wolfertsen van Couwenhoven. He was only three years older than I.

"How can I not think about you? You're always nearby," I teased.

"We're finally alone, my lovely Marie," he winked, approaching me and pulling me close to him. "Ah Marie, you beauty."

My skin tingled at Pieter's touch and my face flushed as he pressed himself against me amid barrels of beer and bags of barley.

"What are you doing to me, Pieter?" I asked, giving in to his kisses for the first time, completely letting down my guard.

He laughed. "Doing what any young man does when he feels smitten. You feel the attraction between us too. Don't you, Marie?" he said as he caressed my face and slickly moved his hand to explore my body. Something inside me knew not to trust the innocent-looking scoundrel, but I was confused. All I knew was that his touch felt good—a feeling I hadn't fully experienced before. "Why not give in to it?" I easily persuaded myself to open my heart and my body to him.

At that time, I really do think that Pieter fancied me. He ignited the passion within me to a full flame of desire. He was a smooth one, that boy.

"I must have more of you, Marie," he stated when his father called out for us to hurry with the beer. "I'll protect you from the rough sailors and soldiers that come into the bar. I won't let them be crass or rude to you. Just let me into your life a little more," he winked and stole one last kiss.

As we made our way back to the main tavern rooms, I smiled at the thought of future rendezvous. I felt freer than I had felt for a long time. I carried on with the rest of my day, humming a little Walloon song about the mating dance of a rooster after a prized hen. My chores ceased to be as cumbersome as they had been that morning.

The Couvenhoven's tavern on Pearl Street was not far from the docks and in view of incoming ships reaching their long journey's final destination. Business was booming ever since the West India Company opened up the fur trade a couple of years before. Throngs of people poured into our little Dutch colonial port town from faraway places of Africa, Europe, and Brazil. With travelers seeking their fortunes in our frontier commodities of wild animal skins, mostly beaver pelts, the town bustled and grew.

Pieter came to New Amsterdam with his father and mother about six years after I arrived in the Dutch colony with my family. They had a little more clout than us Walloons and more money too. His mother never really liked me. She thought I was unrefined. Only briefly having known the culture of Leiden and Amsterdam in my early years, most of my formative years were spent being raised like the Natives we first encountered on Manhattan. It was no wonder I didn't carry myself like the ladies fresh off the ships from Holland. But I had true grit. Why would a man want refinement when strength, endurance, and flexibility were more useful qualities here in the rowdy Dutch colony?

Eventually, his mother saw the attraction between us. I don't think his parents liked it that he had a fancy for me. They thought they were much better than my family of Walloons. Their feelings did not stop our passions. The closeness of the tavern nearly every day and night made Pieter and me became all the more infatuated. His mother, an old scold, was not pleased when we flirted, but her glare couldn't stop us. After all, Papa told me to have fun. Pieter and I were both in our early twenties and ready for an adventurous tryst. It never took us too far from the tavern.

Our affair flourished after our encounter in the storeroom. One night after closing the tavern, Pieter seduced me fully.

"Goodnight. See you tomorrow," I called out to the Van Couwenhovens as I left the wooden building. I hadn't seen Pieter for a few minutes. Walking out onto Pearl Street, he snuck up behind me and whispered in my ear.

"Come with me, Marie. It's time to go somewhere to be alone. Come quickly before anyone sees us," he pleaded.

He grasped my hand and took me to a barn in the back where customers could tie up their horses with the milk cow and a couple of pigs. Leading me past the restless animals, he brought me to a loft. I felt excited to be with Pieter but still wasn't sure that I should play with him in the hay bed he had made for us, hidden within a wall of bales. I didn't have much time to think.

There in the loft, he overtook me quite easily. Pieter felt entitled to have his way with me and I did not resist. I wanted us to discover as much of each other as we could. That is how our relationship began.

The tavern seemed sweeter after that night. A fire deep inside me was ablaze. We sought excuses to be in the back room, hidden in our favorite place between barrels of beer when his father wasn't looking. We weren't very discreet even though we thought we were.

For many days, he would sneak me up to the loft in the barn after closing.

We delighted in the reward of exploring each other there amongst the animals and sneaking intimate encounters in the corners of the tavern when no one was looking. It didn't last long though.

Pieter's mother had other plans for her son. She probably knew what was happening between us and she made it clear in her lack of warmth and treatment of me that she didn't ever want me to be her future daughter-in-law.

With her conniving, coaxing, and planning Pieter soon caught the glance of Hester Symons Dawes, a wealthy widow. She quickly staked her claim on my lover. Her husband Jacques de Vernius, a tobacco farmer, died quite suddenly in October that same year, leaving her with a nice sum of earthly goods. Both Pieter's mother and his father, always thinking of their monetary gain, approved heartily of their budding relationship.

I quickly found out Pieter had never been in love with me. He thought so at first but he was merely using me to satisfy his urges. I noticed his passions waned as Hester's presence increased. He took me to the loft less often until finally one day his mother called me to approach her in the brewery when she was mashing barley and water together to make the wort for the next batch of beer.

"Marie, your time with us must end. We can no longer employ you. We have a cousin who will arrive shortly from Utrecht. He is family and must take your place. You understand?" she said with little care.

I stared at her, stunned. Where was Pieter? I knew he was avoiding me, the little coward of a man.

"Of course, you must know how these situations must end," she continued. "We can keep you until Saturday and then you must go find other work."

I was furious. Pieter had jilted me, letting his mother do the dirty work. I'd hunt him down, the lout.

Past the orchards of ripening peaches and plums, past the strong odors of beaver pelts waiting to be shipped from the warehouses nearby, past the lapping waters of the shore, I raced to get my revenge. I continued to traverse the muddy streets until I heard the whistling Dutch flag of Fort Amsterdam whipping in the wind.

Finally, after looking down several streets, I found him beyond the fort, at the windmill. He was not only getting more grains for his mother, but he was also flirting with Hester as her servant pretended not to notice. A few other townspeople mingled about and spoke with the miller, Abraham Pieterszen. They couldn't help but be taken aback by the storm that had just rolled in.

"Pieter, I want to have a word with you right now. Look at me in the eyes. You be the one to tell me what needs to be said. Not your mother, you immature little beast. I will not stand for this mistreatment!" I yelled.

I looked at Hester.

"Careful, chérie. This rogue and his family only want your money and your tobacco houses. Don't expect anything more," I blurted.

Anxious to be rid of me and hoping to avoid further embarrassment, he grabbed my arm and quickly led me outside.

Pieter looked at me sheepishly.

"I'm sorry, Marie. Our affair was amusing for both of us. I know you enjoyed it too. But I cannot give you anything more," he stammered.

I slapped him on the face as hard as I could.

"No. It is I who would never want to be with someone like you. I am finished with you for good. Don't think of ever being with me again," I shouted.

I stomped off abruptly, holding onto my pride the best I could.

"Marie, I wish you well. I did not wish to cause you any harm. It is for the best," he called out after me.

I kept walking away as fast as I could, not looking back. There was nothing more to say. I had learned the bruising lesson of what it felt like to be used.

Later that day, I went with my papa to collect the last of my earnings.

Leaving Wolfertsen van Couwenhoven's tavern for the last time, I had no idea what was ahead of me. The tavern and its owners had been my teachers in ways that I hadn't expected. I learned a lot about brewing and tavern keeping from them. But more importantly, through Pieter, I learned that I could finally open up to someone in a relationship. It was too bad he was such an opportunist.

In the end, he was right. It was for the best. I deserved better. He'd sown his wild oats with me, but with the influence of his family, he'd decided that I was not good enough to marry. My dowry could never be one like Hester's.

A few short months later, he was married and settled in with Hester Dawes to the satisfaction of his family. Their nuptials confirmed to me that my last suspicions about him were correct all along. It was little consolation as I patted my large round belly, ripe with fruit from Pieter's planted seed.

CHAPTER THREE:

Tinker & Winthrop's Story
Boston, Massachusetts Bay Colony
1637

John Tinker paced the floor of the large English clapboard home of Governor Winthrop. Where was his sponsor? He placed one foot in front of the other going back and forth again in the confined space of the hall.

Wiping sweat from his brow, the young man with the wavy brown hair did his best to remain calm. Before the hearth in the hall of the newly installed governor, he eyed the roaring fire and wished that Mr. Keayne would arrive. Normally not disposed to nervousness, today was a rare day that he gave in to it.

Mr. Keayne, a colleague of his deceased father, a wealthy merchant, and his occasional employer, had put in a good word to Winthrop. The governor needed to hire a worthy and talented young man to help him settle his affairs in England as well as to take care of certain matters in the Massachusetts Bay Colony. Mr. Keayne had been fatherly since Tinker's father had died, aiding him and pushing him in the right directions as he had promised Tinker's mother he would.

Suddenly, Tinker heard the sound of laughter and footsteps heading towards him.

"Well, what have we here? You're a familiar sight!" said John Winthrop Jr. as he patted the young man on the shoulder. A welcoming smile of delight greeted Tinker.

"My dear friend's younger brother! Do you recall? I remember you from London's Inner Temple when you came to visit your brother Robert with your father. I was sorry when I heard of both of their deaths some time ago."

John Tinker did remember him and bowed. He immediately felt at ease. He had forgotten the connection. After all, he was just a boy when he met his older brother Robert's friend during his law studies.

"Of course, young Mr. Winthrop. I do remember you with great fondness. You were quite kind and tolerant of me when I came to visit there. It is so good to see you again," stated John Tinker and shook his hand heartily.

"As it is also to see you! What brings you here today?"

Tinker noticed a leather-bound book cradled in the younger Winthrop's grasp. It was in Latin with Elizabethan lettering. *Compendium Heptarchiæ Mysticæ* by John Dee.

Dr. John Dee? The personal magician and astrologer to Queen Elizabeth? Tinker thought, distracted at seeing the mysterious book. Most curious of all was the symbol on its cover, the moon fused with the sun, Mercury, and another symbol whose meaning he was unsure of.

"Are you all right, John Tinker?" asked Winthrop.

"Aye, of course. I was just noticing your book. Is it the writings of John Dee, famous mathematician and the magus of the dearly departed Queen Elizabeth?" asked Tinker.

"It is! I'm a voracious reader of anything by John Dee. I admire him in more ways than one. He was a rare genius of a man, a man of science, a man of alchemy, a man who also learned the language of the angels," Winthrop said.

"They say the great magus could produce images of people as if he had peered into the depths of their souls," Tinker said.

Winthrop laughed. "Aye, Dee is famous for all his soothsaying and magic, but his studies of the ancient philosophies are lesser known. So tell me, Tinker, what brings you here?" Winthrop asked curiously.

"I wait for your father and Mr. Keayne to discuss settling affairs in England and possibly working for your father here. It would be a great privilege, and I welcome the chance to be a humble servant to your family."

"That would be wonderful! I will put in a good word for you. Have you followed in your brother's footsteps?" asked the younger Winthrop.

"In as much as studying the law, yes. Just as he did, I attended London's Inner Temple. And I was trained by my father to be a merchant as well," Tinker said.

Winthrop nodded approvingly.

A hurried knock at Governor Winthrop's door interrupted their conversation. An indentured servant came out to answer the caller. Tinker sighed. Mr. Keayne in all his glory had finally arrived. Mr. Keayne was a large man with full cheeks and chin. He had a booming voice and assuredness of his place amongst merchants as well as among the religious. He was a prominent figure in Boston. As one of the original investors in the Puritan enterprise of the Massachusetts Bay Colony, he had the respect and the ear of Governor Winthrop.

"Greetings, young Mr. Winthrop. Here you are, Mr. Tinker. I'm sorry to be running late. A foal was newly born at my stable and delayed my departure. I see you have met the distinguished younger Mr. Winthrop," he said, looking at John Tinker.

The younger Winthrop responded quickly and enthusiastically.

"Yes, God has brought an old friend to us! I studied law with his brother Robert in London. It must be ordained that he should be with us!" he said.

As they were talking, a female servant had knocked on the door of the governor's study to announce that everyone had arrived. He was happy to see his son addressing the guests.

"Good day, everyone. I see the Lord has brought you here without incident," the governor said.

Tinker bowed once again in the governor's direction.

"Good afternoon, Governor. This is the young man who has been in my employ for months. His father was a reputable wool merchant from Berkshire. He is the one whom I highly recommend to be of service to you," Keayne said, turning towards John Tinker.

"Father, he is the younger brother of my dear friend Robert who studied with me at the Inner Temple. Unfortunately, Robert was lost to us several years ago. Do you not think it providence that his brother has found us here in the Bay through the introduction of our esteemed friend, Mr. Keayne? Mr. Keayne also knew Robert and the elder Mr. Tinker," explained the younger Winthrop.

"Indeed, it may be, but first let us talk, young Mr. Tinker. Everyone, please sit down. Agatha, please bring our guests some cider," the governor said.

Tinker noted the elder Winthrop seemed more rigid. Perhaps it was the weight of responsibility for the direction of the colony on his shoulders or the dedication he had towards its religious goals. Yet, the colony leader was kind to him. The men talked only briefly before Governor Winthrop decided that John Tinker was suitable for the position. Tinker was slightly nervous. He knew Winthrop would have the highest of expectations of him but would be fair also.

"Very well, John Tinker. It is settled. I would like you to come to live with us. It will make the task of preparing to settle my affairs in England easier for you. Would that be possible?" asked the elder Winthrop tilting his head and clasping his hands together.

Tinker averted his eyes to the mystical tome of John Dee with gold lettering that the younger Winthrop had placed on the table. Intrigued at the prospect of living with and working for such an interesting family, Tinker knew what he must say.

"Aye, sir. The pleasure would be mine. I will be here and available as a faithful servant to do what is expected of me."

Governor Winthrop nodded, pleased that the young man seemed enthusiastic to start his position and relieved that he came with high recommendations from both his oldest son and Mr. Keayne.

It was no surprise that John Tinker became a close and trusted member of the Winthrop family. Tinker often confided in the younger Winthrop and the relationship developed into one of brotherly friendship. For his part, Winthrop was more than happy to be a surrogate brother for his lost friend when he could. He could even predict that he would share some of his alchemical studies with John Tinker but only after he received further signs that his future pupil was ready.

CHAPTER FOUR:

Tinker & Winthrop's Story
Boston, Massachusetts Bay Colony
1637

Tinker and his friend, Winthrop Jr., sat in the hall on a chilly Monday morning. They were both up before the sun rose. Even the hearth was cold, and the fire had to be rekindled. The Indian servant had set out some hot cider and some bread with cheese along with porridge for breakfast.

"Tinker, you don't seem your jovial self today. What is afoot?" asked Winthrop.

"Aye, sir. My demeanor must look a bit baffled to you on this brisk morning. It's my dream, sir. It stays with me. But never mind. I need not pay too much attention and I don't want to trouble you with such frivolous things," Tinker said.

"Please, tell me what it is if you wish. A wise alchemist knows that some dreams are more than nonsense. A rare few hold many hidden keys to the universe," stated Winthrop.

"I am not familiar with what you speak of, but your expertise in the alchemical arts and your reputation is already well recognized in the colonies. I know very little about alchemy, but I have a curiosity to know more. Please take pity on me for I am naught but a man of law, trade, and commerce. For this, you may understand whether my mind speaks in confusion or in hidden messages," Tinker said.

"Aye, of course. What is it then? A nightmare?" asked Winthrop.

"No. 'Tis much more pleasant than that. 'Tis a dream of fanciful colors and a hint of Egyptian pharaohs of old," Tinker described.

Winthrop cocked his head in interest.

"What kind of colors, John?" he asked.

"A magnificent emerald infused into stone. But it's more than just a brilliant color and image. It carries with it a call to come. A deep yearning in me has awoken, yet I know not to what. There is something I must know. If only I knew what it was. Please forgive me for my reverie. I must fully wake up now and let it be. I have much work to prepare for your father today," said John Tinker apologetically.

"Not at all, Tinker. Sometimes, the mind is a window to the spirit world. God speaks to us in these little ways. It will come to you. You will know why one day. You are not alone. Others are seeing images and hints of a life obscured to most. Perhaps we will talk about these phenomena another day. Please come to me if you have visions or dreams like this. I may know what they mean. But for now let us leave it there in the dream world. I'd best be going for I have much work to do today as well," Winthrop explained.

"Aye, of course. I don't mean to burden you with curious imagery," said Tinker.

"No, Tinker. It is not that. It may be a message of great importance, and I may be able to help you with it. I simply must ponder it for a while, as must you. But pay attention to the longing in your heart. Does it fade away? Or does it persist? We will talk more," he assured John Tinker.

"Thank you, sir, we will," Tinker answered.

John Tinker thought about their conversation. It was a strange occurrence. He would take the advice of Winthrop and let the desire for the deep emerald stone at the forefront of his mind linger there longer. Was he desirous to be even closer to it?

For several days, he prepared the documents needed by the governor, all the while surrounded by the energy of the emerald stone that transfixed him. The sensation became stronger with time and did not disappear. The dream of the emerald stone had opened doors to worlds he had known with a vague familiarity yet could not name.

Another mystery unfolded in a dream about a week later. Tinker was standing in open meadows framed by an ancient land forested by great trees. It was bright even though clouds were above. John Tinker observed a pure golden light descending from the heavens. As it reached him, it slowly and gently engulfed him, concentrating at his heart. In the dream, he was filled with perfect peace and calm. Upon awaking, he smiled and prayed. Something spectacular was to come. This was a key of some kind—a key that he knew he should share with his friend Winthrop. Perhaps the governor's son would be ready to comment and share his insights.

Tinker gingerly knocked on the door of Winthrop's laboratory. He was free for the day after preparing many documents for the governor. The laboratory was in an outbuilding with its own furnace. Strange smells emanated from within the structure. There was no immediate answer.

Tinker started to doubt the wisdom of bothering Winthrop with his personal concerns and started to head away. Surely, the young master was too busy for him. He spent hours in his study and laboratory. Even though he assisted his father in some duties of the colonies, he much preferred to immerse himself in his alchemical studies. He was equally devoted to utilizing his knowledge by developing ironworks and other practical endeavors.

At that thought, the door opened. Winthrop gestured to John Tinker to come in.

"I was expecting you, Tinker. I knew you would come. Please enter."

John Tinker walked across the threshold, observing rows of fine books on shelves. Many of Winthrop's cherished volumes were open on tables alongside odd flasks and other glassware. The fire in the furnace was filled with red, hot embers cooking an unknown white substance. An unopened crate contained a curious insignia of the sun, half-moons, and Mercury— the same one he'd seen on the cover of Dee's book.

"Before we go any further, John Tinker, you must know this. Men have died in their quest to learn the secrets of alchemy and thereby the secrets of the universe. There must be absolute secrecy in what we say to each other. God has bestowed his secrets and knowledge of his natural laws into the hands of few men. They have risked their lives to pass on their knowledge. Men such as Giordano Bruno and other great philosophers and seekers have burned in the flames of the Inquisition as perceived heretics. I beseech you; there must be complete trust between us. Are you ready to know and tell more?" Winthrop asked, gazing at Tinker intensely, testing his reaction.

"Sir, I am honored to be in your circle and even more honored that you deem me worthy of such mysteries. I know in my heart that I am ready to tell all," vowed Tinker.

Winthrop smiled in his gentle way.

"Then be not afraid to share your dream. Does it still hold power over you?"

"Sir, the dream of the emerald stone stays with me, and another of equal power has appeared in another dream," said Tinker reverently.

Winthrop nodded, "Go on, what is it?"

"A vision of gold rays from the heavens in a field bordered by ancient trees. They surrounded my heart, providing me with an unfamiliar peace," Tinker said.

Tinker looked intently at Winthrop, feeling more vulnerable than ever before. It was a strange feeling for a confident, intelligent young man of worldly pursuits. He would normally not open up to another in such a candid way. But with Winthrop, he was at ease.

Winthrop paused and sought to clarify the significance of the images conveyed to Tinker in his dreams.

"What you have seen is the Emerald Tablet. It contains the holy works of Hermes Trismegistus. The ancient Hermes was both a great leader of his people and a spiritual teacher. In ancient Egypt, the natural ways of the universe were revealed to Hermes and then passed on by him to his people. Those were times of light and transcendence between the earthly realms and other higher planes. But then the world was thrust into darkness by man's ignorance and destructiveness. The sacred knowledge had to be hidden. It has remained obscured so that it can survive and go forward through the ages through wise men and sages until humankind isready to honor its wisdom again," said Winthrop.

John Tinker listened in awe. He was being drawn into a secret and magnificent world.

Winthrop continued, "The Emerald Tablet was the foundation of the teachings of Hermes, who is of the divine source of the One Mind. It is from this tablet that all his other sacred teachings evolved and were written into thousands of scrolls which he hid in columns of an ancient Egyptian temple before he left this Earth. Many of the writings are gone now, but some were passed on to the ancient Greeks, Arabs, and then Jews. The great library of Alexandria had many of these works of antiquity, but it too was destroyed. But some of those ancient texts that survived have most recently come into the hands of small groups of Christians," explained Winthrop.

Tinker looked perplexed but wanted to know more.

By contrast, Winthrop exuded the serenity of angels as he continued.

"John Tinker, you are meant to assist me. It is part of a greater plan. The sign that you gave me was proof it must be so. The Emerald Tablet is calling you to learn its wisdom. I can teach you, and you can assist me to create a great center of alchemy in this colony."

"A sign, sir? How can I possibly have a sign for you?" Tinker asked.

"God works in mysterious ways, Tinker. But your vision of the Emerald Tablet and your interest in the alchemical arts has clear meaning. What say you? Do you want to turn back or will you come into the light of natural wisdom?" questioned Winthrop.

He pivoted and approached a table near the fire where he picked up an old leather-bound book whose pages had yellowed with time. He leafed through them for a minute until he found what he was looking for.

"Come, Tinker. If you so desire and commit to this journey, if you swear to utmost secrecy, I will show you the meaning of what your soul is trying to introduce you to in dreams."

"Yes, sir, I am committed. I am honored to embark on this journey of sacred knowledge with you. I swear an oath upon my own life that what is discussed between us will not be shared with anyone," vowed Tinker.

John Tinker placed a hand over his own heart.

Winthrop smiled and gestured for him to come closer.

"Please, sit with me now," he said, inviting his new adept.

"Close your eyes and listen to these sacred words—the long-sought words that your dream foresaw that led you to me."

"In truth, without deceit, certain and most veritable.

That which is Below corresponds to that which is Above and that which is Above corresponds to that which is Below, to accomplish the miracles of the One Thing.

And just as all things have come from this One Thing, through the meditation of One Mind, so do all created things originate from this One Thing through Transformation.

Its Father is the Sun. Its Mother is the Moon. The Wind carries it in its belly. Its nurse is the Earth. It is the origin of All, the consecration of the Universe. Its inherent Strength is perfected if it is turned into Earth."

Winthrop continued for several more minutes, also reflecting on the meaning of the sage old words that he had read for himself many hundreds of times.

John Tinker slowly opened his eyes to the dappled light in the room. He was still unsure as to what it all meant.

"With the applications of alchemy, we can achieve worldwide reformation. Through the study of natural laws, an alchemist seeks to know God. And through the means of the alchemist's study of nature and science, God, in turn, reveals himself to man."

John Tinker thought of Copernicus, Galileo, and Dee—men who dedicated their lives to seeking intimate knowledge of the world and cosmos around them.

"The Above corresponds to that which is Below, meaning the Earth can be a perfect likeness of the heavens. However, such a great advancement in consciousness can come only after careful rediscovery of lost knowledge," Winthrop said, rubbing his palm across a gold-embossed book.

"It is said that the brotherhood of the Rosy Cross will, through a process of Christian and Hermetic reformation by study of nature and service to humanity, help to make the world whole again. The Christ-child Jesus brought his light into the world and was of service to mankind out of pure love. And alchemy, as explained through Hermes' teachings, can help us achieve this purity by transforming that which is corrupt."

Winthrop paused, moved by a force far stronger than his own soul.

"In this way, the light shall come again. He shall rise and take His disciples with Him but only when we are prepared," stated Winthrop.

"On Earth, we must create conditions necessary for His coming. Both men and women and people of all races must be trained in basic universal knowledge in order to be ready." Winthrop paused and then explained further.

"The Christ learned from and emulated the principles of Hermes as encoded in the ancient Kabbalah. The Kabbalah encoded the sacred Hermetic teachings passed on to Hebrew mystics. The hidden knowledge continues to come out of obscurity today through Christian philosophers in conjunction with the study of God's natural world. John Dee, through his study, helped to unlock many of the old mysteries through procuring ancient texts and natural magic. Without a doubt, both Christ and nature are the paths to enlightenment."

Winthrop paused again and looked at Tinker who was hanging on to his mentor's every word yet looked exhausted. Winthrop smiled kindly when he saw the young man try to hold back a yawn with no success. Winthrop, like any good teacher, knew when to give his student a rest. Tinker needed to stop, replenish his wits, and ponder the things he learned.

"We will talk more later. There is so much to learn, but all in good time," he said, patting John Tinker on the shoulder.

"The study and manipulation of visible and occult forces can last many lifetimes," he said.

To John Tinker, it seemed that Winthrop was noble in his spiritual pursuits and if they helped mankind he would gladly be a part of his alchemical vision to help the world and establish New England as an alchemical center. Tinker was determined to study diligently until he understood the wisdom of Hermes that many had died to preserve throughout the ages. And even if he never reached such an understanding, he could support his friend Winthrop in doing so. For many believed the Apocalypse was near and man needed to be ready. All he knew was that there was too much pain and suffering in the world. He'd be happy to help usher in more light.

CHAPTER FIVE:

Tinker & Winthrop's Story
Boston, Massachusetts Bay Colony
1638

John Tinker picked up the crisp document, eyed the signature of Mr. Keayne and rolled it up again, placing it into a satchel of important papers. Sitting down at his desk, he reviewed several more in the hand of Governor Winthrop. Everything was in order. He would represent legal transactions on behalf of those powerful men and bring their affairs in England to a close.

He dabbed his quill into the inkwell and wrote the final notes of an agenda that he hoped would be free of complications and hasten a quick return to the Bay. His family relationships and business affairs had been on hold for far too long. He was anxious to bring his cousin to Windsor in Connecticut Colony where the rest of his family had relocated from Dorchester, Massachusetts.

A knock at the door interrupted his concentration. Looking up, John saw the face of Robin Cassacinamon, the Winthrops' servant and a Pequot tribesman. He held a stack of folded clothes in his hands.

"The clothes from the tailor are ready for your voyage," he said, placing the pile of personal supplies into John's hands. His English was fluent.

John rose from the desk and placed the breeches, stockings, and other apparel into one of the many traveling chests that stood open. Only one was for his personal use. The others held items from the New World including Indian masks, the furs and bones of native animals, dried plants, colorful feathers, and other New World treasures to be bequeathed to dignitaries and the King. Robin eyed the opened chests. He had contributed fathoms of wampum to the collection. It was impressive and meant to elicit more support and interest in the fledgling colony.

Tinker's friend, Winthrop Jr., had briefed him about the status of Robin Cassacinamon. The young Pequot man had offered himself as a personal servant to Governor Winthrop. The Pequot War fought the year before had disrupted traditional Indian alliances and all but destroyed the Pequot nation. It was under these circumstances that Robin was forced to become a tributary to his rival, the sachem of the Mohegan tribe, Uncas.

Despite all this, Uncas sent Robin with ten other Indian men to Winthrop's home where they offered several fathoms of wampum for a Pequot woman slave given to Winthrop as a spoil of war. Uncas was desirous of her and wanted to take her as his wife. Winthrop refused the offer, but Robin stayed on.

It was obvious to John Tinker, an astute observer, that Robin had other motives. It eventually became known by both Tinker and Winthrop Jr. that Robin Cassacinamon was more than a Pequot survivor curious to learn the English ways. He was respected and sought out amongst his remaining fellow Pequots and he was also the descendant of powerful sachems. Robin's intelligence and hunger to learn would prove assets to his survival and helped him build a relationship with Winthrop Jr. that was advantageous to both.

Curious to learn all about English ways and culture, Robin was quick to be receptive and friendly with both Winthrop Jr. and John Tinker at their invitation. He was smart and learned the English language quickly, largely with the instruction of Winthrop Jr. The young Englishmen also wanted to learn as much as they could about Robin and the landscape of Indian country. They too had their ulterior motives. The men would help each other.

Furthermore, Robin needed allies. Unbeknownst to the English, his leadership of the few hundred surviving Pequots was beginning to consolidate. His defeated tribe, whose members were massacred or made into slaves of whites or subjugated to other Indian tribes, was not even allowed to legally exist according to the Treaty of Hartford drawn up after the war. Winthrop Jr. was the perfect ally. And he and Robin could support each other.

Winthrop Jr. knew that his relationship with Robin Cassacinamon held the key he needed to establish his alchemy center in the New World. Only the Natives held the knowledge of deeply hidden mineral deposits helpful to Winthrop for his iron metal works and other similar projects. They knew the environment like no colonial settler could, and Robin could greatly aid him with his quest to locate the best place to establish his center.

In addition, Winthrop would need an Indian negotiator who could help with peaceful land transfers and purchases as well as cooperative agreements to ensure safe transport of his mined treasures to his alchemy center.

"Mr. Tinker, have a safe voyage to England. Tell the King the truth about the Pequots. Tell him we can work together."

"Robin, I thank you for your kind words. I appreciate the tokens you gave freely so that His Majesty and his court may learn something good of the Indian ways and the country."

With that pronouncement, Robin gave a slight bow and carried on with his other tasks.

John Tinker had one more thing to accomplish—a last meeting with his employer's son. Winthrop Jr. had promised to come visit before Tinker left for England.

Life had taken interesting turns since John Tinker settled in with the Winthrop clan. He continued to assist the elder Winthrop and local businessmen. He was also being instructed in the art and science of alchemy by the younger Winthrop, all the while keeping his personal life as concealed as his alchemical secrets.

Winthrop Jr. handed the note to one of his father's servants.

"Please drop this off to Tinker in his room."

It looked like gibberish to one uneducated in the cryptic ciphers of the alchemists. But this was no ordinary code. He developed it himself and only shared it with his wife Elizabeth, his good friend Edward Howes, and now,

Tinker. He smiled as he thought of his last test for Tinker to see if he remembered the solution to the elaborate puzzle set on paper.

Winthrop Jr. waited in his laboratory in the early morning hours before anyone else, except for a few servants, had awoken. How long would he wait for John Tinker? Lighting candles one by one, he enjoyed the calm and peace of his mystical and personal retreat from the outside world.

It wasn't long before the expected knock was heard on the thick wooden door. Winthrop hastened to open it, grinning mischievously at Tinker.

"'Twas not a long wait, my dear friend. The adept has reached another level," he said.

The men embraced heartily for the first time in several weeks.

"Aye. 'Tis so at last." Tinker smiled with satisfaction.

"Our messages to each other will not be thwarted by any spy or foe when I am in England," he said.

Since reuniting in the colonies, the two men had become cherished friends. It was just a matter of time before Tinker would be finished working for his father and assist Winthrop Jr. with his own elaborate plans.

Winthrop Jr. made sure that Tinker had become skilled in secret codes and lessons in natural magic. He taught Tinker to complete several operations in transmutation. They talked long hours about finding the Philosopher's Stone, the Elixir of Life, and the coming of Christ, often reading passages aloud from books in Winthrop's library late into the night. Winthrop explained the meaning of the ancient texts and their place in early history as well as forgotten treatises from the early sages.

They were both greatly impacted by the work of John Dee and the sweeping Rosicrucian movement that sought to merge the ancient Hermetic teachings with the reformist view of Christ's teachings.

Aside from being a dutiful and intelligent friend, Tinker had a solid practical side to him. Endowed with the gift of pragmatism that often escaped Winthrop Jr. who was ever immersed in new creative efforts and philosophical quests, he was the perfect compliment. He was the sun to Winthrop's moon. He was earth to Winthrop's fire.

Tinker was someone who Winthrop was always able to count on and would remain so his entire life. Not long into their relationship, Winthrop had known that Tinker's pragmatism and attention to important yet mundane details would unite with his own visions and spiritual dream, allowing them to manifest in a splendid reality, in a perfect transmutation of the Above with the Below. With his assistant Tinker, he would be able to accomplish many things.

From the beginning, Tinker helped Winthrop retrieve supplies or books from English ships sent over by many of Winthrop's alchemist friends in the mother country or elsewhere in Europe. The vast majority of the barrels and crates were stocked with lab supplies, ancient texts, metals, angelic crystals, and other treasures as well as letters of correspondence.

They came largely from Winthrop's old classmate, the alchemist Edward Howes whom he met during his law studies in London at the Inner Temple. Easily recognizable from the insignia of the *Monas Hieroglyphica*, the magical symbol embodying the entire universe and all its elements, the same one Tinker saw on the book by John Dee, Tinker found the barrels and crates in each shipment without confusion.

Winthrop trusted Tinker to such a degree that he sometimes shared the contents of letters he received from Edward Howes with him. Many ideas in the letters were pertinent to their plans to form an alchemical center in the New World. Just as John Tinker was a practical support for Winthrop to realize his alchemical goals and that center, Edward Howes was the supportive friend in England who helped supply what was needed and gave sage advice and guidance. In turn, Howes deemed Winthrop as the spiritual and colonial leader of this endeavor and encouraged his friend in every way possible to make it a reality as a service to all of humanity.

"It pleases me to see you again in good health, Tinker. We have much to discuss. More possibilities and openings are happening. Our plans will move forward quickly once your business is done in England. As Howes had suggested to me, and I find it with good reason, I have learned many important things from Robin Cassacinamon in regards to the Indians. They are crucial in our endeavor," declared Winthrop.

"Aye, I recall Mr. Howes' words to learn from the Natives, to seek out their advice for the best places to settle, for their intimate knowledge of the country, and for their aid in understanding Indian relations."

Winthrop pulled out the letter from Howes and read it.

The more love and respect you gain from the sagamores and sachems, the more love and fear you gain from the common natives. Bestow respect and honor unto such and the lesser will soon come under; so win the hearts of the sachems and you win all.

"Aye. And now it is apparent that Robin comes from a line of sachems, but I worry that if this became widely known among some English, they would go after his life," spoke Tinker.

"You are a wise man, John Tinker. Had his exalted position been known during the war or even shortly after, he would be dead this day. We cannot allow for such a possibility. That brings me to my next point which ties all of our future goals neatly together," he said.

He paused to make sure his pupil and alchemical assistant grasped the significance of what he was about to say next.

Tinker nodded. "Go on, sir," he said.

Winthrop riffled through his letters from Howes, finding the one that made their mission clear.

"I did not share this correspondence from Howes with you before. But now you are ready and must understand the whole of our purpose here in these colonies."

Before Winthrop read the second letter from Howes, he pulled out a peculiar book. The title was *The Circumference of the Earth*, or a *Treatise of the Northeast Passage* by Sir Dudley Digges. The word east had been crossed out and replaced with west.

"I will skip the familiarities and salutations and get to the heart of the matter," Winthrop said and began to read.

I shall and will by God's leave endeavor towards you and the work. Here enclosed you shall find a book of probabilities of the Northwest Passage not in the 60 or 70 degrees of northern latitudes, but rather about the 40th.

"That's near the former Pequot territories and at the center of New Amsterdam!" John Tinker cried out, wide-eyed.

Winthrop continued excitedly.

I suspect the Hollanders will have the glory and benefit of the passage about Hudson's River yet God the Author and Finisher of all works will have the final say for the good of His saints.

Winthrop put down the letter on the table before them and opened the book to Howe's inscription to him. Tinker was trying to absorb the full importance of what Winthrop was describing before him.

Thrice happy I should be if this little treatise should add anything to your knowledge, invention, or industry. I doubt the Dutch will prevent your discovery, for they are the nearest of any that have not as yet discovered the Passage. But doubtless there is a man set apart for the discovery thereof, to communicate more freely, more knowingly, and with less charge, the riches of the east with the pleasures of the west, and the east and the west meeting with mutual embracements, they shall so love each other that they are willing to be dissolved into each other. And so God in Christ through all the world and light shining in thickest darkness, and that palpable darkness being expelled, how great and glorious shall that light appear. With God of his mercy, hasten to accomplish.

Winthrop finished as both men stared at each other in silence.

"Thus far, Hudson and others have tried to find the Passage at higher latitudes and have failed. It's presumed that Hudson and many of his crew died searching for it," said Tinker. "Did he not think to find the passage at a latitude further south?"

"No. When Hudson sailed the North River many years ago, he turned around near Fort Orange and never explored branches that led further inland. I'm convinced the fortieth parallel is the key to finding the riches of the Orient, the key to uniting the East and the West Indies," stated Winthrop.

He paused and continued. "The sacred marriage as applied to the Earth, the unification of all, the completion of the circuit around the globe for the first time will lead to union, great light, and peace in the world. The work of finding the Philosopher's Stone cannot be completed until the union of the world is achieved. It is only then, when humankind is willing to accept the ancient teaching of Hermes, that Christ may come again. I am convinced this must be done by the English, the natural leaders of the reformation," said Winthrop, rubbing his chin.

"Help me to understand," said Tinker. "Are you saying that finding the Passage, a trading route to connect the East to the West, has a much deeper meaning? That it will also bring with it the spiritual goals of the Rosy Cross to bring unity and peace? To foreshadow the ultimate spiritual purification by finding the Philosopher's Stone? To bring total transformation to the world?" asked Tinker in awe.

"Aye, 'tis that important. For our part of it, we must focus on the location of our endeavor. A settlement at Pequot as the location of our alchemical center is vital to our work. It is closest to New Amsterdam at the boundary of English colonial territory on the edge of a great eastern sea. It is to the west of it and closer to New Amsterdam that we may discover the great sea to the west that will ultimately lead to the Northwest Passage. Eventually, the Dutch land must give way to the English who are more suited to do this great spiritual work," pronounced Winthrop.

"But it must not be left to just any Englishman, sir. This you know. It must be done peacefully and in secret with the cooperation of the Natives and the peaceful surrender of Dutch lands along the North River—Hudson's River. This is possible but only through alchemical means. You must accomplish this worthy aim, sir. Howes is correct," Tinker said.

He paused, looking Winthrop in the eye.

"Only you, 'the Sagamore of Agawam' as Howes calls you, can do this. You must lead this important endeavor that will ultimately bring light and peace to the world. It will be the decisive transmutation of the world. Below to be as is the world Above. And as a result, the Philosopher's Stone will be found, and all will be ready for the spiritual coming of Christ. We shall also prosper, and the entire world will benefit for the increased trade and riches of the Orient," Tinker emphasized.

"Thank you, John Tinker. Your faith in the work is important. Your trust and your secrecy are paramount as well. I will work to gain the blessings of Massachusetts to consider the founding of a new plantation at Pequot. If permission is granted, we must also consider the way in which it is done. Again, my dear Howes has encouraged me in dealings with the

Indians to live among them, to truly understand them and their traditions so that the land will truly become ours for the center, so that we have their full cooperation and that we learn as much as possible from them. Most Englishmen are still ignorant of the wisdom of this. We must also educate them in the traditions of the English: our language and the love available from Christ for all men."

"Aye. It is the better way to approach the Natives," Tinker agreed.

Winthrop looked satisfied and humbled by the calling.

"So may it be, John Tinker. We have much to accomplish. Robin will show us where to settle and gain the cooperation of other tribes for what is needed. He has already become an important advisor. He can act as an agent to represent us and help ease any misunderstandings about our intentions."

The eastern sun was starting to show itself just above the horizon and the magnificent beginning light of the day only magnified the significance of what the two men were discussing.

"I will keep all this close to my chest, sir. When I come back from England, I plan to settle in Windsor in Connecticut Colony. I must attend to my mother, sisters, and cousin but I will be closer to you at Pequot and can travel to you to help achieve the work."

"It is all coming together as God hath planned," Winthrop said, sighing contentedly.

"For now, I must give you my list of requested provisions from England. I also beseech you to seek out Edward Howes on my account. Give to him these coded letters in which I express our desires for the next steps of our venture. He will continue to give strength and support to our purpose and to our final mission. I know he will be pleased with our progress. From him, I'm sure you will find further texts and instruments that may be of use to us. It would please me to give him some local treasures to show a token of my loving friendship in return."

"It will be done," Tinker vowed.

"I bid you a safe journey, John Tinker. May God bless you and watch over you. I pray that everything you are entrusted to do for my father goes smoothly. And I thank you for personally assisting me," Winthrop finished.

Tinker left that very day on a tall sailing ship, returning to England for a much longer period than he had anticipated. As stability was starting to form in Massachusetts and Connecticut with new relationships and alliances between Indians and English to the north, life in the town of New Amsterdam was becoming more complicated with the arrival of Willem Kieft, the new Director of New Netherland.

CHAPTER SIX:

Marie's Story
New Amsterdam, New Netherland
1640

As the melons from Papa's farm grew, so did I. My baby and the pumpkins would be ripe together. My daughter, Aeltje Pieters was born the bastard child of Pieter Wolfertsen van Couwenhoven, a brewer on Pearl Street, future orphan master and schepen. My pet name for her was Alida, and she gave me some solace for my lost dreams.

Papa and Susanne stood by me after I realized I was with child. I often wondered if any of this would have come to pass had Papa been stricter with me. My Papa, who always found time for laughter, might have been a little more serious about protecting my innocence. What about my part? No, I would have fought any restriction he placed on me all the same.

Honestly, all I ever wanted was the chance to finally enjoy the affections of a man who I supposed had loved me. I was disappointed in my life and I had a little baby to care for. How I dreamed of a chance to be taken care of by someone else, someone for whom I was more than a practice lover.

I busied myself to contribute what I could to the family, all the while taking care of my daughter Alida. She grew into the image of her father, a little blond angel. I couldn't get away from Pieter. All I had to do was to gaze into my plump daughter's brilliant eyes to see him again.

One day, a much older man came to visit Papa at his little farm. His name was Cornelis Volckertsen Viele. I had known him since he first came to New Amsterdam. He had been friends with Papa from the early days of Manhattan. Now a widower, he started hanging around our farm and seemed more interested in visiting me than Papa.

When he saw me again after many months, he commented about my condition.

"Marie, I see you have gotten into a little trouble since you became a woman. Ah, but the baby, she is a beautiful child," he added and winked, touching my shoulder with a familiar pat.

I sulked and pulled back.

"Now, now, Marie. Don't take me seriously. I heard what happened. The whole town knows of your escapade with that knave of a young man, Pieter. Count your blessings that it did not work out. Had I been your father though, I don't think young Pieter would be as unscathed. It will be fine, my dear. You mustn't worry. Your future can still be bright," he smiled.

And so, that was how Cornelis, a man thirty-three years my senior, inserted himself into my life. Many years a trader and the owner of the great ship *Fortune*, he helped me to form a thousand paintings in my mind of his adventures in faraway places.

From time to time, he would say. "Marie, I am a solitary widower. What I long for more than anything are the kindnesses and the companionship of a warm-hearted young woman," he pleaded.

"Cornelis, I will sit with you as long as you tell me your stories, your splendid stories of places I can only imagine," I'd reply. I was at ease with him but in no rush to be the bride of an old trader. His patience, his kind-heartedness, and the fact that he was half French made our relationship a comfortable one.

Papa encouraged his visits. In Cornelis, he saw a reliable old friend and someone with enough wealth to provide some security to my child and me.

Cornelis also spoke to me about the politics of the day. He treated me with respect and considered my opinions. He did not seem to mind my independence and wit.

One evening, Cornelis and Papa came into our wooden house somewhat agitated. Their faces displayed great concern. That sat at the table to a good meal of fresh bread, a little cheese, fish and some cabbage salad—a testament to Susanne's culinary talents. I brought some beer for both men. Cornelis nodded to me but remained serious.

"Kieft is a fool!" he exclaimed to my father as he slammed his fist down hard on the table.

"His idiocy will lead to the death of this colony and all of its inhabitants," my father agreed. "I've tried to reason with the man, to explain the way our trade deals are negotiated with the Indians, but he is arrogant and stupid. He listens to no one!"

My father was frustrated. He worked with Director Kieft as an official messenger for the West India Company officers when he was not farming or trading Indian goods. We knew he hadn't been happy about the Director, but we hadn't understood specifically why.

"What is it? What has he done?" I asked innocently as Susanne looked on with my brothers and sisters.

"It's complicated, daughter, but no doubt you are smart enough to understand. Ever since the West India Company gave up its sole rights for fur trading, they have been in chaos and not as profitable. As a result, they have cut off important funds to run the fort and pay the soldiers. Kieft's ideas for solutions will only destroy us."

"But Papa, how can this be? New Amsterdam has doubled in size in such a short time. So many people have come here with their trades and to do business. Why should they have such losses?"

I looked at the table where Papa had placed strung sewant beads made by local Indians from quahog shells. English traders that came through New Amsterdam called them wampum beads. Five white sewant beads to the currency of one stiver was the current rate. Purple beads were not as bountiful and fetched a higher value.

"Yes, Marie. It's true, but the Director and the board of directors in Amsterdam failed to account for the results of their own changes. They neglected to devise other ways to make up for their declining revenues. What is needed is a wise man who recognizes the best solutions to this problem, but instead they sent Kieft, a know-nothing simpleton who refuses to learn what the established customs are," Cornelis passionately explained.

"Well, do you know why the imbecile is there residing in the Director's brick house at the fort?" asked Susanne, placing her hands on her hips triumphantly, eager to share some gossip about him.

"I hear the other ladies talking. Kieft has family in high places in the Dutch government and is the nephew to a wealthy merchant tied to the company. They say he has never done anything correctly. He has made catastrophe after catastrophe out of whatever they gave him to do. First, in La Rochelle, they entrusted him to an enterprise that ended failing so horribly that investors wanted to kill him! Then they sent him to the Ottoman Empire on a mission to free hostages where he also failed disastrously.

Papa looked at her and chuckled.

"It sounds like they were desperate to get rid of him in Holland," he said.

"So they thought, why not dump him on an innocent, unsuspecting colony? What possible harm could he do in the wilderness? That is how much regard they have for us!" exclaimed Cornelis.

"Yes, such a lack of respect after we sacrificed and built so much with our bare hands, living in dirt holes those first few years to help this company get started!" Susanne proclaimed emotionally.

"So, what is his brilliant idea now that the Dutch directors have let him loose to wreak havoc here? " I asked, trying to understand the situation.

"Listen to this. The fool has no idea of the Indian ways. He does not understand that you must exchange gifts when you initiate a relationship with them. He considers nothing of their ways in his decision making and this time he has gone too far with his ignorant ideas," Cornelis said and stroked his peppered gray beard.

"Yes. Dr. De La Montagne, our fellow Walloon, is at his wit's end as the only other member of Kieft's pointless governing board of New Amsterdam. The man is so likable it is difficult to defy Kieft, but he can only vote once for a resolution whereas Kieft votes twice. So what does it matter anyway?" questioned Papa.

"Kieft has passed a new directive to demand a special tax on the Indians in these parts for protecting them from hostile tribes—a tribute. They will be livid when they get word of it. They allow us to live here and as part of the agreement to share the land with them and protect their interests. I guarantee they will laugh in his face," stated Cornelis.

As my father and Cornelis predicted, the chiefs from tribes far and wide did just that. Kieft was furious that they did not take his edict seriously and looked for any way possible to start conflicts with them.

Fearing the worst was yet to come, Cornelis decided to take advantage of the booming trade while it was still profitable. He took off one last time for ports abroad. But before he did, he finally succeeded in seducing me. I'd brought him some vittles to take on his trip and was alone with him in his home.

"Please, Marie, give an old trader something to remember you by, something to come back to. You, my dear, are both the sun and the moon to me. You must know by now that you have my best intentions and heartfelt affections."

Perhaps I was weak, but I knew I had started to have feelings for him too. They were calm, not passionate, but I did love the man with his long peppered hair and his keen intellect. He was accommodating to my needs, and I felt relaxed and soothed by him. Certainly, there were worse unions. I gave the charming man what he wanted—a place in my bed. He was pleased by my acceptance of his gentle caresses and a willingness to never tire of his stories.

With his sweet goodbye, Cornelis left for sea a final time from New Amsterdam, hoping to settle every foreign account he had in other ports and close all final business he had in Holland. His intentions were to quit his life as a trader and mariner, immersing himself in a trade with others who made their living on land. The next morning, I waved from the shore as the *Fortune* cast off, not sure if he would make the return journey. I knew that he wanted to, but life had already taught me that nothing is certain.

And the Natives, the Wilden, as they were called by the Dutch, cautiously awaited their fate and prepared their defenses as Kieft seethed in anger. Rebuffed and humiliated by their blatant rejection of his proposal, he looked for any excuse to go to war with them. Indian relations hung on if only by the slightest strand of trust. We, who had lived with, traded with, and understood the Natives the most, carried on in the same ways of mutual and beneficial trade that we had always done and hoped for the best.

To my surprise, I thought of Cornelis more often than I had expected. As I busied myself with the care of my daughter and helping Papa on his farm, I wondered where Cornelis was and tried to imagine details of exciting ports of call. The months leading up to his return went by quickly. One day Papa came from the market near the fort and called out to me.

"The *Fortune* is in the harbor! Cornelis is back, Marie! You must greet him and show him your little surprise. He will be happy to see you, my daughter," Papa said.

"Go to him, Marie," my mother Susanne encouraged me.

I gave a pleading glance to my brothers and sisters to come with me, but they only shrugged their shoulders.

"Come, Alida. You will go with your mother then. Let us meet our dear friend at the water's edge," I said.

I put on her little cloak, tucked her curly blond cherub's hair into her cap and finally, carried her through New Amsterdam's streets until we reached Pearl Street with its little wooden house of a church facing the shore.

A lot had changed since Cornelis left, and more people kept coming, drawn to the many trading opportunities. The shopping district expanded from just a bakery and a few little taverns to many more enterprises. New warehouses stood filled with tobacco, pelts and other items, while more tracts of farmland cut further into the wild forests and meadows along the Wieguasgeck trail at a greater distance to the north from the fort.

The exploding population still needed civil improvements. Most of the homes were made of wood, there was no proper dock, and we suffered walking through the muddy streets where animals of all kinds competed for space. And the fort that we needed increasingly for protection, made of earth and stone, was already falling apart.

The sailors of the *Fortune* had just started to come ashore with much of the cargo from Europe, mostly goods for the Indian trade but some wares for the colonists too. Traders hearing of new merchandise were also at the shore ready with strings of sewant. Coins from many lands mixed with stivers and pounds. The mixing of cultures even in barter and coinage was diverse. Settlers and Indians alike arrived with beaver pelts hanging over their shoulders or on small carts in exchange for trade of duffel cloth, utensils, and any iron tool.

I knew it would be a little while before Cornelis appeared. I counted the wooden crates and the barrels as they were placed on the embankment and stacked into awaiting carts filled by a handful of African slaves and some other laborers. I'm not so sure why I was as anxious as I was. I regretted having any time to think.

Luckily, Cornelis must have noticed Alida and me at the shore from his perch on the ship and left his remaining sailors to organize the unloading of the rest of the cargo. He waved from a small rowboat, shouting to me as he approached. I was about to find out what he thought of my little surprise.

At first, he looked stunned as he approached close enough to see the round belly protruding from my skirts, but then he grinned and hugged Alida and me ever so tightly.

"Marie, you are with child? My child?" he asked, opening his eyes wide with anticipation and surprise.

"Yes. Of course, he's your child, Cornelis. Do you doubt your own virility?" I asked, nudging him as I laughed. All of my nervousness had gone away. He had a manner that eased awkwardness.

"I will take good care of you, Marie. You will see. We shall marry soon," he pronounced.

I pulled back. Marriage was something I was not so sure of. Living under the Dutch, I had the freedom to choose what I wanted. Having one child out of wedlock already, I knew it was possible to have another without the bonds of marriage. I did not mind Cornelis in my life, but he'd have to convince me for quite a bit longer before I finally gave in to his requests for a more permanent arrangement.

"As you wish Marie, but I cannot have my child being taken care of in your father's house. Please, come live with me. We can start a business together. I have wanted to open a tavern for a long time. What do you say, Marie?" he asked, lovingly drawing me closer to him.

"Yes. That's a plan I can live with. Let us see what happens and how we are together after the baby is born," I said.

"As you wish, Marie. You will see. I will take good care of you. You may marry me yet," he winked.

So after that, Cornelis and I started a new life together. I felt more secure than I had ever been. True to his word, Cornelis was a good father to our son who I named Aernoudt, after my grandfather. He was born in May of that year.

With a little prodding from Cornelis, my father helped me to bring Pieter Wolfersen van Couwenhoven to court in a paternity suit. It was overdue. Little Alida deserved to be acknowledged by her father and receive his financial support.

Cornelis was right about marrying me one day. We said our vows in front of Dominie Bogardus, the town minister, the following summer when Aernoudt was a year old. Cornelis had a house built for us on the double highway across from the West Indian Company gardens. Behind it was a big swamp. Within a few years, a big ditch was used to drain it, and that was the beginning of the Heere Gracht, the gentleman's canal.

We bought a tavern near the slip where the ferry went back and forth across from Breuckelen, just at the end of Maiden Lane. We named it *The Salty Rose* in honor of the stands of wild sea roses in bloom we found growing next to it. Cornelis also thought it fitting because he said I was his fair rose, a beautiful one with a salty tongue. Our business at *The Salty Rose* thrived in the beginning.

But just as I was settling easily and comfortably in my family life, opposite forces were playing themselves out in our colony. With so many new arrivals, outward expansion and increased trade, prosperity and hope should have been at our doorstep, but thanks to Kieft and his recklessness, our community faced menacing threats of impending doom and violence.

The same year Aernoudt was born, Kieft found a reason to go after the Natives. He accused the Raritans of stealing hogs from the farm of David de Vries on Staten Island. But David de Vries, owner of the farm, a trader and our friend from the early days, didn't believe the accusations. He even warned Kieft that the Indians would get their revenge if he kept offending them and provoking them.

Ignoring De Vries' advice and to avenge for the supposed theft of the hogs, Kieft sent eighty soldiers led by secretary Cornelias Van Tienhoven to the nearby Raritan village where they killed several Natives. The sachem's brother was taken hostage on a sloop back to the fort where he was tortured by cutting his genitals with a splintered piece of wood.

Just as De Vries had suggested, the Indians hadn't been responsible for the theft. The culprits in question turned out to be other Dutch settlers from Manhattan Island. But it was too late to take back the killings, and Kieft, our fool of a leader, would never have wanted that anyway. He was crazed to keep killing until every last Indian was gone, oblivious to how much destruction would land in everyone else's path.

As predicted, the Natives did exact their revenge while Kieft stayed safely inside Fort Amsterdam. Remaining Natives from the village in which Kieft had ordered the killings promptly went back to the farm, murdered four of De Vries' farmhands, and burnt down his home.

Kieft put out another edict, but this time he hoped to pit Native against rival Native by placing a bounty on the head of any Raritan brought in by any member of an enemy tribe.

Hell surfaced when the elderly Claes Swits was murdered at Deutels Bay. An Indian man had come to his house to trade. But in a bloody moment, for the murder of his uncle several years before, the Indian got his revenge, killing the old man. When word got back to Kieft, he smiled, knowing he would have reason to attack the neighboring Indians.

Immediately, Kieft called an emergency group of twelve men to advise him on going to war with the Indians. They understood a Native war would destroy their families, their farms, their homes, and their trades, putting everything they had worked so hard to create over many difficult and thankless years of toil at risk. They had also been in this wilderness long enough to know that once the Natives decided to exact their revenge, widespread bloodshed would ensue.

Kieft didn't care what they had to say. He only wanted them to agree with him so he was not the only one to blame for the aftermath of such a war. Fearing dire consequences of such violence, most of the twelve men on his powerless council became wary of Kieft and secretly rallied together against him.

Kieft was enraged that his council went against his wishes. Instead of war, they recommended that he make several friendly requests to the chiefs of all villages involved to send the murderer back to the Dutch for punishment. What infuriated Kieft the most was the discovery that his council had decided to meet behind his back. Kieft raged and warned them that clandestine meetings in the future would be viewed as criminal acts.

We were all anxious as to what the future would bring. It unnerved me as I looked at the faces of my two little babies. I did not want to think the worst. Unfortunately, we all found out just how horrible a monster our Director was.

CHAPTER SEVEN:

Marie's Story
New Amsterdam, New Netherland
1643

"Nothing good will come of these Indian wars!" I yelled as I watched New Amsterdam descend into total chaos. People were screaming and crying in the streets. A spirit of doom descended upon the town as the clear realization of the mass destruction of our Native friends at Pavonia and Corlear's Hook took hold. Kieft, that careless fool, had ordered the killing of little babies—babies the same age as my little babies. We first learned about the attacks from our friend Willem de Vries.

It was late February in 1643. I was full with child again, my third one. Our friend Willem came to our house before our tavern opened. He rode his horse wildly from the fort trying to alert as many people as possible to the danger ahead.

I had never seen the man as distraught as he was until that morning. He was tearful and so upset that he looked like he had aged twenty years in just one sleepless night.

Willem had been head of Kieft's disbanded advisory council. He relayed what had passed between them at the fort the previous night just before Kieft's attack on the Native village of Pavonia.

"Marie, Cornelis, I cannot stay long. You must help me after I tell you my story, and sound the alarm to as many others as possible. Let all your family members know, especially those in the open lands. They will need to protect themselves!"

He was wide-eyed and furious as he continued to tell his story.

"I was with Kieft last night at his home in the fort. We dined together. He told me he had made up his mind that only military action would take care of the Indian problems in the colony. I pleaded with him not to attack neighboring Native villages. I told him he had no right to make such a decision. He would be safe in his fort, protected by his soldiers in the days after the attack, but what about the rest of us?"

"I explained that we would anxiously await our fates. But this awful man, one who should never have been sent to us, is too stupid, too proud, and too violent to listen to any reason or logic. He cannot grasp how much time we've spent befriending the Natives in order to trade with them and how important those relationships are to the success of the colony," he said.

Agitated, he broke into a cold sweat. Upon my urging, he quickly gulped down the beer that I brought to him for replenishment.

"What happened?" I asked, alarmed to see him in such a frantic state of mind.

The old man nodded and continued his grim description of suffering.

"Disguised as Indians, Kieft and his soldiers snuck across the river and began the slaughter of innocents. As I watched the smoke thicken and the fire rise across the river in Pavonia, I also heard ghastly shrieks of horror. I feared to know the specifics of the criminal acts that were being committed," he said and continued.

"Survivors, hoping for protection, showed up at Fort New Amsterdam in total confusion and shock after escaping in their canoes across the river. They recounted stories of brutal savagery, including infants being ripped from their mother's breasts and thrown into fires. Other babies in cradleboards were cut, pierced, and tossed into the river to drown as parents watched and then were massacred too."

Willem had to stop. He was so overcome with emotion that he started to cry.

"The Indians in Pavonia were confused at first and thought they were being attacked by their Native enemies. I told them they were not safe at the fort and must go in hiding to friendly villages as far away as possible. They could no longer count on the Dutch for protection, flawed as it had been," he said.

He looked somber as he told us of the horrors committed by Kieft and his soldiers.

"Many of our Native friends are dead, and revenge will be exacted. That is certain," he said in an aggrieved tone.

He had to stop speaking again as he broke down into more tears. I put my hand on his shoulder to give him a little comfort.

Gaining some strength, he composed himself to address the crisis at hand.

"I must go and alert others," he said, looking anxiously down the road.

The distraught older gentleman jumped on his horse again and galloped off. I stood outside our home in disbelief as the pounding of horse's hooves grew fainter and the stirred-up dust began to settle.

"How could anyone be so cruel?" I said.

Cornelis and I had listened, speechless and heartbroken. It was as if the world was ending, and indeed, it was. The world we had all built was crashing down. That event was a dark turning point in the life of New Netherland and her people. The future became ambiguous. Our colony should have become stronger, but instead, Kieft's repulsive actions at Pavonia led us down an unknown and precarious path.

"We must tell your father quickly! They are vulnerable on the farm. Marie, stay here with the babies, bolt the doors, and I will come back as quickly as I can with your family. Your mother and younger brothers and sisters will be safer here in town."

I nodded gratefully, relieved that he would warn them and bring them to stay with us until we knew more.

I did as he said and secured all the windows and doors the best I could, creating a small safe space for us in the back of the house. I pulled my littlest one out of his cradle to comfort him and stop his tears. As he nursed, I could only imagine the horror I would feel if someone broke into my home and grabbed him from me, slaughtering him in the same vicious way that Kieft's army had done to the children of our Native friends. Such evil.

In the fall of that year, the Natives found their revenge. Villages of neighboring tribes banded together and laid waste to farmland, homes, and villages on the outskirts of New Amsterdam. Just as everyone had warned Kieft, the efforts of our labor of over twenty years were lost in the onslaught. Ann Hutchinson, the famous exiled preacher from Massachusetts, died with her family and many countless others in the reprisal for the deeds of Kieft and his soldiers.

New Amsterdam overflowed with refugees from the border settlements—throngs of traumatized people. Some went back to Holland with even less than they had originally brought with them. Others struggled to rebuild their lives on the frontier of New Netherland. Many more preferred the safety of living in town. We all worked to overcome the unnecessary tragedies inflicted on us by Kieft's foolishness and lust for Indian blood.

Recovery from this dark, low point in our community's life was slow and the setbacks harsh. Cornelis and I devised ways to survive, maintaining relationships with Indians we knew and trusted. Not wanting to be targets of their wrath, we continued to sell them liquor even though it was forbidden. We would not change our dealings with them for fear of jeopardizing their trade agreements with us. We wanted to send a message to their communities that they could still rely on us to maintain that which had preceded the wars: our trade agreements and our friendships. In short, we did what we wanted and what was necessary to survive.

With the constant threat of Indian attacks, business soured for us. Fewer people came to New Amsterdam to stay permanently. Still more settlers decided to leave our little colony rather than live in constant fear of more rounds of violence. To keep business going, we kept our tavern open whenever we could, after hours, and sometimes, on Sundays.

Despite Kieft escalating the Indian wars in response to the Native counter-attacks, my body embraced another pregnancy. I had my third baby, a little boy named Cornelis, after his father, and then became pregnant again with a fourth during the perpetual chaos.

It was a cold morning in early spring when the midwife, Tryntje Jonas, came to check on me. The cultivated tulips in the company gardens pushed gracefully through the soil, oblivious to the tensions of the town. Cornelis had gone to fetch more barrels of beer from my brother-in-law Isaac de Forest's brewery, *The Red Dragon*. Cornelis had hired Domingo, a half-freed Angolan slave originally captured from a Portuguese ship, to help watch over the tavern and me during the times he could not be there. Domingo and other half-free men were free to farm and work as they wished but had to pay the company in crops every year so they wouldn't be forced back into full slavery.

That morning, Domingo, had been helping me attend to my customers.

Domingo, taller and sturdier than most men, stopped many would-be delinquents from their malice by simply showing his face and calling out the trouble they'd brought in his deep, even voice. His head hit the tops of doorways if he failed to stoop as he passed through them, and his arms were as thick and hard as the branches of a maturing chestnut sapling. He was steady too, barely batting an eye to the frequent ruckus around him. To this day, I cannot recall a more humble and earnest friend.

"Marie, you work too hard," the midwife clicked her tongue as she eyed me cleaning tables. As usual, there were plenty of spills where drunks had splashed their beers the previous night. Tryntje carefully observed my swollen ankles and the plump bags under my eyes.

"Aw, it's nothing," I replied, knowing the pregnancy itself was the least of my concerns. The constant worry of Native attacks had us all on edge.

She scowled only briefly and then took my hand as a young pretty blond woman walked in the door carrying Trynje's midwifery bag.

"You remember my granddaughter, Sara, do you not?" she asked.

"But of course, you know that I do," I said.

Sara Kierstede, now the wife of surgeon Hans Kierstede and the daughter of Anneke Jans, stepdaughter of our minister, Dominie Everardus Bogardus, accompanied her grandmother sometimes as she made her midwifery rounds. Occasionally, she came to assist her grandmother with the births as well.

Married at fifteen, Sara was knowledgeable about childbirth not only from her grandmother's expertise but also from personal experience. She nodded and smiled. She too had grown up since childhood in New

Netherland and spoke even more Indian tongues than I. She had a knack for learning language surpassed by no one. There was only a tiny group of us who had experienced what New Amsterdam had been like since its beginnings. For that, we had a special bond.

"Hello, Marie. Listen to Grandmamma so she can get a better look at you," Sara said.

The midwife winked. "Yes, come, Marie. My granddaughter knows what's best," she said, smiling.

I guided them to a small room in the back of the tavern. In the exterior wall near the corner was the secret slot where the Indians who wanted a drink after hours placed their deer meat or other trade goods in hopes of a discreet exchange for liquor. My guests couldn't see it since it was well hidden from the inside by a sliding facade.

"Sit, Marie, I need to see those feet. Are you still sick to your stomach?" she questioned.

I took a seat in a tall-backed wooden chair carved as a marriage present from Henri La Chaîne, a furniture maker and friend.

"No, it's passed already. I'm fine, just a little tired but no more than with any other child," I responded.

The midwife carefully placed her hand over my belly. "Do you feel her moving about?" she referred to the baby.

A loud crash emanated from the front of the tavern. The babe in my womb stirred abruptly in response.

"What's this?" she cried.

We ran to the front, the three of us, to see what was the matter. Business in the tavern had been at a lull when I'd retreated to the back only a few minutes earlier.

On my way to the main room, I heard a man with an English accent screaming at Domingo.

"I won't take a drink from a filthy rogue like you. Where's your mistress?" He had just upended a table where Domingo had placed his drink and was ready to turn over some benches in his senseless rage. All my work of cleaning the tavern that morning was ruined in seconds.

"What is the meaning of this, you careless swine?" I screamed, looking into the ruddy face of Captain John Underhill.

"Use great care, Marie. He is a violent and unpredictable man," Sara whispered in warning to me. She grabbed my arm in an effort to shield me from harm.

He pulled out his sword from its sheath.

"Woman, your slave offends me, and for that matter, your stinking tavern offends me too," he sneered.

He was clearly drunk and on an early rampage.

"You're drinking early today, I see. Take your sword, put it back in its sheath, and get the hell out of my tavern!" I retorted.

I was furious and not about to back down.

"You threw a perfectly good mug of beer to the floor. Domingo is a free man, and I have never known him to be rude to anyone. Stop your madness this instant," I yelled, standing firm.

Domingo was at my back and ready to step in.

I turned to Sara.

"Please run toward *The Red Dragon*. Cornelis should be on his way back by now. Go out the back door so the raving lunatic cannot grab you. Tell Cornelis to hurry and bring the authorities," I implored.

I stared down Underhill, staying steady for the brief time I waited until others arrived. The lout had no concern for anyone. He'd come to New Amsterdam at Kieft's invitation. Kieft, in his deadly obsession to kill as many Natives as he could, was determined to enlist Underhill to carry out the murders.

Kieft was drawn to Underhill because of the commander's notorious reputation for having led a massacre of Pequot Natives in Connecticut.

Underhill, a mercenary with a Dutch wife, was only too happy to leave New England to serve the bloody purpose. But his only allegiance was to his thirst for more violence and blood. Rumors abound that the English didn't want him and had kicked him out of New England.

Luckily, one of my regular customers had come to the tavern in hopes of a meal and heard the uproar as he approached. He had witnessed the rampage as he peered in from the window. Realizing it better not to enter, he ran until he reached my father's farm. Hearing the news, my papa ran, axe in hand, until he and a farmhand reached the tavern.

"Stand down, Underhill. Do as my daughter says," he shouted.

He held his axe high, ready to come down hard over Underhill's head if needed. My brave father, one who was prone to avoid conflict such as this, found himself face to face with a trained mercenary and soldier.

Only seconds later, Cornelis rushed into the tavern followed by Van Tienhoven, one of New Amsterdam's own brutes. Underhill had made a powerful friend in Kieft's secretary.

"Come, my friend. Leave the tavern now. We'll go somewhere else where I'll make sure that you're no longer molested. Better to leave things alone," Van Tienhoven said, reasoning with the disgruntled soldier.

Underhill paused, hearing the familiar voice of his friend and fellow Indian agitator. Soon the tavern was teeming with people, and he knew it was best to leave.

"That's it. Put the sword back. Let's take a walk on the waterfront and see what we can find there," Van Tienhoven coaxed.

Papa put down his axe, relieved to avoid a fight with Underhill. Sweat dripped down his pallid, angular face. He wiped it off with his shirtsleeve, looking haggard yet relieved. Fearing the Natives would wreak havoc again, he had just stayed on watch the previous night with my brother. Any slight rumor of more violence put us on edge and on watch. A confrontation with Underhill was the last thing he needed.

Van Tienhoven put his arm around Underhill.

"Come on. Let's leave this little hole. There are better places to go." Finally, calmed by his friend, Underhill let himself be led out of the bar.

Everyone cheered, thankful that the English mercenary was finally gone. I rushed to Papa and hugged him.

"Oh Papa, such a brave stand you took for me. My valiant Papa." The poor old man's hands were shaking as I held them lovingly together.

To stop the trembling, I called for Domingo to unlock the liquor cabinet.

"Pour Papa some fine brandy to steady his nerves. A round for everybody who helped."

Glancing at my brave friend Domingo, I realized he must have been rattled too.

"Domingo, are you alright?" I asked. "You took the brunt of Underhill's wrath," I said. He didn't seem as solid as he usually was.

"He's a terrible man, but I'm fine. I worried more about you, going after him despite being with child. He could have hurt you," he said.

I smiled at Domingo.

"Go get yourself a drink too Domingo. We all need to relax," I said.

When things settled, we sat and drank a toast to Papa and Domingo and talked about the craziness that we had just witnessed.

"The English are probably happy to have gotten rid of the criminal for a while. One day Underhill will betray Kieft and the Dutch. You'll see," I said.

Sara, who had returned to the tavern, sipped some cider and exclaimed, "What a horrible man! "We are lucky no one was hurt."

I nodded, thinking about his childish and violent behavior. No wonder the English had no use for the brute.

Tryntje, my midwife, shook her head. The old woman was horrified. "The man is a beast," she said, nursing her cup of brandy, "You need to rest now, my dear. This was too much for you and the baby."

Eventually, the town of New Amsterdam got a respite from Underhill while he gathered militias on Long Island into a brutal force organized to kill Natives.

The Native tribes of the Wappingers and other tribes to the north were not so lucky to be rid of Underhill. Their populations were decimated after he led his militias to kill, maim, and burn over a thousand Indians in villages near our border with Connecticut and New Haven colonies and in other villages on Long Island.

Indian relations had never been at such a desperate point. What else could one expect after two and a half years of senseless wars? The people of New Amsterdam were furious at the devastation he'd invoked with his ignorance. It was then that a young man named Adriaen van der Donck became involved in all our lives. He was a young lawyer educated in Leiden and he, along with some others, would prove to be the end of Kieft.

CHAPTER EIGHT:

Tinker & Winthrop's Story
Windsor, Connecticut Colony
Summer 1647

John Tinker paced in his tobacco fields. Lines of worry etched deeply into his face of only thirty-four years. His family was at the center of a deadly controversy. Windsor in June of 1647 was a sinister place. The fruit of bitter disagreements and distrust had finally ripened into a treacherous poison of revenge against his family.

No amount of pacing amongst the young tobacco plants would settle his mind. With each breath and each step into well-tilled soil, his concerns exploded many times over.

The aftermath of his beloved cousin Alice's witch trial and hanging was dark. He was devastated that the community of Windsor shunned her and accused her of unfathomable evil. He was shocked by the cruel violence imposed by an angry mob onto her gentle soul. John Tinker and Alice had held a deep affection for each other. His loss felt unbearable.

The rest of the family was also at risk of perceived evil by association with a convicted witch. His brother-in-law William was busy preparing to move to Hartford. His dear sister Mary was afraid for her life as well and looked to relocate to Wethersfield. No one knew when the menacing specter of fear would appear to accuse another person connected to Alice.

John Winthrop must travel from Pequot and put a stop to these tensions and rumors at once lest it turn even more deadly. Tinker thought of his dear friend and employer.

The majority of Windsor residents, the West Country folk, have never trusted us nor approved of Winthrop's plans in Connecticut. Our greatest enemies are here in Windsor he told himself, thinking of Major Mason and Roger Ludlow.

As he neared the edge of the tobacco field, he cast a glance at the meandering Little River.

"If only I could be so peaceful and carefree," he said.

A cardinal flew to a low branch near a sycamore hugging the river and tilted his head as if he were listening. John glanced at the red bird and spoke aloud, relieved to have at least one witness to his anguish.

"I'm afraid my association with the Winthrops has made my family a target for everything bad that happens in Windsor since a pestilence took hold and killed many," he explained, as if the little bird would listen.

Tinker knew the real reasons, the political ones, for why his family had been targeted when sickness spread throughout the community. Even though they were victims of the disease also, the Tinker clan was no longer wanted in town. Too much distrust had already been sown. And new fissures within the family further weakened their position.

Tinker stooped down near the river and picked up a fistful of fresh dirt, letting it sift slowly through his fingers. It was a shame to think of letting go of this property. The deep rich soil of the Connecticut River Valley was the reason so many had come here. His tobacco plantings had done well over the years. But his main reason for leaving Winthrop years ago and being in Windsor was family—ties to family over everything else.

He'd missed both Winthrop and assisting him with his alchemical studies. Tinker had still come to help him from time to time, but love and support of family became his priorities, as were building his trade and farming his land. His new life had been in Windsor. But now the life he'd dreamed of was no more. It had vanished after Alice was murdered, leaving only ghosts that haunted him and pushed him to leave.

"The damn wars against the Pequots had a part in this! Winthrop's new plantation in former Pequot lands is at the heart of their distrust against us," he said aloud. The red bird cocked his head. Uncas and his tribe had aligned with Mason in the war to conquer the Pequots, and both men thought the Pequots should cease to exist or be subjugated.

"Mason, Ludlow, their allies, and other Connecticut people view Winthrop as an interloper into lands that were rightfully Connecticut Colony's. They're convinced he will eventually claim his plantation as part of the Massachusetts Bay Colony," he explained to the little red bird that continued to be his sole audience.

"But what they hate the most is the protections Winthrop has offered to remaining Pequot tribal members. It enrages Mason to no end!" he shouted excitedly, startling the cardinal.

"Fly away then. Of course, you don't care and would rather not hear about it," John stated as the little bird took off in flight.

Tinker recalled how Winthrop had known hostility on the part of Connecticut settlers was a possibility and he was shrewd in how he handled them. Before a decision could be made about who was entitled to the former Pequot territories, Winthrop made his move with Robin Cassacinamon's help. John Tinker remembered meeting him in former Pequot territories to scout out the perfect place for his alchemical center two years before Alice's unnecessary death.

In their quest for the ideal location on Long Island Sound, they followed the advice of their long-time friend Robin, the former servant in Winthrop's father's household and now the official tribal leader of the Pequots. Following Robin's advice and urging, Winthrop located his plantation right next to Nameaug, a Pequot village. It was side by side that Robin and Winthrop could work together for the mutual benefit of their people.

Just a slight bit up the river, Winthrop's plantation sat in a protected location with easy access to the Sound. It suited his purposes perfectly, and he hoped to call it New London one day. From there, he would hold New Amsterdam and Dutch Long Island in his sights.

Winthrop feigned indifference as to whether his new settlement came under Massachusetts' or Connecticut's jurisdiction. He'd long assured Mason and other Connecticut leaders that he only wanted to be a force of stability in the region. But in the end, Mason and his cronies didn't believe him, and the Tinker family and their associates were a near target for Mason's wrath. The Tinkers became "the others." Knowing that John Tinker was a close associate of Winthrop, Windsor's town leaders often cornered him and spoke in threatening tones.

"Tinker, you tell your employer, Winthrop Jr., he can say what he will, but we know his charter was granted from the Massachusetts Bay Colony. We are not ignorant of that fact. This will not stand. We will not allow

Massachusetts to seize what is rightfully ours," said Roger Ludlow, a known enemy of Winthrop's father. He elaborated the thoughts of prominent men in Windsor and other leaders in Connecticut. "Winthrop is an interloper into our colony. Tell him he will meet strong resistance if we observe any steps towards the annexation of former Pequot territories into Massachusetts."

For Mason, what he loathed the most was Winthrop's relationship with the Pequots. Mason approached John Tinker menacingly one morning at Reverend Warham's mill. Mason glared at Tinker before starting his diatribe. He must have recently heard some news that disgruntled him. Uncas was becoming furious that the Pequots were not behaving like obedient tributaries.

"John Tinker, how can you associate with a man who is breaking the Treaty of Hartford by the mere fact of allowing Pequots to take refuge in the village of Nameaug? The only Natives that he should align with are Uncas and his Mohegan tribe members. How convenient for them that Winthrop built his plantation right next to it in order to protect them and create a wedge between the settlers of Connecticut and Uncas, our greatest Indian ally. It's pure foolishness that will serve no Englishman in the end. These Pequots are subjugated to Uncas. They lost the war and would not even be allowed to live if it were up to me," said Mason.

He lurked even closer to John Tinker.

"You and Winthrop are putting us all at risk with this kind of disregard for the treaties of our colony!" Mason spit as he screamed.

No amount of countering his argument had any effect in changing his mind. The threats and hostilities had been building ever since knowledge of Tinker's scouting trip to the Pequot territory with Winthrop had become known publically. They had intensified even more after settlers began moving into the plantation, building their homes, and tilling their new farms with the overwhelming help of Pequots from Nameaug who finally felt safe enough to come out to live in the open under Winthrop's protection. Other Pequots who had been held in tributary status to Uncas began to escape and join their fellow tribespeople. As their population grew, Uncas and Mason were infuriated.

John Tinker wiped the last remaining dirt off on his breeches and surveyed his fields once more. It was the biggest piece of property in

Windsor. The West Country residents also resented him for that. With their rapidly expanding families, they would be happy to see him, a single man, go and would eagerly divide up his land for their own benefit. He hated to leave it. It was a rich land of beautifully rolling hills, a twisting brook trickling its way past the gentle landscape until it picked up speed, combining with a spring near the flatter farming lands and emptied into the Little River. The scene was breathtaking, but life had soured too much in Windsor. Despite its beauty, for Tinker, the country would always be tinged with blood. There was only one thing left to do—leave for good.

Go back to Boston and focus on your life as a trader, he told himself. You must be honest. It is impossible to resume life in this town. No, 'tis not possible to be anywhere near it!

The tragedy that had occurred here suffocated his heart. He needed a new beginning in the wake of Alice's hanging. He had no option but to abandon his land and cut his losses. In time, he'd be ready to sell it altogether.

With the decision made, he walked briskly back to the end of the field where his horse was tied, relieved to desert the town that turned on him and those he loved. He quickly mounted, adjusted himself in the saddle, and rode off full speed to the home he shared with his mother. He couldn't wait to pack his belongings. If she ever survived her current weakness and poor constitution, she was also moving to Wethersfield with his sister.

First, he had to write the letter to Winthrop alerting him to the horrible situation at hand and to let him know that he needed to see him urgently. Tinker hoped to convince Winthrop to meet with colonial leaders to set things right. He rightfully feared for the lives of the rest of his family members.

Even though almost everyone in the Tinker family was leaving, it would take time, and he didn't want their lives to be in jeopardy during the process. His youngest sister Anne and her husband Thomas Thornton had just left Windsor the week before to scout out a new place to live in Stratford. They hurried to leave after everything that had transpired.

His sister, Rhody, was the one exception. She was disheartened at the rest of the family leaving Windsor but decided to stay. She had fallen in love with the widower Walter Hoyt, her neighbor on Backer Row. They could not marry until she had waited a full seven years for her missing husband, John Taylor, to return. But everyone was certain that Taylor, along with his entire ship, had perished in the depths of the sea on a fateful January day shortly after their departure for England.

Rhody had tried to stay out of the fray during Alice's accusation, afraid that her status as a single woman would make her a possible target of witch accusations too. John Tinker knew she would still be vulnerable unless there were some sort of truce. At least her new love, Walter, was from the West Country, a fact that she hoped would shield her to some degree.

John Tinker sat at his desk and began to write with urgency. He imagined talking directly to Winthrop as he wrote the words with a quill pen and ink, taking great care to encode his message in the manner that Winthrop had taught him to.

Once he finished, his friend and assistant, Thomas Hopewell, an Indian of the Nipmuck tribe, took the letter and rode continuously, stopping only to board a boat, until he could deliver the letter safely into Winthrop's hands. Tinker's mentor, the great New England alchemist, would know what was necessary to overcome such a great impasse.

As for his part, John Tinker had done all he could do in Windsor. With the most recent chapter of his life ended, he prepared for his move back to Boston and the search for inner peace, something he could not find from the Windsor pulpit and the tongues of ministers that railed endlessly about the threats of witchcraft. He had no intention of ever setting foot into the Windsor meeting house again.

John's mother sobbed in her sickbed, stroking her long and tangled gray hair in an effort to be more presentable to her only living son. She tried not to lose herself in a torrent of tears. She didn't want it to be his last memory of her.

"Your decision is final, my son? Please, change your mind. Please, I beg of you, stay with your family," she pleaded.

"Mother, you understand perfectly well I can no longer stay after everything that has transpired between us and this town," he said.

"But go with me and Mary's family to Wethersfield instead. Stay with us. Don't go to Boston," Mrs. Tinker begged.

"Mother, Rhody and Walter await to bring me to the shallop for New London. I must go. You know I cannot stay," he said as his voice cracked with emotion.

"When shall we see you again, John?" she asked meekly.

"Only God can know for certain, Mother. But we shall meet again. Fare thee well. God be with you," he said.

After giving her a last kiss on the forehead, he approached the heavy wooden door, pushing it open into sunlight. He knew he had lied. His proud mother would not be around much longer. The life force in her was barely a spark, almost put out with the grief she felt after Alice's hanging.

Walter had already placed John Tinker's belongings in the cart. They rode in silence along the bumpy path toward the ferry. Everything appeared calm: farmers working their fields, breezes gently moving the leaves of trees lining the river, and a few people milling about in the town center doing their business. Reaching the river, Walter whistled for the ferryman to escort them to the other side of the Little River where the shallop bound for New London was secured at the landing and was patiently bobbing in the water while its captain finished his meal in the tavern.

Rhody was waiting for her brother at the dock with Alissa, Alice's only daughter. Alissa was petite like her mother and had the same blue, alluring eyes. She had been forced to live with Deacon Hosford and his wife since her mother's arrest for witchcraft but the girl responded poorly to the situation. She refused to eat, cried out for her mother incessantly, and had all manner of outbursts. No matter the punishment, she fled to Rhody's and sometimes Mary's house where she found comfort in the arms of her cousins and her playmates.

Furthermore, Alissa wanted nothing to do with her supposed father, John Young. She was devastated by his betrayal of her dead mother. So Rhody petitioned the church elders to keep the child with her. Seeing that Rhody was in love with one of their own West countrymen, they relented. She had years to wait before she and Walter could officially be together, so it was easy to take Alissa into her home. Alissa was telling Rhody how much she would miss John's stories when she spotted the ferry bringing him and Walter to the other side of the river.

John Tinker's sister, Mary, and her family also joined them. They gathered closely and spoke as Tinker waited to take his final leave from Windsor. The siblings were solemn and trying to hold on to the last precious minutes together before they began their separate lives without each other in the aftermath of Alice's death.

"Brother, what will we do without you nearby? You will be greatly missed," said Mary.

John Tinker winked at his older sister.

"You know I'll be thinking of my dear big sister often. We shall meet again," he said. He hugged her and his nieces and nephews.

"May God be by your side," said Mathias, Mary's husband.

John Tinker nodded in thanks and patted him on the back.

He turned to Rhody.

"You take care of yourself, my kind-hearted sister. I will never forget how you took in Alice's child. Walter is smitten with you. I pray the time you must wait to be together goes quickly. I know you still mourn your deceased husband, but he would want you to be taken care of," he said.

"Alissa, come to me. I have a secret for you," said John Tinker.

He stooped down to be closer to her. She always loved the man she called her Uncle John. In reality, he was not her uncle but all her cousins called him that so she saw no reason why she shouldn't as well.

"Alissa, listen to Aunt Rhody. She will watch over you until the time comes for you to have your own family. Always remember the love your mother had for you. She was a beautiful soul who loved and healed. Never forget that. That is all you need to know. You must be strong for her, my child. She will smile upon you from her place in another realm. Believe that, child. There is more to life than the ministers and church elders tell you. You must believe that!"

He pulled out a small gold ring from his pocket. "Keep it with you, Alissa. Hide it in the small lining of your skirt. It's imbued with strength to bring you what you need. It will help you to remember your mother and remember the purity of your own heart. I will think of you often, dear child," he said, hugging her and kissing her cheek.

The captain of the shallop had appeared again, his belly now full of hearty tavern food. He clanged the bell for everyone to board. John Tinker said his final goodbyes, entered the shallop, and waved one last time to his family on the dock. The sails caught the wind easily and a swift current whisked him downriver and away from Windsor for a possible eternity.

CHAPTER NINE:

Tinker & Winthrop's Story
Boston, Massachusetts Bay Colony
Summer 1647

The shallop eased away from the shore along the Sound. Onboard, John Tinker sat next to his mentor, John Winthrop Jr. They were each lost in thought as their craft made its way to Boston. Both men recalled their conversation from the day before in New London and questioned the hurdles and consequent outcomes they would face at the meeting of the United Colonies. As soon as Winthrop had received the letter from Tinker, he'd packed his trunks and readied himself for the journey back to Massachusetts. He'd sent a notification with a messenger to his father that they would be coming.

It was mid-July, 1647. As Winthrop waited for his friend's arrival, he considered what Tinker had outlined in his recent letter and was of the same mind. He'd already come to many of the same conclusions on his own about the chasm between Massachusetts and Connecticut over his settlement at Pequot Plantation. He worried that the recent tensions and controversies would be detrimental to his alchemical dreams. Furthermore, he had no doubt that the high emotions his project evoked could have played a part in dark consequences for Tinker's family. He had no choice but to make his case before the members of the United Colonies and assure the contingent from Connecticut that he was not a threat to them.

The previous day, in the quiet of Winthrop's hall in New London, Tinker had explained the torments his family had gone through with his cousin Alice's hanging and the jolting news he had heard en route through Hartford that Reverend Thomas Hooker was dead. Hooker had been the interim minister in charge in Windsor at the time of Alice's hanging while Reverend Warham attended the religious meeting of the Synod in Massachusetts.

John Tinker spoke in exasperation.

"Everyone is anxious and wonders where Satan will appear next. They say Hooker died of the same fever that plagued Windsor. It is also sweeping through neighborhoods in Hartford and Wethersfield. People are afraid. Rumors already enter every home through hushed tones saying Hooker was bewitched by Alice's spirit for his part in her death.

"Mistake me not. 'Tis with great sorrow that I heard of Reverend Hooker's passing. And may God rest his soul. I don't believe Alice's gentle spirit would exact such revenge," added Tinker.

"I presume Alice has as little power in death as she had in life," stated Winthrop sadly.

"Eh, I will tell you this, I do fear that the rest of my family is in danger. It is best that the question of rights to former Pequot land be rectified once and for all. In the meantime, my family won't be taking their chances and will be leaving the town of Windsor to start over. Yes, everyone is leaving Windsor, with the exception of my sister Rhody. She must finish her seven years of waiting since her last husband's death. No doubt she will marry her neighbor, Walter," he added.

"What has become of John Young, Alice's husband?" asked Winthrop.

"What about him? I didn't stop to find out," replied Tinker coolly.

"John, I was deeply troubled by the ghastly news from Windsor and horrified at the lengths of personal destruction that Mason was willing to unleash. His fear and arrogance drive him," Winthrop responded.

"Yes, he and other rivals in town set the rumors ablaze against my family and most precisely against my dear cousin Alice. They sent spies to watch and contrived stories against her to make her look the part of a witch when the sickness took hold. The fear and distrust had spread even more quickly than the fever did. Will it ever stop?" asked Tinker.

Winthrop paused and smoothed his cuffs before commenting.

"Ah, Satan may have been involved, but not as they see it. John Tinker, I assure you, I believe you when you say you know that your cousin was innocent. I also know Mason and his friends will yearn for the death of all perceived witches. Manipulating the forces of nature and the laws of the universe requires years of alchemical training. The possibility that she was aligned with the devil is unbelievable to me," said Winthrop.

He'd met Alice. She was a kind and dedicated herbalist and healing woman. He never sensed the slightest evil in her eyes. He understood Tinker's grief, and it pained him that the politics of the day had played its part in creating such an unstable environment. He was sick to his core to know that she had met such a violent end.

"Aside from protecting your family, there is something else that is of the utmost importance, not only to us but to the rest of mankind. 'Tis one of the most significant reasons for coming to the New World—establishing the alchemical center at New London and finding the Passage. If we cannot appease Mason and other Connecticut leaders to leave us to our endeavors, our grand plan may be in jeopardy.

Tinker nodded. He had no problem understanding how much was at stake.

"We are in a precarious moment in time, John Tinker. Recent events are a test of our spiritual determination and our dedication. We have more challenges with Massachusetts' leaders as well, other challenges. There is even more to be concerned about than Uncas' displeasure at losing his tributaries and Connecticut's hostility over boundary disputes. I must admit it is unsettling that our fellow colonists seem to trust Uncas more," sighed Winthrop.

"What other complications do you see in this mire?" Tinker questioned.

"The other issue is this, my friend, and 'tis equally unsettling. Have you heard the latest developments concerning our friend and fellow alchemist Robert Child?" asked Winthrop.

Tinker looked puzzled. He'd spent so much time worrying about his own lot and that of his family that he'd separated himself from other happenings in the colony for a while.

"The latest I had heard, sir, was that last year, Robert Child brought forth a remonstrance to Massachusetts leaders requesting more tolerance in church membership and greater political empowerment. Word of it was that they were quite displeased," Tinker said.

"Aye. 'Twas damning for Child that he not only presented the remonstrance but also demanded that everyone in Massachusetts should have the same rights they have in England for entry into the church. He alarmed leaders with the threat of letting Parliament know that these ideas are not being respected or offered in Massachusetts," said Winthrop, looking at Tinker.

"Leaders, including my father, responded angrily to his actions. They are furious still that he requested that the church and the state be less restrictive in accepting various men into full religious and governmental participation. He insisted they be open to sharing of different ideas and information as is so important in scientific endeavors," Winthrop explained, shaking his head

"Ah, I imagine the founding leaders of our godly community in the Bay were none too happy with being told what to do by a newcomer! So what has become of it?" Tinker asked intently.

"That is the core of what worries me! He was fined an exorbitant amount for going against Massachusetts' laws and was placed under house arrest. He is not free to leave until the fine is paid in full. I fear he will return to England once this nightmare is over. Oh, how my dear friend suffers. Despite pleading my case to Father, he has warned me to stay clear of it. He tells me many leaders are seeing alchemists as agitators of dissent because of Child's example. My other dear friend and fellow student in alchemy, Richard Starkey, has also been imprisoned of late," complained Winthrop.

"The Bay leaders intimidate to what end?" asked Tinker.

"To the end of purging anyone who might challenge them or present a different perspective. Worst of all, Child, Starkey, and others on the Hermetic path are being maligned as Papists! People talk and rumors spread that they are spies of the Catholic Pope with evil intentions to bring down the governing forces and church leaders," Winthrop said, aghast.

"'Tis madness! Their intentions could not be further from the truth. New England is losing its grasp of common decency and logic!" Tinker agreed.

"Aye, 'tis a difficult situation that brings tension and concern from my own father. The only step left to take is to plead my case, our case, before the meeting of the United Colonies. Come, let us prepare for the challenges ahead with a ritual in the laboratory over the forge," Winthrop had advised.

Winthrop remembered the conversation as they continued on their way to Boston.

Major Mason banged his fist on the wooden table. The veins at his temples bulged out and his face took on a fiery red hue. Mason seethed and shouted at Winthrop Jr.

"This is an outrage, Mr. Winthrop! 'Tis an invitation from Satan to allow more evil into our midst! Why must you meddle further into the Pequot affair that was settled soon after the war with the Treaty of Hartford? The Pequots should not exist! They are lucky to be alive and have no place except as tributaries of Uncas, our only Indian ally."

"Settle down, Mason. Let my son speak his mind," said Winthrop Sr. in a firm and authoritative voice. He glared at Mason until he was silenced.

The meeting of the United Colonies was not going as well as John Tinker and Winthrop Jr. had hoped. The heavy heat of July made everyone cross as they sat in the court chamber.

Winthrop Jr. smoothed out his doublet and looked down at the fine cuffs he was wearing as he waited to speak. He was tired of the unrelenting scrutiny. It wasn't long after he'd started his plantation of New London, in former Pequot lands, that the few remaining Pequots and his neighbors in the village of Naumeaug begged to be released from Uncas.

Robin Cassacinamon, his friend, their chief, was immensely helpful in the establishment of Winthrop's alchemical center. He'd also helped Winthrop to find a location for a lead mine. The lead and silver ore he hoped to find there could be easily transported through waterways to New London with the cooperation of other tribes.

Robin smoothed the way for all of this and was willing to look for a passage to the west of New Amsterdam when the time was right. But none of this could happen with the Pequots remaining subjugated to Uncas. Uncas was too disruptive and increasingly violent in his fierce and stubborn resolve to maintain complete control over his fellow Natives. Winthrop Jr. knew his unique relationship with Robin and the Pequots had caused fierce opposition in Connecticut, but he had to show them just how horribly Uncas had treated his tributaries.

Mr. Hopkins of Connecticut took charge. "Very well then. Allow Winthrop Jr. to speak so as to finish this matter." Among murmurs, Mason huffed back to his seat, glaring at Winthrop who rose to speak again.

"Thank you, good sirs, for allowing me to state my case and present to you the petition that has been signed by many members of the Pequots. As you know, their village of Naumeaug borders my plantation. Their lives have become unbearable under Uncas. His actions are unsupportable," Winthrop Jr. stated.

He pulled out the brown parchment containing the petition that he had helped to create with Robin. On it were the many signatures of over sixty tribesmen aggrieved in endless ways.

"What I propose to you today is to transfer guardianship of the Pequots to me instead of Uncas," requested Winthrop.

The crowd gasped.

The moderator was forced to pound his gavel on the heavy wooden table where the officers of the confederation sat in disbelief.

"The injustices done to the Pequots are long," Winthrop Jr. continued. "These men and women of tributary status endure the unmitigated wrath and injustice of Uncas on a weekly basis in some form or another. They starve because of his cruelty. When they try to fish, he cuts their nets. As soon as they harvest their corn, he steals it. And this is under the enduring stress of extortion, intimidation, and even threats on their lives," said Winthrop Jr.

"Amongst this constant violence, this incessant ill will at Naumeaug, the new settlers at my own plantation feel anxious that Uncas' displays of violence will expand to their own village and to individual properties. They must also be at peace to live their lives. In effect, they question if Connecticut should relinquish claims to Pequot territories under the current circumstances. It is their preference that the plantation of New London become a part of Massachusetts Bay Colony rather than belong to Connecticut," Winthrop said.

Winthrop paused. Etched lines across the young man's forehead were a testament to his worries.

"In the past, I was indifferent to the claims of each colony to this land. I only wanted to be of service as an intermediary agent between the Native tribes, bringing resolution to disagreements amongst them. I have always been happy to work under the government of either Connecticut or Massachusetts. Unfortunately, I must choose now based on the safety of the settlers on my plantation," he explained.

In concluding, he hoped to have gained the sympathies of the group.

"Therefore, I humbly ask that you consider this request to grant guardianship of the Pequots over to me where I will ensure that no further incidents of violence will ensue. I also ask you to consider the proprietary disputes between our colonies once and for all, basing it on what will bring the best conditions for progress. It is only then that both settler and Indian will find peace. Indeed, Uncas has run amuck for too long a time," Winthrop finished.

Some of the Connecticut contingent gaped at Winthrop's requests. The moderator spoke.

"Mr. Winthrop, the leader of these United Colonies and members of its governing council will deliberate on this matter immediately. We ask you to wait outside the chamber whilst we consider our response to your request."

The deliberation went quickly. Tinker knew that it was not a good sign for his mentor when the meeting reconvened after only a few minutes.

The moderator spoke, "Mr. Winthrop, we, the commissioners of the United Colonies have made our decisions on several issues. Firstly, the final decision has been made to honor Connecticut's claim to all former Pequot territories. You say you are indifferent. But how can this be so when you have worked exclusively for the benefit of Massachusetts? We are not naïve to the motivations of men."

He continued. "Furthermore, we have taken note that your close companions, Mr. Child and Mr. Starkey, those with whom you would share many endeavors, are now in custody for their heretical behavior towards the laws of Massachusetts and their unorthodox views. Aye, even papist, blasphemous views."

He paused only a moment.

"The Devil has already worked his hand in Windsor. We will staunchly fight all that is demonic and heretical. The survival of our colony depends upon it. We admonish you to be mindful that you do not follow your friends down the same path in working toward your alchemical goals," the moderator said.

Tinker sat anxiously, knowing his mentor felt despair at the blows being given to him by the governing members of the United Colonies.

"Secondly, Mr. Winthrop, we must state our concern as to the way you have carried yourself in this affair, your resistance to the Treaty of Hartford, and the way you acquired your plantation in the first place. Is it not true that you set about to acquire lands for this plantation while you were still working for Lords Saye and Brook under their patent? The gentlemen of this council find it most disturbing and a conflict of interest that you went forward with acquiring your own land acquisitions whilst under their employ," he stated.

"Finally, your guardianship petition is dismissed. As an ally, it is Uncas' right and also his duty to keep any remaining Pequots under control. Your meddling in his affairs angers him and weakens our alliance. If his measures are harsh to this end, it is of no concern to us as long as he keeps his distance from settlers. The Pequots are brutish and aggressive and must be subjugated by whatever means necessary," the moderator said.

He looked hard at Winthrop.

"They should consider themselves lucky to be alive after being defeated in the war against them ten years ago. Under your guardianship, we fear they would not be held fully accountable for their actions against us in the war. Furthermore, we also fear that they would build themselves up again and show continued aggressions toward us in lands that properly belong to Connecticut," the moderator continued.

"Uncas will be warned to stay clear of the settlers of your plantation. You may tell them that we have communicated our admonishments to him and no further action should be required. Hence, the Pequots must remain as his tributaries. We order you to return the Pequots under your protection to Uncas upon your return. This is our final decision!" He slammed his gavel against the hard oak table to make his final point.

A stunned John Tinker met the eyes of Winthrop Jr. They were both devastated by the proceedings, and all seemed lost. Sullen, they left the meeting in Boston that day not knowing what would ensue. Winthrop was silent on the way back to his father's home. He didn't know what the answer was in the moment, but the gifted magus was sure he would figure out a way to reverse the tide and even more confident that Tinker would be at his side as he did it.

Chapter Ten:

Tinker & Winthrop's Story
New London, Connecticut Colony
1649

John Tinker jolted upright from his featherbed. Bloodcurdling screams of agony awoke the village of New London. He had as of late been a resident of Boston and was visiting the coastal settlement at Winthrop's request.

"What devil's mischief is at hand?" he cried.

Throwing his blanket aside, he jumped from his bed and hastened to put on his deep brown breeches and doublet over his nightshirt. His leather boots were in the corner by the door, but before he could reach them, he heard a thunderous knock.

"Tinker, come at once! It's the Natives. Uncas employs his violent means again to recapture his tributaries. I am sure of it," said Winthrop emphatically.

"Aye. We must stop the madness at once!" Tinker agreed. He donned his woolen winter cloak and joined Winthrop running outside into the new town green to see what was happening.

Outside in the bitter cold, the howl of the winter wind couldn't cover up the bloodcurdling screams of Pequots running towards Winthrop's home for help.

"Shameful," Tinker said, scowling as a young woman, scantily clad, desperate with her child in her arms, ran to avoid capture at a nearby settler's home. Approaching a thick wooden door, she screeched in her native tongue for shelter and safety. She shivered as she waited, not stopping to look back as Uncas and his heavy-handed warriors pillaged and destroyed her village in the distance.

In charity, a man with his rifle in hand and his wife close behind peered outside at their settlement enveloped in chaos as they ushered the young woman into their home.

More Pequots, women and children—some naked, some covered with nothing but furs draped over their shoulders and bare feet in the stinging snow— cried in agony.

"'Tis a moral outrage. I can bear it no more!" screamed Winthrop as he helplessly watched Uncas and his warriors carrying the spoils of their raid: tools of iron and stashes of corn, even the few articles of warm clothing of their rival tribe members.

"Tinker, run to the supply room and get as many blankets as you can to wrap up the women and children in. Try to hide them in the shed in the back of the main house until the danger is over. I will get the constable," Winthrop said frantically.

"It is a sickening sight. This invasion leaves them with nothing again. Uncas must be stopped!" agreed Tinker.

It did not take long before the constable of New London inserted himself into the fray, desperately attempting to stop the aggression. After all, it was his duty to keep law and order in his town and protect its inhabitants.

But it was too late for many. Uncas hollered as he rounded up his escaped tributaries. He tied them to each other in a single chain, dragging them along in the cold snow.

As quickly as he could, John Tinker fetched wool blankets and offered them to the throng of Pequots flowing into Winthrop's settlement, shaking in fear and from the frigid temperatures.

Not far behind, the war yelps caught up to them. Uncas' Mohegan warriors snatched the blankets and their tributaries as soon as they caught up to them. They forced themselves into settler homes and ripped rescued Pequots away for final capture. Very few were able to escape into the woods. The constable was helpless to stop most of the mayhem and focused on protecting the English settlers of the village.

The pandemonium continued as Indian fought Indian. Once again, Uncas had become enraged that the subjugated Pequots did not comply with his wishes. He was even more furious at Winthrop for not abiding by the terms set by the United Colonies. The only salve for Uncas' anger was retribution and revenge.

Off in the distance, on the edge of the upheaval, barely apart from the cries, the tears, and the chaos, appeared Captain John Mason and a few of his soldiers. They watched, unmoved, as the town was laid bare to marauders and thieves.

Winthrop and Tinker saw him from his boastful position atop his horse. Mason watched the bedlam smiling in satisfaction, caring less for his fellow colonial settlers than for getting revenge on the man he despised.

"Look at Mason there!" shouted Tinker

Winthrop darted toward him, leaving Tinker behind. He stumbled in the drifts of snow to reach his rival.

"Mason, what is the meaning of this? You sit smugly on your horse and condone such violence. Do you not see how Uncas and his warriors rip Pequot people away from settlers? Settlers who have come to their aid to give their children shelter, to protect them from the cold now that they have been stripped of the moccasins on their feet and the hides that keep them warm?" shouted Winthrop at his archrival.

"And once again, you, sir, give protection to people who do not belong with you! Uncas must be allowed to take his tributaries. A good year has passed since I came with Uncas to ensure his tributaries were returned to him from this place. Yet, they went back to your plantation, and you do nothing to honor the demands of the commissioners of the United Colonies," said Mason.

Captain Mason had appeared the previous year with a letter from the commissioners allowing Uncas to take back by force any Pequot he found. It was a futile attempt since many escaped back to Pequot Plantation.

"No, Mason, as I recall Uncas violently dragged them from here against their will. This must end. Why do you think they escape again and again? I'll tell you! 'Tis because Uncas takes all that they have and leaves them with nothing to survive," snapped Winthrop.

"Look at the terror in the faces of the townspeople here. You've gone way too far this time, Mason!" Winthrop screamed, quite out of his normal character.

"There's nothing you can do about it, Winthrop. I suggest you abide by the rules set forth! Uncas, let's go," he called loudly to his ally. "Our work here is done."

The last tributaries were being tied together and forced with others to walk in file out of the village. Winthrop shook with rage. Mason scoffed, turning his horse to leave the settlement.

"How dare he continue to support this injustice year after year? This must stop. We will find a way to change course," Winthrop vowed.

As the peril in their village subsided, shaken villagers came outside and joined the constable, Tinker, Winthrop, and other men who had taken arms in shock and dismay. They were weary yet too afraid to shut their eyes in sleep for the rest of the night. They voiced grave concerns for loss of their own lives.

"You have my word that this situation will not stand. Tomorrow, we will survey the damage and make appeals to other leaders in the colonies. They shall hear about this outrage!" Winthrop promised them.

Winthrop was as concerned about his new town's inhabitants as he was about his friend Robin Cassacinamon and his tribe.

In the morning, Winthrop and Tinker walked into the Pequot village of Naumeaug after taking account of the damage in New London.

"The basics of life, food, shelter, and clothing have all been destroyed or stolen in one fell swoop. These people had been deprived of everything they needed to survive several times in their lives, both at the hands of English and now at the hands of Uncas and the Mohegan tribe empowered by Mason," bemoaned Tinker.

"I will make sure the leaders of the United Colonies know about the atrocities committed here last night. We can only hope there will be an immediate reckoning for the actions that took place. Mason and Uncas must be stopped. The townspeople are upset. I am sure they will protest and I will do everything in my power to make sure that their voices are heard," affirmed Winthrop defiantly.

Tinker, after his return to Boston, was relieved when he later heard that the backlash from Mason's actions with Uncas was swift. After settlers from New London complained of Uncas' misdeeds witnessed by Mason, who did nothing, the United Colonies asserted that the Pequots would continue to be tributaries of Uncas but that they could live separate from him. In addition, Uncas had to return all the goods that were stolen from them.

But other developments greatly saddened Tinker. His first employer, Winthrop's father, died soon after and his mentor, incensed by Uncas' raid, thought about moving elsewhere, even back to England. John Tinker understood. In the turmoil of the recent years, he'd also thought of moving back to England.

But Winthrop could never give up his dreams of an alchemical future in the New World. He could never give up the idea of a quest for the fortieth parallel and the possibility to discover the Northwest Passage by way of the North River. He'd also explored his options by talking to Dutch officials on Long Island about the possibility of settling there.

In the end, Winthrop focused his energies on his projects in New London and elsewhere in New England. He decided to scale down his plans for his black lead mine since it would have to go through Uncas' territories. He devoted his time to developing his salt works, animal husbandry, distillation of liquor, ironworks production, and ore processing. He attracted blacksmiths to make tools used to clear land and developed saltpeter production.

For his part, Tinker busied himself in Boston, occupying himself with the life of a trader merchant. He even went back to England for a short time with Winthrop. He continued to help Winthrop with his projects. And in time, he began to heal from the tragedies he'd suffered from in recent years. There was much more work to do.

Indeed, the beginning years of discord in New London seemed to be coming to a close. Meanwhile, in New Netherland, another kind of strife was taking place in the home of Marie du Trieux.

CHAPTER ELEVEN:

Marie's Story
New Amsterdam, New Netherland
1649

My mother handed me a handkerchief to dry my eyes. All my children were around me in the bed. I knew I would have to get up soon to go to the church but I would have preferred to stay under the bedsheets.

"Mama, have a little stew," my dear Alida said as she tried to get me to eat.

"Don't worry, Mama. I will be the man of the house now. Papa will be proud of what I will do to take care of you," said Aernoudt, my oldest boy.

My darling children were so attentive to me even though it was their loss too. Cornelis Volckertsen Viele, who had been such a good father to them, had taken his last breath the previous night.

My sisters, Rebecca, Rachel, and Sarah as well as our mother Susanne, came to comfort me.

"I knew the day would come eventually. Cornelis was so much older than me, thirty-three years older, but I seemed to forget and just enjoyed our life together," I said.

"'Tis a cold fact of life that he was destined to leave this harsh world much earlier than you, chérie. It was a fact of life, but I am happy that you did have a good life with him," said my mother Susanne.

"I'd hoped he could last a little longer. Why not? Why couldn't God give him a little more time, knowing he had little children?" I asked, expecting no answer. "That would only be just, but He does not care."

My womenfolk looked at me tenderly but had no answer either.

"Cornelis always made me feel safe in this crazy world. Now what will I do?" I sobbed. "Three children with a dead father. It won't be easy. At least our little Jacqueline will be with her papa," I said. Jacqueline had already died from a fever at the age of three.

"I have *The Salty Rose*, but I swear it was also the death of my Cornelis in the last year of his life. That pompous Director General Stuyvesant, the son of a minister! He might as well be a Puritan," I complained.

"We spent all of last year battling for the life of our tavern, fighting for our livelihood! It was probably the stress of it all that killed my dear husband!" I cried.

My sister Rebecca grabbed me a little wine out of the cupboard.

"Please, Marie, do not think of this now. It will only upset you more. Leave those thoughts on this day. You must think only of your husband and putting him to his eternal rest," Susanne said.

I nodded and calmed down for the sake of the children, but inside I was not only full of grief and despair. I was also seething with anger. I looked at my poor fatherless children. Our youngest child, Pierre, was only one year old. Cornelis was six and Aernoudt, the oldest, was nine. I could wish for life to be different all I wanted, but who was I to think that Cornelis could have beaten this fate without the stress of Stuyvesant and the ministers trying to get rid of our tavern? I blamed them for shortening his life.

"Thank you for taking care of me, but please, let me be alone with my thoughts for a few minutes," I said.

"Of course, Marie, but you will try to eat a little bit for me in exchange for some time alone, n'est ce pas? Yes? You will do it?" bargained my mother.

"I will try," I agreed and pulled the curtains across the opening to the bed tucked in a wooden frame against the wall.

As I tried to eat a little bit of stew with bread to keep up my strength, the memories of Cornelis and our life together over the decade came flooding into my mind. Cornelis and I had a good life together running our tavern near Maiden Lane. We saw so much change in the wilderness over ten years together. We met so many people in our tavern: the powerful and the meek, the bawdy drunkards and hardworking common folk, respectable leaders and scandalous rogues, Natives and Europeans alike.

Being on the edge of New Amsterdam's hustle, we were a stop for young renegades planning uprisings and insurrections against stubborn rulers. We were the hiding place and the refuge for disobedient servants and outcasts.

And most of all, the Natives, familiar with my family and me, came to drink, getting their fill of wine or other spirits. In later years, they'd sneak their bottles and jugs from the secret side window where they could make their purchases in a clandestine way. Some of them just came to trade deer meat or other provisions.

The first years we ran the tavern, we made our own rules. We did what we pleased and that seemed to work well for everyone. But with the ever-increasing Indian attacks, people were afraid of Natives and what they would do for revenge. Settlers complained that the Indians had no inhibitions about what they said or did once they took to drink. They didn't seem to notice that anybody with too much beer, wine, or other spirits would also lose control of themselves.

We witnessed councils of various members plotting ways to get rid of Kieft and hold him accountable for the damages he'd invoked by starting reckless wars against the Indians. We saw the young lawyer, trained in Leiden, Adriaen van der Donck, come in night after night to sit at a secluded table and write down the many wrongs of Kieft, grievances he would present to the company leaders in Amsterdam in the future. He stayed equally long in a back room with his friends, like Hendrick Hendricksen Kip and Dr. Johannes de la Montagne, to list the rights we should have had as Dutch citizens did back in the fatherland. Van der Donck was a member of the Council of Nine.

Most of our clientele were not as serious. Their main desire was to get a few mugs of beer and play games all night. Some wanted to find a loose woman they could bed. Others just felt like drinking themselves silly to forget whatever problem they had. I knew how to handle all of them. Nobody dared cross Marie du Treux or they were thrown out on their asses. If they weren't repeat offenders, I'd be generous and give them a chance to redeem themselves the next night.

Cornelis was proud of me and called me his grand proprietress, and often reminded me that I was his rose. He teased me relentlessly for my generosity and for my penchant to enjoy some of the finer things in life. Sometimes they were little treasures given to me by traders from far realms in the place of guilders to settle a tavern bill.

We had our favorite customers. The sailmaker, Teunis Jansen, robust and equally as jolly could make me laugh so much I'd cry. The fisherman Hans Gerlude always stopped in his little sloop and saved the best catch for me in exchange for a mug or two of our best beer. Isaac de Forest, a fellow Walloon, was married to my sister Sarah. He was a trader, a brewer, and had a tobacco warehouse. He loved to tell stories that he shouldn't, those that would make my sister blush. And Simon de Groot always lingered on his way home, hoping to find my sister Rebecca visiting me.

Henri La Chaîne and his lovely wife Claire came in frequently for dinner and wine. They were Huguenots and furniture-makers who were reserved, yet very kind and observant. They said they loved to come to *The Salty Rose* and feel the pulse of the town. Henri and Claire often complimented me on my sea roses outside the tavern and begged to know what I did to tend them to such exquisite beauty. It was as if they were trying to unravel a mystery.

Oh, but others were not so pensive. The stories some of my customers and brother-in-law would tell! The best was Isaac's account of Stuyvesant's arrival. Relieved that Kieft was gone, we were naturally apprehensive about who would be the next Director.

"Big hat with a plume, a smirk barely hidden with his thin mustache, the military general limped with his peg leg on the shore as he surveyed the town. I could swear that by his dour expression there was another piece of wood up his ass."

Sarah blushed a crimson red at her husband's remarks. Everyone else in *The Salty Rose* roared with laughter.

"Yes. He said it all with that face. They say a cannonball shattered Stuyvesant's leg while he attempted to retake St. Maarten from the Spanish. The general looked so disappointed with our little ruffian settlement. They say he is the son of a preacher and intends to put this place in order," said Isaac.

"He wants to civilize us!" blurted Claus Brouder. "Bah! We'll show him how to lighten up and be a proper hooligan!"

There was always endless laughter in the tavern once the stories flowed.

Through it all, Domingo helped me keep everyone in line and satisfied at the same time.

As I sat with those memories, I knew I had to bury my husband, but I didn't really want to go to the church. It was only going to make me angrier and not as peaceful as I should have been.

The deacons and ministers had been part of our problem. The new ministers were not as lenient as Reverend Bogardus had been.

Dominie Bogardus, the previous minister of New Amsterdam, had died by shipwreck along with Kieft when their ship, the *Princess*, disappeared into the Bristol Channel on their way back to Amsterdam. Kieft was supposed to answer for his reckless actions in our colony, and Bogardus would have testified against him to the directors of the Dutch West India Company if their journey had not ended so tragically.

The last year of Cornelis' life was far too tense for both of us. The ministers called upon Stuyvesant and the burgomasters and schepens to be stricter with the taverns in town. They said we tappers were luring the populace into the evils of drink and creating poverty by taking items from our customers in exchange for our tavern fare. Stuyvesant and his council drafted new rules and laws to keep us in line, to try to get us to be more pious and upright, a manner they preferred.

We were no longer allowed to tap our barrels on Sundays. The Council forbade the opening of new alehouses. There were about seventeen of us tappers at that time. The church leaders argued that three or four were plenty to meet the needs of the population. They were determined to close the rest of them.

We became a target. Stuyvesant tried to catch us breaking the rules. Soon, trouble surrounded us. A warning here and a fine there, we soon got used to it and devised as many ways as possible to keep some of our activities hidden. Before that, we'd only ever received one warning a couple of years before for selling liquor to an Indian. We tried to lay low and not gather too much attention. But, that changed the day of Cornelis' burial.

My father, who had let the womenfolk do the comforting, finally came into my house. He pulled the curtains back from the bed.

"I am so sorry, daughter. Cornelis was a dear friend and a good husband to you. I grieve with you. It is time, Marie. You must rise for your husband's memorial service and burial," he said.

He grabbed my hand to help pull me from the bed.

"What good is it to go? Why go to the place that represents the reason why life was too stressful for him in the end?" I asked.

"No, Marie. You will go to honor your husband, Cornelis Volckertsen Viele. That is the only reason to go. And you will watch and give your respects as your husband's body is placed into the ground. Put on your proper clothes. We go now," he said, uncharacteristically firm with me.

I gathered my strength and met my waiting family outside to go pay our last respects to Cornelis. I prayed to get through the service quickly, holding my little Pierre on my lap as my other children huddled in close to me. I heard none of the minister's words, only my children's sobs in the church. I was in a dream as we walked to the burial ground on the main highway. Reality struck even harder as I watched Cornelis be put into the ground and said goodbye one final time. I looked at my little ones and resolved I would be strong and go forward.

It was then, after the burial, that Dominie Backerus approached me. As he came towards me, I sensed the storm coming, and my face flushed hot with anger.

"Marie du Trieux, with the death of your husband, God gives you another chance to find a more reputable place for yourself in town other than the tavern. I hope you will do the best thing and let go of *The Salty Rose*. The town does not need it, and your immortal soul would benefit from not spending time there," the minister said, insensitive to my suffering.

He was furthering his own campaign to get rid of more taverns on such a day! Then, he got too personal.

"Your three fatherless boys can learn better ways. We can place the older two in families dependent on other more useful trades. You should let the orphan board place them in more appropriate circumstances, and you should look to marry to improve your situation."

Truth is like a target. When someone tells you a lie or cuts you down with falsehoods, they are way off the target. I feel the force within me to go after such lies with sharp words that direct the truth to come out in the center of the dartboard. So when the minister came up to me to admonish me for my ways on the day of my husband's burial, I was compelled to let the words fly freely. The anger within me was in full steam and forced its way out of my mouth. I did not care that he was a reverend.

"Dominie Backerus, you speak your nonsense directed not only at me but at a dead man on the day he is buried. You're a despicable person and a poor example of a preacher. You helped put my husband into his grave. Cornelis and I provided what the community demands. We only wished to meet those needs. Stop molesting me! I will run the tavern as I see fit and you will have nothing to do with it!" I yelled.

I had to say it. But how unfair it was that after that day Domine Backerus and Stuyvesant were on my tail with their spies, watching me closely and waiting for any slip-up. I wasn't giving up my tavern. It was all I had left of Cornelis. I'd just have to be a little more vigilant.

CHAPTER TWELVE

Marie's Story
New Amsterdam, New Netherland
1650

I mourned for Cornelis for several months. He'd loved me dearly and provided me with a good life. But with three children to care for, I knew I had to be ready to marry again. So many of the men I'd seen in life were louts. I knew there were good ones too, but I preferred to take my time. With some guilt, I realized that resistance against marriage would make life more difficult for my children in the long run. But I wasn't going to force myself to endure a relationship I did not want. So, you can't imagine my surprise the day I met your grandfather, Jan Peeck.

Jan Peeck was a trapper. He'd barely been in New Amsterdam a whole day when he found his way to my tavern on the recommendation of a sailor en route back to his ship.

It was common for unknown travelers to come into *The Salty Rose* along the waterfront near the confluence of the stream at Maiden Lane and the East River. Aside from keeping a generally watchful eye and making sure these customers received their spirits, vittles, and entertainment they came for, I did not give them too much further attention.

But, oh my, when I first saw Jan, my eyes had a glorious feast. I wanted to inhale him into my soul. I did not understand how my attraction to him could happen at all when I still missed Cornelis.

Jan, my brawny man, did captivate me from the first. His mother was English and his father was Dutch. He wasn't like typical strangers, seafarers determined to imbibe themselves silly and take in as much merriment as humanly possible before the hour of their ship's curfew was reached. No, he was clad in furs and moccasins, appearing closer to an

Indian in dress than an Englishman. His face was undeniably English but it was tempered with softer angles and was not as strident and tight with tension as the faces of most of the English. It was obvious that years of trading with Indians had relaxed something deep in his part-English core.

He sat down close to the bar and immediately captured my attention. Laughing and jovial with quick jokes about the news of the day, his boyish grin and handsome face had me transfixed from the start.

I sized him up and down.

"Let me see. From your appearance, you must be the young Prince of Orange come to assess the latest developments in our fine colony, n'est ce pas?" I asked jokingly.

He nodded and egged me on, playing along with my game.

"Or perhaps a young shipping agent on a mission for the West India Company," I said, adding a feigned air of importance to his pretend title.

He continued to grin.

"Not quite. You're very close, my fine pretty tapper."

The truth was, I suspected Jan Peeck might be more trouble than I knew what to do with, but I was shimmering in his presence. He brought out a playful side of me that had been lackluster ever since my fatherly husband, Cornelis, had died a few months before. Jan was strong and virile. He awakened in me the girl of my youth.

Most days, my shoulders hung heavy with the increased responsibility of being sole parent and tapper. Even though I had friends and family, and my barkeeper, Domingo, was my solid rock, it was still a difficult road for a young woman of thirty-one. Jan was a couple of years younger.

I poured myself a frothy brew and sipped.

"The beer is perfect today," I said, staring at him with my intense brown eyes.

"Perhaps you are the master merchant of the great Dutch guild of gold merchants?" I asked.

"Ha ha. You know what I really am, Marie, and I know who you are," he said.

"You do, eh? Well then, you'd better tell me," I exclaimed.

Yes. All cautions to the wind and devils be on the loose, I didn't care. I wanted to surround myself with Jan. I wanted him and I knew at our first encounter we were destined to be together.

Marie, you must be with this man, I told myself in full confidence. I had been a grieving solitary widow for long enough.

I came from around the bar and sat next to Jan. When the patrons got unruly, I yelled my customary warnings but turned my attention back to him immediately. Domingo continued to steadily fill the mugs of beer and keep a watchful eye on everything and everyone, including me. I wanted to close the bar and be alone with Jan but the usual customers would never forgive me. I would not have forgiven myself. I needed the money. I had many mouths to feed. Why was I letting this handsome half-Englishman into my heart so quickly?

Abruptly, I stood up.

"So, what is it that you want? I'm serious now. No more coy games and teasing. I have my children and my tavern to deal with," I said.

"Ah, Marie. Please sit back down. I may look rough. But really I'm a man of honor. Let's do what you want," he said, charming me further.

But he also knew in that moment that this was not an ordinary visit to a tavern. My eyes had already conveyed my innermost desires.

Hoping for him to avoid the full transparency of my soul, I scurried quickly behind the bar again, using Domingo as my excuse.

"Chérie, not now. Look how overworked my loyal Domingo is. I'll work and you tell me more about your life. Your real life, that is," I clarified.

"Anything you desire. Your wish is my command," he joked as I eyed his broad shoulders, hoping they would hold me safe one day.

I tried to busy myself to lower the intensity between us. I checked on other customers and helped Domingo fill more mugs of beer when he rolled an empty beer barrel to the back, retrieving a new one to tap, but I kept coming back to Jan as a moth comes back to a flame. Domingo noticed too. He whispered to me, "Be careful, Marie. It's hard to stop a horse with no reigns."

I always understood that in life many things are out of your own control, even the longings of one's heart. In spite of this, my path had taken a surprising turn. Our alignment was accepted from this first night forward in the same way the moon accepts that it will continue to traverse the night sky among the stars.

Jan and I understood each other. Many things did not need to be said. We fell into each other's arms naturally just as the sun rises above the eastern horizon every morning, just as the tides do not need to tell the shore that they will visit closely once again in a few hours. Some things are just known. And that is how it was with Jan and me from our first passionate meeting.

CHAPTER THIRTEEN:

Marie's Story
New Amsterdam, New Netherland
1650

"Marie, beautiful Marie. I see you too are lazy today," spoke my new husband with an air of slight teasing.

Jan nuzzled up to me under the thick fur blankets in the longhouse. He lavished me with kisses in our wilderness cocoon. I, in turn, embraced the strong body of my love, the one who had made all my previous misery dim in memory. The thrill of his touch and the bliss of being granted a brief sojourn in the woods made my heart leap to heights it had never been.

Jan and I were in our retreat about a day's journey from New Amsterdam. The demands of the tavern and my small band of children were remote for a brief time. Domingo, my sister Sarah, her husband Isaac, and my eldest boy Aernoudt were in charge of *The Salty Rose*.

Jan bought us a property with an inlet where he moored his sloop when he was not traveling to trade with the Natives. We built our house there at the top of the little hill on Pearl. It was close to the tavern and an easy walking distance to my father's farm in Smit's Valley.

There, in Indian country, at a place in a great bend on the North River after a stretch where the river widens to great lengths, we stayed with Jan's Native trading partners of many years.

In their village, we nestled together, surrounded by the glistening snow of February and the scent of hemlock and pines. I wanted to take in Jan and all the peace that surrounded me. I knew our time alone together was only a brief reprieve from all that was expected of us. The daily hardships and grind of keeping our family together in our lawless colony would require our attention.

Most of the Indians in the village where we stayed were awake already. Some Native women stirred the corn porridge for the morning meal in an iron cauldron procured the previous season in exchange for some pelts.

"Come, Marie, we must be good guests and join the others," he said. I felt more blissful and satisfied than I had ever been. I stretched into Jan and then cozied further into him, taking in more of his sweetness. A lifetime wouldn't be enough. Contented for a while, I sighed and stared deeply into his chocolate-brown eyes. He locked his hands into mine and gazed back deeply.

Again, I pondered, who is this rugged young man who has saved me from my hidden despairs? He came to me at just the right moment in time. Despite having given birth to several children already, I realized it was the first time I had ever truly fallen in love.

Love was the crème, the rich crème at the top of the milk but you couldn't expect to have it for yourself most of the time. There was a lot more milk in the container of life. It was fine. It nourished, and I had always been grateful for whatever I had. That I should finally have my turn drinking some of the crème at the top left me content beyond measure.

Jan and I finally emerged from our hidden corner of the longhouse and joined the women cooking in the center. Some women smiled and others giggled, understanding the status of our recent marriage. Only one young woman did not seem amused by our affectionate displays towards each other. I sensed she was not happy about our union for her own personal reasons. I felt completely loved by Jan. But remembering her, I always wondered if there had been something that had happened between them, perhaps an amorous liaison.

The Indians had known Jan for many years from his frequent visits as a trader among them. He also traded with many other tribes. We were with the Sachoes but on further trips up the North River, he also traded with Mohawks, Munsee, Wappingers, and many other smaller tribes.

Even though our trek into the wilderness was a sweet pause from daily life in New Amsterdam, it was also a business trip of trading. Jan wanted to show me some of his world and introduce me to the tribes with whom he interacted. I knew a few of them already from their dealings in our tavern and from my childhood in my earliest years in New Netherland.

This was our last day of trading with them. Jan led me to the fire where an elderly woman gave me a wooden bowl filled with corn porridge to eat and a broth made of warming herbs. She smiled as I ate, never taking her eyes off me.

"Welania is transfixed by you!" Jan said, smiling at the old woman.

Jan had finished eating his food before me and carried some of his newly acquired pelts of beaver, otter, and mink to our boat. When I was finished warming my insides with the nourishment given to me by the old woman's generosity, she took my face into her hands and spoke to me in her native tongue. It is hard to translate perfectly what she said but, in essence, her words were a warning and blessing as well. This is roughly what I think she said.

"Take much happiness into your heart while it is given to you from the Creator. Be grateful for it because sometimes it does not stay long. Also take his gift of strength, for you will need it as well. When happiness can be no more, the Creator will guide you to use your strength. He will help you to see when trickster or coyote is playing with your sight. When the period of strength that is no longer required ends, surrender to the spirits and their wisdom as a rose unfolds into its true beauty."

She let go and smiled once more, turning her head to view Jan making steps in the snow with his fur boots.

As we said our good-byes to our hosts, Welania looked at me again. She nodded silently, captivating my attention, forever etching the moment into my memory. It took us most of the day to travel back to Manhattan with the swift North River current, carefully avoiding chunks of ice where the river narrowed. As we traveled past the highlands of the wide river valley, I thought of her words.

I was taken aback. Why did she make a reference to a rose? How could she know? I was confused. But certainly, some of these Natives knew about my tavern. Perhaps that was what she was referring to. I've thought about Welania's words many times since. In her wisdom, she foretold the rest of my life and her presence penetrated my soul in a way that made me pay attention intently to the foreshadowing of a future that was yet to come.

I knew that Jan had come into my life just in time, but for what reason besides good fortune baffled me. For several weeks, a strange feeling encompassed me. It was ominous, not joyful, and I held a strong sense of something monumental to come. I was unsuspecting of just how personal and close to my own threshold the unwelcome news would come. A tragedy from which I still recover soon cloaked me in a dark coat of human suffering.

Sensing that something had happened, I thought that I had woken up in the middle of the night. I must have been mistaken but my Papa was whispering in my ear in a scene that seemed to be too real to be a dream. Standing just behind him, I saw my brother Philippe Jr. who gave a nod toward a Dutch man with an axe coming toward them. Everything was surreal. It wasn't until morning with the hurried knocks from my mother, Susanne, and my younger brother, Abraham, that I realized the truth about their ghoulish visitation.

"Marie, Marie! Open the door. Something has happened to Papa and Philippe!" cried Susanne.

I'd heard the horse and cart arriving hurriedly to the door a few seconds before.

I ran to see what the commotion was. Seeing Susanne's pallor and the frozen shock on her face, I knew a tragedy more personal than I could bear was about to unfold.

"We found your brother and father dead in the orchard. They were tending to the pear and peach trees when they were killed. The neighbors say it must be Indians, but I do not understand!" she cried.

"No!" I screamed. "This cannot be."

Jan was standing next to me, creating safety by surrounding me with his strong arms. I grabbed my hat. Escorted by Jan with children in tow, we got in the cart with Susanne and Abraham to go back to Smit's Valley, back to Papa's farm.

There had been peace for a few years. Both sides were wary of the toll of war and tired of the accompanying heartache. It was surprising but not unheard of for a lone Native to claim revenge for past injustices done. But Papa had always tried to mind his own business. He was not interested in Kieft's foolish wars. He had forged early relationships with the Natives we lived near, knowing it was good for trade. He also knew it would make our lives easier to get along with our neighbors, neighbors who could help with food and who had intimate knowledge of the land should we get into trouble.

But New Amsterdam was still continuing to pay for the ignorance of former Director Kieft and his brash violence toward Indian tribes previously friendly with the residents of our colony. It was possible that my Papa and eldest brother met their tragic end in this way.

Even in shock, I knew the old Indian woman had seen the incident in the ethers around me on the last day Jan and I were in the Sachoe camp to trade.

We sat in silence on the way back to Papa's farm, shocked and dismayed at what had happened. My boys had heard the story and sat stunned next to me. I yearned for Papa, frozen in panic at the thought of living without him. I was determined to remember as much about him as I could—every detail so that he would not slip away—his scent, the way he held his pipe in his crooked mouth, his impish laugh, his pride in growing the best pumpkins on Manhattan Island.

My papa, Philippe du Trieux, had experienced more than most people, first coming to Holland from Roubaix, France with my mother and then bringing his second wife Susanne and her children to an unsettled wilderness. Only a brave man would do such a thing with his equally courageous family. He was willing to take his chances and had the faith to think we'd be resilient and thrive in a place where no Europeans had settled before.

Papa was the first person to build his house on Beaver street several years before moving out to Smit's Valley. There he bought several morgens of farmland. It was north of Maiden Lane and on the way to Stuyvesant's bowery long before our Director General had his own extensive farm. Papa farmed there for almost fifteen years.

My papa, through his easy demeanor and likability, had risen to be messenger to Director Kieft. It was a useful role. He always had access to pieces of information that were kept out of earshot of most of New Amsterdam's citizens, tidbits of knowledge that might be embarrassing should they become commonly known.

Again, I remembered the words of Welania, the Native elder who had advised me to hold on to happiness tightly when you have it and to be strong when it goes away. Her words had been pertinent. But until now, I had not grasped the meaning of the trickster. As the days unfolded, I remembered that it was a European man with an axe that approached Papa in his visitation to me.

Any suspicions were only confirmed when rumors spread that it was no Indian who killed Papa and my brother but rather a white settler who did not want his secrets known, someone whom my father could expose. Perhaps they had a fight and my father threatened to lay his secrets bare. It was also said that this man had wanted my father's land.

It was believable and we'd seen it happen before, blaming crimes on Indians when the real criminals turned out to be other Europeans. Was the killing of Papa and my brother meant to provoke further hostilities by blaming their deaths on Natives? Alas, we will never know.

We never did find out the specific details of what happened to Papa and my brother. The man in question disappeared for good. What I did learn though from the unspeakable loss of my family was that the words of Welania rang true and I sensed there was more to her message than I could possibly know in that moment in time.

CHAPTER FOURTEEN:

Tinker & Winthrop's Story
New London, Connecticut Colony
1653

John Tinker was anxious to meet with Winthrop again. His life had changed immensely since they'd last met. He'd finally succumbed to societal pressures and had taken a young wife who was ripe with his first child. She was feeling poorly as she neared the last stages of her pregnancy, and Tinker hoped Winthrop could help her or refer her to one of the many healing women he worked with. Tinker had begged her to come on the journey to stay and rest with Winthrop so Mrs. Winthrop could help take care of her, but she dreaded travel and preferred to stay near her parents and brother for the duration of her pregnancy. Tinker understood her need to be near her parents. He was much older than her and, although married, their lives and experiences were drastically different.

Life had changed dramatically for the better in Winthrop's world as well. Ever since his feuds with Mason and the Mohegans had died down, Winthrop was able to focus on mastering his alchemical arts. He was starting to get a respected reputation for healing the sick. He took no monies for his labors and ended up doctoring a good many colonists in Connecticut. As a result, he was able to develop his dream of making New London into both a healing and an alchemical center.

People were starting to show up at his hospital seeking alchemical cures and mystical remedies. Letters arrived from other places in the colony requesting his advice for all kinds of maladies. From smallpox or falling sickness to the king's evil, word got out of Winthrop's talents and generosity. Tinker had longed to visit for many months to witness the changes in his mentor's life.

Despite his concern for his wife, Tinker relished the travel to Connecticut shores. He enjoyed the time alone to smell the salty air and hear the sound of gulls and ocean waves again. It was a peaceful trip, allowing him a few precious rare moments where he could sit aboard the vessel bound for New London and let his mind wander.

"Here we are. New London!" called the captain as they neared the approach into the Thames River.

John gathered his case filled with the multiple documents and ledgers he'd need to go over with Winthrop and a modest bag with some of his belongings. His heart was teeming with excitement at the prospect of seeing his old friend again, of the late-night talks that would be certain to follow, and of experiments in the laboratory.

Winthrop must have seen the shallop from Boston coming in from his hillside home and sprinted to the waterfront to greet his dear friend.

"John Tinker! Over here!" Winthrop shouted, waving to his trusted advisor. "It's a fine feeling to greet a familiar friend," he said, smiling.

"John Winthrop! Look at you! And look at the town. New London has grown since I was last here. Your reputation is spreading, sir. I hear many good things from as far away as Boston! You look calm and happy," said Tinker.

Winthrop smiled. "Aye, Tinker. 'Tis a true transformation. With the past uproar about the Pequots and Cassacinamon fairly settled, I've had God's grace to attend to my alchemical work and to attract needed tradesmen to the town. A good many metal workers have come to take advantage of the mineral enterprises underway. The mill is running and a good many more settlers have come."

"No doubt much of it is due to your doctoring in these parts. I hear people come from far and wide for your healing remedies, and some decide to settle," said Tinker.

"Ah, 'tis true. I will show you." He turned to his servants who had followed him to the waterfront and asked them to bring John Tinker's belongings to the house.

He put a hand on Tinker's shoulder. "Come, man. We'll get you something to eat, and then the hospital and the lab await us. I've much to show you,'" he said.

Cleaned up and well-fed with a hearty mutton stew and brown bread in his belly, Tinker followed the path past Winthrop's home slightly down a hill overlooking the river and farmed hillsides to meet his mentor at his lab. The dirt path led to the group of outbuildings now serving as Winthrop's hospital. Nearby, stood a timber-framed building where his labs were located. Here, Winthrop concocted the remedies gaining attention far and wide as well as conducted his numerous alchemical experiments in their various stages.

Winthrop turned down no one. It was the Rosicrucian way. He felt obligated to use his knowledge to help his fellow man, and asked for no compensation in return. He treated the privileged and their enslaved Africans, English, Europeans, and many Natives too.

He welcomed their stomach pains and back pains, their weaknesses, their chronic swelling, their dental caries, worms, and infections. He treated it all with his specially formulated cures, medical waters, plasters, and eyewashes. They all clamored to ingest the elixirs Winthrop made in his lab, the results of spiritual endeavors inspired by God. So many people came to see him that, at times, there was no available lodging in town.

As time passed, Winthrop was in greater demand to cure the sick and heal the ailing residents in Connecticut. He was widely sought out for his cures made by isolating and concentrating plant essences—cures arrived at by only careful methodical preparation and prayer in the lab of a true alchemist.

Sometimes, Winthrop responded with cures he sent back in color-coded envelopes. Other times, the sick came to him for an in-person diagnosis or on those occasions when they needed to stay for a longer period of convalescence. Winthrop often consulted with local healing women for his herbal staples and advised them to reach ever more people.

It was already late afternoon but the two men had much to catch up on, and Tinker relished seeing the new developments in the labs. The center had been built upon since he was last there. As he entered, he noticed a room off to the right laden with shelves of herbs and other cures.

Jars of herbal medicines lined the shelves: betony, anise, raisins, sarsaparilla, birch, turpentine, ointment of tobacco, saffron, aloes, horseradish, senna, nutmeg rhubarb, agrimony, turnips, china root, and guaiacum, among others.

Others hung dried, ready for further refinement: mugwort, oregano, parsley, verbena, wormwood, sage, roses, St John's wort, and heal all. Tinker had no doubt that Winthrop acquired many from the cadre of female healers he'd worked with.

But those seeking the healing advice of Winthrop wanted something even more. They were entranced by the promises of stronger alchemical medicines. The effects could be strong but they reasoned the healing must be too. So they willed themselves to sweat and vomit until their illnesses had retreated, thanks to such wondrous medicines as minerals and metals.

Other cabinets in Winthrop's apothecary were a testament to that: coral and ivory, deer horn, ambergris, millipedes. Even the rarities of unicorn horn from narwhal and seahorse pizzle were oddities and healing ingredients that graced his shelves. Vials of flowers of sulfur, balsam sulfuris, mercury dulcis, calomel, sal prunelle, sal ammoniac, alum, burnt alum, salt, aqua martis, distillation of vitriol, and blue vitriol—all had their places.

Tinker's gaze upon them was broken when he heard the sound of Winthrop's boots as he walked across the hall.

"You've found your way to the lab again! What do you think, John Tinker?" Winthrop asked as he crossed the room to gesture at the displayed groupings of pharmacopeia.

"Sir, I do believe that you will find the alkahest one day with your dedicated work to the healing of the sick," said Tinker.

"Ah, the alkahest, that magical elixir that can cure all diseases. Only God knows when it will be found, but if I can be of service and discover it, that is what I, among many others, attempt to do," said Winthrop.

"Wouldn't it be rewarding to discover missing medical knowledge lost since the fall of man?" questioned Tinker.

"Aye, Paracelsus, the great medical alchemist, tells us that a physician's powers come directly from the Divine as do a person's medical conditions, so we must rely on this greater power. However, one thing I do know is that the knowledge will not come if man sits idly by," explained Winthrop.

Tinker nodded in satisfaction.

"Just as the alchemist toils to transform the baser metals into precious ones, man must transmute himself to overcome his corrupt nature and find purity of spirit. This is the process that must be achieved. True healing comes from it," said Winthrop.

"I suppose it starts with the Philosopher's Stone," Tinker said. "If you or another alchemist can determine that sought-after substance which turns base metals into precious ones, especially gold, you can also find the elixir of life."

"Aye, immortality would be at our doorstep—the valiant yet elusive goal sought by so many since the great loss of knowledge. I am so glad you are here, John Tinker. I feel we are closer than ever before to so many things that will bring an end to corruption and purify the times. We have almost come full circle back to the Divine. Being here in New London brings the Passage nearer to our sights, just as the alkahest is also closer than ever before," Winthrop stated.

His face lit up.

"Since Underhill claimed the Dutch Fort in Hartford for the English and Stuyvesant ceded many Dutch lands to Connecticut, we are closer to success in our quest for the Passage!" Winthrop added with glee.

"It is splendid, sir. Will you show me the results of your labors here?" asked Tinker.

"Ah, yes! Don't mind me, Tinker. You know how I can go on. I see you've seen some of my apothecary room. The fine womenfolk of the colony leaders, their wives and their sisters, already entrusted to care for the sick in their communities, send me their herbal simples in exchange for some of my powders so that all may benefit. Mrs. Hooker and even Mrs. Mason work with me to heal the sick," explained Winthrop.

"I hope she's somewhat more agreeable than her husband," said Tinker.

"Well, we don't dwell on the past, and most of her interactions are through my dear wife. Her husband has become quieter in regards to me," Winthrop added.

"Thankfully," smiled Tinker.

"Aye," chuckled Winthrop. "Come with me, John Tinker."

He led Tinker through the building where he showed him not just one but also several labs that were managed by Winthrop's enslaved servants.

"This is the lab where I work on the most labor-intensive cures," stated Winthrop.

A putrid smell emanated from a pot near a hearth.

"This, my dear friend, is the black powder you may have heard of that I use as a remedy to heal smallpox, plague, and other fevers."

Winthrop pointed to a clay pot.

"We baked the toads just yesterday. Today, my servants burned the remains in open air. Tomorrow, we'll pound it into brown powder, and from there it will turn black, where we will further refine it. It produces wildly purgative effects," stated Winthrop.

Tinker nodded, not surprised by people's physical reactions to the remedy.

"What are those over there?" asked Tinker, eyeing several instruments of war such as swords and other weapons covered in a salve of some sort.

"Those are the weapons that inflicted a wound that I now attempt to heal from a distance with a specially concocted salve. It is easier that the victim who suffers not travel, so the instrument that has done them harm comes to me here where I apply my salve to it. The victim of the violent event may heal with time if it is God's will," said Winthrop.

They walked to another laboratory on the opposite side of the building. Tinker was relieved to leave the horrid smell of the last lab. It was no wonder that the black powder could induce rapid evacuation of the bowels.

"What have we here?" asked Tinker.

"In this laboratory, the alchemist's most prized ingredients are transformed into their purest forms," Winthrop explained.

Winthrop grabbed a flask off a massive wooden table. "Behold agrimony. It will increase the life energy of the spirit but only when all impurities are filtered out of it. It is a most useful medicine for babies and adults alike."

Then he turned to another vial, lifting it to the level of Tinker's vision. "Nitre, another purgative which I find effective with toothache, stomach problems, and urinary blockages."

Tinker noted Winthrop's reference charts strewn about the table as well. They included the old Galenic system of balancing fire, earth, air, and water—corresponding to blood, yellow bile, phlegm, and black bile. But

Tinker also saw a chart of the alchemist Paracelsus' system of salt, mercury, and sulfur had an exalted place in the diagnostics and treatment Winthrop used.

"Let us go visit the hospital. There are three patients there now. It is time for their Rubila."

Tinker had heard of it. He knew Winthrop had been working on a cure-all for quite some time. Rubila quickly became Winthrop's most prescribed elixir.

"Let me show you," Winthrop said.

Rubila was a red-tinged powder that Winthrop prepared: 4 grains antimony, 20 grains of nitre, plus a little salt of tin.

Tinker was impressed with the progress made at New London. The number of new medicines created by Winthrop and his increased knowledge at distilling them were remarkable.

Little did Tinker know at the time that Winthrop's latest accomplishments would soon lead to a new role as a magical expert in future Connecticut witch trial cases. If only his cousin Alice, the first New England witch trial victim, had had such an expert in the magical arts, a healing champion to testify on her behalf. It might have made the difference between life and death. Winthrop, a renowned and respected physician, differentiating illness from demonic influence, could have been at her side. Tinker stopped himself. Why submit to the desperate wish that life in the colonies would have taken a more benign turn in its beginnings? The tragedy had happened and could not be undone.

CHAPTER FIFTEEN

Marie's Story
New Amsterdam, New Netherland
1651-1656

After Papa died, I became anxious and unsure of myself for the very first time. Jan's mood was more irritable, being bound to stay more often in New Amsterdam under the roof of the tavern instead of roaming in the endless forests under the open skies of the wilderness. We were still passionately in love, but it was never the same, never as peaceful as our first months of marriage before the violent loss of Papa and my brother.

Jan had been a completely free man, answerable only to himself and his desires. All of a sudden, he found himself laden with responsibility and a wife who became even more dependent on him.

It was an awful feeling for me not to be as independent as I had always been. I never imagined that the presence of my papa in life had given me an important and invisible anchor and strength.

Jan was there for me, but he still needed his time away, feeling suffocated by so many new burdens and responsibilities. He was younger than I and so not fatherly to me as my first husband was. The increased tension between us only ignited more passions after our ever-increasing arguments, and I found myself pregnant with babies over and over again.

Our first child together was named Anna after Jan's mother. She was born the year after Jan and I married. Then there was Johannes a couple of years later, followed by Jacob. The last little one was Mary.

I could be honest with Susanne who was also having a difficult time without my father.

"Marie, it will take time to settle into a new way of life for both you and Jan. You will gain your fearlessness back," she said.

With time, Jan developed other interests in the town, became very attached to our children and protective of all of us. He developed the skills of a tapper and was also interested in land speculation. He would buy land on the edges of settlement and sell it for new development.

And I grew my own invisible anchor and became grounded and confident again. My daughter Alida, who received a proper education, taught me to read beyond what my former husband Cornelis had already done, which also boosted my self-assurance.

Our lives revolved mostly around our children and our tavern. Unfortunately, it included the increasing attention of Stuyvesant and the ministers. They'd been on me like a fly to shit ever since I told off Dominie Backerus at the burial of Cornelis. I became accustomed to their spies. They thought they were discreet, but I could smell them from a distance. It was almost like a game for me to spot them. I could easily tell the difference between someone who was simply a stranger and someone who was really a stooge sent to the tavern by Stuyvesant.

To avoid punishment for breaking the rules, we could shut down the tavern in minutes, in plenty of time before the sheriff could obtain his evidence against us. We had a special hidden door for quick exits and hiding places for those patrons who couldn't flee the bar fast enough. Our code was "Salute the flag!" to which everyone scrambled, hiding mugs and glasses, replacing pipes in their rack, and shoving games into a box. Our regular customers knew the drill. Usually, it worked pretty well.

Henri La Chaîne and his wife Claire still came around and took notice of my new reading abilities and my adeptness and intelligence in avoiding Stuyvesant and his spies. They'd chuckle for every snoop I'd discover and expose.

"Marie, you know how to handle yourself with Stuyvesant, at least for now. But maybe life has bigger plans for you than playing cat and mouse with the Director General," Henri said, smiling as his wife Claire looked intently at me.

On the other hand, Jan was not always as perceptive about what was happening. He was busy having a good time too, but I could count on him for protection. He was as wild as a bobcat ready for a fight if he thought any customer was out of his place.

One night, a rogue soldier came into the tavern. He was rude and got too drunk. I told him to get out. He'd had enough to drink and was molesting my other customers.

He grabbed me by the shoulders and shook me, demanding I give him what he wanted. I slapped him in the face and screamed for Jan. Jan came running from the back with a knife which lanced the scoundrel's thigh, forcing him to let go of me. Jan finished him off with several punches until the bastard lay on the rough floor bleeding. With a final kick to his groin, the soldier was dragged to the road.

"Don't throw the bastard anywhere near my rose bushes," I called out.

I was sure Jan had saved my life. The rogue soldier was pulling out his pistol as Jan went to pull him off of me. However, the sheriff, Cornelis van Tienhoven, did not see it that way. He'd been waiting a long time to catch us in some criminal activity. He hauled Jan off to the new city hall, the Stadthuys, where he slept overnight in a jail cell and had to swear to be on good behavior or lose his tavern license. The soldier recovered and thankfully never came back.

Jan started a dance club at *The Salty Rose*. We had a musician friend, Jacques Lambert, a fellow Walloon. He played the fiercest and fastest fiddle you could ever imagine. He gathered folk tunes from all over Europe and aimed to please his crowd. So many people loved it and came to dance for hours on end.

It was easy to stay open beyond the legal hours. Everyone enjoyed themselves. Unfortunately, the music traveled along the East River and one night, some Calvinist stalwarts and their ministers heard echoes of our merriment and, thinking just like Stuyvesant, reported us to the sheriff. Van Tienhoven came and warned us to cease our actions, but we gathered together again and again. The music was the salve our souls needed, and we wouldn't stop.

We needed the money, and New Amsterdam was booming again after respite from wars. It was teeming with new people, and traders from afar came into the tavern hankering for a good time. They weren't all churchgoers. So, why not open our tavern on Sundays? Our Indian acquaintances and friends still came too, but we had to be more careful.

The city had changed a lot after Stuyvesant took over. An increasing population of residents built new shops and warehouses, and built up bulkheads along the East River. Buildings were going up quickly and the swamps were filled in. In their place, a canal mimicked those in Holland and was traversed by several bridges. The mills were constantly running, refining grains and cutting wood to keep up with the demand to shelter and feed the booming population.

We were ready to go forward anew after the menacing threat of war with the English, and the Director General ceded land to New England a couple of years before. The Indian wars had died down for a time, and everyone just wanted their lives to be a little better, to have a little more joy and a lot more laughter.

Not all of us could celebrate. A few enslaved Africans were put to work with other servants to give New Amsterdam cobblestone streets and a wall for protection against invaders from New England, a city dock, and a reinforced fort. They toiled for the company and wealthy residents alike. Some eventually gained half-free status like Domingo, but most worked until their dying day.

The young man, Adriaen van der Donck, who had met his friends and sat for hours in our tavern had helped to bring the biggest changes of all. He had finally presented his petition for representation on behalf of the citizens of New Amsterdam to Stuyvesant. At first, the two men got along. However, Stuyvesant wasn't about to give up any of his power and refused the demands of Van der Donck and those of the Council.

Van der Donck disappeared across the sea for a time to bring his petition to the States-General. He pleaded that New Amsterdam should be properly recognized as a Dutch city in the wilderness and accordingly have all the same legal rights. He argued that the West India Company had been negligent to our needs.

He must have waited for months to bring his case against Stuyvesant and the West India Company, for in the meantime he wrote all about the treasures of New Netherland: its land, its animals, its plants, everything about it, in an effort to create more interest for prospective future settlers and build up the population.

Even with the boom in traders and a surge in the population, we still couldn't keep our population numbers up with the English to the northeast. It was always a concern since Dutch lands on the eastern end of Long Island and those up the Connecticut River had already been steadily encroached upon.

When Van der Donck was on his way back from Patria, the fatherland, a new English aggression arose that interfered with his destiny. The previous autumn, John Underhill, the mercenary soldier who'd help Kieft start the Indian wars, had gone back to the English. After switching his allegiances, he went to Hartford where he posted a notice on the walls of the Dutch fort there.

I, John Underhill do seize upon this house and land thereto belonging, as Dutch goods, claimed by WIC in Amsterdam, enemies of the commonwealth of England and thus, to remain seized until further determined by the said state.

It was posted for any remaining Dutch in Hartford to see. The representatives at the fort were forced to leave. I knew Underhill would turn on the Dutch! I'd predicted it years before.

New Netherland was becoming a little smaller because of the English moving boundary lines and cutting off edges of the Dutch colony for themselves. On the other hand, the citizens of New Amsterdam finally had real representation as directed by the States-General in the fatherland. The town got its municipal charter with burgomasters, town representatives, and five magistrates or schepens. They met most Mondays at the former city tavern—now the town hall, at 9 o'clock in the morning to hear cases.

Because of Van der Donck, Petrus Stuyvesant was finally forced by his superiors back home to allow for city elections.

Poor Van der Donck got the short stick though. Van der Donck returned at the end of the year thinking that he would take over Stuyvesant's role as promised by the directors of the company. But alas, the best plans often do not come to fruition. English aggression caused the leaders in Holland to change their minds and keep Stuyvesant at the helm of the colony.

When Van der Donck returned to New Amsterdam, Stuyvesant, spiteful because of his attempted ouster, forced him out of government forever. The Director General threatened him with imprisonment if he stirred up any more trouble. Van der Donck was ordered to keep his mouth shut. We didn't see too much of Van der Donck after that. He stayed on his vast estate and bowery north of New Haarlem with his English wife, Mary Doughty, the daughter of the minister Francis Doughty.

I was thinking about this and how life can change for the good or bad before the last incident occurred that sent my Jan to jail and then to court. Our dancing clubs became a little too well known for our own good. Jacques was popular and couldn't put down his fiddle once he got going.

The crowd in the tavern was in a merry mood that night. They pounded their feet to the music on my new wood floor. Ladies and men twirled and stomped to the tune at hand, a silly Walloon dance song about a little hen. We tapped our barrels almost dry that night and many moved on to strong spirits and brandy. Domingo poured incessantly.

"A cheer for Marie and Jan. Raise your glasses!"

"My dear wife, you owe me a dance," winked Jan, taking my hand.

I was enjoying the moment and was off my guard. Our bodies swayed together to the rhythm of the music. The hours slipped by so quickly that I had no idea it was as late as it was. Everyone knew Jacques well. He obliged requests for favorite songs and some we all sang together with glee.

We were all enjoying the moment so much that no one had any idea that Van Tienhoven, the sheriff, was slithering outside behind the boarded shutters. He'd managed to find a little crack and peered in from the outside, gathering his evidence of our late-night revelry.

When his patience had run out, he rushed into the tavern. Our amusing little party ended abruptly. The clientele scattered as fast as mice to their homes or back to their ships before he could catch up with them.

"I command that you stop at once!" screamed the sheriff. "I have warned you many times to obey the rules, Marie and Jan Peeck! You will pay for your insolence."

Jan and I looked at each other and laughed, making him all the more irate.

"We'll see how you feel after you spend the night in jail and have to answer for your crimes in court," he snapped at Jan.

Jan was ready to swear at him and let him know what he thought. I could tell the words were coming.

I gave him a stern glance. "No. Chérie, mind your tongue. It is already bad enough for us," I said.

Poor Jan was furious, but he dutifully stayed silent as I advised, not wanting to create more havoc for his family. Van Tienhoven put Jan in his cart with a couple of lingering drunkards that were having a hard time finding their way home. I pitied Jan having to spend the night in jail with the two of them.

The next day, I sat with Jan in court as Van Tienhoven presented our crimes. We were sobered to face the reality of losing our tavern license.

Sheriff Van Tienhoven testified, "I have found drinking clubs with dancing and jumping and entertainment at the establishment of Jan Peeck. I had to move some drunks to jail on a Sunday! They have been warned many times yet there is an endless display of disorderly folk. It is a most scandalous affair that cannot go on! On account of his disorderly house-keeping and evil life, tippling, dancing, gaming, and other irregularities, together with tapping at night, and tapping on a Sunday during preaching. I implore the court to revoke the tavern license of Jan Peeck so that he shall tap no more until he has vindicated himself," said the sheriff.

The bastard sounded so arrogant. It was a pleasure for him to take away our living, the way that we earned our money to feed our children.

We did lose our license that day and did not get it back again until we proved ourselves capable of following the rules. Desperate for a livelihood, I made meals for other taverns. Jan too realized he had to find other work. Of course, I still snuck a few bottles of this and that through my secret window when I was sure no one was looking.

It was only a few weeks before we applied for another license and got it with the promise of good behavior. However, we were affected financially and we both knew for the future it would be better to have other business dealings to supplement our income.

Jan decided to do more land speculation. He took my old home with Cornelis on the main highway, improved it, and sold it. He found other pieces of property that he bought and sold as well.

With so much trade going on and New England just slightly to the north of us, there was a great demand for English translators and brokers. My Jan, fluent in both English and Dutch, was granted permission to be broker and translator between English and Dutch merchants. Luckily his petition to do this was granted. Under his contracts, he would get paid one and a half stiver for every pound, with half being paid by each buyer and seller.

Jan was skilled at his new trade. Soon, the English started showing up at our doorstep, asking for his help with all kind of deals. Sometimes in life the unexpected happens and, because of his new profession, Jan and I found this to be true. I never in my wildest suspicions could have determined that because of Jan's new work, we would develop a rare friendship with a Puritan merchant named John Tinker.

CHAPTER SIXTEEN:

Marie's Story
New Amsterdam, New Netherland
1656

I'll never forget the day when John Tinker walked into *The Salty Rose*. Little did I know what a friend he would become to Jan and me. One afternoon, he stopped by the tavern to find Jan, seeking him out for brokerage services.

When he came walking in the door, he heard me speaking French to my children. I was barking out orders to them to move some barrels and tap another keg. The older boys, Aernoudt and Cornelis, were beginning to learn the tavern keeper's trade.

"Bonjour, Madame. I understand you speak English here. I am in search of Jan Peeck. He is the owner of this establishment?"

I shook my head.

"Yes, he's known as Jan around here. The tavern is mine, but he is my husband. Who are you, and what's your business?" I demanded, placing my hands on my hips, not fully trusting him.

From his clothes, I could immediately tell that he was a prosperous Puritan merchant. He was dressed well in a maroon-colored doublet with a deep purple overcoat of crushed velvet and deep purple breeches. The rest of his attire was black, including a brimmed black hat. He suffered not for want of any material needs, yet he did not possess any airs of entitlement or condescension.

"Good day, fine lady! My name is John Tinker. I come from Lancaster, Massachusetts, where I am a fur trader."

He had yet to tell me that he handled the affairs of the esteemed physician, John Winthrop the Younger of Connecticut.

"I also trade in commodities between the colonies. Your husband Jan was recommended to me by the craftsman, Henri La Chaîne," he said, smiling in a way that began to disarm me from my distrust of Puritans.

I let down my guard slightly more when I heard the name Henri La Chaîne.

"You know Henri, the cabinetmaker?" I asked.

"Yes, Madame. Yes, I do! Henri was commissioned to make a very special piece of furniture, a physician's chair, for my employer. We know each other through various commercial connections."

"Come, Mr. Tinker," I said, pointing to a rack of smoking pipes of many lengths and styles. "Pick the one you like. We have some fine tobacco that just arrived from Virginia and some from another local crop too. Take your pick. It's on the house. Jan is not here now, but I will send one of my sons to find him," I said.

"Thank you," John Tinker pointed to his preference, packing his chosen pipe with the Virginia tobacco.

Lighting it, I asked, "For the moment, what will you have to drink with your smoke, Mr. Tinker? Perhaps you're also hungry from your voyage?"

"A hearty Dutch beer for a simple man will do, kind lady," he stated without bravado. "And of course, I'll try your best local fare of the day," he said hungrily.

"I have the perfect beer for you from a little brewery called *The Red Dragon*. I think you will like it. A Walloon makes it. So even better, eh?" I winked. "I've just made my best coleslaw and fried fish from the morning catch and on the side some cheese and a fine wheat bread from the baker, Joost Teunnissen. If you finish all that, then I'll give you a little apple cake."

John Tinker licked his lips. He told me he'd been traveling for a couple of days and looked forward to some real cooking. This amiable man, once alone at his table, fell deep into thought. On the other hand, his unassuming sense of humor took me by surprise. I'd never seen a Puritan as relaxed or approachable as he was. His smile and good nature were charming. I would even say there was a little bit of daring in that mildly impish grin of his.

When I came back with his beer, I asked him why he needed Jan's services.

"I'm interested in expanding my trading networks and the best way to do that is to make good connections in New Amsterdam. Your husband is highly recommended and I hope will be willing to help me," he added.

Jan and I were lucky. Jan had just been elected by the Council to become a broker of merchants. He served to broker trade between the English and the Dutch. The Council realized the English were eager to trade with us. Their trading networks were not as developed, so the Council wanted to make it as easy as possible for them to trade in New Amsterdam. Stuyvesant agreed. The politics between the colonies never hindered our trade with each other.

John Tinker had barely finished his food when Jan finally got back to the tavern. I nodded to where Tinker was sitting at a table close to the hearth.

"Hello, sir, and good afternoon! My name is Jan Peeck. I hear you've been looking for me and want to do some business here in Manhattan," Jan greeted Tinker.

Tinker stood up and shook Jan's hand. "A good day to you, sir. You're an Englishman then or Dutch? How do you come to be in New Amsterdam?"

"Aye, half Englishman. My mother was English and my father was Dutch. Lost them both when I was a young boy so I decided to try and make my fortune in the colonies. I'm a long-time trader but fell in love with this Walloon vixen a few years back. So now I do brokerage and other such business around here," Jan said as he flashed me a mischievous grin.

"A trader, eh?" said Tinker. "I've brought some New England pelts to use as barter. I've got a monopoly on the fur trade up in Lancaster, Massachusetts. I'm sure you'd know the best people to take them off my hands at the fairest price."

Jan nodded with a satisfied look on his face.

"I've a whole shipment of them waiting in rented space at a warehouse by the docks. Do you think you can broker a deal here with someone to take them in exchange for some commodities like sugar, cloth, candles, ammunition, liquor, tobacco, Caribbean salt, and other staples?" asked Tinker.

"I can connect you to people. It all depends on what you want. But first, have another beer. Tell us about your life in New England, and then we'll get down to business," Jan said.

I took his tankard back to the bar and filled it to the rim. I filled another one for Jan.

"Take the next one on the house," I said.

"Yes, a toast to our future endeavors together!" shouted Jan in celebration.

As the minutes passed, Jan and John Tinker got to know each other better and discussed the business at hand. Jan became his agent and translator.

"Are you making an even barter with the beaver pelts or will you be needing a little credit as well?" Jan asked.

"I hadn't thought about credit. For foreigners too?" Tinker asked, a bit surprised.

"Aye. Everything is set up here. I can get you credit, insurance, and whatever else. Should you have a problem, we've got our courts to settle the matter. But don't worry about that. The goal is trade, my man! You've come to the right place. Just tell me what you need. I'll talk to the right people, and before you know it, you'll be off to Boston, New Haven, or wherever you like with a shipload of merchandise to make you rich," he winked.

"I brought the pelts here on an English ship. It'll be grounded here a little while for repairs before it heads back to England. I'll need to requisition another one to bring any merchandise I find back to Boston," said Tinker.

"It won't be a problem to find one. The market is coming up in two days, this Saturday. We'll see what it has to offer. Also, Marie's brother-in-law Isaac has a warehouse near the dock, loaded with a recent shipment of fresh Chesapeake leaf tobacco. We have it now. Marie, hand me another pipe." Taking it from me, he stuffed a sample into the bowl.

"Here, try this," he said, lighting Tinker's fresh pipe. Smoke billowed overhead.

"Aye, a nice smoke indeed," smiled Tinker, satisfied.

Just then our friend, Caspar Varlet, entered the tavern.

"Halfway through the day, and I had to stop and see what Marie has cooked up for me, he said in Dutch. "My wife thinks I'm spoiled by coming here every day," he chuckled.

Then he turned to Jan and noticed Tinker. In the best English he could muster, he greeted the obvious stranger. He was always ready to sniff out another trade deal.

"Ah sir, you're not from these parts, are you? What does Jan do for you?" he asked.

"You devil, Caspar. Too curious for your own good," I said. "Meet John Tinker from Massachusetts. He comes to trade and Jan is going to help him."

"My wife is right, Caspar. You are an old devil because you came in at just the right moment to make a deal. John Tinker is looking for goods to bring back to New England," said Jan, laughing.

He turned to John.

"John Tinker, I introduce you to Caspar Varlet, known for his fine silk merchandise."

"Pleased to meet you, sir," responded John Tinker.

"Yah, I have silk but I have a lot more cloth too. New England can never get enough of it. Do you want to come to my textile warehouse? We will talk, and I will show you what I have. But first, I need to eat. I have to maintain my lovely full figure," he chucked again, making the comic gesture of grabbing around his large girth and swaying his hips. "I see you've tried the beer, but you need cider too. I treat all of you. Marie, how about three glasses with some citrus and spice?"

"As you wish, Caspar. But I wonder how much business you will do after a glass or two of my strong cider," I winked. The men raised their glasses again and yelled a few other toasts.

"To England!"

"To the Netherlands!"

"To our children!"

"To the future!"

"To Marie's cooking! May it always be better than my wife's so I have a good excuse to come into *The Salty Rose!*" snorted Caspar. Generous laughter followed.

And that is how they commenced their business dealings together.

"We'll have a little more fun here and then we'll go see Caspar's warehouse. We'll put the word out that you need a ship and then we'll go to the notary to sign a contract," clarified Jan, hoping Tinker would not be scared off by Caspar's licentious behavior.

"Of course! To new friends and new trade!" Tinker raised his glass to the others.

Jan gave a sigh of relief. This Puritan was easier to deal with than most.

Within a week, Jan had managed to help John Tinker find the trade goods he desired, brokered deals with other merchants, and hired a ship to take it all back to New England. We would see John Tinker every few months as he arranged for more goods to go to his colony. His demands changed over time but his character did not.

It was just the beginning of our heartfelt friendship with John Tinker. With each deal, each introduction, and each contract, we became closer friends. Our relationship with the gentleman was unexpected. As I would learn later on, there were many startling consequences that would happen as a result of our association with him.

CHAPTER SEVENTEEN:

Marie's Story
New Amsterdam, New Netherland
1656

"A round of my finest spirits for the Varlets!" I raised my glass.

I hated to see Caspar move to Hartford, rascal that he was. He was always one of my best customers and never had a problem with payment. I felt bad for the Varlets because of their recent losses and tended to be on their good sides since their widower son, Nicolas, was courting the sister of the Director General Stuyvesant. A good word from Caspar to the Director General now and again made life a little easier at the tavern.

Petrus Stuyvesant was a true fundamentalist, a religious zealot whose father was a minister. He really should have been a minister himself, but far away from New Amsterdam. If only fates hadn't changed. If the damn war between England and the Netherlands hadn't started, the handsome and free-thinking Adriaen van der Donck would have been in charge right now. It was such a pity that Van der Donck, a man of high ideals, was thwarted by some unfortunate international political events. Everyone would have been better off.

Ah well, such is life. I have my ways to deal with Stuyvesant, I thought to myself.

So, woefully, I had to mind the rules or carry on secretly since I had many little mouths to feed. Caspar had been an ally in my struggles against the ministers and Stuyvesant.

I enjoyed Caspar's good humor. I would miss him raving about my food and miss his jokes too.

"Cheers for Marie!" he cried. "You are the best, Marie. You are my favorite tapper in Manhattan. Raising his hand, he invoked the rest of the throng in the tavern to scream my name.

"Marie, Marie, Marie!" they shouted.

"No, Caspar. It is I who will miss you and your family. But you must go away from here. Hartford is as good a place as any. Sarina, your youngest, needs to be away from the Indian wars. She has been through so much. It is wise of you to take your family to another place. Perhaps in future days we will have peace with the Indians. They are angry and rightly so for past injustices. But your dear daughters had no part in it. And God rest the soul of your son-in-law," I said, laying a reassuring hand on his shoulder.

"Please, Marie. I cannot speak of it. We must go on. As you well know," he responded.

"Another toast. We make merry when we can," he winked.

"We must, we must! Life is to enjoy when possible!" I raised my glass jubilantly.

"That is life in New Amsterdam. Wild, treacherous at times, but we prosper too. I could stay here. In fact, I want to come back again, but I must go to Hartford. There are markets untouched since most of the Dutch have already left the city there. New Amsterdam craves New England beef. There is a good profit to be made. Plus, I might try my hand at distilling spirits too," Caspar said.

He paused and became more serious.

"But you know most of all, my daughters must have peace," he continued. "The Indian wars are died down again, but it seems that any incident, like the stupidity of a Dutchman killing a young Indian woman for taking a peach, could ignite the kindling of war. I need a respite from it, as do my daughters who were caught in the middle of a vicious attack. Marija lost her husband, and Judith is as wild as ever."

I nodded. Everyone was distraught and did not want further Indian wars. The intensity of the constant anxiety was a big reason that my tavern served as a popular pastime. What better thing to do than drink one's sorrows away or celebrate in the moment when that is all we ever really have. Better to do it in good company.

"You'd better keep an eye on your Judith," I said as an afterthought. Caspar's middle daughter was striking and independently fierce. I loved her and saw much of myself in her. As much as she too needed a pause from the Indian wars, I didn't imagine her adapting well to strict Puritan life.

"Ah Judith, she will certainly have to mind her tongue and pay heed to the rules in Hartford," he acknowledged. "But my littlest one, Sarina, is not well. She suffers immensely from head and eye pains. Those Indians that captured her thought to scalp her and then they changed their minds after they started. She will always suffer and will never marry. Mr. Winthrop of Connecticut comes to Hartford often I hear. He has a good reputation as a physician, Marie. He must see her and help her. No one in New Amsterdam can rival his fame," he finished.

Suddenly, I became excited.

"Of course, Caspar! Why did I not think of this! Jan and I have a friend in New England and you know him too! He is the chief assistant to the admired doctor! Do you remember the Englishman whom you sold the cloth to a few months ago? John Tinker! You must know he is there in New England in case you have any troubles. He makes frequent trips to Connecticut to see his sisters and Mr. Winthrop," I explained, eager to offer something helpful.

"He is a decent man. The Dutch are vulnerable with some English in New England ever since that traitor Underhill kicked the Dutch out of our own fort a few years ago. It is best to have an ally in their territory. Ah, but Caspar, you make friends everywhere," I said.

I gave him a little grin to appeal again to his jovial good nature.

"Ah, my dear Marie," he said with a smile, "we will loosen up those English. Then maybe they will relax and enjoy the finer things in life. But I will remember what you said just in case. You never know. We live in unusual times."

"Yes. It's true," I agreed.

"Marie, do you know why your friend John Tinker is so accepting of you? I heard something in passing that might interest you. John Tinker also has no problem selling spirits to the Indians. Word has it that he got in trouble with the Massachusetts authorities for doing such a thing. He is a Puritan, but not so stiff as the others," said Caspar.

I raised my eyebrows. "How do you know this, Caspar? Who told you such a thing?" I begged to know.

"Our former resident Englishman, Isaac Allerton, told me. He heard it at his home in New Haven. It's not far from where Tinker's sisters are from. It's not a secret, and he doesn't care," explained Caspar.

"So, the merchant and trader John Tinker has more in common with Jan and me than I realized. He did not tell me right away that he worked for Winthrop. He is more modest than deceitful, I think," I clarified.

Caspar smoothed his whiskers thoughtfully.

"Do not worry, Marie. I've always been frank with you. I am also quite familiar with the admonishment of authorities. They are after me because my son Guilliam left debts. They hold me responsible. For that reason, a change will be good too. I will beef up my finances in Hartford. Ha ha ha! You understand my joke?"

"Careful with all those bad jokes, Caspar. Who knows what the Puritans will think of them," I laughed.

"Yes, I know. John Tinker is a good contact to have. I thank you for remembering it for me, Marie. You have always given me such helpful advice. I will truly miss my friends at *The Salty Rose*," he said.

Caspar joined the others in the tavern for a few more rounds of merrymaking and songs. Jan had come back after meeting some men from Boston to broker new deals. And Domingo continued to teach Cornelis Jr. and Aernoudt what he knew of the tavern trade.

The crowd was starting to die down but men still played games. A lonely musician shifted his tunes to sweeter melodies from the bawdy ones he had played the previous hour. The old man, Hans Kessel, had lit his pipe tobacco but was slouched and fast asleep in his chair.

"I guess you'll have to carry him home once again," I told Domingo, grateful that Hans only lived two doors down the street.

"That old man wouldn't make it home most nights if I didn't carry him," Domingo said, shaking his head on his way out the door, Hans over his shoulder.

Eventually, Caspar also left as the night became deeper. The stars were bright and the drunks leaving the tavern could still navigate their way through the streets and cross the canal. Sailors stumbled making their way back to their ships docked on the quay. And Jan nuzzled at my ear as the last of our customers left for the night.

"You did it again, Marie. Always bringing people together, always looking out for them. To others, you seem tough, but I know your heart. It is sweet as molasses. Come, my wife, it is time to rest in each other's arms. Boys, it is time to go home," said Jan.

It took a long time, but Jan had finally settled into life with me in our little Dutch city. At last, he seemed content, and I was fully myself again. I thought about Caspar often and hoped he'd find what his family needed in Hartford. I wished for their healing and was sure that they'd get the help they needed from Mr. Winthrop.

CHAPTER EIGHTEEN

Tinker & Winthrop's Story
New London, Connecticut Colony
1658

"Sir, it must have been a shock to be elected to the highest office in the land without your prior knowledge or consent. You have made much progress. I am glad that you finally agreed to fill the post. Connecticut benefits immensely from your wisdom and sage guidance," stated Tinker to his mentor and employer in seriousness as his hair wafted slightly in the wind.

Over time, Connecticut colonists had learned the value of Winthrop's endeavors as an alchemist, doctor, and leader. He gradually came to be viewed as an important healer, government official, and diplomat. Their views evolved from seeing him initially as an outsider from Massachusetts to an integral part of Connecticut Colony. He provided skills that were both needed and practical in a colony transitioning from a land of Native cultures in the midst of wilderness to a place of new communities made in the Puritan image.

Tinker and Winthrop were in New London sitting outside overlooking the Thames River and enjoying the breezes of a mild day. Winthrop had agreed to be Governor of Connecticut and, after several months, was starting to feel torn about the stresses of managing his operations in New London. It was difficult to run his fledgling plantation while spending most of his time in Hartford as he attended to his new duties. He'd temporarily come to New Haven before being elected governor and was dismayed that much of his work in New London had been neglected.

"You've always been a steadfast support to me, John Tinker. And I appreciate our friendship as well. I've asked you to come to New London again in hopes that you will finally agree to help with managing this plantation. I need a trusted friend to help me," pleaded the exhausted leader. The increased lines on their faces and greying hair gave testament to the length of their friendship. It had been many years since they had first met at Winthrop's father's home, but their friendship had also aged like a fine wine that only gets better with time.

Winthrop finished and stared out toward the water, noting the increased numbers of watercraft anchored in front of an ever-expanding town.

"John, only you and a few others fully understand how hesitant I was to take the position of governor. I was content to experiment in my lab and manage this town. The calling of my medical practice has also kept me very busy," Winthrop said.

He paused, sizing up his friend, hopeful that he could convince him to move to New London and take over for him.

"I finally agreed to be governor out of duty to the greater good. I ask you out of this same sense of duty, with the solid foundation of the work we have done together and our strong friendship, to move to New London and help me to continue the many projects here," Winthrop said, examining his friend's reaction.

"The last time I lived here in Connecticut, tragedy took over. I must admit that I hesitate to come back for that reason alone," replied John Tinker tentatively.

He stood up, starting to feel uncomfortable with the prospect of moving back to Connecticut. It had been a decade since his cousin in Windsor was hanged in Hartford, but still the populace sought witches to kill.

Noting that Tinker appeared addled, Winthrop rose from the bench and joined him by placing a hand on Tinker's shoulder to comfort him.

"Come, John, I know of the heartbreak caused by your family's unnecessary calamity. Let us walk to the far meadow overlooking the Sound. It will help to bring you peace of mind and, for that matter, I hope it will do the same for me as well. You must know that part of the reason I agreed to be governor was to address the injustices wrought upon those persecuted for witchcraft crimes. I do it for you, John, and for your lost cousin and the six others who were victims of gossip and vindictiveness," he said.

"I'm grateful for that, sir. But the jackals continue their hunt for the blood of so-called witches. I have faith in you, but how can you as one man stop the lust of the populace to purge more witches out of their midst?" Tinker asked.

He looked down, ashamed that he could not come to terms with a tragedy that happened a decade before and that he did not have absolute confidence in Winthrop. But he could not shake the feeling that his personal tragedy wasn't over—that it would never be over in his lifetime.

They approached a bend at the side of the hill they climbed and passed a herd of cows carefree in their quest to munch more grasses.

"Do you remember the witchcraft case of Elizabeth Godwin of New Haven several years ago?" asked Winthrop.

"Nay. I've tried to shut out any such news," admitted Tinker.

"I have not spoken of this or other cases with you in an effort to avoid bringing up a past which I know causes you so much pain. However, you need to hear about this now. I was asked to consult in the case. The authorities had finally started to respect my role as physician and alchemist and thought I might be able to say judiciously if Goody Godwin be a witch or not," explained Winthrop.

"All right. Go on, sir. Tell me what you must," responded Tinker.

He vowed to listen to Winthrop's words and tried to remain open to what else he might have to say as they continued their stroll along the meadow path.

"Well, like your dear Alice, her neighbors tried to say that she had foreknowledge of the future. They blamed her for an unforgiving illness that devastated the town. She made the mistake of presenting herself as someone who knew about the ways of witches. Before long, her neighbors started having fits. In this case, however, the woman would act as if she was having conversations with unseen forces. The local doctor, Nicolas Augur, wrote me a letter imploring my advice," stated Winthrop.

"And what did you do? Were you able to stop the madness once and for all?" asked Tinker, now looking at Winthrop instead of the path ahead.

"I advised using Christian caution. Most of these cases can be explained by illness, hysterical or otherwise. They can also be the imaginations of people run amuck by their own fear and ignorance. Her original accusation was put to rest by my intervention on her behalf. But alas, old customs and fears resist correction and she was accused again only two years later. They held her responsible for bewitching livestock, disrupting butter churning, and a long list of other preternatural crimes influenced by the forces of evil," Winthrop explained, combing through his speckled grey hair.

"What happened then? What could you do to save her?" Tinker questioned, truly interested in hearing about a better outcome than the one fated to his cousin.

"The court's final decision was that she was not guilty, but that her actions were frowned upon. She was admonished to be on good behavior and keep her distance from others in the town. The important thing to note is this. The townspeople and magistrates in these cases have already been whipped into a frenzy. It is important to approach them using alchemical principles. A specific tactic to not directly confront their fears but rather to diminish them was necessary.

"To direct change, one must apply certain Hermetic principles of natural magic. In this situation, mental transmutation transformed a horrible situation to one of resolution. Using the Principle of Rhythm—that everything must rise and fall, that everything flows in and out as a pendulum swings—it was critical to change the extreme position of the accusers and magistrates who were ready to convict by disarming them. It is not enough to bring proof or logic to those of a rigid mind of fear. One must acknowledge them and listen to their concerns."

Winthrop paused and took a deep breath before speaking again.

"To save innocents from conviction, it is crucial to plant the seeds of doubt, at least enough doubt to disrupt any certainty about convicting. In the end, one must find ways to mollify the community. The community let down their defenses when it was acknowledged that the accused was guilty of certain bad behaviors and that she be chastised for those behaviors. It was important in acknowledging the accusers' concerns that the accused be directed to either leave the town or to be on her best comportment in the future," Winthrop said.

"A shift in the energy and therefore a shift in the outcome. Change the cause and then expect to see a change in the effect. You also applied the principle of cause and effect, did you not?" asked Tinker.

"Yes, indeed. It has been a good many years since we have talked about the Hermetic principles, but you remember them well," Winthrop praised him.

John Tinker smiled in satisfaction that he hadn't forgotten some of the most important lessons his mentor had taught him.

Winthrop was, as were most alchemists, distrusting of most witchcraft accusations. His scientific endeavors and observance of natural magic helped him dismiss credence to most cases. He still believed in witches but thought true witchcraft cases quite rare. He was horrified by the tests of witchcraft: dunking in water, looking for witches' marks or teats, and a whole array of other grisly methods commonly used to identify a supposed witch.

"In the next case of Nicolas Baily and his wife, the same ending came about. They were a vile couple and very disagreeable to their neighbors, but being a person of poor or lewd reputation does not make one a witch!" said Winthrop before adjusting his breeches and continuing.

"The community was satisfied that they were reprimanded for despicable actions. The magistrates required payment of a hefty bond to ensure good behavior. At their trial, they were warned that should they sink back into deplorable behavior, they would be ordered to leave the community. Again, an innocent man and woman did not hang but were dealt with according to their actual transgressions," explained Winthrop.

Tinker and Winthrop had finally reached the end of the meadow and followed the path a little further until the land opened before them. A majestic view of the Sound dappled in sunlight. Their wide-brimmed hats gave much-needed shade.

"Let us sit and rest again, John Tinker. Aside from taking in the lovely natural view, I must share another story with you that gives testament to shifting views," shared Winthrop. Both men eased to sit at the edge of the hillside, taking in the salty sea air.

"Aye. Go on," said Tinker, he was already starting to feel somewhat better after walking and looking at the dancing waves of water along a beautiful undisturbed shore below.

"Did you hear of the recent witch accusation and trial of Goody Garlick of East Hampton? 'Twas the one in which she was accused of bewitching the daughter of Lionel Gardner to death after a childbirth fever?"

Tinker shook his head wearily.

Winthrop continued.

"'Twas just a couple of months ago. Of course, in her case, as in the others, the evidence was flimsy. It consisted of the usual nonsense: stories of her harming someone's cow, causing children to die by making their mother's milk dry up and other tales that described her as a demon of death. The town authorities sent her to Hartford for a trial, ignoring the pleas and defamation suit filed by her husband.

I advised not to convict. For the first time since these trials started, the accused received an acquittal from the jury. Some of the magistrates who had ruled previously to convict in other witch trials were angry with me for giving such counsel but there was nothing they could do. Some of those same men had begged me to become governor, so they cringingly acquiesced to my direction. One of them was Matthew Allyn," he said.

Tinker froze. He despised the man.

"Mr. Winthrop, I advise you to trust nothing in the character of Matthew Allyn. It was with feigned sorrow that he spread rumors about Alice through the town of Windsor to turn the townspeople against her. In later years, my sister Rhody, the last one of my family members to leave Windsor, explained to me that he was also behind the hanging of Lydia Gilbert, the last woman to be hanged from Windsor for witchcraft crimes," Tinker cautioned, his voiced strained.

"Do not worry, John Tinker. I am well aware of the true character of Mr. Allyn. He would privately love to see the brutal death of each and every enemy that challenges him. Innocence is of no concern to such a man, but the fact that he felt he had to shift his view to maintain his status is a good thing. But we must always be on guard for dark natures to take hold with hysteria," Winthrop said.

Winthrop looked up, assessing the reaction of his friend before continuing.

"To this end, I have tried to establish a new pattern that I hope will hold. The first seven persons brought to trial for witchcraft crimes in this colony and New Haven were convicted swiftly. Since I was asked to consult in these cases, no one has died, but we must remain skeptical and steadfast in dismissing the validity of these continuing accusations. You may have a part to play in this if you agree to come back to Connecticut to help me with my endeavors. You must be well informed. I will hide nothing from you should you partner with me and handle my New London affairs," Winthrop said.

John Tinker nodded, still quite wary of the name Matthew Allyn.

John Winthrop realized the conversation needed to take a dramatic turn, so he quickly changed the subject.

"Speaking of Rhody, how are your sister and the rest of your family?" he asked.

Tinker paused and visibly relaxed before answering.

"Rhody moved to Norwalk with her new husband, her former neighbor Walter Hoyt, to join my sister Mary. They have another child together, and Alissa, the daughter of my murdered cousin, Alice, lived with Rhody in Windsor. Alissa ran away from the elder in whose care she was placed after the hanging of her mother. At the time Rhody married and moved away, Alissa also married. She fell in love with a man named Simon Beamon, a messenger to Pinchon, and has started a family with him. I thank the Lord that Alice's child has found some peace in this way," he said, relieved to be able to report a better outcome for Alissa in comparison to the one of her mother.

I was glad she could live with Rhody when she did. Alissa had no reason or desire to live with John Young in Stratford," finished Tinker firmly.

"Aye. I remember treating John Young on more than one occasion. Such strange bouts of illness he has presented," noted Winthrop. "Your brother-in-law, Thomas Thornton, detailed its peculiarity several years ago in a description he sent to me before he left the colony for Ireland," said Winthrop.

Tinker responded, "The one family member that we hear almost nothing from is my little sister, Anne. I fear Thomas Thornton, her husband, is becoming more radicalized than ever. I've been told he's taken up with Cromwell to convert the Irish to Puritan ways and is now a minister there. My sister in Scituate receives a rare letter here and there, but sadly, the rest of us have been cut out of their lives. According to my sister Sarah, the Thorntons have lived in several villages in the west of Ireland doing missionary work, proselytizing to papists, and developing strong ties to the Mathers."

"Interesting," said Winthrop. "And what about the rest of your family?"

"As you already know, my mother died many years ago and William Hulburd, the brother-in-law of my dead sister Ellen, is now in Northampton.

"It saddens me how these witchcraft cases rip families and communities apart. For this reason, a resolution must also attempt to create unity again," stated Winthrop.

"Aye, 'tis true. I admire the work you have done to this end, sir. You've protected the innocent and made the best attempts possible to restore unity as well. I've made my decision. I will transfer my family to New London. I've always been honored to work for you. I am happy to be at your service where you need it the most. I'm ready to come back to Connecticut. I will speak with my wife," said Tinker.

Tinker gestured to the shoreline.

"And not far from here, in a day's journey, I can see my sisters and their families in Norwalk more frequently again. It's time that my family strived to be as close as we once were. At least some of us can be," he smiled.

Winthrop beamed, stood up again, and shook Tinker's hand.

"Thank you, John Tinker. Such a fortunate turn of fates for me and I hope all of us! Come, let us walk back and celebrate with a toast. Tomorrow, I must head back to Hartford. Tell me that you will come with me and we will discuss more of your future responsibilities here in New London. We need a distillery, and I know that is something that you've been thinking of doing for a long time in addition to your trade as a merchant. Would that interest you?" Winthrop asked.

"Aye, I will. The fur trade is slowing down. Since your mineral mines are now in place and working well, it is a good time to move and help you. I'm doing well trading with merchants in New Amsterdam and I could help facilitate more commerce with the Dutch. And of course, I'd be interested in running my own distillery. It would fill a need and I've got contacts for the best molasses in the colonies," confirmed Tinker, becoming excited to begin a new venture.

"I almost forgot. You mentioned new trading partners in New Amsterdam. I recently treated a young woman nearly scalped to death by Indians, the daughter of Caspar Varlet. He says he knows you and sends his regards. Interesting family. His one daughter, Sarina, who was grossly attacked, is withdrawn. But they have another daughter, Judith, who is the most outspoken young woman I've ever met. I pray she will be able to get along with the godly brethren in Hartford. An outspoken young Dutch woman could easily be targeted for being different. Again, we must always be on our guard for disharmony that threatens to disrupt our larger mission," reflected Winthrop.

CHAPTER NINETEEN:

Tinker & Winthrop's Story
New London, Connecticut Colony
April 1661

"The rain does not stop. 'Tis the perfect weather for our alchemical experiments so long as we do not delve into anything that could be affected negatively by excesses of wet and damp elements. The rain has a way of lulling the mind into a still focus to quiet worries of chores unfinished," spoke Winthrop.

"Aye. Always a thought on this vast plantation. 'Tis a pleasure to have the blessed time for meditation and transmutations in the laboratory." Tinker acknowledged. "I know it is sudden, yet it is of the utmost priority that you travel to England."

"John, before we go into the lab, I must clear any misgivings or fears about this trip. There is much I need to discuss with you first. Let us go into the hall," said Winthrop.

As a seasoned alchemist, he knew his state of mind could affect his procedures. The lab was his sacred space to be at one with the Divine and transmute everything, including his spirit, into the purest form it could be. He needed to empty the vessel of his fears and concerns before entering the lab, his gateway to a higher cosmos. He knew his friend and assistant John Tinker would be useful in addressing his concerns.

In the hall, they grabbed two mugs of cider and sat in opposite chairs near windows overlooking the views of the Thames. The water was choppy and the wind was gusting. Winthrop smiled at his friend, Tinker.

"Thankfully, you are here now and will also be here when I journey to England. I will always be grateful for your decision to return to

Connecticut. Aye, the time has come to obtain a charter from the King for our colony. We are on shaky ground. My father-in-law signed the death warrant for the King's father, but we will speak of this to no one. I must and will find a way into the King's good graces. I know His Majesty distrusts those in our colony because rebels have been harbored by Cromwell's greatest enthusiasts in our midst."

"None of our families is free from suspicion of being detrimental to the King's best interests," agreed Tinker. "Word is that my brother-in-law, Thomas Thornton, the renegade preacher working for Cromwell in Ireland, had to flee with my sister Anne and their children. I understand they've come back to Massachusetts for refuge. It will take a long time before the fires of suspicion die down," acknowledged Tinker.

"Aye, exactly the case! I must go soon. I worry that if I do not, there will be trouble and the King will destroy with one misguided decree all the plans that we have worked so hard to fulfill. I fear future royal policies that are not in line with our cause. All could be lost or changed forever. I must beseech the King to grant the charter for Connecticut. I must meet with him and persuade him of all the good we have achieved here. I must convince His Majesty of the glory that our labors bestow upon the Crown and all of England. It is crucial for our divinely inspired plans at the fortieth parallel."

"The charter may be the final step and the key needed to ensure we have a rightful claim to New Amsterdam. It is the key to finding the Northwest Passage and the route connecting East and West Indies—the key to finding the Philosopher's Stone and unification of the world into tremendous light before End Times," said Tinker.

"I have sent word to New Amsterdam that we are coming and alerted my contacts there," said Tinker. They will arrange for you to depart for Holland on a Dutch ship so you can make contact with your cousin, George Downing, the ambassador at The Hague. There you can brief him on the state of affairs in New Amsterdam before fully putting yourself at the mercy of King Charles II," Tinker said.

Winthrop sipped his cider thoughtfully before looking up at Tinker.

"'Tis all coming into place. I've also written to the Director General informing him of our visit, 'a friendly diplomatic visit' I told him. He admired my father and will be happy to take up with me where he left off with him before his death. Stuyvesant will be easy to deal with. Again, the most pressing matter is convincing the King of our colony's support and deep regret of any misdeeds from the past. I must put all of his concerns to rest," Winthrop explained.

"Aye, sir. 'Tis the only way. I have no doubt you will convince him of our righteous endeavors," encouraged Tinker. "But that is not the whole of what concerns you," he continued, sensing that there was so much more to the conversation.

"You know me well, John Tinker. Am I that transparent?" asked Winthrop.

Tinker nodded respectfully at the man he admired, ready to listen and do what he could to help.

"While I am away in England, you must tread carefully with our deputy governor, Major Mason. It would behoove us all to be extremely watchful of him."

Major John Mason, the deputy governor of the colony, and John Winthrop's sworn enemy was about to take the reins for the colony in his absence. Winthrop feared what Mason, the careless bull, would do while he was away in England. Winthrop had ruled the colony with a more moderate hand, but with Mason, one could be assured of a stricter, more authoritarian way of thinking.

"Mark my word, whatever I have done, Major Mason will seek to undo. He has been hostile to my actions for those who sought protections against witchery accusations. He will use the opportunity to pursue a rigid path, one which he deludes himself as righteous," Winthrop stated.

Ah, there it is, thought Tinker to himself. Mason is self-righteous against all and accuses those of witchery who may be his enemies.

Witchcraft prosecutions had changed dramatically in Connecticut after Winthrop became its highest leader. His presence alone gave other magistrates pause, and most convictions came to a halt. Even with a rare conviction, Winthrop refused to see the sentences carried out.

Tinker also worried that without Winthrop's restraining influence, his fanatical deputy governor would swing the pendulum to more extreme views. The colony could not afford that kind of disruption and division again, especially in light of other pursuits for the future and of the colony's vulnerability with the King's recent ascension back into power.

"Sir, the people value your medical skill and your political savvy in bringing this colony forward. It is Mason who must tread lightly with his will lest he disrupt your vision, a vision held in high regard by our colonists because of the great progress made," assured Tinker.

"Aye. And for that, he must also be watched closely in regard to the Dutch. He must not be aggressive towards them lest it create havoc and destroy our carefully thought-out plans for the future. A brash man such as Mason is too bull-headed and ignorant to understand the subtle implications of unnecessary hostility towards the Dutch and Petrus Stuyvesant," lamented Winthrop.

"I rely on you as never before. Your discreet diplomacy with the Dutch and with Mason and his allies is crucial to our cause. Especially so after I have departed for England. Do not be surprised or distraught if they try to blacken your name while I am gone. Stay strong and be true to our mission," warned Winthrop.

"Aye, sir. I am devoted to you and the work. I will be wary of any power plays by Mason or his supporters," said Tinker.

"You have been loyal in every way," acknowledged Winthrop.

Tinker understood all too well. Mason and his crowd had assured the conviction of his dear cousin for crimes of witchcraft, resulting in her hanging, the first such execution in the New England colonies.

Once stationed as the chief military officer at Fort Saybrook, Mason was happy to hear accusations of others for the same crime and had hoped to root out what he argued was evil in their midst. Colonists also deeply respected Mason, for he was their military hero of the Pequot War, a war that allowed for radical expansion into the southern reaches of Connecticut.

Winthrop stood and stared through the leaded glass window where heavy clouds still obscured the rising morning sun and torrents of rain created turbulence and waves on a normally peaceful river. He turned again to John Tinker.

"I fear he may have a powerful ally in the person of Matthew Allyn, the current leader of the United Colonies."

Tinker understood the dynamic all too well. He pulled his brown wavy hair away from his face and grimaced in response. Matthew Allyn, his sworn enemy, was an opportunist and fierce commercial competitor. He was entitled from his birth and resentful of anyone who might get in his way. The damage he had done to the Tinker family had been immeasurable. The thought of it lit a fire of indignation and outrage in his belly.

"I vow to you, sir, I will be one to thwart any miscarriages of justice at the hands of both of them! I will do my best to represent and protect both your interests and the best interests of this colony in your absence," said Tinker passionately.

Who knew what malice would thrive if the two of them, Mason and Allyn, had the opportunity to set into motion their hidden schemes for more power and wealth? Winthrop, and now Tinker, were just in their concerns.

Winthrop continued to look at the steady rain into the Thames River in New London and nodded. It was no surprise that his loyal friend and assistant was quick to understand. He turned to Tinker.

"You are a great comfort to me, my friend," he stated sincerely. "With that out of the way, let us go into the laboratory and work to build strength and purity of purpose."

They headed out into the damp landscape across the yard and down the path to a L-shaped clapboard building on the far edge of the property. In it, other alchemists were granted space and encouraged with their own projects in hopes of benefitting the colony and the town. Slaves carried out preparations for numerous experiments and kept the ever-expanding enterprise running well.

But Winthrop's special personal lab was still locked. Its secrets were well hidden within when Winthrop was not there with the exception of Tinker's occasional inspection. The familiar glyph of the *Monas Hieroglyphica*, the complete energies and ingredients of the universe, newly graced its thick wooden door. The faint aroma of concentrated plant essences and sulfur wafted through the air as the gentlemen opened the heavy door.

Winthrop's alchemical lab was equipped well. He had spared no expense in ordering whatever was needed to ensure that his magical workshop was complete. John Tinker made sure that it was ready when

Winthrop came back to New London to work at it.

To their left was a wall of wooden pegs that held glass blown flasks, cylinders, jars, and other specialized glassware unique to the tasks of an alchemist.

At the center of the room, the tower furnace stood ready for the work of transmutation. It stood about five feet tall. Winthrop, who had traveled to the labs of Europe's most well-known alchemists, emulated their workspaces to the best of his ability many miles away in the American wilderness.

The most important part of his laboratory was an area where he and Tinker would meditate and pray to enhance the processes at work. It was only through this prayer and positive mindfulness that the fruits of their labors would be fulfilled.

A vat of rotting materials was waiting to be transformed into medicines on this day. It had sat for weeks decomposing, and now the life force from it would be transformed into healing substances.

Sometimes Winthrop liked to work in solitary practice, but John Tinker was a soothing presence, and it was useful for him to be there to help make a batch of medications for his patients before he left for England.

Winthrop had no doubts that the diplomacy required would take months. He wanted to make sure his supplies were fully stocked on the shelves of his formulary before he departed the colony.

They worked late into the night. As they prepared medicinal preparations, so too did they ready their souls for what lay ahead: Winthrop for his journey to meet the King and convince him of granting a charter to Connecticut and Tinker for his battle of wits against the destructive forces of both John Mason and Matthew Allyn.

CHAPTER TWENTY:

Tinker & Winthrop's Story
New Amsterdam, New Netherland
July 1661

The trip to New Amsterdam was well underway. Leaving from New Haven Colony earlier that day, Tinker and Winthrop bid farewell to Governor Leete who stood on the pier, waving frantically. No doubt, he realized that Winthrop neglected to take his proposal for the New Haven charter to the King as he had promised. Winthrop thought it was better to feign forgetfulness than to directly deny Leete's request for a separate colony. New Haven might also be crucial to his future alchemical plans.

It was the beginning of July, a crystal clear day with gentle breezes coming in off the Sound. The journey was smooth until the approach to the East River. Tides coming from both the New Amsterdam harbor and the Sound churned the saltwater passage, gently spraying the sides of the boat.

Large tracts of undisturbed forests towered over their passing little shallop. Most of the land opened into scattered marshes interspersed with flower-infused meadows. The land beckoned them with the calls of hundreds of birds ready to feast on fishy delights among the reeds and thousands more in graceful flight overhead.

After several miles, the salty water became more turbulent. Large, jagged rocks scattered haphazardly in the tidal straight warned the shallop of the approach to Hellgadt.

Tidal currents, menacing boulders, tiny islands, emptying streams, and the end of a small river all mingled together to create treacherous conditions—a deadly stew that had led to the demise of many men.

Hellgadt was a graveyard for unschooled skippers and their unlucky passengers. It tested the navigational prowess of any captain that dared attempt to pass through it. For Winthrop, Tinker, and the others on board, the fates were kind that day and the tides were high, allowing for unhampered passage and the continuation of a peaceful voyage.

Local Siwanoy Indians paddled in their canoes, looking for the ideal inlet to fish. Others, already wading at the water's edge with their nets briefly looked up, giving a wave or a nod. However, most of them avoided the gaze of the Englishmen. After years of war, a heavy weariness and distrust of strangers filled the air.

They were deep into the Dutch territory of New Netherland. Eventually, forested land gave way to small farms. Crops, green and lush, ripening, sweetening, and growing ever taller for the future harvest graced their view. Small orchards speckled rolling hills adjacent to animals grazing off marsh grasses and lush pastures.

Corlear's Hook, the last landmark before New Amsterdam, jutted out and created a large bend in the East River. Dutch farms and homes came into view. Vessels large and small flowed toward the docks. The men were relieved to be near the port.

"Almost there," assured Tinker, already familiar with the landmarks that gave a preview to the trading port.

"Aye. Time to adjust to the future," laughed Winthrop, acknowledging that they were arriving at a place ten days ahead of where they departed from in New Haven earlier that day. "Papist, Gregorian time," he clarified.

The English, in their rebuke of anything papist, had kept their old Julian calendar in place both in the New and Old Worlds. They knew to adjust to a loss of ten days on their way to Europe or the colony of New Netherland and to expect a gain of ten days on their way back home to New England or to England.

They'd just rounded the hook and were fast approaching the town of New Amsterdam in the distance. Tinker pointed to the ferry to Breukelen and Peeck's Slip.

"Up the ferry road at Pearl Street is the house of Jan Peeck and Marie du Trieux, my trading partners," Tinker said.

Just a short distance beyond the ferry, joyous fiddle music wafted through the air from a wood-framed building with a painted sign whose only symbol was a rose. Alongside it, the gentle stream at Maiden Lane emptied into the East River.

"There," said John Tinker, gesturing to the shore, "*The Salty Rose*. That is their tavern. Jan has helped me to make many deals and to find buyers for spirits made at the distillery."

"Ah, so that is where it is. *Where waters meet at the crossing by the sign of the rose.*" Winthrop made a mental note.

"Marie's sea roses stand at the front and sides of the tavern. Anyone who dares hurt them must pay the price of her wrath," Tinker said as he smiled.

"It is interesting the details we learn about people and their natures from significant acts large and small," commented Winthrop.

Tinker nodded knowingly.

Once around another small bend in the river, the men on the shallop caught sight of the main port. Vessels of all shapes and sizes merged into the tepid ocean waters of summer. On land near the docks, wagons and carts loaded and unloaded cargo large and small. Behind the docks, a tall stone structure of the former City Tavern, now the Stadthuys or town hall, stood firm to greet them. The sun fading from its heights in the west began to color the skies in gold and oranges, highlighting silhouettes of two windmills and New Amsterdam's fort with its bulging ramparts.

To their great surprise, the men on the English shallop heard sudden rounds of cannon fire coming from the fort. The smoke and noise of cannonballs incited brief alarm as they thundered into the sea, a distance from any ships. Unnerved for a brief few seconds, Winthrop and Tinker soon realized it was a grandiose tribute, a salute to Winthrop, the visiting foreign dignitary.

Out of the Town Hall, Director General Petrus Stuyvesant rushed to receive Connecticut's leader as briskly as he could despite his peg leg. A fresh new plume graced his hat, and he wore his finest stiff lace collar, silk waistcoat, and full breeches. Stuyvesant was filled with glee to learn through Winthrop's letter that the Connecticut governor was coming for a visit. He relished the chance for full displays of pomp and circumstance, eager to boast of his accomplishments at civilizing the former riffraff and unruly populace he'd taken on as New Netherland's Director General.

Perhaps the son of the Massachusetts founder, a proper Protestant like Stuyvesant, was ready to take interest in what the Dutch leader had to say, he thought.

As Winthrop and Tinker's shallop maneuvered closer to the dock, Winthrop murmured, "It would be a great prize for England if this colony could be the center of its holdings in the New World. The Dutch have lost many opportunities to develop and promote it fully."

"Such a fine harbor indeed," confirmed Tinker.

"Precisely at the fortieth parallel," Winthrop said as he stared at Tinker who was fully aware of his meaning and Winthrop's stubborn wish to see his alchemical dreams fulfilled.

If only Stuyvesant knew that the son was different than his Puritan father. His exterior was more mild-mannered in comparison to that of his father, but in his inner workings he was just as dedicated to achieving his own lofty spiritual mission. Stuyvesant was blissfully unaware and thrilled to stoke his own vain ego. His high hopes for increased acknowledgment and status would doom him in the end.

"Welcome to our little jewel of a harbor, gentlemen," Stuyvesant called from the dock as they pulled in. Too overwhelmed at the thought to impress, the Director General could not wait until they had fully stepped ashore.

"Good Day! Director General! Such a fine little city to visit you in," called Winthrop.

Tinker hopped off the vessel and gave a hand to his mentor to climb onto the wooden dock. Two enslaved men of the company gathered the Englishmen's belongings in a cart. While his friend exchanged further greetings and engaged with the Director General in conversation, Tinker ordered the barrels of rum and other strong spirits from his distillery to go to the customs house where he would later pay a tariff and make arrangements for storage in a warehouse near the dock.

Stuyvesant led them to the Stadthuys where the Director General, his staff, and other government officials celebrated their arrival. They toasted to their two colonies and sustained friendships.

For thirteen days, Winthrop and Tinker, serving as his official assistant, stayed in New Amsterdam. The Director General insisted that the

Connecticut governor be his guest at the manor house on his bowery. Stuyvesant was not content until he'd shown Winthrop every detail of the city and his own estate. His bragging rights were on full display, expecting to win over the New Englander. Of course, Winthrop feigned his approval and offered frequent compliments.

"Director General, I've never tasted such a tender delicacy as this! What do you feed the pigs in New Amsterdam to make them so delectable?" asked Winthrop.

At the bowery, Winthrop feasted on the charbroiled tender meats of beasts from the forest and from the stable. He sipped the finest sweet wines and brandies Stuyvesant had in his cellar as well as delicacies from his cupboards. Stuyvesant brought Winthrop into his aviary and cooed at his vibrantly colored exotic birds from Curaçao, calling them also to come and greet his guest. He led the Puritan leader through his orchards teeming with fecund trees overladen with fruit: peaches, pears, and plums. They strolled through fields of grain and discussed their colonies, leader to leader.

Instead of becoming more wary and discerning the reasons behind Winthrop's interest in the Dutch colony, Stuyvesant succumbed to each word of praise with an unbridled need to show the Connecticut governor more. Stuyvesant was oblivious to the glancing looks between Tinker and Winthrop, not understanding that they both were secretly taking careful notes in their minds about the layout of the city and its defenses. At the end of the day, they'd convene to discuss everything and anything they'd seen that might be a pertinent detail for Winthrop's grand future plan.

Stuyvesant was an anxious tour guide, stubbornly needing to prove that New Amsterdam was superior to Hartford, thanks to his own management and leadership skills. The governor of Connecticut and the Director General of New Netherland walked together along the city's wall where Stuyvesant pointed out the latest upgrades and reinforcements. He did the same at the fort, even leading Winthrop through the guard towers and trumpeting the exact number of troops that protected the city. One evening, as they set off to dine within the Director General's brick home in the fort, Tinker quickly walked around it to solidify his memory and write down what Stuyvesant had said in the seclusion of a nearby public house.

In the taverns, Tinker assessed the level of loyalty of local townspeople for the Director General, a populace often disregarded by Stuyvesant as the world's rubbish. Tinker noted townspeople were still furious that their chosen leader Van der Donck was forced out of local government and, sadly, died on his farm during the Peach Tree War. The resentment never died. In fact, Tinker noticed that it only seemed to build with time.

With Stuyvesant wanting his private meeting with Winthrop, John Tinker was afforded some time to visit his friends and business associates. Midway through their prolonged visit, John Tinker snuck off to see Marie and Jan again.

Marie had just finished wiping down the outside tables as she supervised her boys rolling two more barrels from the storeroom into the tavern. Jan smoked a pipe at the side of their building, joking with customers playing a game of ball and pins.

"Well, who do we have here?" exclaimed Marie when she saw John Tinker. "I'd heard you were about and was wondering when you'd get around to coming to see us," she winked.

He laughed at her jest.

"Of course, you knew I was here, Marie. I imagine you know everything that happens in this city," he said.

"Indeed she does!" chuckled Jan in his boyish way, coming around the corner to greet his associate fondly. "You've come for more than visiting, I'm guessing. How's that distillery of yours and life in New London?"

"It suits me well, both the town and the distillery enterprise. And, aye, I've a need for more basic commodities. Do you have a mind to be an agent for me again?" he asked Jan.

"Yes. You know I'm always happy to. We'll get you all set up in a little schooner laden with sugar from the West Indies and other goods you can use and sell in New London. Did you bring any strong spirits for sale that you might give to your favorite agent, a man who is also proprietor of the finest tavern in New Amsterdam with the loveliest wife?"

Marie laughed.

"Have a seat, John Tinker. You'll discuss everything once you've got a good pipe of tobacco in hand and a full tankard of beer. Dare I ask if you're hungry? The Director General must be stuffing you to your fill each day!"

"How did you know? Do I look several stone heavier?" he joked.

"Oh no! You're as handsome as ever! I'll go get your brew and my special fish stew of the day." She walked away and disappeared into the tavern.

Jan sat with him. "I'm glad you showed up now. I'll be here until the winter but then I'm off to the woods again for a while. The town has been closing in on me. Marie agreed. I need to get back to the forest for a time. I'm also going to scout some land deals. There's lots of brokering to do. It's for the best since Stuyvesant keeps giving us a hard time about the tavern."

"From what I hear, Stuyvesant seems to enjoy giving everyone a hard time. Is it true that he's as despised as everyone says?" asked Tinker.

"We barely tolerate him. That's the truth of it. If that young Van der Donck had taken over, we'd be a lot better off. Stuyvesant rules with an iron fist. But it's too late for Van der Donck and for us. The man is nothing more than bones now, taken too early by violence he would have prevented had he been in charge. Aye, it'll be good to get away and disappear into the woods," said Jan.

Tinker stared at him. It was clear that Jan expressed the sentiments of most people in town.

"I'm telling you this so you know not to come looking for me this winter. Until then, I'm at your service. So have we got a deal?" Jan asked.

Tinker nodded and laughed, and Marie came back with his beer and pipe. They discussed deals and joked with each other until well after closing. Tinker came back when he and Jan could make arrangements for his return travel to Connecticut.

After thirteen days of Stuyvesant's hospitality and boasting, John Winthrop left with what he sought—information that Stuyvesant, in his lack of perception to Winthrop's true desires, freely gave away. Winthrop had become familiar with the town layout, its defenses, and many other noteworthy and pertinent details. Of one thing he was certain, the Dutch loved their trade as well as their rich food and drink. Stoic, many were not. Loyal to Stuyvesant, many were not either. As long as the taps kept running, as long as the warehouses bustled with goods dropped off and others were taken to be loaded into ships, the city would keep marching forward whether it was under Dutch or English rule.

Winthrop knew his newly acquired information would be useful to the King. It might even act to convince his majesty just how clever he was, how loyal he was, how deserving of obtaining a charter for Connecticut Colony he was. Perhaps, it was impressive enough to convince the King to include the Dutch lands at the fortieth parallel into his own charter.

Tinker escorted Winthrop to the Dutch ship he would take back to Europe. For himself, he arranged for a schooner to return to New London full of commodities such as sugar and indigo. Other valuable goods were stuffed into the hold.

"God speed, Mr. Winthrop. The months will be an eternity until we meet again. May you be favored and reap all that you seek," said Tinker.

"John Tinker, many thanks for your time here assisting and supporting me. I also thank you for all that you will do when I am gone. Be wary and wise. Until we meet again," said Winthrop, feeling both excited and melancholy.

The two embraced one final time, and Winthrop boarded his ship with the notes and maps they had both compiled secretly together during their stay in New Amsterdam.

As a formal sendoff and final tribute, Stuyvesant ordered fifty-five of his own solders to line up as Winthrop's ship departed. The Director General had no problem commanding them to use twenty-seven pounds of scarce gunpowder to make a final impression on Winthrop from their saluting muskets.

Winthrop was so awestruck that he made sure to give the information to his cousin George Downing, the English ambassador at The Hague, before returning to England for an audience with the King. Confident in his mission, Winthrop was as imperceptive as Stuyvesant to the troubles that lay ahead.

CHAPTER TWENTY-ONE:

Marie's Story
New Amsterdam, New Netherland
September 1662

It was late morning at *The Salty Rose* when I received the stunning news. The last tall ship to depart that day had just hoisted its sails and left New Amsterdam harbor. The only customers were a handful of old men busy gaming and gossiping at an outside table when Captain Nicolas Varlet walked sullenly into my tavern.

Out of puffy red eyes, he looked at me pitifully and in despair. I'd never seen him in such a distraught state.

"Nicolas. What's ailing you today?" I said, motioning to Pierre to grab a full tankard of beer from the tapped barrel. He quickly put it down in front of Nicolas.

"Maybe this will help," I said, concerned about his mental state.

"No, Marie. This is serious. Beer can do nothing for me."

I stared at him. "Speak to me please, Nicolas. Maybe I can help. Your father was always a friend to me," I tried to console him.

I hadn't heard from Caspar Varlet or his family for a while. Several years had passed since they moved to Hartford. Occasionally, Caspar or other family members returned to New Amsterdam to visit or to gather goods that they resold for profit in Hartford. The lengthy period of silence disturbed me, and I began to worry, sensing that something was wrong.

"What happened? Can you tell me?" I asked frantically.

"Marie, I have terrible news. My sister has been arrested for witchcraft in Hartford! Devastated at the false accusations raised against her, my father and mother died suddenly of unknown causes. Such a horrific time for my family. We are in a horrible predicament!" he cried, wiping the cold sweat from his forehead

"No! How horrible!" I screamed, trying to steady myself against the bar.

His words hit me like a lightning bolt. I was in shock, trying to digest the dark news. The tears started to well up and trickle down my cheeks.

He looked up at me again and sighed.

"I wish I could tell you more, Marie. Physically, my parents were fine, but the sight of their daughter being carted away in chains for witchcraft must have caused unimaginable pain and suffering. But was the shock enough to cause both of their sudden deaths?"

I gasped. "What malice lurks about in Hartford? The Puritans and their devils! Which one of your sisters was accused of such heresy?"

I asked the question, but instantly I saw the one who was shackled. Judith and I were sisters in a strange way. We were both feisty and saucy, too outspoken for the typical New Englander to bear. Puritan elite expected that "godly" women should be tame, meek, and obedient wives at their husband's heels. Judith would never fit that expectation.

"Judith was taken into custody with others in the neighborhood on the charge of merry-making with the Devil at Christmas time. The young accuser, Ann Cole, a mere girl of fourteen, is not right in her head. She pretends to be bewitched, mixing in some Dutch words here and there," he said and paused in numb contemplation.

What does the mad girl have against Judith? The free nature of Judith's spirit? Her confidence in rebutting the Puritan men's expectations of her? Oh, poor Judith! What can be done for her?" I asked, reeling from the dreadful news.

"I know not the reason why the young girl acts as she does. I suppose it could be any silly reason for a girl that age. I came to New Amsterdam as quickly as I could to implore Director General Stuyvesant to help us with diplomacy. But things are complicated. Negotiations have stalled. Father's properties and businesses might be confiscated. Perhaps you can help me, Marie," said Nicolas.

"Of course, Nicolas. What can I do to help?" I replied.

"Major John Mason is in charge in Connecticut while Governor Winthrop is away in England. Mason is a haughty and arrogant man who is resolute to punish and kill anyone seen as cavorting with the Devil. It's no surprise that he also hates anyone connected to the Dutch. I hold no hope for Judith's redemption under his charge. So far, he has been unwilling to negotiate fully for her release. Stuyvesant broods at his powerlessness to release her."

"Such a desperate situation! I am so sorry. There must be something to budge that deplorable Puritan, Mason!" I cried out.

"Marie, people say you have a contact in New England. Someone close to Governor Winthrop. Is it possible he could have any sway on Mason and his other unbending allies? I fear for Judith. Under Mason, they've already convicted and killed a woman named Mary Sanford. The Greensmiths and Elizabeth Seager, my family's neighbors, were arrested and thrown in jail too. If there is anything you can do to help, I beseech you to do it now. The fear in Hartford is palpable. No one knows who will be accused next. There is good reason to fear. So many townspeople have had to flee for their lives. The Puritans are swift and fatal in dealing with what they say is 'the Devil's work'," explained Nicolas.

"But of course, Nicolas! You speak of John Tinker. He is Winthrop's life-long assistant and friend. He will sympathize with your plight. He knows from his own experience that these people accused of witchery are really innocent. It is just a vicious ploy to get rid of certain people, people who are not liked for one reason or another," I said.

There was more I could have told about John Tinker, but I refrained. I was not at liberty to divulge what he had told me in confidence about his dear cousin's death.

"So you will tell this John Tinker of my family's tragedies?" he asked. The force of life within him seemed to reignite as I nodded my head in agreement and took hold of his hand.

"Yes. For certain, mon amie. We will try this strategy, but we must be very cautious that no one hears of the plan. I believe John Tinker will help you. Of most immediate importance is that he receives the urgent message right away," I stated.

"In addition, Judith must be released in a way that leads Stuyvesant to believe his own efforts are finally fruitful. He would be furious if he thought an Englishman had arranged everything despite his own efforts.

It would be too great an assault on his vanity," I said.

"I can go to Tinker directly, introduce myself and bring your message regarding the situation," Nicolas offered.

"Nicolas, it is best if no one sees you talking to him. It must appear like your efforts with Stuyvesant ultimately helped persuade Mason to let your sister go. No one from the outside should see that Tinker was involved. Do not worry. I will arrange everything. You visit Judith. Do not tell her specifically what is happening. Convey only that she should maintain her strength for a while longer and that many powerful people are working on her behalf. Do not worry. We will smooth the way to diplomacy through the unseen force of John Tinker," I assured him.

The tavern door swung open, followed by the shuffling boots of two old men who'd been drinking outside. In their hands were empty tankards begging to be refilled.

"Marie, my love, more beer for your favorite customers!" Hans Pietersen called out as his fellow scoundrel, Josef de Luc, gave a hearty chuckle, handing the empty tankards to me.

Nicolas smiled weakly at me just as the two old men who had been playing their game of pins on the green next to the tavern started to leave the building and return to the open air. They had nothing to worry about but games and drinking on that beautiful sunny day. It was a stark contrast to poor Judith sitting in her enclosed dark prison cell in Hartford, all alone.

"Yes. I'll bring all the beer you want out to your table at your game," I assured them as they shuffled back outside.

Once again, I turned to Nicolas.

"The matter is settled. We will talk soon," I said.

He nodded and strode out of the tavern, looking many times lighter than when he had come in.

The last time I had seen Tinker was on one of his commercial trips to New Amsterdam late that summer. Jan had still not returned from his voyage to the north to trade with his Indian friends. I raised my concerns with Tinker that Jan was gone longer than normal on the trading expedition, and I feared for my husband's safety. I'd never forget the kindness Tinker showed me through his reassurances. At his departure, he left me a generous sum of coins to help me buy bread for my children until Jan found his way home again.

That night, I drafted the fateful letter. In it, I pleaded for John Tinker to save Caspar's daughter even though it was too late to save the old man and his wife. I wondered if they really did die from shock or if it was because of something much more sinister. I said a little prayer for Judith before I sent the letter off with a trusted messenger.

It was a message that in the end I hoped would save Judith's life. John Tinker had to receive it quickly or Judith would surely die. Two deaths were already too much for the Varlet family. And their deaths were even more overwhelming for me, not knowing if my Jan, now gone several months without any communication, was also among them in the land of the dead.

CHAPTER TWENTY-TWO:

Tinker's Story
New London, Connecticut Colony
September 1662

On a misty evening as the sun was about to set in New London Harbor, John Tinker received the urgent message from New Netherland. He knew the identity of the sender immediately. Marie had left her mark, the mark of the rose. He had seen her only once since he escorted Winthrop to New Amsterdam on his way to Europe. She had sent the message with Henri La Chaîne, the cabinetmaker from New Netherland, with the excuse of immediate business with clients in New London.

The simple code revealed

Caspar Varlet and wife are dead. Their daughter Judith jailed in Hartford as a witch. Please help her. Mason says no to our leader's request to free her. Varlet home is closest one to Dutch fort. Be discreet. M

John grimaced as he pieced together the coded words of alarm. More witch-hunting under Mason. Hartford must be in a full state of panic. Winthrop had soothed the townspeople's superstitions and fears and put a stop to the madness before he left for England. But Mason and others of his ilk were blood-thirsty to kill more witches, and accusations and inquiries started to grip the populace again mere months after Winthrop boarded his ship for Amsterdam.

Tinker also felt guilty as he read the words, guilty that he had not tried to intervene to stop the hysteria sooner. As someone who was also victimized by the colony's previous witch trials, he wanted to stand up to the madness. Until now he had underestimated its force. Without his powerful ally and friend in Hartford acting as governor, the situation was not halted under Mason.

John thought of the events that started the most recent witch panic in Hartford. In March, just six months earlier, Betty Kelly, a young girl of eight, became suddenly ill with stomach pain. She had eaten hot broth after coaxing from her neighbor, Goody Ayers. Betty's father stated at court that he objected to his daughter eating something so hot, but young Betty ignored his warnings since she was bewitched by Ayers.

Later that evening, Betty cried out in severe terror that Ayers was tormenting her, begging her father to make the torture stop. She barely slept the entire night. And when Ayers came to check on Betty the next day, the sight of Ayers caused the child to be increasingly distraught. The story continued that the sick girl screamed again into the night, insisting that Goody Ayres was pricking her with needles and choking her. Tragically, she died early that morning.

Bray Rossiter, the doctor in Windsor who had also played a hand in the accusation against Alice, did an autopsy on the deceased girl's body. Rossiter, some believed, was not as temperate or skillful a physician as Winthrop. And, as someone involved in a previous accusation, it was unsurprising that he concluded witchcraft as the main reason for young Betty's demise. He claimed the bruises on her body and other physical manifestations were proof that the Devil and witchcraft had played their parts in the calamity.

Like a spark in a dry forest, that conclusion set Hartford ablaze in panic. Winthrop had forewarned that such a reversion to previous witch scares could happen after his departure for England.

Shortly after Betty's death, another level of alarm occurred. An impressionable young woman, Anne Cole, became plagued with hysterical convulsions on a day of fasting and humiliation. Everyone feared demonic possession. She began to speak in tongues, having fits, and accusing many in town of witchcraft crimes. In one of her fits, she laid blame at the feet of Goody Ayers for young Betty's death.

Soon Ayers and her husband were officially indicted for witchcraft and brought to prison. Knowing their lives were at stake, they escaped from jail and fled the colony, leaving their two sons and all their property behind. Tinker reflected that they were wise to do so, considering the outcome of the colony's first indictments that ultimately all led to hangings. Goody Ayers was heard to say, "This will be the end of my life." Who could blame her for such thoughts? The evidence was not in her favor.

Reverend Stone, the senior minister in Hartford, noted that Anne Cole spoke in Dutch at times and must be touched by demonic forces. To Tinker, this was unbelievable for the maid became well intermittently. He knew that the Varlets, the Dutch family in need of his help, lived near Anne Cole. Winthrop had treated Varlet family members. And John Tinker had at times traded with Caspar. Of course, a child exposed to the same language day in and day out would naturally become familiar with it.

Anne Cole's continued ranting and violent fits of suspicious origin led to the destruction of many families. Those who wished to revive hunting witches empowered accusers again. And ministers encouraged new evidence of guilt to address Satan's persistence to infiltrate their flock. Urged on by their ministers, Samuel Stone of Hartford, Samuel Hooker of Farmington, Joseph Haynes of Wethersfield and John Whiting of Hartford, townspeople came forward with horrific stories meant to provide evidence of bewitchments. Their good pastors not only led the witch hunts with zeal but gladly and dutifully took notes, gathered evidence, and interrogated witnesses so that every detail of every story would be used to catch all witches in Hartford. John Tinker heard about their bloodlust, their arrogance, and their pride in getting even the most virtuous to confess.

Thinking about their fervor sickened him. His mind whirled with memories of dear Alice. She was so beautiful in spirit, yet still maligned and brought to her death by an outrageous mob. The clergy did not defend Alice either. They could have pressed for calmer heads both then and presently but they chose the path of fear and ruin for so many.

Poor Alice, what would she say to him if she could speak from the curtain beyond death? Would she be waiting for him to save others in a way that he could not save her?

By May, those in power had compiled a long list of accused townspeople to watch for signs of miscarriages or suspicious behaviors possibly influenced by witchcraft. Among those on the list were Rebecca Greensmith, her husband Nathaniel Greensmith, Elizabeth Seager, and James Wakely.

Their crime was witchcraft based on merrymaking during Christmas time. Anne Cole sputtered in a fit that they drank strong spirits and danced on the green under a full moon. Yet, no one had visited the gallows, despite the ministers' calls to smoke out the Devil in all corners of Hartford. John Tinker had hoped that perhaps calmer heads would prevail at court. Of course, many like the Ayers, also facing an uncertain future, fled.

As for John Tinker, he faced extra scrutiny in the spring of 1662. In March, in the same moments that the first witch accusations reared their ugly faces, William Morton, the constable of New London, accused John Tinker of treason against His Majesty, Charles II of England. It was a slanderous insult, a power-play by Morton and one other, Richard Haughton, who disliked Tinker for his influence as the first town magistrate and as owner of the only distillery in town with sole rights to distribute liquor.

Most people realized the allegations were born out of jealousy and spite. Yet, it was important to address the issue vehemently or word of it might reach England and complicate Winthrop's mission with the King.

If false rumors reached the King's court saying that one of Winthrop's most important associates was a traitor, His Royal Highness, already mistrustful of Puritans for his father's death, would be even more weary, hesitant, and negative toward granting Winthrop the charter for Connecticut. Tinker went to Hartford to counter defamation with countersuits against Morton and Haughton. The issue was brought before the Particular Court during its May session that same spring.

His peers and fellow magistrates quickly dismissed the charge of treason levied against John Tinker. In a small victory, a writ of attachment was issued to Haughton and Morton to appear before the Court at its fall session under a five hundred pound bond. His adversaries would be forced to address their false accusations then. With the court's pronouncement of his own accusation settled, he headed for home.

He felt slightly reassured at his departure from Hartford. The accusations seemed to die down, and no hangings had occurred by the time he left the capital. He hoped the witch panic would calm down even further and peaceful angels would prevail. He was eager to return home to his five young children and his wife. He was in no mood to deal with further complications.

However, only days after leaving, word was sent that more so-called witches were brought to jail to stand trial. Mary Sanford, an old woman, and her farmer husband, Andrew, were swiftly brought to court. Anne Cole had had another one of her fits, quickly escalating the panic again. She'd put the town on edge as more accusations were laid at the feet of those unfortunate enough to be on her mind.

It was a sad reversal of fates the day poor Mary Sanford went to the gallows to hang. Her husband escaped a conviction but was required to abandon the town with haste and return to his family roots near the southern shore. While Tinker tended to his family's needs and fervently wished for normalcy in Winthrop's absence, Mary Sanford became the first calamity of Hartford's witch panic that June.

John Tinker wished that he could have anticipated just how badly things would teeter out of control. He also longed to have more of a calming hand. The full scope of the terrors to come was difficult to understand from his place in New London on the farthest edges of Connecticut's colony. Whisperings against neighbors, terrifying fears, and rejected logic took their toll on the populace.

The summer heat stewed the fear deep into the hearts of the townspeople of Hartford, and by early fall, many who were accused were officially indicted, including Rebecca and Nathaniel Greensmith, Elizabeth Seager and Judith Varlet.

John Tinker looked at the unrolled piece of parchment from Marie again. He inhaled deeply. Now was not the time to hesitate. Mason could destroy everything. Not just the lives of those accused of witchcraft and their families, but also Winthrop's designs on New Netherland.

Not to comply with Stuyvesant's demands and to negotiate for the release of Judith Varlet would stoke mistrust. Mason, in his arrogance and pig-headedness, failed to remember that the Varlets were kin of powerful leaders within the Dutch West India Company. Such hostilities might even sour the relationship completely, providing a reason to declare war on the English colonies and lead to greater defenses of the Dutch colony.

If that happened, the Northwest Passage would surely end up in the hands of the Dutch. But Stuyvesant did not understand the alchemical significance of finding the Northwest Passage as Winthrop did. It would be a devastating blow to Winthrop to lose the Passage all because of failed diplomacy over a witch accusation.

John sighed, thinking of his little ones. He'd have to make up his absence to them when he returned. Despite his forthcoming plans to go to Hartford to seek amends in the slander case against Morton, the latest turn of events required an earlier departure.

The disturbing news of an increase in witch accusations overtaking Hartford posed a threat to Winthrop's long-dreamed plan of finding the opening to the Northwest Passage and demanded that he leave at once. He had no choice but to stand up to Mason and his own long-time archrival Matthew Allyn. Allyn, the leader of the United Colonies, would certainly be pushing Mason and other Hartford leaders to intensify the witch hunt. Allyn had already inserted himself as moderator of the latest trials.

There was no question of the value of Marie's message.

"Act quickly or risk losing the golden prize. Risk losing life itself," he said aloud to emphasize the importance of what he needed to do.

The possibility to realize the alchemical goals set forth by Winthrop and others many years ago weighed heavily on his mind. The time was ripe. Winthrop had already been gone a year and would undoubtedly send news soon. He couldn't let him down.

Even more importantly, he couldn't disappoint Alice, the spirit of his dead cousin, either.

"Silas, secure a boat! We will be leaving for Hartford tomorrow morn."

"Yes, sir. But I thought we weren't leaving until next week," said Silas, Tinker's young law assistant.

"Plans have changed, Silas. Destiny awaits," pronounced John Tinker.

CHAPTER TWENTY-THREE:

Tinker's Story
Hartford, Connecticut Colony
September 1662

Reflective on his way upriver towards the capital, John Tinker dreaded facing ghosts of the past. The journey northward towards the colonial seat of Connecticut Colony always made him melancholy. Hartford held many sad memories for him—most of all the remembrance of a dear cousin lost at the gallows, accused of witchcraft crimes. Unshakable images of her lifeless body swinging from a rope would forever haunt him.

Now he had to go to the same city to calm the witch panic that had taken hold in Governor Winthrop's absence. Such horrendous lies should have been buried long ago—buried in the shallow graves of all the innocents that already hanged.

Feeling unsteady, he quickly sat down. He took out his handkerchief and wiped the sweat from his brow. He carefully and deliberately tried to slow his heartbeat again and fill his lungs with the breath of life. Grabbing his canteen, he gulped thirstily, finally splashing some of the fresh water on his face. Removing himself from the dark memories of his past was not easy. Tinker's young assistant, coming from the other side of the boat, noticed his master's uncharacteristic demeanor and quickly went to him.

"Sir, you're pale as a cadaver. What is the matter? Are you all right?" he said.

"I'm fine now, Silas. It was just the nagging ghosts of the past bearing down on me, supplicating for justice—if not their own, then someone else's. I must admit, I do not look forward to entangling myself in the accusations of witchcraft that have flared once again in the fine city of

Hartford." The responsibility to prevent the death of innocents weighed heavily on his shoulders.

"I should have expected as much with our esteemed Major Mason at the helm," he mumbled to himself, not clarifying this for his devoted young servant.

Witchcraft panic aside, Tinker also had other concerns on his mind. He would face the two men from New London who had accused him of treason against the King. It was nonsense, and the court had cleared him of the charges. Nonetheless, he was en route to Hartford to clear his own name with a slander suit against his accusers. It was a nuisance to have to leave his family of young children to take care of matters that should have never arisen.

He turned to Silas.

"Life is ever so complicated as of late, my dear boy, but do not be worried. Soon enough, the matters at hand will be addressed, and we'll be on our way back to the plantation," he fibbed, knowing full well that the ugly problems might take weeks to address.

"Silas, fetch me some more water. We'll be arriving in Hartford within the half-hour," said Tinker.

They had just passed the cove at Wethersfield and were making good time.

John Tinker and his servant arrived in Hartford late Tuesday afternoon. The captain clanged the bell as they approached the docks, alerting townspeople of a fresh cargo from the shoreline. He had chartered the boat from New London early that morning. The captain made good time, relying on high tide to push the shallop farther upriver to Hartford. Opportune mild winds of late September had also assisted in pushing the boat forward on its course.

A servant from Jeremy Adams's tavern was there to greet Tinker and his man and to carry their baggage up the hill towards the town square and to their lodgings. Once again, feelings of heaviness clouded John Tinker's spirit as they approached the inn.

He resolved to rent a horse from the stables of the tavern keeper to give him ease in getting to where he needed to go as well as freedom to escape from the memories that still dared to lurk in the recesses of his mind. It was needed, for the inn of Jeremy Adams was but a few steps from the town square, the place of not only markets but also of past specters.

The day's market was winding down. Some vendors eagerly called out to the newcomers in hopes of making their last sales of the day. The harvests in Hartford had done well that year as evidenced by the remaining produce being hawked in the square. Apples, persimmons, and kumquats were part of the bountiful offerings. Pumpkins and corn were piled into wooden carts.

A curious-looking thin woman approached Tinker from out of a hidden corner. A tattered blue cape hung over her shoulders, and she wore a worn purse tied around her waist. Reaching her clawed, struggling hands to him, and staring into the whites of his eyes, she grabbed his arm.

"She waits," the haggard woman whispered. She was not old, but life had taken an obvious toll on her.

Stunned, John stared back at her. Lost to the world for several moments, his wits to ask who she was and what she meant were paralyzed. Before he could compose himself and finally clear his head, she scurried off down a lane and disappeared near the river a few streets below.

"She waits." he murmured to himself, ashen once again and trapped in melancholy.

Silas looked puzzled and waited to continue toward the entrance to the inn as the porter, quite oblivious, continued towards the destination. A booming voice jolted John from his daze. Mr. Adams had spied him through the leaded glass windows of the inn and ran out to the street. He greeted John Tinker with a bow.

"Welcome back, Mister Tinker. 'Tis been a while since you have graced us with your presence. You're a stranger to Hartford now that your governor's gone," said the innkeeper.

John Tinker was an honored guest and was always welcome. He, like no other person, knew Governor Winthrop and was given the same courtesies as his highly regarded boss. He had stayed at the inn many times before when not staying with the Winthrops.

But now that the governor was gone to England, he thought it best to be in public lodgings. At the inn, he could observe the goings-on of the townspeople and feel the pulse of the latest happenings. He would quietly do his research before delving into the fray. Besides, court would be kept in the same building.

"Mister Tinker, it's so wonderful to see you again. I've reserved a room for you upstairs in the corner overlooking both the square and the Big River. I hope it will be comfortable for you. Your man may stay with the servants of the other travelers. Let me show you the way," said the innkeeper.

John was grateful to be granted his own private accommodation. It was a rare gesture of respect since most travelers shared rooms. It was all for the better so he could practice his alchemical rituals. Maybe they would help steer the fates to his favor and, most importantly, in the direction of those souls who had so desperately called for his help.

Yes, indeed, SHE WAITS—she of the living and she of the dead. SHE WAITS, Tinker thought.

"I appreciate the hospitality, Goodman Adams. I'm sure it will be the highlight of my trip," he said.

He meant it sincerely, dreading all else. The space would give him some security and grounding in what was expected to be a chaotic ordeal. And if he remembered correctly, the tavern keeper's wife's victuals would also be soothing and settle not only his tumultuous heart but also his grumbling stomach.

Once in his room, John stared out the window. The vendors on the square were putting away their wares and going home for the night. He pensively continued to look out the window towards the river for any trace of the peculiar woman. He looked out until the sounds of the last footsteps and carts were gone. Did the woman know who he was? Did she understand that her words would have meaning to him?

His reverie was only disturbed by a servant's knock on his door who followed with a tray laden with a bowl of hearty mutton stew, coarse bread with butter, and a thick stout. He graciously accepted the offering and closed the door, relieved to have some time alone. He needed to reorient himself to being in Hartford again. Strategizing and fortifying his mind were essential to the tasks ahead.

He hadn't realized how hungry he was until the bowl of stew was finished. The stout was satisfying and helped him to relax and settle into his surroundings again.

And now what will transpire? He thought to himself. Leave the mystery of the strange woman for another time.

He must understand the complexities of the earthly situation set before him. He couldn't stop thinking about Marie du Trieux's desperate message to help. It was convincing. He knew what he was about to do was important to the fate of the colony as a whole. But it would not be easy to face his old foes, the archrivals of both him and Governor Winthrop—foes who were the cause for a gentle ghost to whisper in his ear, imploring him to seek justice.

"I must position myself into strength both spiritually and politically. Now, to the task at hand," he whispered.

He sat in the chair next to the bed and lit a candle on the desk. He stared into the candle and after each breath he repeated his mantra.

"As above, so below. As above, so below," he said, drinking in the strength of the universe with each breath.

"As above, so below."

With each repetition, he could feel himself transmuting into a channel of strength and confidence. The ancient Hermetic wisdom of the ages would feed him and show him what to do.

"As above, so below." The ghost had become more tranquil. "As above, so below."

As practiced so many times with his mentor, "As above, so below."

A trance had taken hold. He knew not how much physical time had passed when he felt strong enough to stop. It did not matter. John Tinker surveyed his guestroom one final time for the night. It looked different. He nodded, satisfied, blew the candle out, and quickly fell into a deep slumber on his featherbed.

CHAPTER TWENTY-FOUR:

Tinker's Story
Hartford, Connecticut Colony
September 1662

John Tinker awoke refreshed and replenished, ready to address the serious task at hand. It would be better to know the background of what had transpired in the Varlet household before confronting Mason and his cronies.

He turned to his young law assistant.

"Silas, please go to the magistrates this morning and gather information about my slander case against Morton. I will put out the flames of that fire once and for all. For now, I must go and investigate another matter of grave importance. Please do not mention it to anyone. That is all I can discuss," Tinker said.

Silas bowed and headed off to contact the magistrates of the court.

On that early September morning, Tinker made his way along the banks of the Great River. Mist arose from it and also cloaked the deteriorating old Dutch fort. It was the place where Captain Underhill brashly placed an eviction notice on the large wooden entrance door a decade before. Some of the fort's previously barricaded walls had collapsed into nothing more than piles of stone and dirt. The massive door was gone, probably used as firewood. All that was left of the Dutch in these parts were the ruins of their trading post, struggling fruit orchards, and a devastated Dutch family.

Finally reaching the Varlet's house, as described by Marie in her message, Tinker discreetly knocked on the door, carefully observing the road for any passersby. He pulled up his collar around his neck and pulled his hat lower to avoid being identified.

A frightened woman in her thirties opened the door with surprise.

"May I help you?" she asked.

"Good day, Miss Varlet. I come from New London, an emissary of Governor Winthrop. I was sent by a friend of your father's in New Amsterdam to help free your sister Judith. Think of me as an ally, but you must let me in quickly to explain."

Marija lost no time in allowing Mr. Tinker in.

"It's Mrs. Schrick," she said. "I am the widow of Paulus Schrick."

No one had come to her family's door for many days. Word had been sent to New Amsterdam to both her brother and Governor Stuyvesant about her sister Judith's predicament.

"Who are you and how can you help us, sir? I was surprised to hear knocking at our door since no one in Hartford will talk to us. They are convinced that my sister Judith is a witch. Major Mason, Reverend Stone, and the other magistrates and ministers vow to have her hanged. I fear there will be no justice." Her voice was low and filled with hopelessness.

"I understand. My name is John Tinker. I know their tenacity and fierceness in hunting witches, especially when someone may be a political foe. My cousin, Alice Young of Windsor, was the first of their victims many years ago. Since Governor Winthrop first came to be in charge, he has cast doubt on the lot of these accusations and saved the souls of those otherwise damned to death."

Marija nodded. "My brother Nicolas told us that current diplomacy looks doubtful to save my sister. Of late, both our parents died unexpectedly under suspicious circumstances—only one week ago! The rest of us are lost and in despair. 'Tis like an angel has come to the door, Mr. Tinker. We are grateful for anything you can do to free my sister. We will make haste to leave Hartford once this nightmare is over—if that is even possible," said Marija, looking sorrowfully at Tinker.

By this time, the rest of the remaining family members gathered in the hall to hear what the welcomed stranger had to say. Tinker noticed packing crates being filled with anything that was unnecessary for basic daily living. He remembered Sarina, the sickly Varlet daughter whom Governor Winthrop had treated for pain and disturbed vision several years before. She still suffered much, having been partially scalped and nearly killed by Indians after a skirmish many years ago in New Amsterdam. She was disfigured and was clearly in pain. He felt pity on them for having to deal with such losses and the current threat against their sister Judith.

Mr. Tinker sat near the hearth and was given a full mug of beer.

"Please, ladies, I need to know exactly what happened and why you are suspicious of your parents' deaths. What led you to come to this conclusion?" questioned Mr. Tinker.

"My parents were both hearty souls. Although I must admit they were sickened by the arrest and detainment of our sister Judith. They were denied seeing her for many days. On the day that we thought the town magistrates had finally agreed they could visit her, they mysteriously died. They had not been sick the eve before nor complained of any particular malady. Truly, Mr. Tinker, we are at a loss for what happened. It was with great sorrow that I had to inform my sister that her biggest advocates were suddenly dead," Marija sobbed as tears began to flow down her cheeks.

Tinker pulled out his handkerchief and handed it to her.

"Was there anything out of the ordinary that happened the day or evening before their deaths or that very morning?" Tinker questioned.

"Ah, nothing. Maybe they were so distressed about Judith it brought them to their deaths," replied Marija, as she wiped the tears from her face.

"Was there anyone in town that wanted to see your father suffer or fail? Were there any grudges placed against him?" Tinker continued.

"We are the only remaining Dutch family here in Hartford now. Some townspeople have been wary of us because of it, but there were always others who got along well with us. Maybe they were just agreeable to our faces and kept their resentments under the surface. Before Governor Winthrop left, he was protective of us. Perhaps it was because he treated my sister for her sufferings wrought by hostile Natives. I don't quite know why," Marija said.

"I remember her case and him talking about your family. He was fond of them," confirmed John Tinker. "I also met your father in the tavern of Marie du Trieux and had some business with him," he acknowledged.

Marija looked at him with even more trust.

"This is good to hear, Mr. Tinker. We have tried to stay hidden from controversy, but my father could not always behave himself. He's always had a colorful personality, and it hasn't helped that the authorities had been scrutinizing him of late for his distillery business. My sister is outspoken as well. No one will ever make her cower in subservience or fear. What is for certain is that we must go back to New Amsterdam. I pray it will be with our sister. Yet, so far, there is no agreement to release her from the authorities here in Hartford. The deputy governor, Major Mason, resisted my brother's requests to free her. Mr. Tinker, I assure you, Judith is no witch!" Marija said, raising arms defiantly.

"So your brother, Nicolas, already spoke to Mason, and our deputy governor refused to release Judith from prison?" asked John.

"Yah, he denied the request. Nicolas begged for Judith's release as a Dutch citizen and as the brother-in-law of Director General Stuyvesant. Mason told him it was not his affair to tell the English what to do in an English colony! 'If witches be on the loose in Hartford,' he said, 'it's best to be prudent to bring them to trial and then to the gallows.' He said there was a wealth of evidence to show that Judith was merrymaking with the Devil and bewitching a young woman to speak in tongues," Marija said, crying again.

Marija paused to compose herself before continuing.

"None of it is true, Mr. Tinker. None of it! Please, Mr. Tinker, since you knew my father and say you're a friend of Governor Winthrop and can help us, I beg you to do it quickly. I worry my sister will die in that jail or worse—die with a noose around her neck," she wailed, inconsolable.

Sarina ran up to her and hugged her. Tinker understood their anguish all too well. He waited patiently until Marija nodded that she was ready to speak again.

"Where is your brother Nicolas now?" asked John Tinker. "Does he stay yet in Hartford?"

"No. He went back to New Amsterdam a couple of days ago. He hoped to obtain a letter from Director General Stuyvesant. Nicolas thought that a direct request to release Judith as a personal favor to a neighboring head of state would carry more importance. Nicolas' wife is Stuyvesant's sister. It is unheard of that Mason would not release Judith if he understood the circumstances," explained Marija.

"Do not fear. Mason will honor Stuyvesant's request. I will make sure of that! Mason is stubborn and arrogant, but he is not beyond persuasion if it's in his best interests. If you so desire, go to visit your sister at the jail. I will make sure you are allowed to do so. Tell Judith to stay strong and endure! She has many friends looking out for her outside the prison walls," he said.

John Tinker finished his beer and placed his brimmed hat on his head after rising to leave.

"Not a word to anyone that I was here," he whispered.

"If you can succeed in freeing Judith, we will be forever in your debt, Mr. Tinker," Marija spoke as Sarina, her sister, looked on, her disfigurement now apparent from light that came in from the window.

"I will do my best. I must!" exclaimed John Tinker.

He tipped his hat and headed out a side door. It was the last time he would meet with the Varlet family. His plan had begun to take shape.

He had one thing left to do to be certain that Judith would live to tell this
sordid tale to her grandchildren in the future, and that was to confront Major Mason.

Traveling back to the inn, he left the dirt road almost immediately, favoring the less-frequented trail near the fort and river. It was a safer way to return to the tavern without being detected too close to the Dutch home. The fog had lifted from the flowing waters, and a shallop with hoisted sail came into view. The sun was shining brightly.

"A sign of Divine Providence." he thought.

Little did he know that the sun helped to cast an ominous shadow over the mysterious man glaring at him from behind the dilapidated walls of the Dutch fort.

After walking several minutes along the worn path and crossing a wooden bridge over a smaller waterway, John Tinker finally reached the main landing for Hartford. From the river's banks, he took the road that led up a hill to the town green, the meetinghouse, and the inn, his temporary shelter.

On that day, the inn was bustling. The innkeeper, his wife, and daughters struggled to keep up with the orders of ale, hearty stews, venison pasties, and freshly made apple pies. From a corner table, Silas spied him coming in the door and waved him over.

"Good news, Mr. Tinker," he eagerly began.

"Yes, Silas? What is it then? What have you found out through the magistrates today? Will they act on the writ of attachment the Court made in May against William Morton and Richard Haughton in response to my suit of slander against them?" He paused and added an afterthought.

"Those two men need to learn that one can't just make an unwarranted accusation against a magistrate for treason against the King! First of all, it was nothing but lies, and second, they chose to do it while Governor Winthrop was in England trying to be in the good graces of the King for our charter. Madness! So, the court agrees?" Tinker asked.

"The matter is not settled yet, Mr. Tinker, but they are to arrange a date to hear the case. However, I think it will go well in your favor based on the preliminary response to Morton's false claims. I have been told that just last week, Mr. Morton, called before the Court, spoke once to say it was his intention to seek justice for the King. The moderator Matthew Allyn, in the governor's stead, taunted him saying that he should have justice to see a dozen like him hang," Silas elaborated.

Tinker stroked the whiskers on his chin.

"Hmm. 'Twas an interesting response. However, one can never distinguish between a dramatic show and actual sincerity with Mr. Allyn."

Silas looked bewildered.

"Silas, you must understand. So much of what Mr. Allyn does is cloaked in his own sinister intentions. It was a curious display. I will never be trusting of that man after everything that my family suffered in Windsor. Perhaps Allyn saw the imprudence of Morton's actions just as the governor is in the midst of securing our charter. It would not present a favorable view to have Governor Winthrop's own assistant accused of treason!" Tinker exclaimed.

"Aye, sir," said Silas, nodding.

"Allyn's true intentions are unknown. Just be observant, Silas. And above all, not too trusting."

All of a sudden, the doors of the tavern burst open with a man named Josiah Cranston recently arrived from England. Having departed from New London where he had taken a shallop to Hartford that morning, he looked invigorated to reach his destination and deliver the exciting news. Beside him stood Major Mason and other dignitaries. In his hands, he held a curious leather box. Inside was a copy of an important document.

"Hear ye, hear ye, Governor Winthrop hath succeeded in acquiring our charter!"

The tavern crowd erupted in glee and relief.

"Huzzah, Huzzah!" Loud cheers rang out in the tavern. People hugged and raised their glasses in toasts. Cranston waited until the applause and shouts died down before continuing.

"On precisely the 1st of May, His Royal Majesty, King Charles II of England, signed the proposed charter acknowledging the rightful existence of the Colony of Connecticut."

"To Governor Winthrop," the crowds cheered.

"To his Majesty, King Charles!"

They felt obligated to raise their glasses.

Winthrop had succeeded in convincing the King to accept Connecticut's proposed charter. The populace was elated.

He turned to Major Mason.

"As acting head of the government in Governor Winthrop's absence, I give ye the charter for the Colony of Connecticut, Major Mason."

More cheers ensued as Mason held the charter and raised it high above his head.

When the din of the crowd had finally died down, Cranston approached Tinker's table. "John Tinker, I presume?"

"Yes?" said Tinker.

Cranston pulled another document out of his satchel.

"'Tis a message from Governor Winthrop for you. He instructed me to see you in New London first and give it to you there, but alas they told me you'd already come to Hartford," he explained

"Thank you, Goodman Cranston. Your effort is much appreciated."

Cranston gave a slight bow and headed off to settle other affairs.

John Tinker eyed the letter with Winthrop's signature seal of the *Monas Hieroglyphica*. It had been several months since any communication, and he hoped that Winthrop had received all his news. What remarkable words did his mentor have to share? He wondered what had taken place behind the scenes at the King's castle to allow His Majesty finally to grant permission for the charter. What alchemy was at work?

"Silas, I bid you a good evening. I must retire to my room. You are free the remainder of this wondrous day. Remember everything I told you and above all keep it in confidence close to your chest. Enjoy the jubilant celebrations with the other revelers," Tinker said.

He handed Silas some extra coins to buy another tankard of beer and promptly left the remaining crowd.

The contents of the letter would not wait.

CHAPTER TWENTY-FIVE:

Tinker & Winthrop's Story
Hartford, Connecticut Colony
End of September to Early October 1662

John Tinker eagerly ascended to his chamber, quickly lit a candle, and carefully opened the letter meant for his eyes alone.

He pulled out Winthrop's invention from his bag. It was a template with empty spaces cut out. When placed over the letter written in Latin, the letters revealed would spell out the secret code of Winthrop's communication in yet another language, French.

Le roi a répondu à l'anneau d'or. Mais le roi n'est pas de caractère ferme. Il change d'avis facilement. Agit rapidement. Notre succès appartient à Dieu. Au quarantième.

The letter was dated in late April, but it was already the very end of September. What was the delay? Did the King and his men try to intercept the message as a test of Winthrop's intentions? In any case, the ingenious code had never been broken by anyone. The fact that it had reached John Tinker without further interference gave him hope that nothing was amiss.

He translated, softly uttering the words.

"The King responded to the golden ring." Winthrop and Tinker had consecrated an ancient ring given to Winthrop's grandfather by the King's father. He said he would only use the ring, forged of pure gold, as a gift and final gesture to coax the King to his favor. It had been necessary. Even the detailed information about New Amsterdam's inner workings and defenses was not enough.

"But the King is not one of firm character. He changes his mind easily." Both Tinker and Winthrop could hang for such words describing the King. For this, the encoded words were essential.

"Act quickly." John Tinker knew that he had to use his strong diplomatic skills to sooth any problems and make everything in the colony ready upon Winthrop's return.

By the last lines, he knew that their final goal had been promised by His Royal Majesty's charter. The force of God was at work.

"Our success belongs to God. To the Fortieth!" he whispered in awe.

God had chosen them to do his grand work of uniting the East and the West. To the fortieth parallel they would go. Winthrop had persuaded the King to include New Amsterdam, all of Long Island, and the rest of New Netherland in the charter for Connecticut! So many years of waiting and now the royal charter would allow for the discovery of the Passage, and with it the next step of pervasive light and union on the Earth, the sacred marriage.

This was most excellent news. It gave him the strength to do what he needed to do next—for the future of the colony—for the future fruitfulness of a divine plan—for the peace of his murdered cousin.

He slept that night with an inner quiet. The heavens felt close, and his heart was more at peace than it had been for a while.

John woke with the sunrise. Calmly he walked the trodden dirt roads of Hartford. He glanced occasionally down toward the riverbanks and the glistening water they framed. The last rooster calls gave way to the rising sun. It was crisp and clear except for the chimneys on each home lot belching fresh smoke from rekindled hearth fires. Servants fetched water and led animals out of their barns. He nodded as he passed a few others also beginning their day.

He passed the governor's mansion, now quiet, and smiled as he thought about his return visit there when Winthrop came home. What joy it would bring after everything that had transpired!

As the road turned, an apple orchard recently harvested and then a great home behind it came into view. He gave a determined and firm knock on the thick wooden door. It was unsettling to know in moments he would finally be face to face with Major Mason. John Tinker chided himself. He must keep his focus.

He had important things to resolve—the future of the colony and saving the life a woman who was key to ensuring that future.

A young enslaved African woman opened the door, revealing Major Mason sitting at a table eating his breakfast with none other than Tinker's old archenemy, Matthew Allyn. The two looked up, startled to see Tinker standing before them looking serious and confident as though he'd caught them at a secret meeting making plans for a final takeover of the governorship and power of the colony. Tinker had no idea what they were really up to, but he did not care as long as it did not interfere with the carefully laid plans of his mentor and true leader of the colony.

Mason waved off the slave girl, not wishing her to hear anything of their conversation. As John Tinker walked into the hall, Matthew Allyn smiled deceptively. His voice dripped with pleasantries. Allyn was the type of viper who wanted you to think him a harmless lamb. But too much water was under the bridge. Tinker would never trust him. He was sure that Allyn had been the instigator, the strongest voice to invoke fears of witchcraft in Windsor many years before.

"Why, Mister Tinker, what a pleasant surprise," stated Allyn.

Mason was too gruff, too obstinate to ever understand flattery or pleasantries. He, on the other hand, grunted before he abruptly spoke.

"What brings you here at such an early part of the day? Court will not convene for another three hours, Mr. Tinker," Mason said.

"Major Mason, it is only appropriate that I come to you now, for I doubt that you would prefer our conversation to be public," Tinker taunted him.

Mason looked at him menacingly, and Allyn looked pleased at the prospect of more drama into which he could insert himself.

"Go on, Mr. Tinker," stated Mason with hostility as he eyed his sword resting near the hearth.

"I am well aware that a woman named Judith Varlet is being held against her will for accusations of witchcraft and that her parents died in a sudden episode for no apparent reason. Much to my dismay, their deaths have gone unquestioned by local authorities. I understand from my sources that Stuyvesant tried to negotiate her release with you through her brother Nicolas, the Director General's brother-in-law. To date, you rebuff the requests of another head of state. Is this true, Major Mason?" questioned Tinker.

Mason seethed in anger and slammed a fist on the table before rising to confront John Tinker.

"How dare you come here and insult my handling of this precarious situation. Devils are on the loose in Hartford! And you stand there on the side of witchery again!" Mason shouted as he stomped across the room to be near his sword.

Tinker retorted, "I have never been on the side of witchery, the witchery of sending innocent people to hang! Now, that's the Devil's true work. Aye, allowing the Devil to speak through your tongues as you malign the innocent to consolidate your own power and privilege. Speak not to me of devils, Major Mason!" yelled Tinker.

John Tinker was actually grateful when Matthew Allyn inserted himself into the dispute as predicted. He knew he needed to stay calm and give nothing away. The precious few seconds would allow him to regain his composure despite being baited by Allyn as well.

"Why surely, Mr. Tinker, you would not be so scandalous as to accuse Major Mason of inappropriate actions and slander his name in such an unjust way. I warn you to stop immediately. Mason is righteous in ridding this town of demons, be it the Dutch woman or anyone else!"

John Tinker was well aware that Allyn's feigned disgust was nothing more than a ruse. He had used a poor woman, Lydia Gilbert in Windsor, to relieve his own son Thomas' guilt in the shooting death of Henry Stiles a few years before, masterfully manipulating the town folk into believing that she, who was not even at the site of the shooting, was responsible for it. Of course, he had been as sly as a fox, making suggestions behind closed doors to the foolish and the gullible until a wave of accusations broke out against the woman. Three years after the fatal discharge, the rumors led to her conviction for witchcraft crimes and a hanging at the gallows. He had trained his sons well, and now his oldest son was one of those weighing evidence of witchcraft crimes on the court.

Tinker stood firm, ignoring Allyn and refusing to be drawn into his net coated in poison. He addressed Mason directly.

"For what reason is it that you encourage discord among the populace when Governor Winthrop is away? What have you to gain from it? At least on the face of it, our citizens should appear united or the King is apt to think differently of our new charter," stated Tinker.

"It will affect nothing!" Mason hissed, while his face reddened with anger. "How dare you come to this place and accuse me of such when I am taking great care to ensure our colony stays on a godly path! As for Caspar Varlet and his wife, there have been no reports of foul play. I resent the implied accusations."

"Major Mason, let go of your pigheadedness and your blindness that prevents you from seeing the situation in its entirety," said Tinker.

Mason grabbed his sword and went to lunge toward Tinker but was stopped when Matthew Allyn pressed his palm against Mason's chest.

Mason did not fully stop, and Allyn adjusted his long bony fingers and pressed harder.

"Mason, let him speak. His words may be used against him for slanderous assault," Allyn calmed him.

"And as for you, Mr. Tinker, I would proceed with great caution."

"You have read the charter now. In it, the King claims New Netherland as part of our colony of Connecticut. Once word gets out, it will put our neighbor to the south on edge. They will cautiously assess their defenses. Stuyvesant will carefully calculate his best options. This will allow time for Winthrop's return and a slow and subtle yet sure path to the taking over of New Netherland," said Tinker, parsing his words slowly to emphasize their importance.

"What does this have to do with the wayward Dutch woman and her deceased parents? Your harassment has no bearing on my decision!" shouted Mason.

Allyn gave Mason a stern glance to silence his peer and nodded at Tinker to continue.

"Have you no sense of who this woman is? Who her family is? Her connections and her losses could be the downfall of all that Governor Winthrop has so carefully worked for?" Tinker emphasized.

Mason and Allyn looked dumbfounded as Tinker continued convincingly.

"I implore you to accommodate Stuyvesant's request to free Judith Varlet, the sister of his brother-in-law, for she is also the niece of one of the most powerful directors of the Dutch West India Company! The death of his niece may be the final incident that compels the company directors and the Dutch government to send defenses strong enough to curtail our new charter! I also suggest you fully investigate any reports of suspicious actions regarding her parents' deaths. The Dutch must be assured that we have taken proper care of this situation and have not shown prejudice against them. Do not disrupt our course, Major Mason. There is no time to waste!" demanded Tinker.

Mason and Allyn were speechless as they stared at Tinker.

A black raven landed on a branch outside near the closest window and let out a caw. Was it a sign that Tinker had convinced them? A warning to take heed of his message? Mason finally appeared to grasp the fact that his actions could undo the King's claims and hinder the solid grounding of the English further to the south. He had to relent, but he was furious.

"Very well then. Upon receiving an official request from Stuyvesant, I will release her. But you will claim no credit in this. You will stay invisible and only alert Nicolas Varlet that I have reconsidered his proposition," seethed Mason through clenched teeth.

John Tinker insisted, "I assure you, Major Mason, I only wish to stay in the shadows. I am alerting you to the hazards at hand. Make a big display of graciousness as a courtesy paid to one leader from another. It bothers me not. I only wish to keep our colony on its due course. Letting Stuyvesant think he has the upper hand will only serve our colony in the end by softening his vigilance against us."

Allyn approached him.

"Your reasoning was masterful, Mr. Tinker, but heed this warning. Do not interfere with other decisions concerning what I, as head of the United Colonies, and what Major Mason, your acting governor, deem as necessary for the protection of our citizens' souls," warned Allyn.

"Mr. Allyn, you have missed an important part of the discussion. No good will come of these further witchcraft accusations if justice is not served. Each case should have a proper review. I call on you to wait for Winthrop's expertise on the matter. We will discuss it another day. For now, let us greet our brethren from our southern border with hospitality and not venom when they arrive with a letter from Director General Stuyvesant. I will send word of your willingness to reconsider his request," Tinker said, pausing only briefly.

"And another thing, Major Mason. I think it wise to wait to ratify our charter until after the Dutch have completed their mission to free the Varlet woman. The populace will be buzzing with news of Connecticut's expanded territory. Better that the buzz happens after their departure so as not to feed hostilities, and to buy us some time," he added.

Allyn and Mason nodded in understanding, albeit begrudgingly.

"I bid you a good day, gentlemen!" Tinker gave a slight bow and departed.

He was eager to send the fateful note that Judith would be freed upon the receipt of an official letter from Stuyvesant. It was still early in the day, so he was hopeful that his message would arrive in New Amsterdam by the day's end.

He felt lighter with each step. A large burden had dissolved from his shoulders. Even so, the business would not be finished until he saw Judith released from jail into the arms of her brother.

He prayed that Winthrop would be able to return quickly. His only tactic for the others being accused of witchcraft crimes was to stall and delay.

John Tinker was so engrossed in thoughts of Winthrop's return and his success in changing Mason's mind that he failed to notice the cloaked figure that lurked behind him on his way back to the tavern. The sinister character lagged purposefully at a distance, casting the same distinctive shadow as he had behind the Dutch fort's crumbling walls.

CHAPTER TWENTY-SIX:

Tinker's Story
Hartford, Connecticut Colony
October 1662

Captain, Varlet, Judith's brother, was flanked by two Dutch governmental officials when he arrived at the court in Hartford to secure the release of his sister.

Tinker noted the horror on Captain Varlet's face as he watched an emaciated Judith being dragged into the court session by the constable. She was disheveled with tangled hair, sullen face, and dirty clothing. It disheartened Tinker that the young woman had been treated so poorly while in English captivity.

Captain Varlet presented the official letter imploring Judith's immediate release to Captain Mason as the court began. Director General Stuyvesant's letter from New Amsterdam was dated October 13th, 1662, in Gregorian time. Varlet and his associates carried it to Hartford the very next day. Crossing back ten days to Julian time, the day reverted to October 4th when it was presented in Hartford.

"Read Stuyvesant's letter to the Court for all to hear," commanded Mason to the secretary.

Honored and worthy sirs:

By this occasion of my brother-in-law being necessitated to make a second voyage to aid a distressed sister, Judith Varlet, imprisoned, as we are informed upon pretended accusation of witchcraft, we really believe, and out of her well-known education, life, conversation and profession of faith, we dare assure, that she is innocent of such horrible crimes, and, wherefore, I doubt not he will now, as formerly find your honor's favor, and aid for the innocent.

"It is signed by Director General of New Netherland, Petrus Stuyvesant."

Captain Varlet listened intently, assessing Mason's reaction. The message he received from Tinker in New Amsterdam earlier in the week was positive for Judith's release. Mason's barely veiled rage did not make the situation appear so hopeful.

Mason looked up and glared at John Tinker from his place on the court. He could not hide his hostility at being forced to go against his natural inclinations. Tinker stood straight and strong, staring back hard at Mason in warning.

Exasperated, Mason called the constable to bring the prisoner forward. The deputy governor addressed her.

"It is not my wish to free a woman known to many to have consorted with Satan. However, I have no choice but to release you to your brother as a courtesy to Director General Stuyvesant and the Council of New Netherland. The guilt will rest on their souls for not punishing such deeds, and the responsibility will lie with them should any future acts of evil occur and disrupt your Dutch community. But it will not be my affair. God must judge you, and men will deal with you in New Amsterdam. Connecticut wishes to assert no further quarrel with the Director General in this matter. Be gone with you, woman. May you never set foot in this colony again!" proclaimed Mason.

"Guard, release the prisoner from her chains."

As the constable unlocked Judith's chains, Mason looked directly at her brother.

"You have forty-eight hours to take your family and leave Hartford forever. Assign an agent to handle the sale of your family's properties. Now go. Disrupt this settlement no more!" Mason declared.

After Judith was freed, she struggled to run to her brother. She had been brought to such a weakened state by her time in jail that he had to carry her out of the room as she whimpered in both relief and trauma.

Tinker was satisfied and comforted that Mason did not go back on his word. In a strange way, he felt some peace with his own past and his dear Alice's death by helping to free the Varlet woman. His work was almost done in Hartford.

The next day, as the Varlets hurried to pack the final contents of their homestead and load up their commissioned shallop for New Amsterdam, the General Court ratified Connecticut's new charter. For the rest of the day, excited discussions ensued as to how to notify the English towns of Long Island. Governor Leete was furious at the news of New Haven Colony being absorbed into Connecticut, and ways to proceed with him in completing the union between the two colonies had to be considered carefully. They fretted and calculated ways to entice New Haven to embrace the monumental governmental changes.

Tinker's case against Morton and his associate, Haughton, for slander had not yet been resolved. The case was delayed a few days until more important considerations of the colony concerning its charter were resolved.

For John Tinker, it was a welcome respite and an opportunity to check on a dear relative in Agawam the following morning.

CHAPTER TWENTY-SEVEN:

Tinker's Story
Hartford, Connecticut Colony
October 1662

The young enslaved girl, Emma, found it a bit strange to make only a small sweet cake with strict orders to make no extra batter for any other cake. Her command of English was far from perfect. Perhaps she didn't understand. Her master's nephew seemed intent to watch her. Stranger still was the order given by him to leave the hearth at the end of preparing the batter. Before she could place it in the beehive oven, he called out.

"Emma, you're needed in the hall with the children." Yet, when she went there, her missus queried as to why she had left her cooking. Upon returning to the table next to the beehive oven, the young master was holding her prepared mixture and insisted on placing it in the oven himself. As she peered into it, the batter seemed a little different. She didn't know how, but something seemed amiss.

Unbeknownst to her, he had quickly stirred a hefty dose of belladonna and laudanum into the mixture.

"Emma, hurry. This is a special gift to a dear friend from England. It is cake from our home region. He departs soon. I must get it to him before his shallop is ready to depart. He will be so pleased to receive such a tasty treat from our native homeland."

It was strange, but what could she do? The ways of these people were foreign to her. Questioning, even in an effort to understand, only led to unwanted harshness and unbearable punishments later. It was best to ignore his peculiar behavior to survive.

Barely out of the oven, the master's nephew snatched the sweet miniature spice cake, wrapped it in a linen cloth, and started out toward the center of town. Before the master's nephew left, he spoke to her in a most menacing way.

"You shall speak of this to no one. It must be a complete surprise. Do you understand me?"

She nodded in desperation to halt the assault of his icy glare. Emma wanted nothing more to do with the bizarre incident. Much to her shock, he hummed gleefully as he put on his cloak and slammed the entryway door.

After a few minutes of walking down the lane, the strange man encountered another slave. Toby was a captured African bound to take care of another family's stable and animals. The mysterious man hissed at Toby to come forward. Pulling out a silver shilling, he put it in Toby's palm.

"For this, you will say nothing to anyone and deliver this present to John Tinker at the inn at daybreak," said the stranger.

"I swear I will kill you if you mess this up or say anything to anyone. Do as I say perfectly. John Tinker rises early. The room he stays in is the corner room on the left overlooking the square. From a distance, observe to make sure he opens the door to retrieve his gift, but do not speak to him directly. I, in turn, will be watching you and distracting the innkeeper or his servants if need be. Is this clear?"

Poor Toby nodded. He felt trapped. No one would ever believe him over the well-dressed white man. Threatened with his life, he also felt like he had no choice but to go along with the stranger's plans.

John Tinker woke famished from going to bed early and missing supper after the fatigue of the previous day's session of the General Court. He had commanded Silas to ready their belongings for travel again to Agawam and to arrange a shallop. It was still so early that darkness enveloped Hartford with only a hint of dawn on the eastern horizon. He wondered about the Varlets and hoped they were able to leave town within the timeframe afforded by Mason.

He lit a candle, sat at the desk, and started to respond to Winthrop's last letter. He would send it by boat to New London before leaving Hartford. From New London, his wife could send it by ship to England.

It was then that he heard an insistent knock on his door. Sensing something urgent, he arose to answer, but when he opened his door, no one was there. Only a small item wrapped in linen cloth with a brief note was placed in a basket at the threshold.

Tinker read the unsigned note.

In gratitude for your service Mr. Tinker

"It must be from the Varlets," he said softly. They knew not to make public his connection to the resolution of Judith's case. With that thought, he opened the cloth and delighted to find the spice cake. He was still extremely hungry and had not wished to awaken the innkeeper for food at such an early hour.

He devoured the little cake quickly. It was extra sweet and filled with the strong taste of nutmeg, clove, and other powerful spices. Satiated, he returned to the writing desk to continue the letter.

Some time elapsed before John Tinker became unable to write more than a simple salutation. His sight became blurry and his heart began to race. Alarmed, John Tinker realized that he must have been poisoned.

"Dear God, what have I done? Will I ever see my children again?" he murmured, becoming more heated with each second. He wanted to vomit and expel the poison.

But the toxic blend had already taken hold of his nervous system, and it was too late to stop its course of action.

Overwhelmed by thirst, he was hot and dry with eyes dilated.

He chided himself for lack of due vigilance. He knew he was about to die.

"She waits no more," he whispered for the very last time.

As he tried to stumble towards the door for help, his body slowly succumbed to total paralysis.

His thoughts quickly became confused as he lost control of his body and then his mind.

Barely functioning, he finally fell to the floor, going in and out of consciousness. By the time Silas came to his room to announce the readiness of his preparations for the trip to Agawam, John Tinker lay on the floor, barely breathing and unable to speak. He was deep in the throes of hallucinations, moaning and terrified.

Silas tried to shake him awake but to no avail.

"Mr. Tinker, wake up! Mr. Tinker, talk to me!" Silas screamed frantically from the door.

"Help! Come quickly! Help! I fear Mr. Tinker is dying! Someone call a doctor! I beg of you! It is urgent!" he pleaded.

Silas picked up his mentor and placed him on the bed, desperately trying to think of what to do next. He grabbed a cold cloth, begging John to suck water from it and then wiped his face with it. John Tinker was still unable to respond.

"Please pull through, Mr. Tinker," he sobbed, as other travelers ran into the room.

"The innkeeper sent for a doctor. Mr. Rossiter's in town for the court session," spoke an old woman. She took over and put cool compresses over John's feverish body. They tried to nurse him to the best of their abilities until Rossiter arrived. Tragically, John's breathing slowed even more. He was unable to swallow even small drops of water and completely unable to move his limbs.

The old woman was wrong. Rossiter had left Hartford after the charter was read the day before and was no longer available to help. A young medical apprentice was the only one they could find. He concluded that John Tinker had had a stroke. No one saw the linen cloth and the note attached to it. John had hidden them away, mistakenly thinking that he was protecting himself and the Varlets in doing so. The young doctor in training did the best that he could, but he lacked the experience to understand what Tinker's correct diagnosis was.

Silas refused to leave John Tinker's side and was full of remorse for not finding him sooner. He did whatever the medical apprentice suggested, but ultimately their efforts were futile. John Tinker took his last breath that morning.

Silas slowly covered John's body and face with the blanket. "God bless you, Mr. Tinker. Walk with the angels," he said as tears streamed down his face.

Hartford greeted the news of Tinker's death with shock. He was forty-nine years old and one of the most respected leaders in the colony as well as Governor Winthrop's most loyal assistant. The General Court declared that all of the costs related to his illness and funeral expenses would be paid from the treasury of the colony. John Tinker was laid to rest in the burial ground near the meetinghouse in Hartford.

There was one man who smiled and nodded with approval when he heard the news. "It is finished," he grinned. "Just as planned. No more interference from Mr. Tinker."

No one suspected foul play—no one except for certain enslaved servants after hearing about Mr. Tinker's death. They eventually shared their stories of the disturbed and agitated man they had encountered before Tinker's death.

For Emma, she feared that as an enslaved African she would not be believed except by those of her own kind. Ever so carefully, she offered an account of the strange trajectory of what took place to only fellow slaves whom she most trusted.

Toby had similar concerns. He had just been allowed to marry his dear wife Eliza, a new maid in the household. He was afraid of being sold off for slander should he choose to tell his story and risk losing his wife, the woman whose existence was the sole reason he survived. It was with great alarm that Eliza confided in him a similar story that she had heard from Emma as they were washing their family's clothes in the Little River.

The information weighed heavily on Toby who knew it had to spread outside of Hartford if there were ever to be justice for Mr. Tinker. As they talked low and soft one night in their loft space, Eliza had an idea. She would visit Isabel, the enslaved woman of the Varlets who was left behind with her uncle until Nicolas Varlet's final return. She was their hope. In New Amsterdam, she might be able to figure out a way to get the story to someone who could bring forth justice without having to know where it had originated.

Their plan was conceived in the nick of time. Nicolas Varlet returned again the next afternoon. Eliza casually called out to the young woman pretending to want nothing more than a companion to wash clothes with.

"Isabel, you still be here in Hartford? Come with me to the river. I need someone to keep me company today."

The shy girl came out of the barn.

"Eliza, I wait for Mr. Varlet. He comes back soon. I cannot go with you. My washing days are done in Hartford," she replied.

Eliza quickly grabbed the girl's arm and pulled her into the barn. "Listen here, young Isabel. That man John Tinker everybody talking about, the man who some slaves say saved your Judith, he's dead. You listen good to my story now. His only hope for justice is you passing the story to someone who can help. You tell Judith. She owe him something."

"Yah. She owes him her life. I'll do it. You tell me everything. Maybe Judith can get the story to Governor Winthrop. They say that man loved John Tinker like a brother. He needs to know."

Eliza hugged her.

"Thank you, Isabel. May the sun shine on you."

She lost no time in telling Isabel as many details as she could recall.

"Now be safe, Miss Isabel. I wish for you a better life in New Amsterdam," she said, as she waved and snuck away again, satisfied that she and her new husband Toby had done everything they could.

Their story would not die in Hartford with John Tinker but would reach someone in New Amsterdam who might be able to seek justice for Tinker's death.

CHAPTER TWENTY-EIGHT:

Marie's Story
New Amsterdam, New Netherland
1662

The days passed painfully and slowly since Jan's disappearance. There were some land acquisitions that he had been working on in the northernmost region of New Netherland, but he had slipped into the forest, never coming out again to finalize them.

My sons, Aernoudt, and Cornelis, in Beverwyck had looked for him and spread the word to many tribes they traded and interacted with that Jan was missing. I tried to keep *The Salty Rose* going as well as I could without my husband, but his disappearance weighed on me heavily. It was still unbelievable to me that Jan had vanished without a trace into the wilderness over eight months before.

In my mind, I went back to the time of our romantic retreat in the forest. What happened to Jan? Could he have run off with the young Indian woman who seemed unhappy about our union? Or was it an unexpected accident that befell him? I wished I could know something. Not knowing was the worst. How could this man whom I loved, fought with, had children with, and worked with so closely for over ten years cease to exist in my life so suddenly?

I was weary but grateful to have family and friends around to support me. My sisters often took care of my younger children, and a few customers who were already regulars came and sat with me in the bar for hours, much longer than they normally did. They knew how difficult my life had become and visited me more frequently at the tavern. Henri La Chaîne and his wife Claire were among them. Of course, Domingo was a strong presence, and Pierre and my daughter Anna were learning tapping and helped as much as they could.

Even though times were tough, a tapper never runs out of thirsty customers. I was busy wiping tables diligently, trying to remove layers of scum encrusted into the little lines of the game boards carved into our tables when Caspar's rescued daughter, Judith, walked through my tavern door.

At first, I did not recognize Judith. After weeks in a dirty Hartford prison with barely any food or room to move around, her eyes seemed hollowed out and her once voluptuous curves were replaced with a bony frame. Judith was still very weak and relied on the steady arm of an enslaved young African woman owned by her family to move around. Her sister Marija had also braved the harsh end of autumn to come to pay her respects.

"Marie!" she tried to shout, but it was barely a whisper, her face laden with emotion as tears began to well up at the edges of her haunted eyes.

"You saved my life! I've come to thank you! I heard what you did. I will forever be grateful for your appeal to the brave Englishman, John Tinker," Judith cried.

A moment of silence ensued as Judith looked at the young, dark-skinned women at her side who returned the glance in a way that made me think she was witnessing a specter. I knew in that moment that something was wrong. A fog of confusion coated my thoughts as I struggled to distinguish reality.

I went up to Judith and hugged her, puzzled by her expression and the scared reluctance of her enslaved companion.

"Judith," I cried. "It is a comfort to see you again. We were frantic over your ordeal. I am very sorry for all you have gone through, including the death of your dear parents. It is a tragedy. So many traumas and so much heartache you have endured!"

I turned to her sister, Marija, as well.

"I cannot imagine the pain you must feel. But I am so happy you are back!" I said.

"But why did you come to me in such a fragile state? It is already cold outside."

I brushed off a few fallen leaves from her cloak with tender care. It could have waited until you were stronger, chérie," I soothed.

"Thank you, Marie. You are very kind. But my heart was bursting once Marija and Nicolas told me the story behind my release. I am overwhelmed," said Judith.

Marija interjected, "I must be honest, Marie. Her brother Nicolas and I wanted her to wait, but when we told her of your own trauma, she insisted that she could not."

"I had to see you!" Judith cried out.

"Ah, yes, my Jan. He is gone. Everybody knows, yet no one has found a trace of him."

The wind howled just then, shaking the windows of the tavern and affirming that our chances of finding him were grim.

"If only I could help you, Marie," Judith said with deep sadness.

I took her hand.

"Judith, seeing you here and alive makes me feel much better, but the fact that you are here is the doing of John Tinker, your brother Nicolas, and Director General Stuyvesant," I said.

Judith shook her head.

"You must give yourself more credit, Marie. I understand that John Tinker ultimately saved me, but what led to such an outcome was the initial kindness you showed despite your own hardships. If you had not communicated with John Tinker about my peril, I would also be dead," said Judith.

She paused, not wanting to cause me any more pain, but knew it had to be said.

"Marie, I am so sorry to hear that Jan is gone. Unfortunately, I must tell you some other grave news."

Again she looked at her enslaved servant. Both of their expressions were of gloom and dread. She introduced the woman to me.

"This is Isabel, Marie. She is part of our household and was in Hartford too. She stayed a little longer to help my brother and another servant pack up the last of our belongings into crates and barrels. I must tell you what she heard. It is horrible, but you must know now before you hear it passed on in rumors," she said.

My heart sank. It had to be severe for her to act in such a manner.

"No, please, Judith, say no more. Come to a table in the back. You must sit and we need privacy before you go any further with your story," I said.

Judith nodded, and Isabel slowly escorted her to a more secluded place away from the larger public area of the tavern. Marija followed closely behind. I beckoned for Domingo to bring us drinks and asked him to stay, perceiving from his eagerness to help and be near the conversation that he may have already heard something about Judith's impending news.

Once we were quietly tucked into a private corner in the back of the tavern, I was ready to hear Judith's update.

"What is it, Judith? You must tell me now that we are out of the earshot of my patrons," I implored her.

I turned to Isabel. The poor girl was very nervous. She looked to Judith to speak for her.

"Marie, John Tinker is dead," Judith blurted out. "Could I have been the cause? Did someone murder him because he helped to free me?" she asked, bursting into tears.

I was shocked.

"He's dead? There must be more information," I pleaded. "But that is also why you are here, n'est ce pas? Please tell me everything," I begged, feeling my spirit turning into a hollow shell.

"Of course, Marie. I am so sorry to be the bearer of bad news. Isabel said another slave woman came to her a couple of days after I left. They were packing our last belongings into crates and barrels. I cannot go on. Please, Isabel, please I beg of you courage to speak about what happened next," she said as she squeezed her arm.

"Go on. Nice and slow, Isabel. It'll be all right. No one gonna hurt you. Just say what happened," Domingo assured her.

"'Tis sad, Missus Marie. I was in the barn when a neighbor slave woman came up to me. She called me over and told me to do some washing with her by the Little River. I told her I had no time. I had to hurry and get everything packed. Right then, she pulled me into the barn. I knew she was serious. She told me she knew that John Tinker, the man who helped Judith go free, was dead. Said it had to be murder. Said her husband told her of a strange story about a man who cornered him early on the morning John Tinker died," she said.

Isabel was racing frantically through the story now, frightened and eager to get it over with. Yet, she overcame her own fears in telling it as she had promised she would do.

"That's good. Take your time, girl. You not gonna be in any trouble," Domingo encouraged her.

"Yes, Domingo is right. Be brave. Tell us everything you know. You will be safe. We only want to know who the killer was if that is possible. John Tinker was a dear friend of mine. I owe it to his family to find out what happened," I said, still feeling like I was floating above my seat from the shock of the discussion.

"Ma'am, I'll tell you what else I know so long as nothing happens to the messengers. I know who John Tinker was 'cause he came to talk to Marija before Judith was let free. Nice man he was. They say he had young children he wanted to get home to," said Isabel.

"Yes, so sad," acknowledged Judith. "Please, Isabel, start where you left off."

Isabel nodded sullenly and continued her story.

"So, the slave woman who come to me say that John Tinker was dead. Told me she thought it was murder. Her husband was made to help a man that morning who was suspicious. Didn't know his name but he had real curly red hair and was about thirty years old. Never seen him before in Hartford. He threatened her husband's life if he dared tell anybody about it. Told him he'd get him in trouble with his master and make his life hell if he didn't do what the freckled, red-haired man wanted. He made him deliver a spiced sweet cake to John Tinker real early in the morning at the inn while the red-haired man distracted the innkeeper. It was just a few hours later that people got word Tinker was dead. Said he had a horrible fit as he died. He was drooling and couldn't talk no more. Was barely moving when his helper found him. Her husband thought it had something to do with that cake," Isabel said.

"Take a breath, Isabel. Here, a sip," Judith handed a mug to her.

"I agree it does sound strange," I assured them. "Was there any other information?" I asked.

After catching her breath, Isabel was ready to tell me more.

"Yes, ma'am, the whole slave community was talking. There was a young woman who lived at the home of the lady, Missus Lucy Smith.

They said her husband was the uncle of that man with the red hair. He was staying with them. One of the girls who cooks for them and sometimes helps care for the children passed on some other strange information to my friend. She said the same man, the one with the curly red hair, instructed her to make the spice cake. Didn't want her to say nothing to nobody 'bout it. Threatened her life if she did. She wasn't gonna say nothing either, but when she heard the other strange story, she had no choice. Please promise you won't give away how you heard this, Missus Marie?" Isabel said, looking up at me pleadingly.

"No, no, of course not. You are doing a good thing. I will seek out justice for John Tinker, but nobody will be the wiser of how I found out. Is there any more detail you can give me?" I asked.

"Yes, Missus Marie. The slave girl who baked the cake said something was weird about it aside from the threats. She say that red-haired man was evil. He made her leave the kitchen, and when she come back the spice cake was different. Smelled different and looked different too. She was sure he did something to it. He also scolded her and told her not to let the children try any of it. Said it was all for his friend, a little sweet spice cake to remind him of home."

"My dear God!" cried Marija.

"It had to be murder. I was not aware of all these details. While you were in prison, Judith, a man with curly red hair of about the same age Isabel described came to speak to our parents. Sarina let him in. He said he had to speak about business with them. Father seemed irritated. I did not pay much attention. Papa seemed to not want him in the house and led him to the barn. What followed was muffled shouting that could not be easily understood from inside the house. Papa never explained what happened. Not long after that incident, both Papa and Mama were dead," Marija explained.

Everyone gasped. Who was the devil whose appearance foreshadowed both John Tinker's and the Varlets' deaths?

"We thought it strange that both of them died together without any warning, but the authorities in Hartford wanted nothing to do with us. We found them both dead in their bed one morning. We didn't investigate it further, thinking that they both died from severe grief," Marija explained.

She looked into the air as if searching for answers—revisiting the scene in her mind. She startled as if she had just remembered something important.

"There was a carafe—a small carafe with the remnants of wine. My parents stayed up late into the night talking about Judith's fate. The rest of us had already gone to bed. The wine must have also contained the same poison that killed John Tinker! Starting to feel ill, I imagine they slipped into bed before it took its full effect on them. That explains the one glass that fell on the floor and the way they slept on top of their featherbed holding on to each other," she cried. "I should have known something was very wrong. I should have pieced it together!"

Marija became inconsolable.

Poor Judith joined her. Their hearts were broken.

I had an avalanche of feelings. I was shocked and angry about the deaths of my dear friend Caspar and his wife. I felt joy that Judith survived her close brush with death but also experienced intense grief and sorrow at the loss of John Tinker. I felt responsible for sending him into danger.

Was someone vengeful that he had secured Judith's freedom, vengeful enough to order a murder? Who was it that wanted him dead? Who had a grudge against John Tinker? In their zeal to kill all supposed witches, did the Puritan leaders become assets of the Devil themselves? These were all questions that I knew must be answered. I was devastated to lose my friend and would not rest until I had answers.

"I will tell you this," I said firmly, pounding a fist on the table.

"I will make sure that whoever was behind the murder of John Tinker and your parents will pay the price of justice for his misdeeds! There will be an atonement of some kind. If it is the last thing I do, I will make sure that happens. God be my witness!" I would never forget Tinker's kindness towards me when I first told him of Jan's likely disappearance. I owed it to him to make sure his killer was found. I turned to Isabel.

"You will be protected for your courage in speaking the truth. I commend you for your bravery. There is a way to make sure Governor Winthrop finds out about these disturbing crimes. But, all of you must simply trust me for now. Not a word about our conversation to anyone—not a single soul!" I whispered, surveying the other astonished faces around the wooden tavern table.

CHAPTER TWENTY-NINE:

Winthrop's Story
Hartford, Connecticut Colony
Summer, 1663

As his tall ship headed into New London's small colonial harbor, Winthrop smelled home. It was a warm June day in 1663. The charter had preceded him to the colonies. He had received word that his trusted advisor, assistant, and friend was found dead in his room at Jeremy Adam's tavern. The news had cut his heart like a knife. The loss of such a trusted friend was shocking and disheartening.

As he strode down the plank to disembark, it struck him hard. Tinker was not there to greet him. As happy as he was to see his wife and children again, his home still seemed empty as they ate their late meal that afternoon. It was emptier still when he went into his lab.

The next day, he'd gone to Tinker's home and visited his wife and their five young children. What to say? There were no adequate words.

"I loved your husband like a true brother. I will never be able to repay his loyalty to me over many years. Should you need anything, you must come to me for help in Hartford or send word to my wife," he said, trying to console Tinker's family.

Settling into Hartford again that summer was harder than John Winthrop ever could have imagined. His capital was in chaos and its populace more divided than it had ever been. Differences in church doctrine caused a massive exodus to Northampton, Massachusetts, where previous inhabitants had moved to start a new church more aligned to their beliefs.

The sufferings and anxiety of the extended witch hunts also led many other residents to leave Hartford. Aside from a divided population, only the ghosts of four executed witches remained. Were it not for the interventions to save the Varlet woman and the daring escapes of the Ayers, the Palmers, and James Wakely to Rhode Island, there would surely be more phantoms lurking about.

Rebecca and Nathaniel Greensmith, who hanged together with Mary Barnes of Farmington, had gone to the gallows on a cold January day just a few months before. The Natives who came to trade in Hartford made a point to avoid the Greensmiths' home near the meadow next to the Great River. It wasn't far from the same place where rumors of drinking sack and dancing around a fire in merriment at Christmas time led to the Greensmiths' ultimate demise.

On the other hand, the husband of Mary Barnes was not the slightest bit haunted by his previous wife's spirit. Instead he focused instead on enjoying the new, shapely young wife at his side.

Mary Sanford was gone too, the earliest victim from June of the previous year. Andrew, her husband, barely escaped a conviction. Of those who stayed to face their supposed witch crime, only Elizabeth Seager received a narrow acquittal. Six jury members found her guilty and six found her suspicious—not enough to convict.

However, voices of moderation were still at bay. The townspeople of Hartford were not content to let Elizabeth Seager be. They had smelled the blood of witches, and it eased their fears to see those witches die.

It wasn't surprising to hear that Seager was indicted again! Winthrop would often see the poor woman, haggard from her status as a pariah, walking around the town square in her tattered blue cape. She often mumbled to herself as if she were in another world.

This time, she was indicted for adultery, blasphemy, and witchcraft! Of course, Matthew Allyn and his son John were involved. Allyn and his sons reveled in hunting witches. It gave them great satisfaction.

Winthrop was much aggrieved. Disgusted at how far his fellow colonists had slid back into their contentious attitudes, he wondered how he would ever piece his colony together again. He was alarmed at the way the Hartford community was splintering before his eyes. He knew in his heart that it would be more difficult to extinguish the fires of the witch frenzy than it had been before he left. Too much damage had already been done.

Winthrop walked grimly past the place of their murders in an effort to understand the senselessness of what had transpired while he was away, determined to stop its continued history. It was clear that Mason had acted rashly in his absence of almost two years. He was sure his deputy governor's fundamentalism had only encouraged the frenzied hunt and the harsh judgments that followed. Winthrop knew it would be a slow and painful process to lead his town and colony to a calmer, more rational state.

Winthrop longed for more details from a moderate voice.

If only Tinker were here. If only I could talk to him about what happened, he thought.

But upon thinking these words, Winthrop realized John would have left him with the record of what transpired. His journal would be hidden for his mentor to find. Just as John Dee and other presumed Rosicrucians had kept their journals in duplicate, Winthrop had taught John Tinker to do the same: the first one, if found, contained false information designed to mislead. The second, one of truth, would always be hidden and coded with the real account of what had transpired.

Winthrop hurried home with the insight of what was waiting for him there. He knew exactly where to look for his hidden treasure. He and Tinker had communicated in this way before. It was only a matter of minutes before he entered his library with a door leading to a garden outside.

Standing before his voluminous desk, he gazed at a wall panel at the left side of it, a nondescript one looking like all the others but with a few taps of his formed fist, the panel opened, and Winthrop entered a cloistered space with some old furniture. Inside another desk that was much older, Winthrop felt underneath for another secret compartment. Feeling carefully with his fingertips, he came across a hard oblong object.

Excitedly pulling it out, Winthrop knew he'd discovered exactly what he was looking for. He carried the newly revealed little journal back to his study and placed it on his desk. He sat on his alchemical chair that depicted the symbols of the universe and the seven levels of spiritual development found there. He held the book and said a prayer.

"The last testament of John Tinker was written within these pages," Winthrop whispered. He leafed ravenously through the journal until he found the last entry.

It was dated October 1662. "He must have left this last entry immediately after the Varlet woman's release," he said softly.

"Dear Tinker, I am listening now through your words that you left for me," he murmured.

Winthrop sensed the spirit of his friend at his side, the hairs on his arms standing erect.

In that space of the sacred, Winthrop looked again at the opened little book. With intensity and reverence, Winthrop began to decipher and read the coded text.

Dearest Excellency John Winthrop, Governor of Connecticut

I express my deepest thanks and admiration in bearing witness to the charter secured for our great colony. I had full confidence in your endeavors. The Passage is closer than ever before. I pray it will give a turn to the unfortunate events I must describe.

As I write this, I fear for the lives of many souls. A cloud of black death has come to Hartford, brought to us by devils turning neighbor against neighbor in the guise of righteousness. As we had feared, Major Mason is content to upend all the peace that once was. Matthew Allyn is his helpmate in the destruction. I've come to both of them on behalf of word from the one at the sign of the rosy cross. Mason, with great anger, released Judith, the daughter of Caspar Varlet.

But, methinks something has gone awry here. At September's end, the Varlets, both husband and wife, were found dead. The remaining daughters are in shock and testify they had no preceding illness. I pray Caspar and his wife find peace in the afterlife.

As for me, I am eager to return to my family but first I must continue to quell the fires of these horrible witch suspicions. I will keep my promises to you, sir. There is more to do afore others hang. Up to now the person of one Goody Sanford was killed for witchcraft crimes, but others are at risk of joining her. God rest her soul.

I also await the trial against Constable Morton and Goodman Haughton who have wrongfully tarnished my name with lies accusing me of treason against the King. I have heard the happy news that it is likely I will be vindicated with my countersuit against them for slander. I can only hope all this viciousness and scandal will clear shortly and harmony will revisit the city. Again, I long to be home to be with my young family. I will hope that it will be mere days before my return and not weeks.

May God keep you, sir, and may your travels back to Connecticut be safe and secure. I will cherish the day we can meet again.

Your most humble and loyal servant and friend,
John Tinker

Winthrop began to weep uncontrollably, hearing John Tinker's voice again in the text of his written hand. He was even sadder to think about John's fatherless children. Indeed, the town of Hartford had gone mad.

He needed to be even closer to John Tinker, so he walked outside to the garden, cut a handful of summer flowers, and headed to his friend's grave in the burying ground across from the town green.

CHAPTER THIRTY:

Winthrop's Story
Hartford, Connecticut
Summer, 1663

The burying ground was quiet and empty in stark contrast to the town green at a near distance. Winthrop placed the bouquet of daisies and other summer flowers respectfully on the ground where John Tinker was laid to rest not far from a lone oak tree. Winthrop was so engrossed in his own thoughts that he did not notice a figure come to him from behind the solid oak tree.

"We meet again," said a voice.

Winthrop looked up to see a man in the dress of a Frenchman.

"Governor Winthrop." The man with the well-groomed beard bowed and took off his hat with a slight flourish.

Winthrop stared, scarcely believing his eyes. His friend, a French Huguenot and a fellow alchemist, was a most unexpected sight.

"Welcome back to the colonies. I hear you secured a big success with the English King. It is opportune for all our holy plans. The marriage of East and West that we all dream of may come to pass. But that is something we must discuss later. For now, I have news," said the Frenchman.

Winthrop finally aroused from his stupor.

"Henri La Chaîne! What a great surprise! My dear old friend from the days of the siege at La Rochelle. My fellow brother of Hermes, what news brings you here?"

"I know the identity of the killer of John Tinker," he said as he solemnly bowed toward his burial.

Winthrop startled, grabbing his chest.

"Murder, you say! I must know more," he cried in disbelief.

"Unfortunately, Tinker's life ended prematurely," said Henri sadly.

"There must be justice," Winthrop croaked.

"Let's go over to the bench over there. It will be even quieter," motioned Henri.

"But how can you know what happened to John Tinker?" Winthrop questioned him, rather baffled.

"Are you sure you are ready for me to tell you the whole story? Perhaps you would prefer to speak in your home?" Henri asked, looking around to make sure they were alone.

"No. This is private enough. No one else is here now. You must tell me in front of the corpse of John Tinker. You will be his surrogate voice. If you forget anything, his spirit will call out to you to remember every last detail," said Winthrop.

"Very well. I will tell you all, and his spirit will be witness. John Tinker's death was not one of innocence. Someone wanted him dead. Unfortunately, we suspect that the death of the Varlet couple may have also been carried out by sinister means. That person wanted Tinker out of the way and the Varlets too so he could carry forth his nefarious plans," said Henri.

"Please, how do you know of this?" demanded Winthrop.

"A tapper named Marie du Trieux called on me to help. She wanted to make sure you knew. She was also a friend of Tinker."

"Aye, I knew they were friends already. Her husband translated for Tinker when he went to New Amsterdam to trade. But how in this world did Marie learn of the exact circumstances of Tinker's demise?" asked Winthrop stunned.

"Through a vast network of slaves both here and in New Amsterdam, Governor Winthrop. I cannot be more specific about their identities for they fear for their lives. Marie only knows the identity of one and has promised absolute secrecy, but I have confidence in everything that was conveyed to Judith Varlet and those in her network through Marie du Trieux to me. I have verified all of it," assured Henri.

"Please tell me everything that you know," begged Winthrop. "There must be justice."

"One of the people involved told Judith that on the eve before leaving Hartford to join the rest of the family in New Amsterdam someone came to visit her. Servants in the neighborhood were talking about two bizarre incidents.

The first concerned a man with curly red locks and a hostile and impatient demeanor. He had forced, under threat of death, a male servant to do his dirty work. He made him drop off a spiced sweet cake to John Tinker in the early dawn hour at Jeremy Adam's inn. It was only a few hours later that Tinker was found almost dead in his room," Henri said, pausing and wiping his brow while Winthrop looked on, entranced.

According to the network, around the same time, a young woman told a story about the same red-haired, angry man. He forced her to cook a spiced sweet cake but was very peculiar about it, saying it was for a friend. Yet, he was fierce in his wishes that only one cake be made with the batter. The woman suspected that he had added something vile to it. He had called her out of the hearth room before she could put the cake into the beehive oven to bake, and when she came back, the batter looked different. It smelled different too. He also threatened to kill her if she said a word to anyone.

"Someone had heard both stories and had put it together to form suspicions of foul play against John Tinker by the same red-haired man. Of course, talk of Tinker's death circulated through the town and everyone knew about it, especially after the honorable burial he was given. The public understanding of what happened did not match what certain persons had witnessed in private," Henri explained.

"Luckily, Marie gave me all the information she had in a timely manner. I dispatched immediately to Hartford to do a little detective work. I knew how important this would be and how much of a trusted assistant John Tinker was to you," Henri said.

"Thank you," said Winthrop, in a hushed, melancholy tone. "Please continue."

"My first stop was the inn of Jeremy Adams. I asked him if he had seen the red-haired man. He had. He identified the man as Hugh Dyer, the nephew of the Smiths. It turns out Hugh Dyer had been staying with the

Smiths for more than a month. He'd arrived from New London mid-September.

"Wait a minute! I know whom you speak of. He held a grudge against Tinker for being granted the monopoly on his distillery business in New London," said Winthrop.

"Yes," said Henri. "Once I knew his identity, I followed his footsteps and found something rather curious. Witnesses said that he had also known the Varlets. He had wanted to buy out the Varlets' Hartford distillery at a robber's price. A neighbor testified to me that Dyer had visited Caspar Varlet the night before his death and that there was shouting from the barn. The next day both Caspar and his wife were dead. Their daughter Marija reported finding an empty carafe of wine that she hadn't seen before. She thinks the poison was placed in it and left at the door as a false gesture of neighborliness at the time the family was dealing with Judith's witchcraft indictment," said Henri.

"Undeniably, the motivation behind the killings of John Tinker and the Varlets was greed for the profitable business of making strong spirits!" exclaimed Henri.

He paused, respectfully looking at Tinker's grave and then continued.

"Hugh Dyer was a jealous man who coveted John Tinker's license to have the only distillery in New London. He also wanted a share of the distillery business in Hartford. Caspar Varlet owned a big chunk of it. I also found out that Hugh Dyer first tried to get Tinker out of the way by offering a small share of his future distillery business to Morton and Haughton if they brought forth a false claim against Tinker saying that he made treasonous statements against the King," said Henri.

"Did those two knaves have any knowledge of Dyer's lethal plan?" asked Winthrop?

"To my knowledge and from the evidence that I've discovered, no. They are innocent of Dyer's darkest motives and actions. However, they will still be dealt with at court for their false accusations against our friend," explained Henri.

"Ah, it's starting to make sense. My natural suspicions would not have gone to Hugh Dyer nor murder," said Winthrop sadly, still waking to the full extent of the destruction that had occurred in his absence.

"Dyer thought he could hide his actions and the real motivations behind the killings since the witch trials were capturing everyone's attention and time. He thought that if people suspected foul play at all, perhaps they would think it was from witchery alone," Henri clarified and continued.

"I wanted to bring attention to the authorities sooner, but I didn't trust Mason. And I certainly didn't trust the sheriff in New London, Morton, the man coerced by Hugh Dyer to make a false claim against Tinker. I thought I'd have to find other allies or wait until you came back. I prayed for justice. I begged to the heavens for resolution. I envisioned the archangels shifting the innate forces of earth, air, fire, and water to bring natural justice for John Tinker," said Henri looking up at the sky, smiling.

"Certainly, the heavens could not wait for it. Not long after that, news came of an accident that killed Hugh Dyer instantly. A sudden rash storm tossed his vessel over turbulent waves. Hugh Dyer—drunk off the distilled spirits he so loved—fell overboard and was never seen again! He was drowned for sure," said Henri, satisfied with his eerie account of justice.

Winthrop sat stupefied by Henri La Chaîne's story.

"I am sorry for the shock of all of this, but you had to know the truth," said Henri, putting his arm around Winthrop.

He walked towards John Tinker's simple, sandstone grave.

"And I am sorry that it had to end so violently, John Tinker. You were a good man. I hope you will now be at peace."

He knelt down and placed his hands over the dirt of Tinker's final resting place. Winthrop joined him.

"Be at peace, John Tinker," whispered Winthrop.

They stood for a few minutes in silence before the grave. Finally, Henri turned to Winthrop.

"Winthrop, it was Marie du Trieux who became involved to save Judith Varlet and she did so again when she heard of John Tinker's suspicious death. She enmeshed herself in these affairs to help others despite her own hardships. Her husband Jan has been missing in the wilderness for over a year. Marie of *The Salty Rose* at the East River ferry crossing in New Amsterdam may be the rose whom we have been looking for, the Rose of New Amsterdam, the key to the Passage.

CHAPTER THIRTY-ONE:

Marie's Story
New Amsterdam, New Netherland
November 1663

I could not sleep for long. My restless dreams disturbed me to the point of wakefulness. New Amsterdam was silent, but my soul was not. I could not lie to myself anymore.

"Jan is lost to you forever. He is not coming back!" a voice screamed within my head. I sensed impending doom, but still I refused to grasp it fully.

In those wee hours of the morning, I realized that my life was about to change dramatically. The loss of Jan hit me harder than it ever had. He'd been gone for months and the seasons had even started to repeat themselves.

As I sat awake in my bed still not wanting to venture out into a silent world, I desperately tried to remember the dreams that had unnerved me. Was it Jan who spoke to me in warning? I tried to remember to no avail. However, my forlorn heart had fully opened, and I cried more than I had ever let myself before.

For months I'd held the remains of our life together, always hoping that my Jan would return from his trek into the wilderness. The duties at the tavern never ceased. I tried to be the best mother I could to all my children. The financial burdens only increased.

That morning I was late in opening up *The Salty Rose*. Sara Kierstede, the wife of the company surgeon, Hans Kierstede, came to see me. She must have sensed my nightmares.

Sara and I had known each other since childhood, and she had been at the tavern with her grandmother and her aunt Trynje Jonas during my many pregnancies. But our paths in life had diverged greatly. At fifteen, Sara had married well, as had her aunts and sisters, into the most powerful of families in New Amsterdam. Sara, also knowing the language of the neighboring Natives since childhood, was recently asked to be a translator. The powerful chief of the Munsee, Oratam, trusted few Dutchmen who had translated in the past. They were all connected to previous wars in some ways. That is when the Director General and some of the other New Amsterdam leaders turned to Sara for her help.

"Sara, what brings you here? Such a surprise visit so early in the day," I said. We didn't move in the same social circles anymore, and her visit was completely unexpected.

"Marie, I've come to give you a warning. I am aware of all your recent troubles. I know you have a good heart and do not wish to see more pain come to you," she explained. "Please forgive me for being frank, but Judith wanted me to come and explain to you what is happening in the colony. She fears for you. May I come in, Marie, where we can discuss this quietly?" she asked.

I led her to two solid carved wooden chairs by the hearth. The fire was still burning and gave off much-needed warmth. I called for my daughter, Anna, to bring Sara some warmed cider.

As we warmed ourselves by the fire, I continued the conversation.

"I don't understand. Why would she fear for me? I have told her many times not to worry about me," I said.

"Marie, you can be stubborn, and your transgressions with the law were quickly forgiven in the past, but the times are different. I must warn you what is at stake."

"I'm listening. State your case," I said, becoming a little irritated.

"Marie, you may have heard that I'm translating for the Munsee leader, Oratam, of the Hackensacky. He represents many Native villages, including areas on Staten Island. With other leaders, he has become increasingly concerned about our settlers going to the Indians with drink to sell. The Native leaders are loathe to see the behavior of their young after they have imbibed European drink such as wine or beer. They say it makes them crazy. They are not used to drunkenness. Oratam is adamant that Stuyvesant pass harsh penalties to those who are responsible for bringing liquor into Native communities," she explained.

"But why would Stuyvesant care and why can't individual Natives decide for themselves? I've had some of the same Indian customers for years. Why does he suddenly care now? Why do any of the leaders care now?" I asked.

"They care because Oratam's word is powerful among many Native communities. Stuyvesant needs his cooperation to avoid any further war with the Esopus. Stuyvesant knows his power is weakening. He suspects an uprising afoot, be it from the English settlers on Long Island or among his own kind. At the same time, he fears the English creeping further into Dutch territories and a possible takeover by the New Englanders. If he can't hold on to cooperative agreements with the Hackensacky and the Munsee tribes, further Indian wars will weaken his position and threaten his survival as leader of our colony," she said.

I stared at her. Of course, it had to do with Stuyvesant's survival. He may have put the false face of propriety and morality on it, but his position stank of self-interest.

"Marie, do you understand? Oratam's main condition among others is that European drink must be kept away from his Native communities. He complains of increasing violence and rebellion. He says that brandy and wine are turning once-peaceful villages into places of knife fights and neglect," she stated, desperately hoping that I would understand.

I turned away in an effort to shut out what I did not want to hear. Sara continued, hoping that her insistence on conveying the information would draw my attention to the severity of my situation.

"Marie, please listen to me! Indians are anxious for their young adults who they say become crazy once they start to drink, so crazy that they have to have more of it. They witness some of their tribespeople becoming indebted and poor, neglecting to take care of their families and their responsibilities. The families are being driven apart from what Native leaders like Oratam see as the demon alcohol."

I turned away from her, not wanting to listen further.

"Marie, please look at me. With increased populations in the town, the Native leaders worry that tribespeople will have more access to it and will be weakened. They are firm on this point, Marie. If you sell any more brandy, wine, beer, or other spirits to these Natives, you will be severely punished this time. The tides have changed, Marie. That is all I can tell you. You risk your own livelihood should you continue on a path of serving alcohol to Natives," said Sara.

"Everyone looks to their own survival, Sara. I have my own to attend to as well," I said. "It's not that I don't have pity for the problems in Native villages. It's just not for me to decide what they can have or what they can't have. The people who come to me have been friends for years. They trust me. What kind of reputation will follow me if I give to some and withhold from others?" I questioned.

I placed my hands on my hips in defiance.

"They are not children. They should have the freedom to decide for themselves what they wish to do. Why should I be made to enforce the rules of someone else's community? You have my word. I will not go looking for them," I paused, becoming angrier.

"There are plenty of others who go directly to the Natives. I know who they are. They sneak their contraband into canoes and paddle into Indian villages. I do no such thing. It is those people who Stuyvesant needs to focus on. It is unfair that he has placed his target on me. Now please, give me your word that you will make that recommendation," I requested.

"Very well, Marie. I will make your suggestion, but I fear it will not take the attention away from you. You have been warned. There is nothing more that I can do to help you," she said, shrugging her shoulders.

Sara got up to leave and turned to me once more at the door, "Marie, mind what I say. The diplomatic situation is serious this time."

With that pronouncement, she crossed my threshold and never looked back. She'd done her duty by Judith and by me as a childhood friend.

In that moment, I couldn't quite believe that anything was so different from the way it had been before. I'd been in New Amsterdam since the beginning. Sara's warning seemed like just another threat without any teeth.

CHAPTER THIRTY-TWO:

Marie's Story
New Amsterdam, New Netherland
January 1664

I tried to control myself with some level of restraint: breathing, slowing down, and compacting all my anger into my fists. I was fully aware of the havoc that would ensue as a result of my forthcoming, unleashed temper. I had walked in earlier by the back door and had heard commotion upfront in the tavern area. Listening carefully, I became angrier by the minute.

"What have we here?" I bellowed.

"How dare you come stalking into my place and threaten my workers and family? How dare you, sheriff? You know what we have been through this past year with the loss of my beloved. What kind of a man are you to swoop in and threaten in this way? Never mind! I already know what kind of lowly man you are! Domingo! Quick, go get my brother-in-law, Isaac. Tell him it is urgent," I directed him.

Domingo listened intently in the corner near the end of the bar. He had been hunched over drying newly washed mugs when the sheriff forcefully marched in with papers for my arrest and appearance in court. No longer the young man that first arrived on the shores of the New World in shackles, years of hard work had slowed him down slightly.

"Yes, Madame Marie. I'll go to Monsieur De Forest right away," he said. Then he briefly glared at the sheriff.

The sheriff looked down his crooked nose at the massive man knowing he was the one with real power despite Domingo's size. He stood straight, giving the message that he resolved to be firm with me that time. The Deputy General and the Council of New Netherland had demanded it. Never mind if I had children to feed or not.

The sheriff finally spoke.

"So, Marie, you heard what I was saying to your daughters then? You have broken the law again and again. The Director General will no longer tolerate your defiance and total lack of respect. You must go before the Council and the court for your justice. Do not bother me with your insults. I have turned a blind eye these many years," he said, glancing at the rings on his stubby fat fingers.

"Ah, yes. So this is the kind of treatment I get after my husband is gone. You would dare to prey on me, sheriff? I will have none of this! You should know by now. I cower to no man. How many free beers have you had at my expense? And how many of your own sins have I ignored while you were enjoying the delightful spirits of my fine establishment? You never had any difficulty

drinking your fill, eh? So what makes you so different now?" I demanded.

The people of New Amsterdam were weary of the Indian wars. Everyone had lost someone, including me. But desperation causes people to do what is necessary for their own survival. Now it was my family's survival in opposition to the whole of New Amsterdam.

There was no choice in the matter any longer. And in all honesty, I knew. I'd hoped for protection from the Varlets, but Judith had warned me of the consequences of continuing my contraband ways. They'd already intervened multiple times to help me. I know Judith did plead on my behalf but diplomacy with the Munsee chief, Oratam, had prevented giving me another chance. There was nothing I or anyone else could do. Sara Kierstede had been right.

"Marie, now your own needs are pitted against the needs of this community. We have been accommodating. You and Jan have gotten into trouble many times. You were given countless extra chances. Conditions are different now. I am a hard man but I am not a heartless one, as you suggest. Marie, I must obey the order of the Director General this time. We have all had many opportunities to do whatever we wanted. But now the Munsee chief, Oratam, will have no trouble waging further Indian wars on all of us if you do not abide by his rule to deny spirits to his Indians. We have no time for further disruptions," he said arrogantly.

I turned away from him. My daughters' expressions showed their concern. Wasn't there something that I could do? Did they want me to humble myself before the town sheriff? Perhaps just one more time he could turn a blind eye if I were not so defiant.

Anna, my youngest daughter, working in the tavern, recognized the moment. Wide-eyed and observant, she quickly moved to the taps and poured the sheriff a fine brew nursed with just the right amount of hops and a barely discernible pinch of citrus.

Her sister Alida spoke to him.

"Please, sheriff, come get off your tired feet. Rest on the bench while we wait for Uncle Isaac. This is the freshest brew we have. See if it quenches your thirst. Please, I beg of you, see if it is to your liking."

Anna eyed me from behind the tap while the sheriff was suddenly engrossed in the charms of Alida, my most hospitable daughter.

I gave her a quick wink. I knew what she was up to. The scene had played itself out many times before. I chuckled to myself, knowing what usually came next. The anger inside me was subsiding but the defiance was not. My daughters had subtly reminded me of the most successful path of rebellion, sweetness and charm. If they could get him a little bit drunk before Isaac arrived, then perhaps they could alter our fate.

"Why not have a drink, sheriff? Maybe it will trigger your memory, and you will recall the generosity that we have offered you over so many years. Please, sheriff, partake in as much as you want. It is really my pleasure to help you do that," I said with a sly smile.

"Of course, I enjoy your beer, Marie, but enough of this. Nothing will change. The papers are signed by the Director General and request your appearance at the court. There is nothing—absolutely nothing—I can do for you this time. The complaint has been made. I will bring nothing further to their attention but, Marie, this is it—the end," retorted the sheriff, also versed in this game that we had played so many times before.

"We shall see," I said firmly. "Isaac must be on his way. So drink your beer and let me see the paper."

He obligingly handed me the summons with the charges outlined against me. The Director General had signed it himself this time. I sighed as I read the complaints. Once again, giving spirits to the Indians and tapping after hours were my main crimes.

Realistically, I knew my time in New Amsterdam was waning. I had succeeded in accomplishing many things that most people were unaware of. I needed to make some quick decisions. But they would be on my own terms, not those placed upon me by the Director General.

"Alida and Anna," I said, motioning them into the back room, "You wait here with the sheriff. I must also go and see someone quickly. I will be back. Hopefully, near the time Domingo brings in Isaac," I whispered. With that command, I threw on my cape and slipped out the back door.

CHAPTER THIRTY-THREE:

Marie's Story,
New Amsterdam, New Netherland,
January 1664

I combed through my long mane of hair and tightly pulled it into my cap, uncharacteristically trying to look the part of the remorseful citizen. For years, I'd run my tavern with playful disregard of the law, but I never did anything that the average townsperson did not want me to do. I provided a valuable service, but now I was desperate. I was down and out. But that is when the Director General made me suffer the most.

Wasn't it enough that my Jan had disappeared, leaving his children without a father and leaving me with the only means to provide for them—my tavern? Stuyvesant was attacking my family and my livelihood. The bastard had no heart. I'd go along with it, though. Isaac had warned me there was nothing I could do to change things. In reality, it would work out. I had to believe that.

I wondered if Stuyvesant was suspicious of me because I had a connection to Governor Winthrop through John Tinker. But in the end, I reasoned he was resentful of me for my blatant disrespect of his laws and his moral code. With the Munsee chief's threat, it was clear that he had no more patience for dealing with the likes of me, desperate situation or not!

This was it. I knew I wouldn't be able to believe my situation until I had to face it, pleading my case before Stuyvesant and the Council of New Netherland.

It was mid-morning when my family and I arrived at the fort for the Council session. We were bundled up in our woolens to keep warm in the coldest part of winter. Even the weather reflected the darkness of my personal ordeal. I trudged through the snow, silent with my children and my sisters surrounding me. It was a sullen day as gray as it could be. "To match my heart," I said sadly.

We walked into the building already filled with throngs of spectators eager for gossip. I approached the front bench and sat with my family members. Across from us were the wooden tables of the Council members and in the middle, another wooden table for Stuyvesant and his assistant. Stuyvesant looked cheerful, uncharacteristically smiling and talkative. It was clear he was keen to see me go. The sheriff had already shuttered my tavern and placed a notice of closure on its door.

The Council of New Netherland was called to session.

"Marie du Trieux, present yourself before the Council."

I stood and tried to appear calm although inside I was burning with rage.

"Hear the charges brought before you, Marie du Trieux."

"The defendant has a long history of disobeying the laws of tapping in New Amsterdam. She and her husband, Jan Peeck, were charged several times before for disorderly conduct, tapping after hours, tapping to Indians, tapping on the Sabbath. The defendant has been previously fined and disciplined. She has been given considerable chances repeatedly to correct her wayward actions, yet she chooses to go back to her aberrant and illegal behavior each time. After several warnings and continued infractions of the law, the Council petitions that the defendant be disciplined in a final and irrevocable sentence. What say you, Marie du Trieux? Please address these grievances to the Council of New Netherland a final time."

FINAL

That word rang in my head. I knew that there was nothing I could say to sway the court in my direction again. It was finished. Without thinking, I came forward and vowed to say whatever came to mind. They had already decided my fate. At least they thought they had.

"Gentlemen, you sit here and are supposedly representatives of justice, yet I know your minds are already made up that I should be punished a final time with no further chances," I said, my voice quivering.

"What kind of justice can be described if it is void of any compassion?" I asked.

I paused, hoping pointlessly that my question would sink into their hearts and move them to change their minds.

"Every single one of you knows that my husband has disappeared. I do not know if Jan is alive or dead!" I exclaimed, raising my fists in the air.

I stopped and took a couple of breaths, trying to stay strong.

"What I do know is that I am now a single woman who must use my assets to care for my children. You create laws that make it impossible to earn a competitive living. I am only catering to the citizens of New Amsterdam and their wants. The tavern is my only resource. Jan sold many of the properties he had been acquiring before he went missing. So you see, I must use my only resource to provide for my children. I have no other option. It is because I take my responsibilities for my children seriously that I have kept my tavern open. Please consider this," I said.

I glared at each of them, never taking away my gaze.

"Look into the faces of my children who rely on me. Go on, look at them!" I pleaded, gesturing to the space where my crying children sat witnessing the spectacle.

I went to sit down on the hard bench and heard all the murmurs and gossiping. My sister Rebecca squeezed my hand, and my youngest, my namesake, scrambled to sit on her mama's lap.

Stuyvesant talked to the Council and weighed the evidence against me. It was not long before Stuyvesant, in a rare move, requested to deliver the sentencing himself. He stood, fists clenched, relishing the moment where he could finally deliver his brand of justice to me.

In that instant, I knew. Stuyvesant had somehow believed that my tavern harbored all the rebels against him. How could he not know that almost the entire town opposed him when his back was turned? His measures to make peace with the Indians had come twenty years too late.

He stood stiffly and unrolled his decree against me.

"Marie du Trieux claims to break the law in order to care for her children. In effect, she is saying that she is teaching her children not to abide by the law and, in addition to that, to allow lax moral standards in her household. In consideration of these moral and legal admissions, the Council finds that it would better that your youngest children be placed into better care!" he declared arrogantly.

"Marie du Trieux, you are hereby banished from New Netherland FOREVER!" he pronounced.

"The Council members and especially I can no longer be tolerant of your antics! The Council will allow the orphan master to appoint a godparent to be guardian for your youngest children. They may stay in New Amsterdam with their guardians. Your older children may travel and settle in the colony as they wish," he said.

His last words to me were even more painful.

"As for you, Marie du Trieux, you may no longer reside in this city or the colony of New Netherland and have one month to decide what other alternative plans you wish to enact. You will come before the Council again in one month and request permission to either return to the fatherland or relocate to another place altogether. Until that time, it is ordered that your tavern, *The Salty Rose*, continue to be boarded up and be eventually sold in order to raise funds to care for your dependent children," he said, smug as he could be.

"That is all! Next case, please!" he shouted.

He stomped his wooden peg leg down on the hard wooden floor as if it were a gavel.

My family cried and surrounded me, sullenly filing out of the fort and into the deep cold. The finality of Stuyvesant's words stung me. His lack of compassion and false morality unnerved me even more. How can a man be so heartless as to not understand that if not for lack of bread, I might have been more willing to abide by the rules?

I didn't need a month to make a decision about where to go next. I resolved to act remorseful and plead to stay in the colony in its northernmost reaches. My older boys were in Beverwyck. Aernoudt was to be married, and Cornelis worked with him. Pierre was old enough to come with me and start a new life.

At my final appearance in front of the Council, I received permission to go north to be with them. My sisters begged the Council to be able to take care of my younger children, Anna, Johannes, Jacob, and Maria, until I could arrange to care for them in the upper reaches of the colony. Their requests were granted.

Late that afternoon, I made my way over to the cabinetmaker's workshop of my friends, Henri La Chaîne and his wife Claire. They had been preparing me for this moment and assured me to face the inevitable on the day the sheriff came with my arrest warrant. They were the ones whom I sought out while my daughters occupied the sheriff, and we waited for Isaac, my brother-in-law.

Now I would wait in Beverwyck for further directions and consider taking part in a life-altering mission. I hoped to make my way back to New Amsterdam one day despite Petrus Stuyvesant and his Council members. Convinced I was desperate, Stuyvesant, that clueless, proud leader, was completely unaware of what my return might mean.

CHAPTER THIRTY-FOUR:

Winthrop's Story
Long Island, New Netherland
June 1664

Winthrop rode his dark bay horse toward the next Long Island county to survey the lands given to Connecticut in its new charter. He would also meet with leaders in the closest town, ask for their pledge of allegiance to Connecticut, and instruct them to pay taxes to the colony as well.

The female Native leader, the powerful sachem, Quashawam, had already worked well to form agreements with English leaders in Southampton and other areas on eastern Long Island on behalf of the Montauk and Shinnecock tribes. Foolishly, the Dutch under Stuyvesant had failed to recognize her authority among her people and her networks, causing her to turn to the English instead. Based on his extensive communication and work with other Native leaders in New England, Winthrop thought he would be successful in negotiations with her as well.

Comfortable in that assessment, Winthrop let his mind roam to be with the concerns of his heart. He still couldn't stop thinking about John Tinker's death. It fed seeds of guilt that continued to sprout in his chest. Knowing for certain that foul play was involved, he sometimes questioned himself. Would Tinker's murder have happened if he hadn't stayed in England so long? Maybe John should have come to assist him in London.

No, he thought. That was impossible. Tinker kept watch over Mason and for certain one more life would have been lost during Hartford's witch panic had it not been for Tinker's involvement in the matter.

The only solace he had was the relief that Hugh Dyer had met his just end. Winthrop was glad that Henri La Chaîne communicated the details of his crime and bore witness to the fates who righted wrongs. Tinker could now rest in his grave, knowing that the criminal did not succeed in his evil plans to take over Tinker's business and ruin his family.

"You will not have died in vain, John. With the new charter, we are closer to finding the Passage. If it exists in reality, we are in a better position to find it than we have ever been. Be with me in spirit, dear friend. Be with me. Help me from above," he said, tilting his head upward toward the heavens.

Winthrop was also satisfied in having secured the release of Goody Seager and having restored some semblance of normalcy again in Hartford. Winthrop knew Seager's accusers still needed to be taken seriously in their doubts about her character, or they would continue their quest to see her hang by a noose.

With Winthrop's intervention, she was found guilty of adultery but not witchcraft. The townspeople were willing to listen to their newly returned governor. They were happy with him for bringing back the charter and were willing to go along with his recommendations. After all, Connecticut was on solid footing with the King and was expanding into new territory thanks to Winthrop.

Winthrop talked to many settlers and let them know that Long Island was soon to be unified under colonial Connecticut. He'd requested them to declare independence from New Netherland. Most of the English there were happy to hear that they would be citizens under Winthrop's new charter and were ready to pledge their allegiance to Connecticut and to the English Crown. But as he came towards western Long Island, word spread about his activities until it touched the farthest reaches of New Amsterdam and the fort.

Stuyvesant was becoming increasingly alarmed and sent word to the directors in Holland beseeching them to send more troops and supplies. The Dutch directors had responded that the English had contacted them, assuring them through the English ambassador, George Downing, that the fleets about to take off for America from England were only a practice show of force in order to have the backing needed to reorganize their colonies in New England under the King.

Winthrop as well had no idea what the English were really up to. Having been promised a generous charter, he was busy making that reality happen. Just a few miles from Hempstead coming from the east, he was caught off guard when John Underhill galloped up to him bearing a letter. Hearing the rapid beat of horse's hooves, Winthrop stopped and turned around.

"Governor Winthrop, sir!" Underhill shouted and slowed his horse to stop next to him. "I must speak with you immediately. I've an official letter for you, sir."

"What is it, Underhill? I'm in the midst of letting the Long Islanders know their land is now under Connecticut's jurisdiction. What do you want?" he asked.

"A change is coming, sir. The English are on their way to settle the government and to reduce the Dutch," Underhill explained.

"What? You say a fleet of English ships is on its way?" asked Winthrop in disbelief.

"Aye, King Charles, in counsel with his brother, realized you weren't going to be uniting the New England colonies for him any time soon. So much for the charter! He gave most of Connecticut to his brother, James, the Duke of York. All of what you see now belongs to James. Aye, the whole of Long Island and more! James must have been pushing his brother hard—not letting him forget everything that the colonists did to help those that killed their father. James doesn't believe a Puritan would help a Royal do anything. He reminded Charles of this, I'm sure. And now four ships, all under the command of Colonel Nicolls, are coming to help James, the Duke of York, claim his land for him.

"And what of Connecticut and its standing? What of Connecticut's charter precisely? What of its borders defined therein?" demanded Winthrop, stunned by the massive blow to his plans.

"Connecticut's been cut down to a smaller size, sir. Territory west of the Great River is now under the jurisdiction of James, Duke of York. His patent also includes land to the north as far as Maine and to the south as far as the Delaware River," said Underhill.

Winthrop must have looked shocked. His body was charged with alarm. The months spent on political maneuvering in England before the King, and the gift of his grandfather's golden ring. The death of his trusted friend John Tinker. Could it have all been in vain? he thought.

"No! How can this be?" he shouted incredulously.

"Aye. It is. I must tell you," answered Underhill. "The fleet of four English ships has come with five hundred soldiers and a thousand small arms. The King has abandoned the agreement he made with you. Massachusetts will resist the King's authority. I do not doubt that," said Underhill, taking off his hat before continuing.

"As for taking over New Netherland, it could be a bloody fight. Our English have been waiting to squash the damn Dutch and their stubborn leader Stuyvesant. And James wants what was gifted to him by the King. He's declared as much, and he's directed it be taken by whatever measures complete the task. The Dutch have no idea of the sheer force that's coming their way. The English are ready to claim their empire.

"Listen to me, Captain Underhill, there will be no bloodshed and no violence if I have anything to do with it. There must be another way," shouted Winthrop, still distraught by the distressing news.

Winthrop reeled in his laboratory, thinking of the radically changed charter. Over half of Connecticut was to be taken away and given as part of the patent to James, the King's brother. Even New Haven was to be a part of the royal brother's acquisitions. Governor Leete would no doubt be stunned by the news as well.

Winthrop was advised to return to Connecticut and await further instruction. It was a humid evening in July when Winthrop finally received a packet of letters from the British fleet anchored at Nantasket Point close to Boston.

Staring at the packet that his servant, Mercy, placed on his desk that afternoon, he was loath to open it. He wished he could ignore the letters. But Winthrop, wise as he was and well-seasoned in diplomacy, knew it best to discover the contents and then assess the damage to his own plans. One after the other, he took a deep breath as he carefully opened them.

The first from his colleague, the President of the Royal Society, implored Winthrop to assist Colonel Nicolls on his royal mission for the

King and to cultivate their relationship through a commonality of natural philosophy. He implored Winthrop to come to the aid of Nicolls, clearly letting him know that actions in any other direction would be foolish.

"My fate is now set in another direction than had been promised. What can I do but acquiesce to His Majesty's demands?" he asked somberly.

Another letter held the seal of the King. It was a demand letter sent to each governor affirming the intentions of the Crown to reorganize colonial administrators in a way most befitting to the royal goals of expanding the empire and taking firmer control of its colonies. Any hope of an alternative plan was quickly evaporating as he read on.

Finally, a letter from his long-time friend, Robert Boyle, dated from April strongly advised him to cooperate.

"Make yourself available to Colonel Nicolls, the envoy of the King. Be useful to His Majesty's service. Show loyalty and affection, not merely obedience."

Boyle assured him that the Crown did not mean to completely abolish his charter or dissolve religious freedoms so long as the colonies would grant liberty of conscience to all citizens in accordance with current English laws. In this, Winthrop knew cooperation with Colonel Nicolls would be the only way that he could maintain any autonomy of his colony.

It was a lot for Winthrop to take in. He wished John Tinker was still around to speak with him in secrecy about the unexpected dilemma. After much turmoil, he wrote letters back, stating his intention to help Nicolls. It was only from a standpoint of good graces that he could go on unmolested and hope to succeed with his own plans, albeit altered ones. The messages in the letters were clear; it was necessary to be deferential to the English Crown's plans or risk losing everything.

Winthrop retreated to his study and read volumes of philosophy and alchemical works. In the evening, he returned to the open skies over Hartford with his three and a half foot telescope. He still needed a spiritual sign, a heavenly nod that this was the path he must take.

On the 6th of August 1664, while looking through the largest telescope ever brought to New England, Winthrop saw a majestic sight. Along with four known moons, the fifth moon of Jupiter appeared.

Observing the night sky, he was stupefied by what he saw. He wondered if he could be mistaking it for a star. But every time he looked and tried to discern if the object was simply conjunct to the great planet by a slightly greater light, it was not.

"It must be another moon," he murmured.

He looked to the great beyond with awe and wonder.

"A message from other dimensions that all will work out well," he whispered in reverence. "It makes sense now. Jupiter, the ever-expanding planet, mirrors the expanding British Empire. Jupiter brings with it opportunity, generosity, and goodness. It commands the night sky and is a great benefactor of divine grace and light."

He paused, thinking of the meaning of five moons.

"Of course, the five comes out of the four of stability and upsets the status quo. It signifies movement and instability at first. Five signifies something new and the unexpected, with huge changes ahead," he said aloud, amazed by the symbolism.

"The heavens have spoken. The fates are sealed. I must follow the path that's been laid before me."

And so it was with a sense of inner peace that Winthrop was able to go meet Nicolls on Long Island. He hoped to extend that peace to the populace of New Netherland and avoid unnecessary bloodshed and war.

He'd make plans to leave a little earlier. There was something that was important for him to do before he met Colonel Nicolls in Gravesend.

The fifth moon of Jupiter danced in his heart and assured him on his journey.

CHAPTER THIRTY-FIVE:

Marie's Story
Beverwyck, New Netherland
Summer, 1664

By messenger, I'd received word that my sons, Cornelis, Aernoudt, and their little brother Pierre, were on their way back from their trading expedition to engage the Mohawks. Pierre had tagged along to learn what he could. Of course, I agreed to let him go with them shortly after we arrived in Beverwyck.

Excited to see my boys again, I got a kettle going with water. Singing an old Walloon song of homecoming way too loudly, I thought about our impending reunion. I soaked rags in the warmed water, cleaning our modest wooden cottage in anticipation of their arrival. I was curious as to why their trip was shorter than originally planned.

I hadn't anticipated that their premature return was the result of the news about my beloved Jan, lost to the wilderness for over two years. Aernoudt, through his many Native contacts, sent word of his disappearance and made inquiries. Weeks passed, but finally an emissary for the Mohawk tribe showed up at my sons' trading camp bearing news of Jan.

As my boys entered our cottage, I sensed immediately that something was wrong.

"Hello, Mama." Aernoudt kissed me and then took my hands gently as the other two boys looked on somberly. Aernoudt placed an intricate necklace of bone and beads into my hands.

"What is this?" I asked. "Tell me right away. You know something about Jan," I guessed, with both anguish and relief in my voice.

They nodded grimly before proceeding to tell me the story.

In the late spring of 1664, after an early thaw, Jan's frozen body, previously hidden under ice and snow in a crevice, pinned against a bolder, and largely decayed from the previous two seasons, sat waiting to be discovered at the base of a mountain. I understood it was a grisly sight, but those who had traded with Jan verified that it was he, without a doubt. He'd worn the distinctive necklace of bones and beads traded in the spring of 1662 from a chief in the Mohawk tribe. His skeletal remains, adorned with that unique ornamentation around his neck, held the final proof that the cadaver was my Jan.

The Mohawk emissary had explained to them that it looked like Jan had lost his balance at the edge of a cliff. Up from the cliff where he fell were remnants of where a large rock dislodged, tumbling after Jan on his fall down the mountain. When it caught up to his body, it pinned him against the rocky precipice near the ground where he was found.

"No! My Jan! How can this be?" I collapsed into my Aernoudt's arms and cried uncontrollably with the painful knowledge of Jan's bitter end. "You are really gone, my love."

I had already grieved for almost two years, not knowing whether Jan was alive or dead, not knowing if he'd run off with an Indian maiden to leave me alone with the struggles we'd once faced together in the tavern. Although I hated that Jan died in such a gruesome way, I was glad that his death was instantaneous and he was probably on his way home to me when the accident led to his mortal end. I could finally be at peace, knowing what happened and that my husband was still true to me.

I could see the moon, full and large through the little window near my bed that night. "We will still think of each other when we see the moon, my love," I whispered, recalling the last conversation we had before he left on his trading trip. We promised to think of each other every time we observed the celestial orb. It would connect us. As I looked at it more intently, remembering my love, I knew what he would want me to do.

With the realization that Jan was forever gone from this world and that I bore sole responsibility for keeping my family together, I made the final fateful decision to leave Beverwyck and seek out Governor Winthrop.

I turned the corner and hurried to the little bakery. I needed some extra bread for the journey. With travel arranged for Pierre and me, I needed to take care of some provisions. I wanted to think clearly, and hunger would not help me accomplish the mission. Mathias, the baker, caught my glance his way.

"Good day, Mr. Van Ginkel. I'll take four loaves of bread today. My sons are about to leave on another trip up north. They'll need it for their sustenance," I explained.

The grizzled old baker peered at me with a quizzical expression from behind his simple display of breads, pretzels, and sweet rolls. Moments passed in what seemed like an eternity.

He stared at me as if he knew I was lying. Indeed, I would be the one traveling under disguise to reach Governor Winthrop.

Damn the old baker, I thought. Just give me the bread! I screamed inside my head, trying to remain as outwardly calm as possible. He took my basket in slow motion and filled it without saying a word, finally raising four fingers to indicate how much I owed him.

I placed the coins in his cold hands, relieved that he didn't question me for more details. I thanked Mr. Van Ginkel, clasped my basket, and rushed home to make the final arrangements with Pierre.

Without the constant worry for Jan, my mind was free to contemplate my own destiny and go back to the life that I was desperate to reassemble. I hoped it would be possible. News from downriver had become increasingly fearful that the English would strike at the heart of New Amsterdam. Travelers from there brought news of heightened anxieties and concerns.

It was almost time to go to John Winthrop—almost time to reveal my identity and set my plan in motion. I knew that there might be something I could do to help my family at the same time I acted to bring safety to help the town I loved. Finding out Jan was dead only strengthened my resolve to be a part of something much bigger than myself. Jan's death was a sign that cast out all doubt about my participation to take New Amsterdam in a new direction.

My plan depended on Winthrop. Would he recognize my name when I presented myself to him? Would he understand the role I had already played in finding his former assistant's assailant? Would he appreciate my role in bringing some justice to John Tinker's killer and in the colonial drama unfolding? Thoughts tumbled over my brow only to be revisited minutes later.

Days before, I sent an Indian scout to determine the whereabouts of Winthrop. As governor of Connecticut, he normally resided in Hartford. The word was that months after courting the royal ego of the King, Winthrop, with his finesse and charisma, had coaxed a new charter for Connecticut from the King's hands. It was a charter that included all of Long Island and the biggest prize of all, the jewel of New Amsterdam.

I knew that New Amsterdam was completely unprepared for an English invasion. The dilapidated fort and a populace in love with trade and distasteful of war would not serve as barriers to an English takeover. Winthrop's own amiable charm with the English settlers on Dutch parts of Long Island would be a challenging match for the certain resistance and stubbornness of Stuyvesant to preserve the land he lorded over for almost twenty years.

I would take advantage of the history about to be made. I wanted to grab it by the reins and be the queen of my own destiny instead of the victim of it. It was the only way for me to return to my beloved town and the only way to save it from both Stuyvesant and English aggressors. Winthrop wasn't like most of the English. That was my understanding of him from both John Tinker and Henri La Chaîne.

I had received news the previous night from Henri and Claire that it was time for me to go to Winthrop directly with his current location. Their previous plan had changed suddenly and they stressed that it was critical I see Winthrop in person.

I hurried to finish getting ready so that I could connect my own path with his. I'd heard previously through my friends that Winthrop was confident with his charter and decided to go to Long Island to talk to his new citizens. He started in the east but was slowly making his way to Flushing to see Reverend Doughty, the archrival of Stuyvesant, the man who brought grievances of religious intolerance, the father-in-law of the late Adriaen van der Donck.

I hoped to play my part as requested by my friends Henri and Claire La Chaîne. However, I'd make sure that what I valued the most would be my ultimate prize for helping them—a return to the center of my family in the town I loved. Only Winthrop could ensure this fate so I'd make sure to convince him of the need to include me in his plans.

Returning home with the bread, I called out to Pierre who had agreed to go to New Amsterdam ahead of me.

"Pierre, son, make haste for your mother. We have work to do. I have business to take care of on Long Island. I've arranged for a vessel that is waiting at the dock to take you to New Amsterdam where you will go back to the rest of the family. It is only temporary. You may come back to be with your brothers shortly if you so wish."

Pierre came to me. He was loyal and steadfast in his support for me. I asked him to forego another trip with his brothers up north to help me a final time. He agreed as a dutiful son does. I was his mother, and he would fiercely defend me and be at my side until the end.

I gently held his chin in my hand.

"Pretend that the only purpose of your return to New Amsterdam is to visit family. Once you get there, you will find Domingo. Do not give information about this to anyone," I instructed him.

"Is that all you ask of me, Mama?"

"No. It's not that simple," I said. "Once you see Domingo, tell him to meet me in the shed behind the tavern with extra provisions. I'll need a place to hide and a boat ready to take me to Long Island. Your absolute silence and discretion will save my life. Revealing anything to anyone other than Domingo may put me in great jeopardy. Do you understand?" I questioned him firmly.

"Yes, Mama. And what happens after that? Is there nothing else I can do?" Pierre asked.

"You will stay in New Amsterdam with your sisters and younger brother in your Aunt Sarah's home and say only that you've come for a visit. Tell them I send my regards. They know I am forbidden from returning so will not question my absence," I said.

Pierre nodded in understanding and quickly prepared a satchel with some of the bread I just purchased.

I was satisfied with my decision. I would find Winthrop and offer my assistance, knowing that he had the power to help me return home, the power to guide New Amsterdam gently from the hands of rigid Stuyvesant into a future of peace and prosperity. But he'd have to meet my conditions and understand the unique and important ways that I could help him take control of the new territories outlined in his charter.

I reasoned silently. It will be a future without the rigid rule of that peg-legged tyrant. He cared too little for the citizens that built New Amsterdam.

Stuyvesant's disdain for Jan and I will be avenged. How could he come after me as he did, vulnerable without my husband who had disappeared into the wilderness without a trace? He knew I had young mouths to feed, yet he cared not. I will never forgive him for that. Life in New Amsterdam will be better without him!

I kissed Pierre on the cheek as he left and urged him not to worry. "We will be together soon enough," I assured him. "There is no need to worry. You shall see," I winked and ushered him out the door.

Returning to my preparations, I put a few more provisions into my sack, a drinking cup and some dried meat and berries. I pulled out my light linen traveling cloak with a hood and my French cap, tucking my brunette hair inside it for disguise. There was one last thing I needed.

Out of a decorated little box, I grabbed a tiny velvet bag and pulled out a ring given to me by Jan. I knew wearing it would ensure my success.

As I tied my traveling sack closed, I knew I had transformed to more than a rebellious tavern keeper. I'd made up my mind to become an agent and informant for a secret society, a society that supported Winthrop and his dream of finding an important passage to the East.

It all started with the disappearance of Jan, the love of my life, and the appearance of friends who led me to my fate.

After Jan had disappeared into the woods forever, I was afraid. My life had collapsed into ruins. The orphanage had threatened to place my youngest children in the care of their godparents if Jan did not appear again soon. It was a low and desperate point in my life.

So, it was by grace that I still aspire to understand why Mr. Henri La Chaîne and his wife, Claire, regulars at my tavern, revealed their true selves to me. They were from France and had lived through a Catholic siege against Protestants at La Rochelle, the same kind of persecution that had led my father to bring his family to Holland years before.

Before they came into my tavern on that fateful day months after Jan had vanished without a trace, it was quiet. Domingo was outside chopping wood. I had just been warned again not to sell spirits to my Native friends. Rumors abound, and people around town knew I was being watched mercilessly. Even regular customers started to come less frequently to avoid an association with my troubles, hoping to evade any consequences for their own indiscretions.

I rarely cried but I did that day. Stopping my tasks to rest at one of the empty tables, I allowed a torrent of tears to run freely for the first time in years. I no longer had the backbone to take anything that came my way. I'd endured my whole life but the reality of missing my love and his probable death in the woods, drowning in a flooding river, or worse—desertion, hit me hard that day. I let down my guard, believing no one would come into my tavern. It was in that moment of despair that my two angels found me.

Henri and Claire came up to me directly. They spoke to me in the language close to my mother tongue, a dialect similar to what I knew as a child with parents from northern France.

Claire placed a soft hand on my shoulder.

"There now, Marie. Let it out, you will be whole again. We know all about you, dear Marie, more than most of your customers," she smiled.

Startled, I looked up with reddened eyes and studied the compassionate faces of old customers who now looked different to me. They know something about me? What does that mean? I tried to imagine what other trouble I might find myself in. But quickly I felt even calmer around them than I normally did. I was not afraid of what came next.

"Do not worry. We mean you no harm. We are here to help you," assured Henri. "We are more than cabinetmakers, Marie. There are others like us. We are inviting you to be one of us," Claire said.

One of them? I thought in a state of confusion.

"There is also more to you than you realize in this moment. But we have seen the signs. We were led to you for a special purpose. Outside your tavern are the beautiful sea roses that you safeguard and spread with care," said Henri.

"Yes," I murmured, still perplexed. "Almost impossible with some of the drunkards I serve, but everyone knows not to touch my roses."

"Even the name of your tavern, *The Salty Rose*, speaks to your destiny and its place at the crossing into New Amsterdam from Breukelen." Claire added.

"When my first husband named the tavern, it was after me. He called me his sassy, salty rose. He said the sea roses were an extension of me," I smiled, still unsure of what was taking place. At least I felt momentarily better in their presence.

But as I looked around at my largely empty tavern, a feeling of hollowness and doubt overtook me again.

"What destiny? You mean destitution, which is where I will be if my husband is not alive and does not return shortly. If I do not figure out a way to earn a better living, my youngest children will be taken from me. I can find nothing of importance in my life which would lead you to seek me out," I said, still baffled by our conversation.

"No, no." Henri shook his head, "Out of darkness, light will emerge once more. It is the law of nature. You are a flame for justice, Marie. You sought justice for both the Varlets and John Tinker. In making sacrifices to help both of them, you have gained powerful allies. Sometimes those who pull humanity forward suffer the most. But it will not be in vain. And you will have peace in your final years," he offered.

"Dear Marie, you must listen carefully, you must prepare because there is something important you must do a few months from now. Things do not always appear as they really are. You may be separated from some of your children in the near future, but they will be back with you sooner than you realize," explained Claire.

But how can you know of this? How can this be real?" I asked, still confused.

"Dear one, we will teach you everything you need to learn. Please know your actions will save the lives of hundreds of people and bring great prosperity and safety to your community. And you will become that which you were destined to become, a wise woman who will lay the spiritual stonework of a path leading to the future," Claire assured me.

As Claire finished speaking, I felt bemused. In that moment, I could not begin to understand the depths of human history and spirituality that they were trying to present to me. I know they were sincere and had thought they'd seen the correct signs, but me fulfilling a spiritual purpose? I did not see such a vision.

"I do not see myself as you do. In fact, I cannot imagine what you see but I have come to love both of you, my dear friends, over many years. As long as what you envision brings peace instead of endless war, I will consider helping you in your quest, but I will need more information," I said

"The details will come in time. We will tell you everything you need to know," Claire assured me.

A dragonfly gently flew over the dancing waters of the East River in that moment, twinkling from rays of sunlight. Despite my doubts about Henri and Claire's assertions of my destiny, they were kind and willing to help me out of my dire circumstances. And thus was my introduction to the ideas of the members of the Rosy Cross, the Rosicrucians, and their efforts to recruit me to their cause—changing the governance of New Amsterdam to forge a destiny that involved bringing the world together and finding a special passage. I did not quite understand it but thought my involvement with them might be my only path to come back home.

With those memories, I lifted my traveling sack to my shoulder and left the cabin. I took the path down from the fort where a small boat was waiting for me in the shadows of a large willow tree. Excited and nervous, I hoped to find my way to Winthrop.

CHAPTER THIRTY-SIX:

Marie's Story
Long Island, New Netherland
Summer, 1664

The boat dropped us off at the landing in Flushing not far from Reverend Francis Doughty's home. Domingo insisted on escorting me there. He had been a friend to me in my greatest hour of need. Once we arrived at the dock, his friend, who agreed to take me there on his tiny sailboat, escorted me off of it and wished me well.

I felt it better that Domingo went back to Manhattan lest someone recognize us. I was afraid somebody would place him from the tavern. I thanked him and assured him that we would meet again soon, even if I wasn't sure exactly when.

I was happy. It seemed that everything was going according to plan. I sensed invisible hands along my path that kept me safe from harm's way and assured me of the success of my mission. I like to think they were Jan's. I walked alone on the dirt road close to the dock for only a short time before meeting someone who guided me to what I thought would be Reverend Doughty's home.

During my brief time alone I thought of John Tinker and the things I remembered about him. As I learned more about the Rosy Cross and the alchemists and helpers that were part of this society, it slowly became clear that he worked in alchemy too. I once noticed the strange ring John Tinker wore that matched the symbols on the boxes he brought to his boss but brushed it aside without much thought. But now I knew that Winthrop was considered a master alchemist. I learned that he started New London as an alchemy center and John Tinker, my dear friend, had devoted most of his life to helping this man to achieve his visions in the New World.

I'd seen Winthrop once before when he came to New Amsterdam on his way back to England to meet with the new king. Would he be willing to see me? I still had to be careful because nothing was for certain. If my plans went the wrong way, I could be named as a traitor and then the only part of New Amsterdam I would see would be the inside of the jail at the fort.

On the other hand, Winthrop could dismiss me, paying no mind to a simple tapper who'd been banished as a criminal. For the first time in my life, I felt a little daunted at meeting such a man, someone who had the admiration of many. I knew the significant moment when we met would set the stage for the rest of my life and those of others as well.

"Madame, I am Annette. We have been waiting for you. Claire advised me of your coming," a slight woman of blonde hair and angelic blue eyes explained. "I recognized you from your linen traveling cloak. It was given to you by Claire, was it not?"

"Yes," I told her, finally realizing that what was about to happen was so much bigger than I had ever fathomed.

She stared at me and nodded slightly.

"Welcome, Marie. You will have what you need. Winthrop has been advised that you are coming to see him. We cannot meet at Doughty's home. There are too many people there, and some may recognize you. I am taking you to another place that is necessarily clandestine," she whispered.

I looked carefully at my surroundings. A little Dutch cottage with three dormers peeking out from its roof came into view. It sat on the edge of woods overlooking rolling hills of farmland and the vast sound of Long Island to the north. I sensed that we were walking at the most remote corners of the county. As we approached the cottage, my heart raced a few beats faster.

After a sharp curve on the dirt road that led to a barn, I saw a man of small stature sitting in a chair next to a garden in full bloom. A table was before him. As we approached him, one book was ajar as he took notes onto a parchment. An apple tree laden with ripening fruit stood behind him, completing the scene that will forever be etched in my mind.

As he heard the faint, gentle strides approaching him, he stood from his chair and turned to receive us. He nodded as we curtsied in greeting.

"I have been waiting for you," he said.

Annette officially introduced us.

"Governor Winthrop, this is Marie du Trieux. Marie, this is Governor John Winthrop of Connecticut."

"A pleasure," I stated. "Governor Winthrop, I knew it was fate that I must see you."

He calmly regarded me and, with a faint smile, answered.

"Aye, I received word of your arrival, Madame du Trieux. Please come sit by the garden.

He was charming and smooth as well as reserved and intelligent, a master statesman. He had to be, in order to be able to talk the King of England, Charles II, into exactly what he wanted and even more.

"Governor Winthrop, please call me Marie.

"Please leave us for a time," Winthrop instructed Annette, the young woman who brought me there. She nodded and obliged. He paused until she had disappeared into the house.

"Tell me fully why you are here. Have you made your decision?" he said.

I nodded slowly. "I do not know what you know about me, but I was a friend of your associate and assistant, John Tinker, as was my husband, Jan Peeck, a fellow trader and part Englishman."

"Yes, Madame du Trieux, Marie, I'm aware of that friendship. I am also aware of the many kindnesses you and your husband bestowed upon him. John Tinker was dear to me. He was my most trusted ally, someone who worked for my father and then for me for twenty-five years. His death was a shock and a personal tragedy. I am also aware of your conveyance of information about what happened in his untimely and unnatural death. I found out that you sought justice for it, making sure I received pertinent information. It is for this that I am most grateful to you," he explained.

"Yes, sir." I stopped and drank a sip or two of cider that was offered to me from the table as he studied me even more.

"All right, Marie, now that you know of my benevolence toward you, have you decided to help us?" he asked, assessing my intentions.

"Sir, all of New Amsterdam, in actuality all of New Netherland, knows of the charter you procured from the English King that logically makes you governor of Long Island, New Amsterdam, and New Netherland, should the English enforce that charter. Frankly, everyone fears it is a matter of time. The Dutch don't care for war, sir. Stuyvesant is weak. I tell you nothing you do not already know and, for this, I will not feel treachery against my own former home," I said.

"Former home? Please tell me what happened Marie."

"I was banished, sir, but please do not think of me as a common criminal. My husband, Jan, disappeared into the wilderness. I now know he is dead for certain. With no bread and many mouths to feed, I sold spirits at my tavern when I could to whoever was thirsty. I was warned many times by the Dutch authorities to abide by their rules."

I paused and smoothed my skirts, hoping that he would understand the predicament I'd found myself in.

"In truth, it had never mattered before. It was a new pact with the Munsee Indians that changed the colony's leaders' approach to me and other tavern keepers. The Munsee sachem complained that alcohol was hurting his community, and Stuyvesant was desperate for an agreement with him to keep further Indian wars at bay. It's complicated, sir, but a mother must feed her children. I want to come back to New Amsterdam when the English take over," I stated.

"I assure you, I will help you with a peaceful transfer to the English if you can promise me that and rights for my people," I continued.

Winthrop listened intently to me, posing questions to better inform his decision. Even though I was talking quickly and fighting for my ultimate salvation with every word, I sensed that he already knew most of what I was confessing to him.

"What became of you after you were forced into banishment?"

"Governor Winthrop, I went to Beverwyck with some of my sons near Fort Orange. They are traders and translators. Since they were little, they've known the Indians in that region. But I miss my little ones, most of whom stay with my sister Sarah and her husband, Isaac de Forest. He is a brewer and a burgomaster. You see, Governor Winthrop, none of that matters now," I said. "What matters is that I can help you."

"Tell me specifically how you can help me," Winthrop requested.

"Governor, I know everyone in New Amsterdam, from the lowly servant to the wealthy merchant to burgomasters such as my brother-in-law. I have connections to almost everyone in town. And more than that,

I know their secrets as many good tavern keepers do. I can convince the populace, with the right conditions, that life would be better under English rule. I am the connection you need to the people of New Amsterdam for I am trusted despite my banishment. Most importantly, I can be the one to go directly to the wives of important Council members—the people closest to Stuyvesant," I said, convincing him of the desirability of my involvement with his plans.

He nodded and studied my face carefully as I spoke.

"Governor Winthrop. You must already know, sir. Henri La Chaîne and his wife Claire aided me and requested that I be an informant for your movement. It is through them that I became introduced to members of the Rosy Cross. I pledge my loyalty to you and Connecticut, Governor Winthrop. But I further ask that you protect my family, my friends, and all the citizens of New Amsterdam. They will not fight you if you preserve their lives and their way of life. Please, if the English take over as I know they will, make it peaceful and free of bloodshed," I beseeched him.

His eyes became a little brighter with compassion, and he smiled gently at me.

"I understand your wishes, Marie. I will do what I can but I cannot give an absolute promise to anything. Have you not heard? The desires of the King have changed my plans. The power to annex New Amsterdam and the rest of Long Island into Connecticut rests no longer in my hands. The King, disappointed that I did not use the charter to place all of New England under one rule, gave most of what he promised to Connecticut to his conniving brother James, Duke of York, instead. Underhill notified me that ships sent by James are already on the way. My only assurance to you is that I will work with Colonel Nicolls, the man who has command of those ships, to negotiate a peace," Winthrop explained.

I was stunned. This new information had to be the reason Henri and Claire requested that I see Winthrop in person. Before that moment, I thought Winthrop could do anything. But even he, despite his charms, his intelligence, and the power of his alchemical practice, was also at the whims of the King of England. As powerful as Winthrop was, he also knew betrayal.

"Marie, I know Henri La Chaîne well, as I do Claire and others who have been protecting you and coming to your aid. I was there when the

Catholics seized La Rochelle. It greatly impacted my life, and I have held a kinship with those that were there and resisted, including Henri and Claire. Be faithful and remember that a peaceful unification of the two colonies is still possible," Winthrop said.

I listened intently, trying to understand what else I could do.

"Will you still pledge your loyalty to me and agree to work for the Rosy Cross in an underground capacity? No one will give up, but we will need to work secretly. I will strive to make the transition into English hands as peaceful as possible and also request that your return be granted, but you must promise me several things first," he clarified.

"Yes, of course, Governor Winthrop. I want nothing more than to give my assistance, provided my own conditions are met. Henri and Claire told me I had a part to play. I have made my decision to be involved and ensure the transfer of New Amsterdam is peaceful. Whether that transfer happens under the government of Connecticut or the King of England, I am committed to a peaceful end result.

It was genuine. I truly wanted to help in a way that was most conducive to peace, given the fact that the King's brother would take over no matter what. I knew New Amsterdam would not have the reserves or the will to fight. The Dutch West India Company had treated us as orphans from the fatherland. Stuyvesant had warned them of English hostilities to no avail. Despite some attempts to protect us, Stuyvesant ruled with too much disregard of his citizens. He was too much of an autocrat for our liking. As long as the English left us alone to live as we had for decades, I hoped a peaceful takeover would be possible.

"This is what you must do for me, Marie. Say nothing of our meeting. Keep your secret knowledge of the Rosy Cross, its members and its ancient teachings hidden. You will stay here at this house until you are called upon. I understand John Tinker helped to save Judith Varlet's life from witchcraft conviction before he died. And for that she is indebted to you," he said.

My gaze did not wander from Winthrop's face. I listened intently, trying to grasp every word.

"John Tinker left me a coded letter that explained your role in notifying him of the Varlet woman's peril when negotiations between Stuyvesant and Mason were unfruitful. You also played a part in convincing Nicolas to bring the situation to Stuyvesant's attention again in a way that convinced him that it was through his renewed diplomacy that Judith was finally released."

"I wanted to help them. It was not hard to do," I said.

Winthrop smiled.

"It wasn't hard for you but it would have been difficult for others. You did not shy away from involvement. Furthermore, you convinced others to be of help as well. In light of this recent history, I agree that you will be an important connection between the English and the people of New Amsterdam. Are you ready for your mission?" he asked.

I beamed with pride and renewed confidence as I faced him.

"Yes, I've been ready," I said.

He nodded and continued.

"As the English ships approach, you will notify and convince your brother-in-law Isaac and the Varlets, through Judith, that a peaceful agreement can be made without firing a single cannon shot," he said.

"You are right, Marie. Your position as a former tavern keeper in New Amsterdam who has connections there will be invaluable in making the takeover as smooth and peaceful as possible," he added.

He was silent for a few moments as he stroked his chin in thought and stood up.

"Being quite familiar with the proud Stuyvesant, I recognize that only voices from inside the gates of New Amsterdam will have any impact on the stubborn man. Yours will be the voice of reason from inside New Amsterdam. It will be the voice that reassures the townspeople and lets them know that peace is still possible—that preservation of their way of life is still possible," he said. "With the assurance that they are on board with a new direction under the English, I can better negotiate with Colonel Nicolls for a peaceful transfer, an advantageous one to your people."

I stood up also, wishing to show him that I was up to the task he was describing.

He continued. "You will know best the means to convince them. More communication will follow. For now, I will not reveal your true identity to the leader in command. I will only say that you are an informant from the other side. I will ask that the terms of capitulation be as generous to the citizens of the Dutch city as possible."

My heart felt lighter in that moment. I was convinced that if anyone could pull off this feat it would be Winthrop. He was no fan of war or bloodshed either. He was unlike Englishmen such as Underhill who reveled in murder and subjugation.

"Yes, I can do that, Governor Winthrop. Is there anything else?" I asked.

"Aye, Marie. Your elder sons, the traders, the ones who frequently explore the Indian lands to the Northwest at the edges of the North River, have they ever mentioned a passage that leads far north from somewhere in the interior of New Netherland, even near New Amsterdam itself?"

"I know not, Governor Winthrop, but I do know the Dutch have only just begun to explore what is there. Their armies have stayed close to the North River. With all the Indian wars, people hesitate to journey too far into the interior, fearing more trouble," I explained.

"My sons say the wilderness stretches well beyond anything that one can imagine. They've recounted to me tales of multiple green valleys, rich forests, and waterways tumbling into ever-deepening wilderness. Perhaps with established peace between the Dutch and the English more jewels of nature will be known, and passages to new and wonderful places can be explored," I said.

He smiled more widely than he had all day. I felt the warmth and promise of it settle on my face.

"And may your sons be a part of the great discoveries, Marie. Perhaps they will be involved in helping to find the Passage, that great trade route which will connect the East Indies to the West Indies, he said and continued.

"It is prophesied that when the completed circle of the world is navigated, the elusive Philosopher's Stone can finally be found, bringing forth conditions for spiritual purification, unification, and worldwide reformation. Did Henri and Claire teach you about the Stone?" he asked.

I nodded my head. "Yes, sir, they told me of its importance," I said.

"The magical substance that can change lead into gold, the elixir of life that can heal all illness and purify the hearts of men. I am happy to be part of the noble quest to enable it to be found," Winthrop said.

Winthrop grinned and seemed pleased. I'm sure he was hopeful that with the imminent fall of New Amsterdam, he would be that much closer to finding the Passage. I hoped my sons could share the honor of finding it with others after the English took over.

"If our mission is successful, will you recommend and include my sons in expeditions to look for the Passage?"

"I will indeed," he said. "I must go now. You will stay here in this cottage until you are called upon. It won't be long. Annette is here to help you until that time," said Winthrop.

With that, he closed his book, placed it and his rolled-up parcel into his case. A man whom I hadn't seen before came out of the barn with a horse freshly saddled for Winthrop to ride. He mounted the horse and took off his hat in a gesture of final greeting to me. That was not the last time I saw Governor Winthrop. It was quite an impression that he had on me. I hoped he'd remember everything we'd talked about. But, ultimately, it was out of my control. There was nothing left to do but wait and hope that peace would prevail and I'd return to my home in New Amsterdam shortly. I'd eagerly wait for my next move.

CHAPTER THIRTY-SEVEN:

Marie's Story
New Amsterdam, New Netherland
August 1664

She was almost next to me before I heard her footsteps. To my great surprise, I saw my old friend from *The Salty Rose*.

"Marie, it is time," she said. Claire appeared on a day of oppressing heat at the end of August. I was in the front of the farmhouse under the apple tree in an attempt to stay cool. I admired the deepening colors of its fruit, ripening for a September harvest. I had been preparing myself for my own harvest of sorts.

I turned to see her there standing next to Annette. I could barely believe that I was about to begin my role as an informant for their group.

"Claire! It brings me such joy to see you! Where is Henri?" I asked.

"Marie, we all have our part to play. I cannot tell you for your own protection, but do not worry. You will meet him again," she explained.

"The important thing to know is that it is time for you to help change the course of history. It is time to go," she said.

It was the notification I'd been waiting for.

Annette clarified, "Governor Winthrop has left for Gravesend to meet Colonel Nicolls and his fleet of ships. You must make haste for New Amsterdam. A small vessel is waiting to take you to the ferry across from your old tavern. We have people who have told your sister to be there waiting. From there she will bring you to her home near the waterfront. It will be the central location where you may meet with others who can influence Stuyvesant. If you go back to your own home, people may alert the authorities. In any case, you must be closer to the fort and the city center," she explained.

I nodded. My heart was racing, caught up in the intensity of the moment as Claire continued.

"Marie, you must coordinate this perfectly well. You must warn your kin of what will happen, but there must not be enough time to alert Stuyvesant. He is in Beverwyck. The townspeople of New Amsterdam should come to terms with the fate they desire before he can return," she stressed.

I understood. Stuyvesant was the one who needed to be surprised. With the knowledge that peace was possible, I was positive that my family, my friends, and almost everyone else in New Amsterdam would choose peace over war. The suggestions I put forward to Winthrop, ones he'd promised to abide by to the best of his ability, would only sweeten the townspeople's resolve to convince their stubborn leader to surrender.

"I understand, Claire," I said with a faint smile of acknowledgment. I clasped her hand and continued.

"Come, take me to the bateau. I'm ready to dance with fate," I said.

True to Claire's words, my sister, Sarah, was waiting for me in Breukelen near the ferry to the island of Manhattan. I saw her for the first time in months next to a tree by the ferry dock. She ran to me and embraced me.

"Oh, Marie! We worried what had become of you," she whispered and led me on a path due north.

"Madame La Chaîne said it was critical that I meet you here and take you back to my home. The children have missed you so much. Pierre said you would be safe. What is going on, Marie? Please tell me! Maybe Isaac can help you. In fact, he will meet us on the other side of the ferry. He has a delivery cart with his barrels of beer. We can hide you there among the barrels until we get home," she explained in hushed tones.

She held my hands and gave me a heartfelt and familiar smile.

"Soon, Stuyvesant will not care if I am here or not, little sister. The Council will have their minds focused on other more important matters than a defiant tavern keeper," I explained.

I'd always been the outcast and Sarah the respectable one. Even still, our differences would serve New Amsterdam well. I, the black sheep, the troublemaker, cast out and desperate to get back home, had found a secret calling to protect my people and a mighty friend in enemy territory. Sarah, the respected wife of a brew master and Town Council member, had come to my aid many times. She, who was accepted and loved by all, she who fit flawlessly into New Amsterdam's more reputable circles, knew me and could see the good in me.

Through Sarah, I could help my beloved town to avoid bloodshed and preserve a large degree of our way of life. I knew my dear little sister would help me back and, through her, others might finally see the good in me too.

I pulled her head close to me and whispered in her ear.

"The English warships are on their way, Sarah. They want New Amsterdam. They will not go away until they get what they want!" I warned her.

Sarah gasped and looked at me in horror.

"Please, stay quiet. Do not let fear betray you. You must do exactly as I say so we stay safe and keep the lives we know, unmolested. First, let's go away from here. We must guard against any spies," I calmly directed.

She stared at me, nodding her head, and then motioned me further down the path.

"Come, the ferry leaves to the other side. Wait until it has departed and fewer people are about. Isaac has arranged another vessel to take us across that is less conspicuous. Take care to cover your face with the hood of your linen traveling cloak. We will continue walking until I see the fishing boat waiting for us. The fisherman has never met you and will not know the difference," she said.

In a few minutes, Sarah spotted the fisherman and led me to the river's edge to board his little boat. We sat in silence as the vessel slowly approached a private dock not far from *The Salty Rose*. My tavern sat abandoned without a license to function, yet my beautiful roses outside still bloomed. Sarah would later tell me that my daughters often came to check on them. I interpreted their fully open, mature blossoms as a sign of a positive outcome.

As we pulled to the dock, I saw my handsome Pierre, looking proud and assured that his mother was back. Isaac stood by, pretending not to see us. Sarah greeted him as I walked past like a stranger and then quickly slipped into the back of the wagon in between some barrels and under a coarse cloth. Isaac clicked his tongue at his horse that began to pull the cart in the direction of the city center. My dear sister sat beside her husband. Pierre grabbed a perch at the edge of the wagon in the back to make sure I was safely tucked in among the barrels of beer.

As I sat crouched in my hiding place, hearing my breath and bracing my body as the cart rolled over cobblestoned streets, I should have been nervous, but my heart was full. I was grateful to see my family again. I was also thankful to be a part of history being made. I knew these moments would permeate every crack and each crevice in New Amsterdam for years, becoming the force for the ghosts who will try to tell this story many years into the future.

CHAPTER THIRTY-EIGHT:

Marie's Story
New Amsterdam, New Netherland
September 1664

Sarah's brick home near the waterfront bustled with activity and reflected the prominence of her family in the city. Her home mimicked a fine house in the Netherlands with its distinctive architecture, its large glass windows, and numerous fireplaces encased in delft blue tiles. Children, hers and mine, played in the yard and our good-hearted and obedient daughters helped with the cooking and chores. In the front room, Sarah greeted some important friends, women married to influential men on the Council of New Netherland and in the church.

Outside, the town was quiet but would soon be in chaos, with English ships lurking in the distance. My plans were slipping from the realm of dreams as a new reality emerged more clearly by the minute. We were on the cusp of something that would influence the fates of all of our children and grandchildren and maybe even their children. I felt it deeply in my soul.

I knew I had to make my move quickly. Sarah helped me by inviting several ladies over, telling them she had critical information. Knowing it was unlike Sarah to be so forceful in her insistence that they come to meet with her, they must have sensed it was of great urgency.

"Be a sweet niece and bring your auntie's friends some beer," Sarah directed my Anna.

She turned to the women seated at the table. Looking at them intently, she began to speak.

"Ladies, I asked you to come here today to address matters of life and death. Everyone is anxious with the rumors that the English may come at any time. Someone is here who knows what is happening, but you must vow to keep her presence hidden," Sarah emphasized.

New Amsterdam's finest women nodded.

"Marie, come out," Sarah instructed me.

I entered the room and came face to face with both joy and shock.

"Ah, Marie, you are back! How we missed you!" cried Judith Varlet, getting up quickly to hug me.

She'd never forgotten my role in saving her from the witch-crazed Puritans.

"Dear Marie, Stuyvesant will have you in chains to find you here in New Amsterdam again!" warned Hillegond Megapolensis van Ruyven.

Hillegond was the daughter of the minister, Johannes Megapolensis, and was married to Cornelis van Ruyven, who had been Secretary to the Director General for over ten years. She was a stickler for rules. What else could you expect from a minister's daughter and the privileged wife of a top leader?

"Stuyvesant has forgotten all the kindnesses and favors my father did for him as his messenger. I've come here to help, but Stuyvesant is too proud and arrogant to listen to me. That is why you ladies are here. You must hear me out for your own survival and that of your children," I stated without any hesitation. "I know I come at my own risk, but I assure you, you will be happy I did."

I heard their sighs and observed the quizzical expressions on their faces, curious to know more. I paused and glanced more thoughtfully at the other friends and acquaintances my sister invited, those she thought would have the most influence on the men in their lives, the men who could try to reach through the thick skull of Stuyvesant.

Lydia van Dyck de Meyer seemed to be the one listening most intently, even though she cradled her two-month babe, Deborah, in her arms. I remembered when she came with her father, Hendrick van Dyck, to the colony in the early 1640s. Her father was a ranking military officer for the West India Company. He played a brutal role in siding with Kieft against the Indians, a stance I'm sure he now regretted in the wake of its pointless and bloody aftermath. He'd also been on the Council for many years. Her husband, Nicolaes de Meyer, was currently on the Town Council. He had much in common with Isaac, my brother-in-law, being an established brewer as well as a trader and merchant.

Lydia was serious and impeccably dressed in fine satins brought by traders all the way from the Orient. She knew she had a high place among the women. It was she along with Hillegond who I thought would hold the most influence over their men. They were smart and quite capable of calculating their risks in any given situation. I knew them to be as shrewd as any man.

"Marie, how is it that you, an outcast and someone in constant trouble with the leaders in this colony, can have information that would be of any use whatsoever?" Lydia asked skeptically.

Hillegond nodded in agreement. They were friends with Sarah, but of course, everyone still knew I was the black sheep of the family.

"Judith may help you to recall that I became friends with a trader named John Tinker many years ago. Jan often translated for him when he was in New Amsterdam on business. We also did personal transactions with him for the drink in our tavern because he had a distillery in New London. He was a fine gentleman, and we got on very well. But what was most notable was that he was a loyal assistant to Mr. John Winthrop, the governor of Connecticut Colony. He knew him better than any man and was often at his side," I said.

Then Judith spoke up, tossing dark strands of hair away from her face.

"It was John Tinker who helped save me from the clutches of the Puritan witch frenzy. Marie, through her friendship, sent a message and convinced him to save my life by preparing the magistrates and the deputy governor, Major Mason, to accept Stuyvesant's requests for my freedom," assured Judith. "Without him and Marie, I would not be sitting here alive and breathing."

Hillegond put down her mug of beer and folded her hands together.

"I did not realize he did so much for you, Judith, or that Marie was so instrumental in helping him to become involved. But what does that have to do with our present moment?" she asked.

"Everything," I said. "Please, just listen to me. It will all make sense," I stated, hoping for their patience.

"Go on, Marie," the women encouraged me.

"Not long after Judith was released did we receive the tragic news that John Tinker had been murdered. No one would have been the wiser to this deception had it not been for a courageous group of slaves who knew what happened. It was through them we discovered the treachery behind his death," I explained.

"He paid for his kindness to me with his life!" cried Judith.

"I imagined that Governor Winthrop would be devastated when he came back to England to find his most trusted advisor and associate departed from this Earth," I continued. "I'm sure he would have given anything to find out what happened to John Tinker. I could not rest until I knew Winthrop had the detailed clues I received from the network of slaves.

"It was with that information that his associate was able to figure out the culprit and convey the facts to him. Justice was served to the criminal in the form of fate before Winthrop even had the chance to bring the man to justice. I discovered many months later through another friend that Winthrop was grateful to me for my efforts. I also learned that the English King's charter gave Winthrop rights to New Amsterdam.

"I wanted to find out if it was true, so I searched for Winthrop."

"This next part I tell is for your ears alone. You must never divulge that you received this information from me. You must pretend it came from a young soldier or farmer on the edge of our current border with the English, someone who would be the first to see and report English movement," I said.

Lydia was indignant.

"Marie, have you betrayed us to the English? How could you do such a thing?" Her baby stirred.

"No!" I shouted. "I am not guilty of treason. It was inevitable that the English would come to our doorstep. I just thought it would be Winthrop because of his charter. I thought I could convince him to come in peace only. Do not forget that my youngest children are here. I would never do anything to threaten their existence!" I cried out and continued defiantly.

"You should be pleased that Winthrop felt gratitude toward me for helping him to find out the fate of John Tinker. It was from that goodwill that I begged him to consider the best interests of the good citizens of this city and the rest of New Netherland. He is a shrewd man but one of higher spiritual aspirations, and he values peace. But alas, our fate is not in the hands of Winthrop as so many had previously thought. The stars have shifted once more to give the ultimate power to another," I said in a hushed tone.

The ladies became silent, hanging on my every word.

I slowly continued my explanation and warnings at a steady pace, hoping desperately they would understand what to do.

"Through messengers, I soon learned that the English Crown decided to send warships. The King has already promised New Netherland to his aggressive brother James, the Duke of York, on a whim. The royal promises to Winthrop meant nothing. But, you see, even as the King turned his back on Winthrop and disrupted his plans, his envoys seek his help and therefore, are under his influence to some degree. They are likely to listen to his recommendations for a peaceful solution in their conquest of New Netherland."

"But how can you be sure of this, Marie? And even if you are right, do you not think Stuyvesant will want to try to fight off the English?" Hillegond demanded. She paused, finally realizing the peril they could all be in.

"Ah, Stuyvesant will be taken off guard. He is not even here. He's gone to Beverwyck and Fort Orange to ensure a truce with the Munsee," said Hillegond, nervously biting her lip at the thought of impending conflict.

"Trust me when I say that Winthrop will be there as a negotiator. They know Stuyvesant was a friend of his father and that the younger Winthrop was once entertained for several days by our leader," I said.

"They will use him to accomplish their ends, but Winthrop is clever. Who knows what his cooperative efforts will bring him?" I said.

Isaac, my brother-in-law, had been listening on the edges of the room and came forward.

"Marie, how do you know that you can trust Winthrop to deliver satisfactory terms of surrender to the Dutch and others living here?" he asked.

"John Tinker was my friend. It is hard to explain, but he held Governor Winthrop in the highest esteem. I know deep in my heart it will work out for us. Think about it. How good has it been under the Dutch West India Company? We begged for defenses, for representation, and for consideration, but the company cared little, ignoring pleas to right past wrongs from unwitting and unscrupulous leaders. What have we got to lose under English rule?" I asked.

Making sure they were tied to each word, I pulled out a small scroll.

"Dear friends, these are the requests I asked of Winthrop. I must tell you that there is no hope for a military victory over the English. Four navy vessels are coming. They've arrived at Gravesend already, and their frigates will be here shortly. The English have over five hundred troops, and many English on Long Island have already pledged their loyalty to the English King. They've sworn to come fight against Stuyvesant and his forces to bring our land into English hands. Without cooperation, you will lose even more than you did during our futile Indian wars of the past.

"Let me see the scroll, Marie," Hillegond demanded. I gladly handed it to her. She read carefully through the terms that I had requested.

The people of New Amsterdam will remain on their property, their land, their homes, their businesses, and their farms, unmolested.

The people of New Amsterdam will be free to speak in their native tongue and attend their own churches. They will not be forced to live as English.

All previous punishments may be reconsidered, and former exiles may request reentrance into the community."

"No doubt you requested the last demand for your own benefit in order to return to this city," said Hillegond.

"Well, of course, and you would do the same to be with your children if you were separated from them," I retorted.

Judith intervened on my behalf.

"Now listen to me. Marie has gotten in trouble from time to time, but it was only because she needed to survive for her children. The good she has done for me and in helping others has far outweighed any rules she has broken. She comes again not only to save her own children but to save yours as well. She has information that will now help us to survive. We must pay heed to her warnings."

The women considered her words.

I knew they would be loyal to their community and put the needs of their families and neighbors first.

Lydia responded.

"Marie, you see my Deborah cradled in my arms and see clearly what is at stake. I do not believe that you could face me, looking at my babe, and lie to me. And I know, as any mother does, that you have concern for your children. I will convince others of our predicament," she said.

Sarah smiled and gave me an approving glance.

"For my part too, I will work to negotiate what is best for New Amsterdam. May we use your scroll, Marie? This is good, but we may have other demands. We must see what happens," added Hillegond.

Just as she finished her sentence, the frigates came into view in the main harbor. Their ominous approach sent the populace into the streets, screaming to warn others as they rushed towards the fort. The top command at the fort sent an emergency messenger to Stuyvesant imploring his immediate return.

"We must go now. We will be in contact with further information and communications as the situation ripens," said Lydia, looking down and stroking the head of baby Deborah.

The ladies rushed home to get their households in order. They beseeched their husbands to listen to what they would describe as the words of farmers on the outskirts of New Amsterdam. Our lives hung in the balance of a final reckoning between two colonial powers.

CHAPTER THIRTY-NINE:

Marie's Story
New Amsterdam, New Netherland
September 1664

I stayed hidden within my sister's home, waiting for what seemed like an eternity. At times, I feared the worst, but luckily, those moments did not overcome me, and I was able to maintain overriding hope. It was hard to stay concealed when the city was in chaos. Rumors and gossip abounded that the citizens of Long Island towns were organizing as foot soldiers on behalf of the English.

Word of the English invasion was sent immediately up the North River to Stuyvesant who returned with a vengeance from Fort Orange. Once home, it was reported by neighbors that he paced along the walls of New Amsterdam's fort stomping his peg leg against the stone walkway where he could peer over the walls into the harbor.

He raged at his soldiers to be ready to send cannon fire straight to the bows of the English ships for any provocation. He glared at them with his military looking glass and grimaced, thinking of his options. Tormented with the English fleet lurking so menacingly close, Stuyvesant dictated a blunt letter demanding that the English colonel explain the meaning of the foreign fleet's presence.

Isaac and other city leaders had met Stuyvesant and the members of the Council of New Netherland in the fort. He told me that old Stuyvesant had also been working hard to encourage the populace to take up arms and to swear that they would fight for New Netherland to the bitter end. Of course, most townspeople were less than enthusiastic. After all, the West India Company had abandoned us. They never recognized New

Amsterdam as a fine pearl. It was Brazil that the company viewed as the gemstone of their western territories.

The fur trade had died down, with fewer and fewer pelts available for trade. Beavers were no longer found in local areas. The only ones left were at the farthest reaches of the colony. The real riches were being made on the gold coasts of South America and in the spice trade. So, it wasn't surprising that the people of New Amsterdam didn't feel much allegiance to the West India Company or to Stuyvesant. They did not have a sense of urgency to preserve anything for the West India Company either.

Isaac took Sarah and me aside and warned us to be ready for anything.

"Stuyvesant has gone mad inside the fort. He won't give up the colony easily. The English naval leader, Colonel Nicolls, sent an immediate response to Stuyvesant demanding surrender to the Crown of England in order to spare bloodshed, but Stuyvesant refused to respond because the letter was unsigned and he sent it back."

"I thought I saw a messenger go back and forth several times," I sighed.

"Yes, well, the signed letter is in his hand and he's calculating how to hit his English targets. But in the end, no good will come of it, and we'll be as devastated by war as we were with the incessant Indian conflicts," said Isaac.

"It need not be that way! Somebody must reach out to the English when Stuyvesant is not looking. I promise you, bloodshed is unnecessary. Please keep him from doing anything in aggressive retaliation or all will be lost. Are Hillegond and Lydia at the fort also?" I asked.

"Yes, they came to learn about the latest developments, but they are also trying to reason with their husbands. The men, in turn, are trying to convince Stuyvesant of the futility of fighting the English. We all know Stuyvesant is stubborn. He is not ready to capitulate to the English. This may go on for several days. Ladies, keep the children safe and calm. I must get back to the fort. I will apprise you of further developments later."

"I should go to the fort and talk to him," I said.

"No, Marie!" My brother-in-law stood firm. "Stuyvesant will have you chained up immediately. He'll be furious to see you in defiance of your banishment. We must not take that chance. You must stay hidden but available to help negotiate."

"Dear Isaac, you are right, of course. My sister did well to marry a man of such common sense," I said in acceptance of his advice.

Sarah smiled at me and nodded. She kissed her husband's cheek.

"We'll be fine here devising the best way to break through the recalcitrance of our leader!" she assured him.

Sarah and I spent the rest of the day busy with preparations for all possible scenarios. In any case, we'd need bread for sustenance, and the bakery shelves were bare. Rebecca, another younger sister, joined us. It was good to occupy our hands and speak our minds together as sisters during such a pivotal time.

Desperate for a reprieve in events, Stuyvesant wrote another letter back to Nicolls telling him that he would only believe that the takeover of his colony was sanctioned from the Crown if he heard directly from the King himself. Again he asserted Dutch sovereignty, much to the exasperation of Nicolls.

Isaac, Hillegond, and Lydia were back speaking with me again that afternoon to tell me of Stuyvesant's determination to do his duty to the West India Company and stand his ground against the English.

"Nicolls will no longer communicate with Stuyvesant unless it is to accept surrender. Stuyvesant is still promising to fight at any cost," stated Lydia. "He is refusing to speak with the English colonel."

"The Council has barely held him back from releasing gunners at the fleet. This standstill must come to an end! I fear as time goes on we lose positive ground to make better demands. Nicolls will tire of this and lose his patience. We do not want to see our businesses lost to destruction again!" Isaac stated with deepening lines of worry etched above his brow.

"Everyone knows we are outnumbered and that there is not enough gunpowder for the cannons to be of any use against the English. The English have more men coming from Long Island, probably double the number of the Dutch troops. It's no use. Marie, we need to see the generous terms of capitulation you've promised. Maybe Stuyvesant fears losing his home more than anything. If the English would allow him to stay with his own family unmolested, we might be able to talk him into surrendering," reasoned Hillegond.

Judith had come too.

"The Council is pleading with Stuyvesant to no avail. The terms must be favorable, or there will be unnecessary bloodshed in the end. The ones who have Stuyvesant's ear have told him about the rumors of the English bringing forth favorable conditions of surrender, but he will believe none of it and says it does not matter anyway," said Judith.

"I know what must happen now," I said, excited to present another solution.

"Stuyvesant has a wonderful life in this town. Has he not? He imagines himself as a type of king. Hillegond, you are right. He fears losing the life he has built here, and his pride would never let him bow down to anyone. If he can be reassured that even he, the enemy leader, will be allowed to keep his vast estate, his tropical birds, and his way of life, he will do it," I stated.

"What you say makes sense," confirmed my sister Sarah.

"He loves the country and the pleasant life he has. But, I know this pompous man and I know he is full of hot air. I don't think he cared for New Amsterdam except for the improvements he made that he could boast about. He is full of bluster. If you present him an ideal offer, one in which he keeps his property for his heirs in perpetuity, it may satisfy him," I said, smiling slyly before I continued.

"But most pleasing and comforting of all is that he will no longer be obligated to deal with all the conflicts between settlers and the West India Company. Present it to him in terms of letting the English deal with the rabble-rousers while he retires to his beautiful estate to run it and enjoy it for the rest of his life. That is his soft spot, and he will surrender once that is in place," I finished.

"Yes. That is his weakness, Marie. I know he will fall for it. If only the English will agree," said Judith.

"We must speak to Winthrop! And he must come here with the terms of surrender you spoke of, Marie, and more, of course, to convince Stuyvesant," said Lydia with no hesitation whatsoever despite still having baby Deborah swaddled onto her chest.

Hillegond matched her bravery.

"Yes, as the sun sets and the darkness makes it harder to see, we will sneak past the line of West India Company soldiers. We will go to Gravesend to negotiate with the English leader there. As women, we will not be accused of treason, so we will secretly go to negotiate a truce on behalf of our citizens. We've discussed it with our husbands, and they support us. They are making no progress with Stuyvesant. We must preserve our way of life for our families and our friends. After everything we have been through, we must protect the safety of those we hold most dear," said Hillegond.

Lydia nodded and looked down at the babe whose head she caressed gently.

I smiled proudly, happy to know these great women.

"That is a plan. God be with you. But so will I," I said.

True to their word, Hillegond and Lydia slipped out of the fort once more as the moon began to rise. I joined them that night as planned, and we stowed away in a simple sloop where a local English fisherman who had now pledged allegiance to the Crown brought us to Long Island. Awaiting us there was Henri La Chaîne who led us to Winthrop at a tavern on the edge of Gravesend, overlooking the bay.

Henri smiled at me and kissed me on both cheeks.

"We meet again, Marie du Trieux," he said, clearly happy that I had decided to become involved.

"Come, you ladies have work to do," he said, leading us to the front of the tavern.

Marie's Story
New Amsterdam, New Netherland
September 1664

Lydia, Hillegond, and I glanced at each other with a mixture of fear and determination. It was too late to turn back. The fate of New Amsterdam was in our grasp. We arrived in the evening at the English tavern, escorted by Henri La Chaîne.

"We will accomplish this mission," stated Hillegond forcefully.

"Yes. For the peace of New Amsterdam and all her residents," Lydia said in confirmation, squeezing Hillegond's hand.

They were unwavering in their mission and quickly opened the heavy tavern door. I nodded and acquiesced to their leadership. I was there as a guide. They would be the final negotiators.

English officers, New Englanders, and Gravesend residents sat drinking and smoking their pipes when we arrived at the tavern. Henri approached the tapper and indicated that people were there who wanted to speak with Winthrop. Lydia's baby, Deborah, was fast asleep and nestled next to her mother's bosom.

Winthrop soon arrived with another man my fellow women guessed to be Colonel Nicolls, the commander of the British forces. Henri La Chaîne had sent word that they would be coming.

Upon seeing Winthrop approach, I turned to him.

"Greetings, Governor Winthrop, thank you for meeting us here this evening. I bring with me two wives of leaders in New Amsterdam," I said.

He nodded and smiled at me.

Before I had a chance to introduce them, Lydia spoke up.

"I am Lydia van Dyck de Meyer, and this is my friend Hillegond Megapolensis van Ruyen. We represent both the leaders in the church and the colony government. We wish to speak with you, Governor Winthrop and Colonel Nicolls," said Lydia firmly. "We have information for you from our husbands and the people of New Amsterdam."

"I am Colonel Richard Nicolls whom you speak of," said Nicolls.

"Please, Colonel Nicolls and Governor Winthrop, we have much to say which may help to turn the tide of Stuyvesant's mind. We wish to speak with you privately about the future of both our nations," Hillegond demanded.

Nicolls signaled to Winthrop to lead us to a private meeting space in a back room of the tavern where his officers had congregated for strategic planning. Henri La Chaîne nodded encouragement, and we followed them to a private corner room.

The paneled chamber contained small leaded-glass windows overlooking the bay that led to Manhattan Island. Flickering candles in sconces lined the walls, revealing a large wooden table.

"Come sit here," spoke Winthrop as he cleared papers that had been strewn about.

"Governor Winthrop and Colonel Nicolls, we are grateful to have the chance to meet with you," Lydia said.

He smiled and nodded but said nothing through his words alone. It was clear now. The word was out. The people of New Amsterdam would be willing to go along with the English takeover provided they were treated well.

Colonel Nicolls ordered his officers to bring us some ale and then sat with us.

"Governor Winthrop has come to help negotiate terms of capitulation. I must say this is somewhat of a curiosity to see you ladies here. Stuyvesant has not made it possible to go forward. I am interested in hearing what communications you have for us from New Amsterdam."

"What do you have to say that would have any bearing on this situation? What messages do you carry from your husbands?" Nicolls asked.

"Colonel Nicolls, we are not naïve. We know the English aim to take over our colony and our city. It can be easy for you or it can be extremely difficult. The choice is yours. We prefer peace to war, for we do not want our children to suffer. However, if you want your takeover to be easy, you, in return, must also make our lives easier," said Hillegond.

Winthrop quickly cut in.

"Madame, as I'm sure you were told, the terms of capitulation we have been discussing are generous. You will be free to continue to live your lives in almost every way you did under Dutch rule. Or should I say under the Dutch West India Company?" said Winthrop.

"People will be free to speak Dutch or any language they choose?" asked Lydia.

"Aye," he said.

"And what about keeping our businesses? We must also be free to continue to attend the churches of our choice," added Hillegond.

"Aye. You will have all that and so much more. The English invest more in their colonies than the West India Company ever did. Your lives will be better in many ways," said Winthrop.

"All that is good, but you know it will still not happen until you make personal assurances to our recalcitrant leader. He will not give up his life in New Amsterdam without a good fight. The only clear way for you to go forward is to promise him everything that he enjoys now," advised Lydia.

"Madame, that is only possible if he abdicates his power. There will be an English colonel who will take over the fort. The English will be in charge of the colony. Your Director General must face that outcome," clarified Nicolls firmly.

"But what of our citizens' rights to control the laws of this colony through its own governance?" asked Hillegond, wary of the answer.

"Aye, the city of New Amsterdam will have the right to self-government, but only if its citizens agree to be English subjects and acknowledge the ultimate power of the Crown. You must pledge your allegiance to the King of England."

"We understand these conditions, sirs. And we also request that those who were previously banished, like our friend Marie du Trieux, will be allowed to come back," added Lydia.

I shifted uncomfortably in my seat.

"If someone is determined to come back and they are in good standing with the English, then they may certainly come back despite previous quarrels with the Dutch leader," agreed Nicolls.

"I can allay your fears, ladies. I give you my word that the conditions will be surprisingly favorable. You must beseech your husbands and other members of the Council to convince Stuyvesant that this is the best outcome of many possible ones," stressed Winthrop.

"We understand. As long as the conditions we stated are honored, and the terms are in the best interests of everybody, including Stuyvesant, you have a chance," said Lydia.

"We ask that you be patient with us. Stuyvesant is as strong-willed as they come. Believe me, the Council may not be fully happy to capitulate, but they will do it reluctantly because we want to preserve what we have," emphasized Hillegond.

"Please tell them that we beseech them to cooperate. We will make the transition as smooth as possible as long as the people of New Amsterdam do their part to work together. As for Marie, I will personally vouch for her with the new government," stated Winthrop, giving me a reassuring glance.

"So what will happen now?" questioned Hillegond. "For our part, we will let our husbands know what was discussed so that it can be conveyed further. Hopefully, Stuyvesant will listen to reason."

"Even Stuyvesant will be entitled to his farm. I will draw up our generous terms of capitulation this evening with the approval and feedback of Captain Nicolls. They will be laid out as we discussed. I will present them to Director General Stuyvesant personally in the morning. He admired my father and saw him as a friend. Hopefully, remembering that history, he will soften his stance and hear what I have to say," explained Winthrop.

"Aye, your leaders will be hearing from us tomorrow. This deadlock must end. King Charles II awaits! Ladies, thank you for coming to share the true sentiments of the people of New Amsterdam. Your concerns and demands will be considered as we discussed. Look for Winthrop tomorrow. Hopefully, we will then have an agreement for a peaceful surrender," Colonel Nicolls said.

"And we thank you, ladies, for helping to stop this horrible impasse," said Winthrop.

"Thank you, sirs, for listening to our requests," said Lydia.

"Yah. Thank you," reiterated Hillegond.

Hillegond, Lydia, and I bid our hosts goodnight, found Henri, and headed back to the waiting sloop.

We held hope for a peaceful solution. However, one never had absolute certainty about assurances when dealing with the English.

CHAPTER FORTY-ONE:

Marie's Story
New Amsterdam, New Netherland
September 1664

It was mid-morning when I noticed Winthrop on a small boat with several other New Englanders. He was waving a white flag as he approached the town at the dock near the Stadthuys. As he stepped on the pier, I discreetly glanced his way from the stoop of Sarah and Isaac's home. He looked in my direction, noticed me standing there, and gave a slight nod.

Then, turning his attention toward the fort, I saw him pull out a rolled parchment. I was sure it was the document that contained the favorable terms of capitulation. Several soldiers approached him. He motioned to the fort in what was a gesture to request a meeting with Stuyvesant. They led him towards *The Purple Grape*, a tavern near the fort.

Townspeople crowded out into the streets to stare. Almost everyone in the town must have had their eyes on him and his companions. I'm sure most people recognized him from his visit a few years previously. That earlier visit, filled with fanfare and celebratory gun salutes, was in stark contrast to the scene I saw before me.

Instead of greeting Winthrop as an honored guest, Stuyvesant stayed in his fort, hiding from the inevitable fate that Winthrop represented until his anger got the best of him. This time, even one cannon blast would ignite a torrent of violence that we would all regret. I had no doubt Stuyvesant saw Winthrop as he floated across the water on his way to speak to him. Stuyvesant was in no hurry to greet Winthrop this time, for he was more of an intruder than a true guest in the Dutch leader's eyes.

What saddened me the most was not seeing John Tinker there, knowing that he would have been a part of this moment had he not been murdered.

I had expected that Winthrop would come sometime that morning. I knew he would be true to his word. I was giddy at Winthrop's reassurance that he would defend my return to New Amsterdam. I hoped for a peaceful resolution to the conflict for all of us—at least I did until I saw Stuyvesant huffing down the shore, accompanied by more of his soldiers. In those eyes, I saw a man defiant to the end, a man who was not going to give anything up to the English. He held his head high, with the plume of his general's hat placed proudly.

Stuyvesant then greeted Winthrop briskly and ushered him into *The Purple Grape* near the fort where he utilized the private room in the back perfect for confidential meetings.

It was only Petrus Stuyvesant and John Winthrop in that private tavern room together that morning. Some speculate that after reading Winthrop's letter, our stubborn leader must have realized Winthrop's proposals would be too sweet, too accommodating for the populace to consider fighting to a bitter and hopeless end. We all recognized that it was at that moment when Stuyvesant knew that he didn't have a morsel of hope of holding onto New Netherland and his own power in the colony. Surely, that had to be the reason why he didn't want to show it to anybody—not even his secretary nor his Council members after Winthrop departed.

After about an hour of discussions in the tavern, I saw Winthrop gather his entourage and board a small boat that led him to the ship where Colonel Nicolls was waiting.

In the heat of the afternoon, Sarah and I sat busying ourselves with some mending. It was then that Isaac sprang through the door.

"Oh Isaac, I thought Stuyvesant would never let you out of that fort. It seems like you've been there forever!" my sister hugged her husband.

"People are demanding a meeting at the Stadthuys tonight. Everyone is insisting on figuring out what's in the document that Winthrop gave to Stuyvesant. It must be the terms of surrender. No?"

"Yes. That's it. It must be that which we discussed secretly with Winthrop last night. Stuyvesant will not show it to you?" I asked, perplexed.

"I thought it would soften him to surrender. He is even more stubborn than I realized. What is he waiting for? We are far outnumbered in fighting forces. When we went to see Winthrop yesterday, it became clear just how many English under Dutch rule have already turned their backs on the Dutch West India Company. They are organizing forces that will more than double English manpower," I added.

"We will get to the bottom of this later today. The Town Council has demanded a meeting at the Stadthuys for late afternoon. The Town Council insists that Stuyvesant must show the terms of capitulation as outlined by Winthrop to the populace. They must know. It is their right to decide if it is worth it to fight the English." Isaac said, holding his pipe and inhaling sweet tobacco.

He was exasperated with Stuyvesant's constant resistance to the Town Council's demands. He had been up most of the night with others, and the bags under his swollen eyes were evident.

"Drink a beer, my dear. Rest your weary body. It is too much, all of this stress," soothed Sarah.

Isaac squeezed my sister's hand and then looked at me.

"Marie, come with us to the meeting at the Stadthuys tonight. There will be so much commotion going on that it will be easy for you to blend in on the edges. It's only right that you go. Even if you are noticed, I don't think anyone will pay any mind. You have friends here, and certainly everyone is focused on the future of this colony," he said.

"Yes, please, Marie, come. You should see this moment," reiterated Sarah.

"I wouldn't miss a minute of it," I cried.

I stayed out of the way at the meeting. I listened in at the back of the large hall behind swarms of anxious townspeople crowded around the long tables of the Council members.

After a superfluous speech about the nature of the historic moment at hand and the importance of every family in New Amsterdam defending their colony, Stuyvesant was interrupted. The Council members had lost all patience. Nicolaes De Meyer quickly got to the point. There was no doubt that his wife had told him of the favorable terms Winthrop had outlined before us. Lydia stood near him, nodding as he spoke and giving her emotional support.

"Director General, there has been more than enough talk. The public must know what is written on the parchment delivered to you by Winthrop earlier this day. You must show it to them. I demand that you share the contents of the document with the citizenry at once!" he said.

"It's time, Director General. Give us the document if you won't read it yourself," Isaac cried out.

Hillegond's husband, Cornelis van Ruyven, had had enough and went straight towards Stuyvesant's panicked face. He'd defended Stuyvesant in the past as his secretary and often tried to smooth things over with townspeople. He'd reached a point of no return. His stubborn boss was going to cause a calamity of deaths if he did not intervene.

"Give me the document now!" he roared in his superior's face.

Stuyvesant looked stunned and then, like a cornered animal, he darted in and out, pointlessly hoping for a futile escape from the angry mob and their demands. With no route open to him, he tore up the parchment in plain sight of the entire town.

"You pig-headed fool!" I shrieked, no longer able to contain myself. My rant was barely noticed as the entire hall, filled with the town populace, was screaming and shouting. All hell broke loose as the rest of the Council members jumped up and out of their seats, trying to tackle their stoic leader.

"Give me the pieces of paper!" another defiant Council member demanded.

The Director General paid him no mind and threw the pieces to the floor.

One by one, each Council member gave Stuyvesant a piece of their ire and shared their grievances that had collected from the seventeen years he held the position as head officer for the West India Company.

"How can you ask us to fight for you and for the company when you cannot even have the decency to show us what the English have to say?" an angered Council member questioned.

A noisy crowd agreed.

"This is our future and our lives!" Isaac screamed.

"How dare you, Director General?" shouted another angry voice amongst the crowd.

In between the boisterous shouts and incriminations against our fallen leader, Sarah was hastily gathering the torn-up pieces of Winthrop's letter and eventually delivered them into the hands of Nicasius de Sille who pasted them together again with great care. The crowd stirred with tension as he did so.

Nicolaes de Meyer, Lydia's husband and one of the most important people on the Council, read the terms of capitulation as proposed by the English in Winthrop's hand and under his influence.

All people shall still continue to be free denizens and enjoy their lands, houses, goods, ships, wheresoever they are within this country, and dispose of them as they please.

All public houses shall continue the uses for which they are now.

If any inhabitant has a mind to remove himself, he shall have a year and six weeks from this day to remove himself, wife, children, servants, goods, and to dispose of his lands here.

The crowd cheered as each of the terms was read.

The Dutch here shall enjoy the liberty of their consciences in Divine Worship and church discipline.

The town minister, Johannes Megapolensis, and his son sighed in relief.

No Dutchman here, or Dutch ship here, shall, upon any occasion, be pressed to serve in war, against any nation whatsoever.

The Dutch here shall enjoy their own customs concerning their inheritances.

All inferior civil officers and magistrates shall continue as now they are (if they please), till the customary time of new election, and then new ones to be chosen, by themselves, provided that such new chosen magistrates shall take the oath of allegiance to His Majesty of England before they enter upon their office.

That the town of Manhattan shall choose Deputies, and those Deputies shall have free voices in all public affairs, as much as any other Deputies.

There were others outlining the rights of the West India Company and the States-General and the rights of citizens in regards to soldiers. But the questions related to our biggest concerns, keeping our homes, our businesses, our land rights, and our way of life in general, were answered to the relief of many.

The terms were generous. I knew Winthrop would come through. I had no doubt he'd honor my requests and, in fact, he made the agreement even sweeter with the additions asked for by Lydia and Hillegond.

Once they realized what old Stuyvesant had been holding back from them, the crowd was furious. A nest of hornets couldn't have been more irate than the crowd of my fellow citizens before me that evening. Some of them buzzed out of the Stadthuys, quickly spreading the news to anyone not at the meeting who would listen.

Unwilling to withstand further humiliation, Stuyvesant huffed back to the fort. I can't imagine what he was thinking, but someone thought they heard him mumbling something about "treasonous ingrates." His performance at the meeting united the entire town against him.

At the behest of city leaders, people who were in favor of the terms of surrender signed a petition. Poor Balthazar, Stuyvesant's seventeen-year-old son, even realized the senselessness of his father's position. With meager defenses and no help from the West India Company or the fatherland, he also knew that fighting was futile and signed the petition with great sorrow.

As the final crowds dispersed from the meeting, I ran to Isaac.

"You don't think he will do something crazy, do you? After everything that has happened, I am concerned the fool will act in a rash and provocative way. It will surely start a war if he cannot show some restraint."

Hillegond's father and brother, the two ministers Megapolensis, heard me.

"Marie, you have our word that we will do everything to deliver the town to a peaceful solution. Hillegond has spoken of your bravery and your influence in such positive terms of capitulation," said her father.

"We will say nothing to Stuyvesant about you, but we must rush off to the fort now and plead reason for the peace of our town and the wellbeing of our families," added Hillegond's brother and they quickly ran off to the fort to deal with our recalcitrant and unyielding leader.

Colonel Nicolls must have seen the town in chaos as he looked from his perch on his ship. He'd ordered that the fleet move in a little closer. The river was impassible. Stuyvesant stood ever defiant near a cannon with one lone soldier at his side glaring at the English fleet coming menacingly closer. It was a pitiful sight and one that inspired terror in all who stood watching him.

"Please, dear God, do not let him provoke the English with a stupid stunt. Their firepower will never be matched by our side," I pleaded to the heavens.

Sarah held on to me tightly. The children were ordered to stay in the house or in the garden in the back until we knew the final scene of the drama ensuing. The English citizens of New Netherland on Long Island who had already pledged loyalty to the English Crown were waiting in view from the opposite shore, ready to assist their fellow Englishmen.

"Where are the ministers? They must keep talking to him!" Sarah reasoned in a panic. "How can our fates rest on the shoulders of such a stupid, obstinate man? Dear God, help us!" she prayed.

We watched nervously until finally the two ministers appeared in sight. In what seemed like an eternity, they gestured and talked to him until he left his perch by the cannon. I imagined they compared visions of bloody corpses in the streets, shops looted, the fort and town hall plundered into total destruction to the more positive option of living peacefully as a gentlemen farmer on his vast bowery.

"Imagine, Director General, you sitting in your beautiful aviary with the birds you so love, surrounded by family. Your children will have their own children, and you will be the patriarch of so much. There, you will watch your grandchildren grow up and play games among the fruit trees. Do not give up such a life. You have no other choice, truly. There is no action you can take without losing everything. The West India Company did not come to your aid, and even when you advised Holland of the perilous situation we found ourselves in, surrounded by covetous English, you received no help. Please, Director General, you have done all you can. The people are happy that they can live under such generous terms."

That is what I imagined the ministers said to Stuyvesant in the fort that day. Sometime during those hours, the petition pleading for Stuyvesant to surrender to the English rather than risk the rape, murder, and ruin of his fellow townspeople was presented to him. He must have scowled at the ninety-three signatures on the page before him. I'm sure the ultimate blow was seeing his son's signature among them.

It was said that Stuyvesant still told the ministers that they should fight to the end, but they were able to lead him away from the ramparts and eventually prayed with him. Ultimately, he acquiesced to the English, much to the relief of the populace. Some said they heard him muttering that the people of New Amsterdam deserved English rule. He was a broken, bitter man.

Stuyvesant agreed to send a group of six men from New Amsterdam to make plans for the transition of power. They met at Stuyvesant's farm the very next day. Among them were Governor Winthrop and five fellow New Englanders, including Samuel Willis who witnessed Judith's torments during the witch panic in Hartford. Judith's brother, Nicolas Varlet, and Sam Megapolensis, Hillegond's brother, were among those negotiating the transition from the Dutch side. I thought to myself how interesting it was that some of the same players had met again for a different drama.

The morning after the Articles of Capitulation for the transfer of New Amsterdam were signed, we all saw the Dutch flag go down. The final Dutch troops left their posts one last time and marched out of the fort.

Tearful faces of a diverse group of people looked on. It was strange seeing something we had known our entire lives go away.

If our circumstances had been different, we would have loved to stay as a Dutch colony, but we were forgotten by the company, ruled carelessly, and ignored when we wanted to be treated like proper Dutch citizens. It had been this way for a very long time. Colonel Nicolls made his way to the shore, accompanied by his own soldiers in their red uniforms. They marched into the fort, and we soon saw the English flag go up.

My friends, Claire and Henri La Chaîne, joined me freely for celebrations of peace in what was now New York. I remembered Jan in one of the toasts to our new life.

I thought of Winthrop and my old friend John Tinker. I hoped that Winthrop would find the passage I knew he was looking for. It also occurred to me that New York was part of a greater plan. Even if the final outcome did not make sense for us on that day, another generation would understand why it all came to be.

CHAPTER FORTY-TWO

Marie's Story
Schenectady, New York
1671

After the fall of New Netherland, I went back to New Amsterdam, whose name changed to New York, to join my youngest children. Just as Winthrop had assured me, I was allowed to rejoin my community under English rule.

The Salty Rose, which had been boarded up for months, came to life again. Music and song graced its interior, and my family came together to help me run it. The wild sea roses in front and along the side of the tavern where the old men played their games of ball and pins thrived even more with my loving care. The tavern was successful in New York for a few years, but ultimately, it wasn't the same without Jan or some of the friends who no longer came. After several years, I decided to sell it and moved to Duke Street.

Henri and Claire had moved slightly north to the town of New Rochelle founded by French Huguenot immigrants. I imagine they connected with other furniture makers, craftsmen, and possibly other members of the Rosy Cross. I think they were disappointed that I never became a disciple of the order. Nonetheless, they were grateful that I had committed myself to helping them with the peaceful transfer of power from the Dutch to the English. I will always have a warm place in my heart for them.

After they left town, I never interacted with members of the Rosy Cross again. In fact, I'm not even sure if they exist anymore. But one can never really know since they exist in secret for the most part.

To my knowledge, the mystical trade passage has not been found. However, true to his word, Winthrop recommended my sons for several expeditions into the interior. Aernoudt has plans to go to a place called the Ohio River Valley in the future. One day, they might find the Passage. They tell me the country and its wilderness is so vast that it is hard to imagine where it ends.

The last time I talked to Winthrop was when he met us in Gravesend the fateful night when Lydia and Hillegond gave final demands for an agreement with the English. I hear he is still busy with his duties as Governor of Connecticut.

So was a great peace achieved after the English took over you may wonder? Well, yes and no. The English came in without a single cannon shot, and the Dutch were able to maintain their way of life. But the English and Dutch warred with each other again back in our father countries after the takeover.

I observed the English women who came to New York and noted they had fewer rights than those given to women living under Dutch rule. I can say the same for my African friends—the slavery enforced by the English is just as tortured and cruel if not more so, and the number of slaves has increased. I feared for my friend Domingo before his natural death and for the other half-freed slaves as well. The English have no such status and give no partial rights. I was relieved Domingo had escaped a worsening fate through dying peacefully in his sleep one night. I'll always miss him.

When I returned to the city of New York, I tried to take pity on old Stuyvesant. He disappeared for months back to Holland. They demanded his presence and an explanation for why New Netherland had fallen to the English. Realizing that it was partially their fault for not sending supplies and for being duped by the English, the States-General let him return to his home and his family on Manhattan Island.

With tortured soul, he turned into a recluse on his farm, forever humiliated from defeat by the English. I imagined him stewing over his losses and his betrayal by the Dutch West India Company who directed him to make reinforcements and build up his troops but didn't provide the means to do so. I could see him secretly talking to the tropical birds in his aviary as counselors who would cock their heads and squawk at the injustices thrust upon him.

The few times I did run into him on the waterfront or near the market, the rancor within me rose again, and I quickly lost any compassion I'd imagined that I had. That stubborn man had almost delivered the town into the musketry of the English. We narrowly slipped out of harm's way from his pigheadedness. So, let him sit brooding as a hermit on his little bowery. Let him sit among his fruit trees with nothing but the scowl on his face.

He showed me no mercy when I was forced to leave, and he showed the townspeople no understanding when they asked to be represented. It mattered not to me whether the place was Dutch or English. I just wanted my world to come together again. And in my struggles to do just that, I learned many lessons.

I came to realize that many things happen in life that we may not understand, but are the objective result of previous events—consequences of the past ripened. John Tinker's death was senseless, yet not in vain, nor was my allegiance to Winthrop. It allowed the way for the English takeover but in a way that the heart of New Amsterdam could still beat. If not for my friendship with John Tinker and his influence in releasing Judith Varlet from her accusations of witchery, Winthrop would not have known to trust me.

Some sages looking at the stars of the future have predicted that a new nation will be born, a nation not possible under solely English influence, a nation that carries within it part of the spirit of New Amsterdam. It's hard for me to imagine such things, but the soothsayers also foresee it will be born of Hermetic principles and the wisdom of the Rosy Cross. I do not really know about this.

What I do know is that you can never go back to exactly where you were because change is constant. To observe nature and the mystery of how it unfolds from season to season, as is the way of the alchemists, is to observe change—constant change. Nature moves on, and so must we.

Be comfortable with change if you want to enjoy your life, my granddaughter. Embrace it as a new adventure with great promise to unfold as many blessings. Just remember what you learned and what you will always hold dear from your past.

In the end, after fighting so hard to return to New Amsterdam, I could never fully fit into the fabric of my own home city again. The best thing in the end was to return to my changing and growing family near Beverwyck, now called Albany, where I was needed. But I had to have the experience of going back to what was once New Amsterdam that final time. I had to feel what it was like and I was not the only one who came to understand this.

Most of my sisters and brothers did not stay in the city of our childhood either. Most wanted to leave too. We realized that being together as a family was better than living apart. Coming to settle in Schenectady with my sons and watching my brood grow has been most fortunate.

Life will always continue to transform. Resistance to change is useless. And those who do not accept change as part of life will suffer. We can never go back. NEVER.

As you look so intently at me, your aging grand-mere, the strength you see in me is also your own.

Take my hand, chérie. I will always smile upon you, for I share these secrets with you alone. You, my child, are my sun and my moon. I know not how much longer I have to live. It is through you, my little Rose, that my spirit will carry on.

CHAPTER FORTY-THREE:

Winthrop's Story
Boston, Massachusetts Bay Colony
1676

Mercy dabbed Governor John Winthrop's face with a moist cloth to bring down the fever as his son looked on. He had been going in and out of consciousness, and the family knew the time was near for him to meet his Savior.

He was on his way back to home when a sudden cold had overtaken him. He remained Governor of Connecticut despite two failed resignation attempts, and his body was weary after so much continued commitment and work on behalf of his community and colony.

He mumbled. The others in the room saw nothing, but John Winthrop on his deathbed was face to face with the ghost of the great magus John Dee. He looked just like Winthrop had imagined him to be. Dee was dressed in a long artist's gown. His face was thin with fine, clear skin and perfectly white hair accompanied by an equally white beard that reached his waist. He reassured Winthrop at the same time he spoke the final truths to the dying man about the life he had lived.

"I have spoken with the angels—Uriel, Raphael, Gabriel, Michael, Madimi, and many others. You must not worry. The goal could never have been met. It was a worthy aim, but unattainable."

"Hundreds of years will pass before man finds and is able to traverse the Northwest Passage. And even when that happens, the East uniting with the West will still not bring oneness and the bright light of purification into the world."

"After all that time, man will still not be ready. In the future, people will continue to be blinded by their own shortcomings, divisions, and imbalances," said the spirit of John Dee.

"But what of the Philosopher's Stone?" Winthrop asked.

"In this period, it was never possible to find. Again, it will be hundreds of years before it can be discovered and completely different than what you imagine it to be now."

Winthrop was perplexed. He had so many other questions.

"Was our Rosicrucian mission for naught? The great alchemical work?" Winthrop whispered.

"You achieved much, dear man of faith. Your heart opened to the sickness and suffering of others. In service to your fellow man, you tended to the ill and gave hope in doing so."

"You saved an entire people, an entire tribe, from annihilation.

Perhaps you had other personal motivations that you considered even more important, but in the end, that was the result. You saved the lives of those thought to be consorting with evil when there was no evil, only fear. You led your people with dignity even though you preferred to contemplate and experiment in your laboratory and study in your library. And so, dear adept, your purpose was largely actualized."

Winthrop continued to gaze at Dee's spirit. His words were not what Winthrop had expected. Dee continued.

"You, John Winthrop, are no different than any other man or woman. You have been noble and steadfast in your quest to be of service and transform the world into a place more aligned with the heavens, but please hear this.

"Human beings neglect to recognize their own failings. For that, they are forgiven. The Creator bestows Grace to us to allow our souls to keep learning and overcoming our limitations just as the prophet and teacher Hermes laid out in his lessons in the early times of humanity—those most spiritual of times in ancient Egypt."

Winthrop murmured again, lost in his vision as Mercy, his enslaved servant, continued to attend to him.

John Dee spoke his final words.

"John Winthrop, your time has come. May God have Mercy on your soul! May you see where you have been blind to your own shortcomings and ignorance."

Winthrop opened his eyes, suddenly fully awake. He looked at Mercy, a woman bound to him through no choice of her own, a woman who had emptied his chamber pots, cleaned his vomit, and bandaged his wounds. His tears began to form.

"Mankind was not ready. I was not ready to find the Passage or the Stone."

His words were barely audible.

"Yes, may God have Mercy and many others like her on my soul. Forgive me."

The words had taken another meaning—his final code deciphered. He understood and was now free to depart the earthly realm.

Winthrop could not keep his eyes open any longer and inhaled his very last breath before crossing over to the astral plane of the Great Above.

Author's Note:
Real History *vs.* Fiction

The Salty Rose: Alchemists, Witches & A Tapper In New Amsterdam is a sequel to *One of Windsor: The Untold Story of America's First Witch Hanging.* However, I also wanted it to be available as a stand-alone novel. With that in mind, I made sure that the reader would not have to read one in order to enjoy the other and was careful not to give too much away from the first story.

It was a pleasure for me to learn about the real people who were modeled as characters in *The Salty Rose.* I found it equally fun to invent new ones and find ways to present some early colonial American history through a fictional story.

Marie du Trieux, the main character in *The Salty Rose,* depicts a real tavern keeper in New Amsterdam. Banished in the winter of 1664 for selling liquor to Native Americans, she went to her older sons in Beverwijk (Albany under the English). It is not known if her son Peter, Pierre in the story, went with her at the time of her banishment.

Marie came to New Netherland as a young child with her father, Philippe du Trieux, and her stepmother, Susanne du Chesne, a cousin of her deceased mother. They came with a group of Walloons, the earliest settlers in New Netherland. Marie had her first child out of wedlock with Pieter Wolphersen van Couwenhoven who later agreed to acknowledge paternity and to be financially responsible to his daughter Aeltje.

Marie's first husband was Cornelis Volkertsen Viele, a man thirty-three years her senior. They started a tavern in New Amsterdam and had four children together: Aernoudt, Cornelis, Jaqueline, and Peter. Jaqueline died at age three, and Viele died around 1649. At that time, there was a concerted effort by Stuyvesant and the clergy to limit the number of taverns.

In 1650, Marie married a man named Jan Peeck. Peekskill, New York is named after him. He had his trading camps with the Natives there. The old Peek Slip on the East River in New York City was the place where he parked his sloop on a cove he and Marie owned. In between trading trips, Jan helped Marie with their tavern at the end of Maiden Lane. I do not know what the real name of their tavern was. *The Salty Rose* is an invented name for the book. They also had four children together: Anna, Johannes, Jacob, and little Marie. Jan Peeck was also named as an agent to English speakers who came to trade in New Amsterdam. He disappeared from the records a few months before Marie was banished. The date of his death and its circumstances are unknown.

The Native leader, Oratam, did request that the Dutch not sell liquor to the Native communities he represented. Sara Kierstede was his translator and was extremely important in negotiations with him. Historian Susanah Shaw Romney describes this relationship in detail in her book *New Netherland Connections: Intimate Networks and Atlantic Ties in Seventeenth-Century America.* Their negotiations to stop the sale of alcohol in Native communities and the Dutch request that Oratam and tribes he spoke for not be involved in the Esopus War coincided with the time that Marie du Trieux was banished for selling liquor to Natives.

The Varlets moved from New Amsterdam to Hartford in the late 1650s. Their daughter Judith was indicted for witchcraft crimes. Her mother and father died in Hartford while she was in jail awaiting trial. Judith was released based on a letter from Petrus Stuyvesant demanding her release. Although John Tinker was in town at the time, it is unknown if he did anything behind the scenes to secure her freedom. In her historical novel, *Days To The Gallows*, Katherine Spada Basto recounts the entire saga of the Hartford Witch Panic.

While the incident of Lydia van Dyck de Meyer and Hillegond Megapolensis van Ruyven going past enemy lines to negotiate peace with the English has been described by historian Susanah Shaw Romney in the same book just cited. There is no evidence that Marie du Trieux participated in actions with them that would help turn the Dutch colony over to the British. However, it is clear that she did want to return to New Amsterdam after her banishment. English records for New York indicate she lived on Duke Street after the British took control.

The time of Marie du Trieux's death is unknown, but she left New York City and settled with most other family members in Schenectady, New York. At least two sons had taverns of their own: Aernoudt in Albany with Storm van der Zee and Cornelis in Schenectady, New York.

John Tinker, an immigrant from Windsor, Berkshire, England, started working for John Winthrop Sr. in the late 1630s. He took care of the elder Winthrop's business in England and also worked for Robert Keayne. I am unsure how Tinker came to be hired by Winthrop. He could have met John Winthrop Jr. during his employment with his father. Tinker worked for Winthrop Jr. for many years. While I do not know specifically how close Tinker was with Winthrop Jr., there are several letters that exist between the two, and Tinker follows the path of Winthrop for most of his life, taking care of Winthrop's business along the way. Letters written in the hand of John Tinker to both Winthrops can be found in the *Winthrop Family Papers*. John Tinker died in October of 1662 with honors in Hartford, a time that coincided with the height of the Hartford Witch Panic and the release of Judith Varlet. He would have to be buried in the Ancient Burying Ground.

John Winthrop Jr. was an alchemist and was interested in the works of John Dee and many other alchemists and philosophers. Dee was the astrologer and magician to Queen Elizabeth as well as a famous mathematician. John Winthrop Jr. first became interested in alchemy while in school and was friends with Edward Howes.

Howes supported Winthrop Jr. from England, sending books and supplies to his friend. Howes' letters to Winthrop Jr. are archived in the Winthrop Family Papers, Volume 3 that appear in this novel. Howes' original letters to Winthrop Jr. are in the italicized print in chapter five. This author did not invent them. They are attributed fully to Howes. Historian Walter Woodward depicts Winthrop's alchemy practices and how they shaped much of Winthrop's world and the New World, including his stance on the witch trials, in his book, *Prospero's America: John Winthrop, Jr., Alchemy, and the Creation of New England Culture: 1606-1676.*

While there is plenty of evidence to show that Winthrop Jr. was an alchemist, Tinker's involvement in these beliefs and practices is unknown. However, one of his signatures is very interesting and appears to contain a lot of symbolism that hints at this interest. Howes mentions Tinker coming to see him while he is in England handling the Winthrops' business affairs.

John Tinker moved to Windsor for several years to join other immediate family members after he had helped settle the affairs of the elder Winthrop. While in Windsor, Tinker with his brother-in-law, John Taylor who was married to his sister Rhody Tinker Hobbs, bought a large tract of land together from the local Natives. The introduction of tobacco coincides with his time there.

While in Windsor, Tinker would have witnessed the accusations of witchcraft against Alice Young who became the first hanging victim from a witch trial in Hartford. Alice was married to John Young. While the precise relationship between the Tinkers and Youngs is not known, it is not an outlandish assumption to say that the Youngs and the Tinkers could have been related in some way either through the husband or through his wife to other members of the Tinker family or their husbands. One of the Young properties, their home lot, was located on Backer Row in the middle of John Tinker's three sisters' home lots. After Young's hanging, the entire family moved out and left Windsor for good. This story is told in my first novel, *One of Windsor: The Untold Story of America's First Witch Hanging.*

Only a month after Young's murder, Winthrop Jr. made his way to speak with the United Colonies where he pleaded his case concerning the Pequots that resided next to his village, Pequot Plantation, later called New London. He also hoped to settle which colony had jurisdiction over his plantation. Winthrop Jr. did start New London as an alchemical center. He also took great interest in healing and became a doctor to a large number of residents in Connecticut Colony. His most famous formula was Rubila, devised by alchemical means.

At that time John Tinker was in Lancaster, Massachusetts, the town that had been built near Winthrop's lead mine. He was given a monopoly on the fur trade there. He married first in Boston in 1648 to a dying woman, Sarah Barnes, and second, to a much younger woman named Alice Smith. Her name was not mentioned in the novel to avoid confusion with Alice Young, a woman with the same first name and John Tinker's cousin in the story.

John Tinker moved to New London shortly after Winthrop Jr. became governor in Connecticut. Tinker was granted sole rights to operate a distillery, and he also continued to handle the affairs of the new governor. In 1661, John Winthrop Jr., then Governor of Connecticut Colony, understood the need for a charter after the reinstatement of the monarchy in England. He left the colony in the hands of his deputy governor, Major John Mason, the veteran leader of the Pequot War. Winthrop Jr. obtained the charter for his colony in the spring of the following year and spent more than six thousand pounds of his personal finances to achieve this goal. The charter reached New England in September of 1662. It included much of Long Island, New Haven, and all lands directly west of Connecticut Colony.

As Winthrop Jr. was surveying the new land promised to him for Connecticut Colony, he heard from Underhill that King Charles II had reneged on his word and had given most of the land west of the Connecticut River and Long Island to his brother, the Duke of York. Winthrop decided to cooperate with Colonel Nicolls, leader of the English fleet on the advice of friends. He participated in negotiating an agreement between the Dutch and the English that helped to prevent war. Winthrop Jr. thought that he might have seen a fifth moon of Jupiter only a few weeks before the British takeover of New Netherland and reported it later to the Royal Society, the oldest scientific organization in the world.

Slavery was sadly common in the era that is depicted in this novel. The West India Company owned a few slaves, and wealthy citizens owned more. The first enslaved people in New Amsterdam were taken from a Portuguese ship. Half freedom was a status in New Amsterdam for a few formerly enslaved people.

The English did not have any condition pertaining to slavery that allowed for partial slavery. It's true that both Governors Winthrop owned slaves. Early colonial slavery also included some Native people in New

England. A new project led by historian Katherine Hermes and her team was undertaken recently at the Ancient Burying Ground in Hartford to identify people of color buried there. It tells the story of some of Hartford's early African and Native Americans—some from the period in the book, most of them later.

The brutality, violence, and injustice toward not only Africans and African Americans but also Native people in early colonial America cannot be overstated. The author tried to bring specific events that greatly affected Native people, including episodes that would have impacted characters in the novel, to the forefront. John Winthrop Jr. took a much different approach toward Native people than many others during his era.

There are no records known to indicate that John Tinker or Marie du Trieux and Jan Peeck were friends or business associates. The author created this relationship, recognizing that as a special agent to the English it was in the realm of possibility that Jan Peeck might have made the acquaintance of John Tinker, a trader, if he came to New Amsterdam for his profession.

Several characters were imaginary. In the interest of not wanting to accuse an actual person for the death of John Tinker, this author devised the character of Hugh Dyer. The causes and details of John Tinker's death are unknown. The characters of Henri and Claire La Chaîne were also literary inventions from the author's imagination. However, Winthrop Jr. was at the siege of La Rochelle in France as a young man and was greatly influenced by it.

As far as early Rosicrucianism in America, it is hard to know the full extent or influence of this thought since these movements were largely secretive. The author did research some of the early alchemical teachings for this book but barely scratched the surface as far as what this philosophy and belief system contain.

If you'd like to learn more about early American history, there are numerous archives available. The selected sources on the next pages are a great place to start.

Beth M. Caruso
August 14, 2019

Monas Hieroglyphica

John Tinker's
Alchemical Signature

Selected Sources

Even though *The Salty Rose* is a work of historical fiction, it required months of research to depict an accurate historical background of the events that transpired in New England and New Netherland in mid-seventeenth century America. The characters in the novel were largely based on the lives of actual people, including Marie du Trieux, Jan Peeck, John Tinker, John Winthrop Jr., and others. Although many resources were used, my most frequently referred to are the ones listed here. Please note that new information about New Netherland is still being published each year. Having been largely neglected in the first centuries after the English takeover, the records are still in the process of being properly translated. The many completed ones are available through the New Netherland Institute.

Demos, John Putnam. *Entertaining Satan: Witchcraft and the Culture of Early New England*. New York, NY: Oxford University Press, 1982.

Hartford's Ancient Burying Ground. *Uncovering Their History: African, African-American, and Native-American Burials in Hartford's Ancient Burying Ground, 1640-1815*. http://theancientburyingground.org

Hall, David D. *Witch Hunting in Seventeenth Century New England*, Boston: Northeastern University Press, 1991.

Hoadly, Charles Jeremy, and Trumbull, James Hammond eds. *The Public Records of the Colony of Connecticut Prior the Union With New Haven, May 1665*. Hartford: Brown & Parsons, 1850.

Kamel, Neil. *Fortress of the Soul: Violence, Metaphysics, and Material Life in the Huguenots' New World, 1517-1751.* Baltimore, MD: The Johns Hopkins University Press, 2005.

Manwaring, Charles William, ed. *A Digest of the Early Connecticut Probate Records: Hartford District, 1635-1700.* Hartford: R. S. Peck & Co., 1904.

The Massachusetts Historical Society. *Winthrop Family Papers.* http://www.masshist.org/publications/winthrop/index.php

New Netherland Institute. https://www.newnetherlandinstitute.org

Shaw Romney, Susanah. *New Netherland Connections: Intimate Networks and Atlantic Ties in Seventeenth-Century America.* Chapel Hill, NC: University of North Carolina Press, 2014.

Shorto, Russell. *The Island At The Center Of The World: The Epic Story of Dutch Manhattan and the Forgotten Colony That Shaped America.* New York, NY: Random House, 2004.

Woodward, Walter W. *Prospero's America: John Winthrop, Jr., Alchemy, and the Creation of New England Culture: 1606-1676.* Chapel Hill: University of North Carolina Press, 2010.

Acknowledgments

An author is never alone in their quest to present the perfect story. That was certainly the case in bringing forth *The Salty Rose: Alchemists, Witches & A Tapper In New Amsterdam*.

With much gratitude, I'd like to thank the staff at New Netherland Institute for pointing me in the right direction with research about New Netherland, the early Dutch colony.

I'd also like to thank readers Steve Watton, Susanne Aspley, Brianna Dunlap, Liz McAuliffe, Ricki Aiello, Mary Hotaling, and Elaine Bentley Baughn for their corrections, insightful feedback, and suggestions for tightening and improving my story.

A cover artist is essential in creating artwork that can generate interest in a story. Sue Tait Porcaro is a talented Windsor artist who was able to capture a pivotal moment in *The Salty Rose* on the cover.

I'm equally grateful to Bill Harris, my wonderful copyeditor. He's efficient, generous, detailed, and always careful to improve my voice and not change it.

Patrick Schreiber helped me with his expertise in book design and graphics. He was able to work with a myriad of special requests and give *The Salty Rose* its custom look in both the interior and on the cover. A special thanks goes to him.

Brewing is an art and a science. Many thanks to modern-day brewmaster, Mike Klucznik, and his tapper wife, Sheila Mullen, of Fat Orange Cat Brew Company in East Hampton, Connecticut for showing me some of the intricacies of their trade.

Most of all, I'd like to thank my family, Chazz, Sky, and River who have seen much less of me than I'd prefer as I researched for, worked on, and completed this historical fiction novel over a four-year period. They really are the best!

BETH M. CARUSO

About The Author

The Salty Rose: Alchemists, Witches & A Tapper In New Amsterdam is Beth M. Caruso's second novel and was inspired by the discovery of Marie du Trieux, a distant great grandmother in her husband's family tree as well as from information she gathered from previous research. Her first historical fiction novel is *One of Windsor: The Untold Story of America's First Witch Hanging,* a book that tells the tale of Alice Young and the beginnings of the colonial witch trials. Beth is passionate to discover and convey important and interesting stories of women from earlier times.

Beth grew up in Cincinnati, Ohio and spent her childhood swimming and writing puppet shows and witches' cookbooks. She studied French Literature and Hispanic Studies, earning a Bachelor of Arts from the University of Cincinnati. After spending two years in the Peace Corps in northern Thailand, she obtained Masters degrees in Nursing and Public Health. Beth's other interests include aromatherapy, travel, gardening, and exploring and protecting our beautiful natural world. She lives in Connecticut with her family.

Feel free to reach out to Beth in the following ways:

Website: https://www.oneofwindsor.com

Email: oneofwindsor@yahoo.com

Twitter: https://twitter.com/oneofwindsor

Facebook: https://www.facebook.com/bethmcaruso

Made in the USA
Middletown, DE
23 November 2020